The Broom-Squire by Sabine Baring-Gould

Sabine Baring-Gould was born on January 28th, 1834. The family had its own manor house at Lew Trenchard on a three-thousand-acre estate, in Devon, England,

His bibliography is immense. 1200 items at a minimum including the hymns 'Onward Christian Soldiers' and 'Now the Day Is Over'.

The family spent much of his childhood travelling in Europe and he was educated mainly by private tutors although he spent two years King's College School in London and a few months at Warwick Grammar School. Here he contracted a bronchial disease that was to plague him throughout his life.

In 1852 he gained entrance to Cambridge University, earning a Bachelor of Arts in 1857, and then a Master of Arts in 1860 from Clare College, Cambridge.

As early as 1853 he had decided to become ordained. In 1864, after his education and several years teaching, he took Holy Orders.

He became the curate at Horbury Bridge in West Riding. Here he met Grace Taylor, the daughter of a mill hand, aged fourteen. During the next few years they fell in love. His vicar, John Sharp, arranged for Grace to live with relatives in York to learn middle-class manners. Baring-Gould, meanwhile, relocated to become perpetual curate at Dalton, near Thirsk.

He and Grace were married in 1868 at Wakefield. Their marriage lasted until her death 48 years later, and the couple had 15 children.

Baring-Gould became the rector of East Mersea in Essex in 1871. In 1872 his father died and he inherited the family estates which included the gift of the living of Lew Trenchard parish. Upon its vacancy in 1881, he took the post, becoming parson as well as squire.

He wrote many novels, his usual writing position was whilst standing, including The Broom-Squire set in the Devil's Punch Bowl (1896), Mehalah and Guavas, the Tinner (1897), a collection of ghost stories, and a 16-volume The Lives of the Saints.

His studies in folklore resulted in The Book of Were-Wolves (1865), a frequently cited study of lycanthropy.

The popular work Curious Myths of the Middle Ages, published in two parts, in 1866 and 1868. Each of the book's twenty-four chapters deals with one medieval superstition, its variants and history.

Grace died in 1916. He had carved on her headstone: Dimidium Animae Meae ("Half my Soul").

Sabine Baring-Gould died on January 2nd, 1924 at Lew Trenchard. He was buried next to Grace.

Index of Contents

CHAPTER I. — AT THE SIGN OF THE SHIP

On a September evening, before the setting of the sun, a man entered the tavern of the Ship in Thursley, with a baby under his arm.

The tavern sign, rudely painted, bore, besides a presentment of a vessel, the inscription on one side of the board:—

"Now before the hill you climb,
Come and drink good ale and wine."

On the other side of the board the legend was different. It ran thus:—

"Now the hill you're safely over,
Drink, your spirits to recover."

The tavern stood on the high-road side between Godalming and Portsmouth; that is to say the main artery of communication between London and Portsmouth.

After rising out of the rich overshadowed weald land, the road had crossed long sandy wastes, where population was sparse, where were no enclosures, no farms, only scattered Scottish firs; and in front rose the stately ridge of sandstone that culminates in Hind Head and Leith Hill. It was to prepare the wayfarer for a scramble to the elevation of a little over nine hundred feet that he was invited to "drink good ale and wine," or, if he were coming from the opposite direction was called upon to congratulate himself in a similar manner on having over-passed this ridge. The wayfarer with the baby under his arm came from the Godalming side. He looked up at the sign, which appealed at once to his heart, for he was obviously a sailor, no less than did the invitation commend itself to his condition.

He entered, tumbled the baby on to the tavern table that was marked with wet rings from beer cans, and upset a saucer containing fly poison, and said, with a sigh of relief—

"There you are! Blowed and all of a lather!"

He pulled out a blue cotton pocket-handkerchief, mopped his face and shouted, "Beer!"

"Well, I never!" exclaimed the landlady. "Whoever heered afore or saw of a babby lugged about wrong side uppermost. What would you say if I was to bring you your tankard topsy-turvy?"

"I wouldn't pay for it," said the sailor.

"'Cos why?" asked the woman, planting herself arms akimbo, in front of the wayfarer.

"'Cos it 'ud capsize the ale," he answered.

"Very well, ain't babbies got no in'ards to capsize?" asked the landlady, defiantly. "And chucked in among the pison for killing them dratted flies, too!"

"Never mind about the kid," said the man.

"I do mind about the child," retorted the woman; "look at him there—the innocent—all in the nasty slops. What'll the mother say to the mess and crumple you've made of the clothes?"

The landlady took the infant from the table, on one arm, and proceeded to the bar to draw the beer.

Presently she returned, kissing the child and addressing it in terms of affection. She thrust the pewter full of foaming ale on the table towards the customer, with resentfulness in her action.

"He's a stomachy (sturdy) young chap," she said, patting the babe with the now disengaged hand.

"He ain't a he at all," retorted the man. "He's a she."

"A girl, is it!" exclaimed the hostess; "and how came you by the precious?"

"Best rights of all," answered the man; "'cos I'm the kid's father."

"Her mother ought to be ashamed of herself letting you haul about the poor mite under your arm, just as though she was pertatoes."

"Her mother can't help it," said the man. "She's dead, and left me wi' this here child a month or six weeks old, and I've been sweating along the way from Lun'non, and she yowlin' enough to tear a fellow's nerves to pieces." This said triumphantly; then in an apologetic tone, "What does the likes o' me know about holdin' babies? I were brought up to seamanship, and not to nussin'. I'd joy to see you, missus, set to manage a thirty-pounder. I warrant you'd be as clumsy wi' a gun as I be wi' a kid."

"D'r say," responded the landlady, "and where be you a-g'win to with this here angel? Takin' her to sea to make a mermaid of her?"

"No, I aren't," said the mariner. "Her mother's dead—in lodgin's down by the Katherine docks, and got no relatives and no friends there. I'm off to sea again when I've dispodged o' this here incumbrance. I'm takin' her down to her mother's sister—that way." He indicated the down road with his thumb.

"It's a wonder you ain't made a crook of her backbone, it is," said the woman. "And if you'd gone and crippled she for life, what would you think o' that?"

"I didn't carry her like that all the road," answered the sailor. "Part ways I slung her over my back."

"Wonder she's alive. Owdatious strong she must be. Come in, my cherry beam. I'll give you as good as mother's milk. Three parts water and a bit o' shuggar. Little your father thinks o' your wants so long as he gets his ale."

"I let her suck my thumb," said the sailor, timidly.

"Much good she got out o' that," retorted the landlady. "Yes, yes, my syrup. I'll give you something."

"If you can stop her yowling, I'll thank you."

With a contemptuous look at the father, the hostess withdrew.

Then the sailor planted his elbows on the table, drank a long draught of beer, and said, sententiously, "It's an institootion is wimin."

"Woman is the joy of our lives," said a lanky, dark-haired man at the table.

"'Tain't exactly that," answered the sailor, now first observing that there were other men in the room. "'Tis that there's things for everything—there's the capstan for hawlin' up the anchor, and there's the woman for nussin'. They was ordained to it—not men—never, no—not men. Look at my hand." The sailor extended his arm across the table. "It's shakin' like a guitar-string when a nigger's playing—and all along of that kid's yawls. Wimin likes it."

"It's their moosic," said the lanky man.

Then in rushed the landlady with flashing eyes, and holding out both palms before her said, "The child's mouth be that purple or blue—it's fits."

"It's blackberries," answered the seaman. "They was nice and ripe, and plenty of them."

"Blackberries!" almost shrieked the hostess, "and the child not six weeks old! You've killed her! It's upset her blessed little inside."

"I thought I'd done wrong," said the sailor, timidly, "that's why I was a-carryin' of her topsy-turvy. I thought to ha' shooked the blackberries out again."

"If that child dies," exclaimed the landlady, solemnly, "then where will you go to, you unnat'ral parient?"

"I did it wi' the best intention," apologized the man.

"That's what Betsy Chaffers said when she gave wrong change. Oh that heaven should ever a created man. They's terrible monsters."

She disappeared again after the child.

The sailor drank more beer, sighed, wiped his brow, then his upper lip, and looked appealingly about him at the men who were present. Of these there were four and a half. That is to say, four men and a boy. Three of the men were at the table, and of these the lanky sallow man was one.

These three men were strange, unpleasant-looking fellows, dressed up in scraps of incongruous clothing, semi-nautical, semi-agricultural. One was completely enveloped in a great-coat that had belonged to a very tall and stout man, and he was short and thin. Another was incompletely dressed, for what garments he had on were in rags that afforded glimpses between them of tattered lining, of flesh, but of no shirt.

The third man had the unmistakable lower jaw and mouth of an Irishman.

By the fire sat an individual of a different type. He was a young man with heavy brows and a large mouth devoid of lips, set tight as a snapped man-trap. He had keen, restless, watchful eyes. His hair was sandy, thrust forward over his brow, and hanging low behind. On the opposite side of the hearth crouched a boy, a timid, delicately formed lad with a large head and full lustrous eyes.

"Come from far?" asked one of the ragamuffins at the table.

"Didn't yur hear me say from Lun'non town?" answered the sailor. "Lagged that there dratted baby the whole way. I'll have another glass of beer."

"And what distance are you going?" asked the lanky man.

"I shall put into the next port for the night, and tomorrow on to Portsmouth, and stow away the kid with my wife's sister. Lord! I wishes the morrer were well over."

"We're bound for Portsmouth," said the man in tatters. "What say you? shall we keep company and relieve you of the kid? If you'll pay the shot here and at the other end, and at the other pubs—can't say but what we'll ease you."

"It's a bargain," exclaimed the sailor. "By George! I've had enough of it from Lun'non here. As to money, look here," he put his hand into his trousers pocket and pulled out a handful of coins, gold, silver and copper together. "There is brass for all. Just home, paid off—and find my wife dead—and me saddled with the yowling kid. I'm off to sea again. Don't see no sport wider-erring here all bebothered with a baby."

"We are very willing to accompany you," said the tattered man, and turning to the fellow with sallow face and lantern jaws, he said, "What's your opinion, Lonegon?"

"I'm willing, Marshall; what say you, Michael Casey?"

"Begorra—I'm the man to be a wet nuss."

The sailor called for spirits wherewith to treat the men who had offered their assistance.

"This is a mighty relief to me," said he. "I don't think I could ha' got on by myself."

"You've no expayrience, sir," said Casey. "It's I'm the boy for the babbies. Ye must rig up a bottle and fill it with milk, and just a whisk of a drop of the craytur to prevent it curdling, and then stuff the mouth with a rag—and the darlin'll suck, and suck, and be still as the evenin' star as I sees yonder glimmering at the window."

"You'll have to start pretty sharp if you want to get on a stage before dark," said the man by the fire.

"It's a lone road," threw in the boy shyly.

"What's the odds when we are four of us?" asked the man whose name was Lonegon.

"And all of us pertecting the little cherub from ketching cold," threw in Casey.

"We ain't afraid—not we," said the ragged man.

"Not of bogies, at any rate."

"Oh, you need not fear bogies," observed the man at the fire, dryly.

"What is it, then?" asked Michael Casey. "Sure It's not highwaymen?"

The man by the fire warmed his palms, laughed, and said: "It would take two to rob you, I guess, one to put the money into your pocket and the second to take it out."

"You're right there," answered the Irishman, laughing. "It's my pockets be that worn to holes wi' the guineas that have been in them, that now they let 'em fall through."

The man by the fire rubbed his palms together and made a remark in a low tone—addressed to the boy. Lonegon turned sharply round on his seat and cried threateningly, "What's that you're hinting agin us? Say it again, and say it aloud, and I'll knock your silly, imperdent head off."

"I say it again," said the young man, turning his cunning head round, like a jackdaw. "I say that if I were going over Hind Head and by the Punch Bowl at night with as much money in my pocket as has that seaman there—I'd choose my companions better. You haven't heard what I said? I'd choose my companions better."

CHAPTER II. — WANDERING SOULS

The long, lean fellow, Lonegon, leaped to his feet, and struck at the man by the fire.

The latter was prepared for him. He had snatched a brand from the hearth, and without losing the sarcastic laugh on his great mouth, presented it sharply in the way of the descending fist, so as to catch Lonegon's wrist.

The sparks flew about at the clash, and the man who had received the blow uttered a howl of pain, for his wrist was torn by the firewood, and his hand burnt by the fire.

With an imprecation and a vow to "do for" "eyes, liver, and lights" of the "clodhopper," he rushed at him blindly. With a mocking laugh, the man assailed thrust forth a leg, and Lonegon, stumbling across it, measured his length on the floor.

The man called Marshall now interfered by snatching the pewter tankard from the sailor, and aiming it at the head of him who had overthrown his mate.

At the same time the boy, terrified, began to scream. "Mother! mother! help! pray! they'll murder Bideabout."

The hostess speedily appeared, set her arms akimbo, planted her feet resolutely on the floor, and said, in commanding tones—

"Now then! No fighting on the premises. Stand up, you rascal. What have you done with the pewter? Ah, crushed out of all shape and use. That's what Molly Luff sed of her new bonnet when she sat down on it—Lawk, a biddy! Who'd ha' thought it?"

Lonegon staggered to his feet, and burst into a torrent of recrimination against the man whom the boy had called Bideabout.

"I don't care where the rights are, or where be the wrongs. An addled egg be nasty eating whether you tackle it one end or 'tother. All I sez is—I won't have it. But what I will have is—I'll be paid for that there tankard. Who threw it?"

"It was he—yonder, in tatters," said the boy.

"You won't get money out o' me," said Marshall; "my pockets—you may turn 'em out and see for yourself—are rich in nothing but holes, and there's in them just about as many of they as there are in the rose o' a watering can."

"I shall be paid," asserted the hostess. "You three are mates, and there'll be money enough among you."

"Look here, mistress," put in the sailor, "I'll stand the damage, only don't let us have a row. Bring me another can of ale, and tell me what it all comes to. Then we'll be on the move."

"The other fellows may clear off, and the sooner the better," said the landlady. "But not you just now, and the baby has dropped off into the sweetest of sleeps. 'Twere a sin to wake her."

"I'm going on to the Huts," said the seaman.

"And we're going with him as a guard to the baby," said the Irish fellow.

"A blackguard set," threw in Bideabout.

"What about the color so long as it is effective?" asked Casey.

By degrees the anger of Lonegon was allayed, and he seated himself growling at the table, and wiped the blood from his torn wrist on his sleeve, and drawing forth a dirty and tattered red kerchief, bound it round the bruised and wounded joint. The man, Bideabout, did not concern himself with the wrath or the anguish of the man. He rubbed his hands together, and clapped a palm on each knee, and looked into the fire with a smirk on his face, but with an eye on the alert lest his adversary should attempt to steal an advantage on him.

Nor was he unjustified in being on his guard, judging by the malignant glances cast at him by Lonegon.

"Whom may you be?" asked the tattered man.

"I'm Jonas Kink," answered the young fellow at the fire.

"He's Bideabout, the Broom-Squire," explained the landlady. Then with a glimmering of a notion that this variation in names might prove confusing, she added, "leastways that's what we calls him. We don't use the names writ in the Church register here. He's the Broom-Squire—and not the sort o' chap for you ragamuffins to have dealings with—let me tell you."

"I don't kear what he be," said Lonegon, sullenly, "but dang it, I'd like a sup o' ale with your leave," and without further ceremony he took the new tankard from the sailor and quaffed off half its contents.

The hostess looked from the drinker to the seaman and said, "Are you standing tick for they?"

"I'll pay for their drink and they'll help me along the road with the baby," said the sailor.

The landlady shrugged her shoulders contemptuously, and asked, "If I may be so bold, what's her name?"

"What's whose name?"

"The baby's."

"Ha'n't got none," said the seaman.

"What, ain't she been christened yet?"

"No, I reckon not," answered the father. Then he proceeded to explain. "You see my poor wife she was down in lodgings and hadn't no friends nor relations no'ther nigh her, and she took ill and never got over the birth of this here babe, and so it couldn't be done. But the kid's aunt'll see to all that right enough when I've got her there."

"What! you're trapsing about the country hugging a babe along under your arm and slung over your shoulder and feeding her o' blackberries and chucking her in among fly poison, and not a Christian yet! My! What a world it is!".

"All in good time, missus."

"That's what Betsy Cole said o' her pork and 'ams when the pig wor killed and her hadn't salt nor saltpetre. She'd see to it some day. Meanwhile the maggots came and spiled the lot."

"It shall all be made right in a day or two."

"Ah! but what if it be too late? Then where will you go to some day? How can you say but that the child wi' being hung topsy-turvy and swinging like a pendiddlum may die of the apoplexy, or the blackberries turn sour in her blessed stomach and she go off in convulsions, or that she may ha' put out the end o' her tongue and sucked some o' that there fly paper? Then where will you be?"

"I hope I shall be on board ship just before that comes to pass," said the sailor.

"Do you know what happens if a child dies and ha'n't been christened? It becomes a wanderer."

"What do you mean?"

"It ain't a Christian, so it can't go to heaven. It ain't done no evil, so it can't go to hell; and so the poor spirit wanders about in the wind and never has no rest. You can hear them piping in the trees and sobbin' at the winder. I've heard 'm scores of times. How will you like that when at sea to have your own child sighing and sobbin' up in the rigging of the vessel, eh?"

"I hope it will not come to that," said the sailor.

"That's what Susan Bay said when she put a darnin' needle into the armchair cushion, and I sed, said I, 'twas a ticklesome thing and might do hurt. She did it once too often. Her old man sat down on it."

She brought some more ale at the request of the seaman, and as she set down the tankard said:

"I won't be so bold as to say it's in Scriptur', but it's in the Psalm-book I dare swear. Mother, she were a tip-top tearin' religious woman, and she used to say it to me when I was younger than I be now:—

"'They flies in clouds and flap their shrouds
When full the moon doth shine;
In dead of night when lacketh light,
We here 'em pipe and pine.

"'And many a soul wi' hoot and howl
Do rattle at the door,
Or rave and rout, and dance about
All on a barren moor.'

"And it goes on somehow like this. You can think on it as you go over Hind Head in the dark:

"'Or at the winder wail and weep,
Yet never venture nigher;
In snow and sleet, within to creep
To warm 'em at the fire.'"

The child began to cry in the adjoining room.

"There," said the landlady, "'tis awake she is, poor mite without a name, and not as much Christianity as could make a cat sneeze. If that there child were to die afore you got to Portsmouth and had her baptized, sure as my name is Susanna Verstage, I'd never forgive myself, and I'd hear her for sure and certainty at the winder. I'm a motherly sort of a woman, and there's a lot o' them poor wanderers comes piping about the panes of an evening. But I can do nothing for them."

"Now then, lads, let's be moving," said the mariner.

The three men at the table rose; and when standing exposed more of their raggedness and the incongruity of their apparel than was shown when they were seated.

The landlady reluctantly surrendered the child.

"A babe," said she, "mustn't be shaken after feeding;" then, "a babe mustn't be allowed to get its little feet cold, or gripes comes;" then, "you must mind and carry it with the head to your shoulder, and away from the wind." Presently another item occurred to the good woman, as the men left their places at the table: "You must hold the child on your arm, between the wrist and the elbow-jint."

As they went to the door she called, "And never be without a drop o' dill water: it's comforting to babies."

As they made their exit—"And when nussin', mind, no green meat nor fruit."

When all had departed the landlady turned to the man by the fire, who still wore his sarcastic smirk, and said "Bideabout! What do you think of they?"

"I think," answered the Broom-Squire, "that I never saw three such cut-throat rascals as those who have gone off with the sailor; and as for him—I take he's softish."

"I thought him a bit of a natural."

"He must be so to start on one of the lonesomest roads in England, at fall of night, with such a parcel of jailbirds."

"Well, dear life!" exclaimed the good woman. "I hope nothing will hap' to the poor child."

"Mother," said the boy, timidly, "it's not true is it about the spirits of babies in the wind?"

"Of course it is. Where would you have them go? and they bain't Christians. Hark! I won't say there be none flying about now. I fancy I hear a sort of a kind o' whistling."

"Your boy Iver, he's coming with me to the Punch-Bowl," said the Broom-Squire; "but I'll not go for half-an-hour, becos I don't want to overtake that lanky, black-jawed chap as they call Lonegon. He ain't got much love for me, and might try to repay that blow on his wrist, and sprawl on the floor I gave him."

"What is Iver going to the Punch-Bowl for?" asked the landlady, and looked at the boy, her son.

"It's a snipe's feather Bideabout has promised me," answered the lad.

"And what do you want a snipe's feather for at this time o' night?"

"Mother, it's to make a paint brush of. Bideabout ain't at home much by day. I've been over the road scores o' times."

"A paint brush! What do you want paint brushes for? Have you cleaned out the pig-stye lately?"

"Yes, mother, but the pig lies abroad now; it's warm in the stye."

"Well, you may go. Dear life! I wish I could see that blessed babe again, safe and sound. Oh, my!"

The good-hearted woman was destined to have her wish answered more speedily than she could have anticipated.

CHAPTER III. — THE PUNCH-BOWL

The Broom-Squire and the boy were on their way up the hill that led towards the habitation of the former; or, to be more exact, it led to the summit of the hill whence the Squire would have to diverge at a sharp angle to the right to reach his home.

The evening had closed in. But that mattered not to them, for they knew their way, and had not far to go.

The road mounted continuously, first at a slight incline, over sand sprinkled with Scotch pines, and then more rapidly to the range of hills that culminates in Hind Head, and breaks into the singular cones entitled The Devil's Jumps.

This is one of the loveliest parts of fair England. The pine and the oak and the Spanish chestnut luxuriate in the soil, the sand tracts between the clumps are deep in heather, at intervals the country is furrowed as by a mighty plough; but the furrowing was done by man's hand to extract the metal of which the plough is formed. From a remote antiquity this district of Surrey, as well as the weald of Sussex, was the great centre of the iron trade. The metal lies in masses in the sand, strangely smooth and liver-colored, and going by the name of kidney iron. The forest of Anderida which covered the weald supplied at once the ore and the fuel for smelting.

In many places are "hammer ponds," pools of water artificially constructed, which at one time served to turn wheels and work mechanism for the beating out of the iron that had been won on the spot.

The discovery of coal and iron together, or in close proximity, in the North of England brought this industry of the counties of Surrey and Sussex to an abrupt end. Now the deposits of ore are no longer worked, no furnaces exist, only the traces of the old men's mines and forges and smelting pits remain to attest that from an age before Caesar landed in Kent, down to the close of the last century, all the iron employed in England came from this region.

Another singular feature of the district consists in the masses of hard stone, gray with lichen, that lie about, here topping a sandhill, there dropped at random in the plain. There was at one time many more of these, but owing to their power of resisting heat they were largely exploited as hearthstones. These masses, there can be no doubt, are remains of superincumbent beds of hard rock that have been removed by denudation, leaving but a few fragments behind.

That superstition should attach to these blocks is not marvellous. The parish in which lies the Punch-Bowl and rises Hind Head, comprises one such Thors-stone, named perhaps after the Scandinavian Thunder god. One of these strange masses of stone formerly occupied a commanding position on the top of Borough Hill. On this those in need knocked, whereupon the "Good People" who lived under it lent money to the knockers, or any utensil desired in loan, on condition that it was returned. One night, a petitioner, who was going to give a feast at the baptism of his child, went to the stone, and knocked, and asked in a loud voice for the loan of a cauldron.

This was at once thrust out from under the stone, and was carried away and used for the christening feast. Unhappily, the applicant for the cauldron neglected to return it at the time appointed, and since then no more loans have been made. The cauldron, which is of copper, is now preserved in Frensham parish church. It is two feet in diameter, and stands on an iron trivet.

After the road had ascended some way, all trees disappeared. The scenery was as wild and desolate as any in Scotland. On all sides heathery slopes, in the evening light a broken patch of sand showed white, almost phosphorescent, through contrast with the black ling. A melancholy bird piped. Otherwise all was still. The richly-wooded weald, with here and there a light twinkling on it, lay far below, stretching to Lewes. When the high-road nearly reached the summit, it was carried in a curve along the edge of a strange depression, a vast basin in the sand-hills, sinking three hundred feet to a marshy bottom full of oozing springs. This is termed the Devil's Punch-Bowl. The modern road is carried on a lower level, and is banked up against the steep incline. The old road was not thus protected and ran considerably higher.

The night was gathering in, fold on fold, and obscuring all. The Punch-Bowl that the Broom-Squire and the boy had on their right was a bowl brimming with naught save darkness. Its depths could not be fathomed by the eye at that time of night, nor did any sound issue from it save a hissing as though some fluid were seething in the bowl; yet was this produced solely by the wind swirling in it among the harsh branches of the heather.

"So your mother don't like your drawing and painting," said the Broom-Squire.

"No, Bideabout, she and father be terrible on at me to become a publican, and carry along with the Ship, after father's got old and gived up. But I don't fancy it; in fact, I hate the thought of it. Of course," added the boy; "if they forces me to it, I must. But anyhow I wouldn't like to have that there Ship sign at our door so bad painted as she be. I could do better if I had the paints."

"Oh! drinkers don't care for beautiful pictures at the door, but for good ale within."

"I don't like that there ship, and I wouldn't stand it—if the inn were mine."

"You're a fool," said the Broom-Squire contemptuously. "Here's the spot where the turn comes off the road to my house. Mind where you walk, and don't roll over down the Punch-Bowl; it's all a bog at the bottom."

"There's no light anywhere," observed the boy.

"No—no winders look this way. You can't say if a house is alive or dead from here."

"How long have you had your place in the Punch-Bowl, Bideabout?"

"I've heard say my grandfather was the first squatter. But the Rocliffes, Boxalls, Snellings, and Nashes will have it they're older. What do I care so long as I have the best squat in the lot."

That the reader may understand the allusions a word or two must be allowed in explanation of the settlements in the Punch-Bowl.

This curious depression in the sand range is caused by a number of springs welling up several hundred feet below the summit of the range. The rain that falls on the hills sinks through the sand until it reaches an impervious bed of clay, when it breaks forth at many orifices. These oozing springs in course of vast ages have undermined and washed away the superincumbent sand and have formed the crater called the Devil's Punch-Bowl. The bottom is one impassable swamp, and the water from the springs flows away to the north through an opening in the sand-hills.

At some unknown date squatters settled in the Punch-Bowl, at a period when it was in as wild and solitary a region as any in England. They enclosed portions of the slopes. They built themselves hovels; they pastured their sheep, goats, cattle on the sides of the Punch-Bowl, and they added to their earnings the profits of a trade they monopolized—that of making and selling brooms.

On the lower slopes of the range grew coppices of Spanish chestnut, and rods of this wood served admirably for broom-handles. The heather when long and wiry and strong, covered with its harsh leafage and myriad hard knobs, that were to burst into flower, answered for the brush.

On account of this manufacture, the squatters in the Punch-Bowl went by the designation of Broom-Squires. They provided with brooms every farm and gentleman's house, nay, every cottage for miles around. A wagon-load of these besoms was often purchased, and the supply lasted some years.

The Broom-Squires were an independent people. They used the turf cut from the common for fuel, and the farmers were glad to carry away the potash as manure for their fields.

Another business supplemented farming and broom-making. That was holly-cutting and getting. The Broom-Squires on the approach of Christmas scattered over the country, and wherever they found holly trees and bushes laden with berries, without asking permission, regardless of prohibition, they cut, and then when they had a cartload, would travel with it to London or Guildford, to attend the Christmas market.

Not only did they obtain their fuel from the heaths, but much of their victual as well. The sandy hills abound in rabbits, and the lagoons and morasses at the foot of the hills in the flat land teem with fish and wild fowl. At the present day the ponds about Frensham are much in request for fishing—at the time of our tale they were netted by the inhabitants of the neighborhood when they felt a hankering after fish, and the "moors," as marshes are locally termed, were prowled over for ducks, and the sand burrows watched for rabbits, all without let and hindrance.

At the present date there are eight squatter families in the Punch-Bowl, three belong to the branches of the clan of Boxall, three to that of Snelling, and two to the less mighty clan of Nash. At the time of which I write one of the best built houses and the most fertile patches of land was in the possession of the young man, Jonas Kink, commonly known as Bideabout.

Jonas was a bachelor. His father and mother were dead, and his sister had married one of the Rocliffe's. He lived alone in his tolerably substantial house, and his sister came in when she was able to put it tidy for him and to do some necessary cooking. He was regarded as close-fisted though young; his age about twenty-three years. Hitherto no girl had caught his fancy, or had caught it sufficiently to induce him to take one to wife.

"Tell'y what," said his sister, "you'll be nothing else but an old hudger (bachelor)."

This was coming to be a general opinion. Jonas Kink had a heart for money, and for that only. He sneered at girls and flouted them. It was said that Jonas would marry no girl save for her money, and that a monied girl might pick and choose for herself, and such as she would most assuredly not make election of Bideabout. Consequently he was foredoomed to be a "hudger."

"What's that?" suddenly exclaimed the Broom-Squire, who led the way along a footpath on the side of the steep slope.

"It's a dead sheep, I fancy, Bideabout."

"A dead sheep—I wonder if it be mine. Hold hard, what's that noise?"

"It's like a babe's cry," said the boy. "Oh, lawk! if it be dead and ha' become a wanderer! I shu'd never have the pluck to go home alone."

"Get along with your wanderers. It's arrant nonsense. I don't believe a word of it."

"But there is the crying again. It is near at hand. Oh, Bideabout! I be that terrified!"

"I'll strike a light. I'm not so sure about this being a dead sheep."

Something lay on the path, catching what little light came from the sky above.

Jonas stooped and plucked some dry grass. Then he got out his tinderbox and struck, struck, struck.

The boy's eyes were on the flashing sparks. He feared to look elsewhere. Presently the tinder was ignited, and the Broom-Squire blew it and held dry grass haulms to the glowing embers till a blue flame danced up, became yellow, and burst into a flare.

Cautiously Jonas approached the prostrate figure and waved the flaming grass above it, whilst sparks flew about and fell over it.

The boy, shrinking behind the man, looked timidly forward, and uttered a cry as the yellow flare fell over the object and illumined a face.

"I thought as much," said the Broom-Squire. "What else could he expect? Them three chaps ha' murdered him. They've robbed and stripped him."

"Oh—Bideabout!"

"Aye. What other could come o' such companions. They've gone off wi' his clothes—left his shirt—have they? That's curious, as one of the blackguards had none."

Then the child's wailing and sobbing sounded more continuously than before.

"The baby ain't far off," said Jonas. "I suppose we can't leave it here. This is a pretty awkward affair. Tell'y what, Iver. You bide by the dead man and grope about for that there baby, and I'll go down to the houses and get help."

"Oh, Bideabout! I dursn't."

"Dursn't what?"

"Not be left alone—here—in the Punch-Bowl with a dead man."

"You're a fool," said Jonas, "a dead man can't hurt nobody, and them rascals as killed him are for sure a long way off by this time. Look here, Iver, you timid 'un, you find that squalling brat and take it up. I don't mind a brass fardin' being here wi' a corpse so long as I can have my pipe, and that I'll light. But I can't stand the child as well. You find that and carry it down, and get the Boxalls, or someone to take it in. Tell 'em there's a murdered man here and I'm by the body, and want to get home and can't till someone comes and helps to carry it away. Cut along and be sharp. I'd ha' given a shilling this hadn't happened. It may cost us a deal o' trouble and inconvenience—still—here it is—and—you pick about and find that creature squealin' its bellows out."

There was callousness unusual and repulsive in so young a man. It jarred with the feelings of the frightened and nervous boy. Tears of alarm and pity were in his eyes. He felt about in the heather till he reached the infant. It was lying under a bush. He took the poor little creature up, and the babe, as though content to feel itself with strong arms under it, ceased to cry.

"What shall I do, Bideabout?"

"Do—cut along and raise the Boxalls and the Snellings, and bid them come and remove the body, and get someone to take the child. Confound the whole concern. I wish they'd done it elsewhere—or I hadn't come on it. But it's like my ill-luck."

CHAPTER IV. — WITHOUT A ROOF

The boy, Iver, trudged along carrying the infant in his arms. The little face was against his cheek, and the warm breath played over it. Whenever the child cried, he spoke, and his voice reassured the babe, and it was quiet again. He walked cautiously, as the path was narrow and the night dark. A false step might send him rolling down the steep slope with his burden.

Iver had often been to the squatters' quarters, and he knew very well his direction; but he was now agitated and alarmed.

After a while he reached bushes and could see trees standing black against the sky, and caught the twinkling of lights. Before him was a cottage, and a little garden in front. He opened a wicket and went up to the door and rapped. A call of "Who is there?" in response. The boy raised the latch and entered.

A red peat fire was burning on the hearth, and a man sat by it. A woman was engaged at needlework by the light of a tallow candle.

"Tom Rocliffe!" exclaimed the boy. "There's been a murder. A sailor—he's dead on the path—there's Bideabout Kink standing by and wants you all to come and help and—here's the baby."

The man sprang to his feet. "A murder! Who's dead?"

"There was a sailor came to our place, it's he."

"Who killed him?"

"Some chaps as was drinking with him, so Bideabout says. They've robbed him—he had a lot of brass."

"Dead—is he?" The man ran out.

"And what have you got there?" asked the woman.

"It's his baby."

"How came he by the baby?"

"I heard him say his wife was dead, and he were going to carry the child to his wife's sister."

"What's the man's name?"

"I don't know."

"Where did he come from?"

"He was a seaman."

"Where was he going to put the baby?"

"I don't know 'xactly—somewhere Portsmouth way."

"What's the man's name?"

"I don't know."

"How'll you find her?"

"I don't know."

"Portsmouth is a large place. Are you sure she's in Portsmouth?"

"He said Portsmouth way, I think."

"Then there be a difficulty in finding her?"

"'Spose there will. Will you take the baby?"

"I-I—" The woman stared. "What's its name?"

"It ain't got none."

"Is it a boy or girl?"

"I think it's a girl."

"How old is it?"

"I think he said about six weeks."

"Is it healthy?"

"I don't know."

"Maybe it has the smallpox."

"I do not think so. Will you take it?"

"I—not I. I know nothin' about it. There's no saying, it might bring diseases into the house, and I must consider my own children. Is it terrible dirty?"

"I—I don't think so."

"And it hasn't got a name?"

"No; the sailor said it was not baptized."

"What's the color of its eyes?"

"I don't know."

"Has it got any hair?"

"I have not looked."

"P'raps it's an idjot?"

"I don't think so."

"And is deformed?"

"Oh, no."

"Well, I can't have no baby here as I don't know nothin about. You can take it over to the Snellings. They may fancy it. I won't have nothin' to do with a babe as ain't got no parents and no name, and ain't got no hair and no color in its eyes. There is my Samuel snorin'. Take the child away. I don't want no measles, and smallpox, and scarlatina, and rickets brought into my house. Quick, take the nasty thing off as fast as you can."

Iver shrunk away, left the house, and made his way, carrying the baby, to another cottage a hundred yards distant. There was a lane between them, with a stream running through it, and the banks were high and made the lane dark. The boy stumbled and fell, and though he probably had not hurt the child, he had frightened it, and it set up loud and prolonged screams. With brow bathed in perspiration, and heart beating from alarm, Iver hurried up to the second squatter's cabin, and, without knocking, burst in at the door.

"I say," shouted he, "there's been a man killed, and here's a baby yelling, and I don't know what's the matter with it. I stumbled."

A man who was pulling off his boots started to his feet.

"Stop that darned noise," he said. "My wife—she's bad—got the fever, and can't abide no noise. Stop that din instantly, or I'll kick you out. Who are you, and what do'y mean rushing in on a fellow that way?"

The boy endeavored to explain, but his voice was tremulous, and the cries of the infant pitched at a higher note, and louder.

"I can't hear, and I don't want to," said the man. "Do you mind what I sed? My wife be terrible bad wi' fever, and her head all of a split, and can't bear no noise—and will you do what I say? Take that brat away. Is this my house or is it yours? Take that 'orrid squaller away, or I'll shy my boot at yer head."

"But," said Iver, "there's a man dead—been murdered up in the—"

"There'll be more afore long, if you don't cut. I'll heave that boot at you when I've counted thrice, if you don't get out. Drat that child! It'll wake my wife. Now, then, are you going?"

Iver retreated hastily as the man whirled his heavy boot above his head by the lace.

On leaving the house he looked about him in the dark. The cottages were scattered here and there, some in hollows by springs, others on knolls above them, without a definite road between them, except when two enclosures formed a lane betwixt their hedges.

The boy was obliged to step along with great care, and to feel his way in front of him with his foot before planting it. A quarter of an hour had elapsed before he reached the habitation of the next squatter.

This was a ramshackle place put together of doors and windows fitted into walls, made of boards, all taken from ruinous cottages that had been pillaged, and their wreckage pieced together as best could be managed. Here Iver knocked, and the door was opened cautiously by an old man, who would not admit him till he had considered the information given.

"What do you say? A man murdered? Where? When? Are the murderers about?"

"They have run away."

"And what do you want me to do?"

"Would you mind taking in the poor little baby, and going to help Master Bideabout Kink to carry the body down."

"Where to? Not here. We don't want no bodies here."

The old fellow would have slammed the door in Iver's face had not the boy thrust in foot and knee.

Then a woman was heard calling, "What is that there, Jamaica? I hear a babe."

"Please, Mrs. Cheel, here is a poor little creature, the child of the murdered man, and it has no one to care for it," said the boy.

"A babe! Bless me! give the child to me," cried the woman. "Now then, Jamaica, bundle out of that, and let me get at the baby."

"No, I will not, Betsy," retorted the man designated Jamaica. "Why should I? Ask for an inch, and they'll have an ell. Stick in the toe of the baby, and they'll have the dead father after it. I don't want no corpses here."

"I will have the baby. I haven't set my eyes on a baby this hundred years."

"I say you shan't have nothing of the sort."

"I say I shall. If I choose to have a baby, who's to say me nay?"

"I say you nay. You shan't have no babies here."

"This is my house as much as yourn."

"I'm master I reckon."

"You are an old crabstick."

"You're an old broom-handle."

"Say that again."

"I say it."

"Now then—are you going to hit me?"

"I intend to."

Then the old man and his wife fell to fighting, clawing and battering each other, the woman screaming out that she would have a baby, the man that she should not.

Iver had managed to enter. The woman snatched at the child, the man wrenched it away from her. The boy was fain to escape outside and fly from the house with the child lest the babe should be torn in pieces between them. He knew old Cheel and his wife well by repute—for a couple ever quarrelling.

He now made his way to another house, one occupied by settlers of another family. There were here some sturdy sons and daughters.

When Iver had entered with the babe in his arms and had told his tale, the young people were full of excitement.

"Bill," said one of the lads to his brother, "I say! This is news. I'm off to see."

"I'll go along wi' you, Joe."

"How did they kill him?" asked one of the girls. "Did they punch him on the head?"

"Or cut his throat?" asked Bill.

"Joe!" called one of the girls, "I'll light the lantern, and we'll all go."

"Aye!" said the father, "these sort o' things don't happen but once in a lifetime."

"I wouldn't be out of seeing it for nuthin'," said the mother. "Did he die sudden like or take a long time about it?"

"I suppose they'll inquitch him," said one of the girls.

"There'll be some hanging come o' this," said one of the boys.

"Oh, my! There will be goings on," said the mother. "Dear life, I may never have such a chance again. Stay for me, Betsy Anne. I'm going to put on my clogs."

"Mother, I ain't agoing to wait for your clogs."

"Why not? He won't run away."

"And the baby?" asked Iver.

"Oh, bother the baby. We want to see the dead man."

"I wonder, now, where they'll take him to?" asked the mother. "Shall we have him here?"

"I don't mind," said the father. "Then he'll be inquitched here; but I don't want no baby."

"Nor do I nuther," said the woman. "Stay a moment, Betsy Anne! I'm coming. Oh, my! whatever have I done to my stocking, it's tore right across."

"Take the child to Bideabout," said one young man, "we want no babies here, but we'll have the corpse, and welcome. Folks will come and make a stir about that. But we won't have no babies. Take that child back where you found it."

"Babies!" said another, scornfully, "they come thick as blackberries, and bitter as sloes. But corpses—and they o' murdered men—them's coorosities."

"But the baby?" again asked the boy.

CHAPTER V. — MEHETABEL

Iver stood in the open air with the child in his arms. He was perplexed. What should be done with it? He would have rubbed his head, to rub an idea into it, had not both his arms been engaged.

Large warm drops fell from the sky, like tears from an overcharged heart. The vault overhead was now black with rain clouds, and a flicker over the edge of the Punch-Bowl, like the quivering of expiring light in a despairing eye, gave evidence that a thunderstorm was gathering, and would speedily break.

The babe became peevish, and Iver was unable to pacify it.

He must find shelter somewhere, and every door was shut against the child. Had it not been that the storm was imminent, Iver would have hasted directly home, in full confidence that his tender-hearted mother would receive the rejected of the Broom-Squire, and the Ship Inn harbor what the Punch-Bowl refused to entertain.

He stumbled in the darkness to Jonas Kink's house, but finding the door locked, and that the rain was beginning to descend out of the clouds in rushes, he was obliged to take refuge in an out-house or barn—which the building was he could not distinguish. Here he was in absolute darkness. He did not venture to grope about, lest he should fall over some of the timber that might be, and probably was, collected there.

He supposed that he was in the place where Jonas fashioned his brooms, in which case the chopping block, the bundles of twigs, as well as the broom-sticks would be lying about. Bideabout was not an orderly and tidy worker, and his material would almost certainly be dispersed and strewn in such a manner as to trip up and throw down anyone unaccustomed to the place, and unprovided with a light.

The perspiration broke out on the boy's brow. The tears welled up in his eyes. He danced the infant in his arms, he addressed it caressingly, he scolded it. Then, in desperation, he laid it on the ground, and ran forth, through the rain, to the cottage of an old maid near, named Sally, stopping, however, at intervals in his career, to listen whether the child were still crying; but unable to decide, owing to the prolonged chime in his ears. It is not at once that the drums of hearing obtain relief, after that they have been set in vibration by acute clamor. On reaching the old maid's door he knocked.

For some time Sally remained irresponsive.

"I knows very well," said she to herself under the bedclothes, "it's that dratted boy who has been at the Rocliffe's."

Iver persisted in knocking. At length she appeared at the casement, opened it, thrust forth her nightcapped head, and said peevishly, "It ain't no manner o' use. I won't have no babies here, not to my time o' life, thank'y. I sez I won't, and wot I sez that I sticks to like toffee between the teeth. You may knock them there knuckles of yorn into dimples, but open I won't. I won't. I won't."

The old woman stamped on her bedroom floor.

"I do not ask that, Sally," pleaded the boy. "I have set the baby in Bideabout's barn, and there's no knowin', it may get hold of the chopper and hack off its limbs, or pull down all the rick o' broom-handles on Itself, or get smothered in the heather. I want a lantern. I don't know how to pacify the creature, and 'tis squeadling that terrible I don't know what's the matter."

"Is it a drawin' of the hind legs up, and stiffenin' of the back?" asked the old maid.

"I think so," answered the boy, dubiously; then, with further consideration, "I'm sure of it. It wriggled in my arms, like a worm when one's gettin' it on a hook out fishing."

"That's convulsions," said Sally. "'Twill go off in one of they, sure as eggs is eggs and ain't inions."

"Do you really say so?"

"It's that, or water on the brain. Wi' all this pouring rain, I shouldn't wonder if 'twasn't the tother. Not, you know, that I've any acquaintance wi babies. Only I've heard wimmin talk as has had 'em just like rabbits."

"Do they die when they have water on the brain?" asked the boy.

"Always. Babies can't stand it, no more nor can goslings gettin' their backs wetted."

"Don't you think that perhaps it's only hunger?"

"Can't say. Has the babe been a grabbin' and a clawin' at your nose, and a tryin' to suck it?"

"Once, Sally, when my nose got into the way."

"Then there's hunger too," said Sally, sententiously. "Them babies has terrible apertites, like canibals, and don't know what's good for 'em."

"Will you help me?" pleaded the boy. "Have you a feeding bottle?"

"Presarve and deliver us—I! What do you take me for, you imperant bye?"

"I think any medicine bottle would do, if well washed out. I shouldn't like, if there was any castor oil or senna tea dregs left, you know. But properly washed out, it might do, with a little milk in it."

"You'll choke the baby like that," said the old maid.

"I have seen how it is done. You stuff a bit of rag into the throat of the bottle, and leave a tip o' rag hanging out."

"Dare say, but you byes seems to understand these things better than I."

"Won't you come down and help me, Sally?"

"I'll come down presently when I've tumbled into some of my clothes."

Then the head disappeared, and the casement was shut.

After the lapse of a few minutes, a light appeared at the window of the lower room, and the door was slowly unlocked and unbarred.

Then the old woman appeared in the doorway. She wore her huge white-frilled nightcap, that fluttered in the wind about the shrivelled face it enclosed, but she presented an extremely limp and attenuated appearance in her person.

"I've been a turnin' over in my head," she said, "and ten chances to half-a-one, if that there child hev been squealin' so long, it's either broke a blood vessel, or will die o' 'plexy. There'll be a purty expense to the parish. There'll be two buryings laid on it that oughten't to be. That means an extra penny in the rates. If them there chaps wanted to murder a man, why didn't they go and do it in Hampshire, and not go a burdenin' of this county an' parish? There's rayson in everything."

"Do you really suppose the child will die?" asked the boy, more concerned about the life than about the rates.

"How can I say? I've had precious little to do wi' babies, thanks be. Now, sharp, what is it you want? I'm perishin' wi' cold."

"May I have a bottle and some milk, and a lantern?"

"You can have wot you wants, only I protest I'll have no babies foist on me here." Then she added, "I will not trust you byes. Show me your hands that you ain't hidin' of it behind yer back."

"I assure you the child is in Bideabout's shed. Do be quick, and help. I am so afraid lest it die, and becomes a wanderer."

"If I can help it I will do what I can that it mayn't die, for certain," said the woman, "anything but taking it in here, and that I won't, I won't, I won't." Again she stamped.

Iver provided himself with the requisites as speedily as might be, and hastened back to the outhouse. At the door a cat was miawling, and rubbed itself against his shins. When he entered the cat followed him.

The child was still sobbing and fitfully screaming, but was rapidly becoming exhausted.

Iver felt the arms and head and body to ascertain whether any bone was broken or battered by the fall, but his acquaintance with the anatomy of a child was still rudimentary for him to come to any satisfactory conclusion.

He held the bottle in one and, but was ignorant how to administer the contents. Should the child be laid on its back or placed in a sitting posture?

When he applied the moistened rag to its mouth he speedily learned that position was immaterial. The babe fell to work vigorously, with the large expectation of results. Some moments elapsed before it awoke to the fact that the actual results were hardly commensurate with its anticipations, nor with its exertions.

When roused to full consciousness that it was being trifled with, then the resentment of the infant was vehement and vociferous. It drew up its legs and kicked out. It battled with its hands, it butted with its pate, and in its struggles pulled the plug out of the mouth of the flask so that the milk gushed over its face and into its mouth, at once blinding and choking it.

"Oh, dear, oh, dear, what shall I do?" he exclaimed, and began to cry with vexation.

The cat now came to his assistance. It began to lick up the spilled milk.

Iver seized the occasion.

"Look, see, pretty puss!" said he, caressingly, to the child. "Stroke pussy. Don't be afraid. You see she likes the milk that you wouldn't have. Naughty pussy eats little birds and mousies. But she won't touch babies."

The cat having appropriated the spilled milk looked at the infant with an uncanny way out of her glinting green eyes, as though by no means indisposed to try whether baby was not as good eating as a fledgling bird, as toothsome as a mouse.

Iver caught up the cat and scratched her under the chin and behind the ears.

"Do you hear? The pussy purrs. Would that you also might purr. She is pleased to make your acquaintance. Oh do, do, do be quiet!"

Then casting aside the cat he endeavored slowly to distil some of the milk down the child's throat without suffering it to swallow too much at once, but found the task difficult, if not impossible for his hand shook.

"Wait a bit," said he. "There are straws here. I will cut one and put it through the rag, and then you can tipple like a king upon his throne."

He selected a stout barley straw, and finding a knot in it endeavored to perforate the obstruction with a pin. When this failed he looked about for another straw, and at last discovered one that was strong, uninterrupted by knots, and sufficiently long to serve his purpose.

For awhile he was so engrossed in his occupation that the child remained unnoticed. But when the straw had been adjusted satisfactorily, and the apparatus was in working order, as Iver ascertained by testing it himself, then he looked round at his charge.

The babe was lying silent and motionless.

His heart stood still.

"It is dead! It is going to die! It will become a wanderer!" he exclaimed; and putting down the feeding bottle, snatched up the lantern, crept on his knees to the child, and brought the little face within the radius of the sickly yellow light.

"I cannot see! O, I can see nothing! There is no light worth having!" he gasped, and proceeded to open the door in the lantern side.

"What is do be done?" he asked despairingly. "I do not know if it be dying or be in a fit. O! live! do, do live! I'll give you a brass button and some twine out of my pocket! I promise you my next lollipops if you will. Nasty, cross, disobliging thing." He went to the barn door and looked out, saw that the rain was coming down in torrents, came back. "Is it true," asked he, "that you must be a wanderer, if you die unchristened? Shall I ever hear you yowling in the wind? It is too, too dreadful!"

A chill came over the boy's heart.

Iver had never seen death. He was vastly frightened at the thought that the little soul might fleet away whilst he was watching. He dared not leave the child. He was afraid to stay. If he were to desert the babe, and it expired—and to run home, would not the soul come crying and flapping after him?

He considered with his hands to his head.

"I know what I will do!" exclaimed he, suddenly; "I'll make a Christian of it, anyhow."

There was standing on the floor an old broken red bowl of coarse pottery, out of which fowls had been fed. It was now empty.

Iver took it, wiped it out with his hand, and went with it to the door, where a rude "launder" or shoot of wood carried the water from the thatch immediately over the door, and sent the collected moisture in a stream down one side. The boy held the vessel under the shoot till he had obtained sufficient for his purpose, and then, returning within, said, "I'll stop your wandering," went up to the child, sprinkled some water over it and said, "Mehetabel, I baptize thee—"

The cat made a spring and dashed past.

Down went the contents of the bowl over the babe, which uttered a howl lusty, loud enough to have satisfied any nurse that the baptism was valid, and that the devil was expelled.

CHAPTER VI. — MEHETABEL IT MUST BE

In at the barn door came Mrs. Verstage, Iver's mother.

"Iver! Wot's up?"

"Oh, mother!"

"Where's that babe?"

"Here, mother, on the ground."

"On the ground! Good life! Sowsed, soaked through and through, whatever have you been doin'? Holdin' it under the spout?"

"Baptizin' it, mother."

"Baptizin' of it?" The woman stared.

"I thought the creetur was dyin'."

"Well, and wot then?"

"Mother. Lest it shud take to wanderin'."

"Baptizin' of it. Dear life! And what did you call it?"

"Mehetabel."

"Mehetabel! 'Taint a human name."

"It is, mother. It's a Scriptur name."

"Never heard on it."

"Mehetabel was the wife of Hadar."

"And who the dickens was Hadar?"

"He was a dook—a dook of Edom."

In the churchyard of Thursley stands a large white stone, on which is carved a medallion, that contains the representation of a man falling on the ground, with one arm raised in deprecation, whilst two men are robbing and murdering him, and a third is represented as acting sentinel lest the ruffians should be surprised. On the ground are strewn the garments of the man who is being killed. Beneath this rudely sculptured group is this inscription:—

IN MEMORY OF
A GENEROUS, BUT UNFORTUNATE SAILOR,
WHO WAS BARBAROUSLY MURDERED ON HIND HEAD,
ON SEPTEMBER 24TH, 1786,
BY THREE VILLAINS,
AFTER HE HAD LIBERALLY TREATED THEM AND PROMISED THEM
HIS FARTHER ASSISTANCE ON THE ROAD TO PORTSMOUTH.

In the "Royal Huts," a tavern, in which now very good entertainment for man and beast may be had, a tavern which stands somewhat further along the way to Portsmouth than Hind Head, may be seen at this day some rude contemporary paintings representative of the murder.

The ruffians after having killed their victim, robbed him, not only of his money, but also of his clothes, and hastened on their way.

A hue and cry were raised, when the corpse had been discovered, and the men were arrested upon the following day at Sheet, near Peterhead, and were found in possession of the clothing of the deceased. In due course of time they were tried at Kingston, and on the 7th of April, 1787, were hung and gibbeted in chains on Hind Head Hill, beside the old road and close to the scene of their crime.

A cross now marks the summit, and indicates the spot where stood the gallows, and a stone for some time pointed out the locality where the murder was committed. When, however, the new Portsmouth Road was cut further down the hill, skirting the Punch-Bowl at a lower level, then the stone was removed to the side of the new road. At present it is an object visited by vast numbers of holiday-makers, who seem to take almost as lively an interest in the crime that was committed over a century ago as if it were an event of the present day. At the time the murder aroused the greatest possible excitement in the neighborhood, and pre-eminently in the parish of Thursley.

As may be gathered from the wording of the inscription on the tombstone that covers the victim, his name never transpired. No relations claimed the right to bury him. None appeared to take charge of his orphan child.

The parish fretted, it fumed, it protested. But fret, fume, and protest availed nothing, it had to defray the cost of the funeral, and receive and lap the child in its parochial mercies.

A deceased wife's sister undoubtedly existed somewhere. Such was the conviction of every parishioner. The poor man was on his way to Portsmouth to deposit his child with her when the tragic event took place. Why did she not come forward? Why did she hold her tongue?

Had there existed in her bosom one particle of natural feeling she would not have remained mute and motionless, and allowed the parish to bury her brother-in-law and encumber itself with her niece.

So the parish talked, appealingly, argumentatively, blusteringly, objurgatively, but all to no purpose. The deceased wife's sister kept mum, and invisible. Reluctantly, resentfully, the parish was finally obliged to face the facts, pay the expenses of the interment, and settle that a weekly dole should be afforded for the maintenance of the child, and as that deceased wife's sister did not appear, the parochial bile overflowed upon the hapless babe, who came to be regarded as an incubus on the ratepayers and a general nuisance.

The one difficulty that solved itself—ambulando, was that as to who would take charge of the child. That was solved by the hostess of the Ship.

The parish endeavored to cajole the good woman into receiving the babe as a gift from Heaven, and to exact no compensation for her labors in rearing it, for the expense of clothing, feeding, educating it. But Mrs. Verstage was deaf to such solicitations. She would take charge of the child, but paid she must be. Eventually the parochial authorities, after having called a vestry, and sat three hours in consultation, and to "knuckle under," as the hostess expressed it, and allow a trifle for the entertainment of the little waif.

So the matter was settled.

Then another had to be determined. What about the christening performed in the shed by Iver? What about the outlandish name given the child? The landlady raised no question on these heads till it was settled that the little being was to be an inmate of her house, and under her care. Then she reasoned thus—"Either this here child be a Mehetabel or she bain't. Either it's a Christian or it's a heathen. What is it? Is it fish, is it flesh, or is it good red herring? It ain't no use my calling her Mehetabel if she bain't nothing of the sort. And it ain't no use teachin' her the caterplasm, if she ha'n't been made a Christian. I'll go and ax the pa'son."

Accordingly the good woman took Iver by the shoulder and dragged him to Witley Vicarage, and stated her case and her difficulties. The Vicar had already had wind of what had occurred. Thursley was at the period a chapelry in the extensive parish of Witley, and the church therein had, before the Reformation, been regularly served by the monks of Witley Abbey. It was afterwards more or less irregularly supplied with sacred ministrations from the mother-church, and had no resident pastor.

In former days the parishioners were never very sure whether there was to be a service in Church at Thursley or not. The sexton was on the look-out, and if he saw the parson's wig glimmering over the hedge top, as he rode along, then he at once rushed to the bell-rope and announced to such of the parishioners as were within hearing, that there was to be divine service. If there were no service, then those who had come from a distance in expectation of devotion, retired to the tavern and drank and gossiped, and were not disposed to cavil. The Church of Thursley is curious, it has a central bell-tower supported on huge beams of oak, such oaks they must have been as are never seen now. Those desiring to see the parson had to seek him in the Vicarage of the mother parish.

Mrs. Verstage accordingly had to go with her boy to Witley.

"If the boy gave a name," said the parson.

"He did, your Reverence, and such a name."

"What is it?"

"Mehetabel."

"Wherever did you pick up that name?" asked the Vicar, turning to the boy.

"Please, sir, we was doin' the Dooks of Edom in Sunday-school. We'd already learned David's mighty men, and could run 'em off like one o'clock, and—I don't know how it was, sir, but the name slipped out o' my mouth wi'out a thought. You see, sir, we had so many verses to say for next Sunday, and I had some of the Dooks of Edom to repeat."

"Oh! So you gave it the name of one of the Dukes."

"Please, sir, no. Mehetabel was the wife of one, she was married to his Grace, Dook Hadar."

"Oh, Hadar! to be sure, quite so; quite so! Very good boy, glad you are so well primed in all things necessary to salvation."

"And is the child to be called Mehetabel?" asked the woman.

"That depends," said the Vicar. "How did the boy perform the sacred function?"

"Please, sir," said Iver, "I did it as your Honor does, after the second lesson on Sunday afternoon, and the churching."

"He hadn't no surplice on," argued the mother.

"You had a bowl of pure water?" asked the parson.

"Yes, sir, rain water. I caught it out of the spout."

"And the words used?"

"The same as you say, sir; exactly."

The parson rubbed his chin.

"Was it done in thoughtlessness—in irreverent folly?"

"Oh, no, sir! I did it in sober earnest. I thought the child was going to die."

"Of course," said the Vicar, "lay baptism is valid, even if administered by a Dissenter; but—it is very unusual, very much so."

"I didn't do all that about the cross," observed Iver, "because the cat jumped and upset the bowl."

"Of course, of course. That belongs to the reception into the church, and you couldn't do that as it was—"

"In Bideabout's basin," said Iver.

"You are certain the water touched the child?"

"Soused her," responded the hostess. "She caught a tremendous cold out o' it, and has been runnin' at the nose ever since."

"I think the very best thing we can do," said the Vicar, "is that I should baptize the child conditionally, in church,—conditionally mind."

"And call her by another name?" asked the woman.

"I do not think I can do that."

"It's a terrible mouthful," observed Mrs. Verstage.

"I daresay that in practice you will be able to condense it. As for that boy of yours, ma'am, I should like a word with him, by himself."

"So, the creetur must bide Mehetabel?"

"Mehetabel it must be."

CHAPTER VII. — FALSE PERSPECTIVE

As this story concerns that child which received the name of Mehetabel, it has been necessary to begin de novo with her as a babe, and to relate how she came by her name—that is her Christian name—and how it was that she had no surname at all. Also, how it was that she came to be an inmate of the Ship, and how that her fortunes were linked at the very outset of her career, on the one hand with Iver, who baptized her, and on the other hand with the Broom-Squire, whose roof—that at least of his shed—had sheltered her when every door of the squatter settlement in the Punch-Bowl, was resolutely closed against her.

But although this story begins with Mehetabel before she could speak, before she could assimilate anything more substantial than milk, yet the author has no intention of inflicting on the reader the record of her early days, of her acquisition of the power of speech, and capacity for consuming solid food. Neither is it his purpose to develop at large the growth of her mental powers, and to describe the evolution of her features. Suffice it then to say that Mehetabel grew up in the Ship Inn, almost as a child of the hostess and of her husband, with Iver as her playmate, and somewhat consequential patron.

By the parish at large, whether that of Witley or of its subdivision Thursley, she was coldly regarded. She was but a charity girl, and kind as Mrs. Verstage was, the hostess never forgot that.

Iver was fourteen years older than Mehetabel, and, above all, was a boy, whereas Mehetabel was a waif, and only a girl.

Iver, moreover, regarded the child with gracious condescension. Had he not baptized her? Did she not owe her name to him? Had he not manufactured her first feeding-bottle?

As Mehetabel grew up, it is not surprising that she should regard Iver with admiration and affection, that she cherished every kindness he showed her, and in every way sought to deserve his notice.

The child had an affectionate, a clinging nature, and she threw the tendrils of her heart around the handsome boy, who was both patron and playmate.

It is a matter wholly immaterial whether Mehetabel underwent the ordeal of the customary childish maladies, measles, chicken-pox, whooping-cough for certainty, and scarlet fever and smallpox as possibilities, for none of them cut short the thread of her life, nor spoiled her good looks; either of which eventualities would have prevented this story proceeding beyond the sixth chapter. In the one case, there would have been no one about whom to write, in the other, had she been marked by smallpox or deafened by scarlatina, the interest of the reader could not have been claimed for her—so exacting is the reader of fiction. A heroine must be good-looking, or she will not be read about.

Indeed, it is more than probable, that had the author announced his story to be one of a very plain woman, he might have looked in vain for a publisher to undertake the issue of the story.

Before proceeding further it will be well to assure the reader that, from an early age, promise of beauty was given, and not of beauty only, but of intelligence and robust health.

Mehetabel was sent by Mrs. Verstage not only to a day school, kept by a widow, in Thursley, but also on the Lord's Day to the Vicar's Sunday-school at Witley. The Vicar was an excellent man, kindly disposed, earnest in his desire to do good, so long as the good was to be done in a novel fashion, absolutely untried. Sunday-schools were but a recent introduction, and he seized on the expedient with avidity. Hitherto the children had been catechised in Church after the second lesson in the afternoon, before their parents and the entire congregation. But as this was an usage of the past the Vicar rejected it in favor of the new system. According to the traditional custom the children had been instructed in the Creed, the Lord's Prayer, and the Ten Commandments. But this did not please the innovating Vicar, who cast these out of his curriculum to make way for a knowledge of the geography of Palestine, and an accurate acquaintance with the genealogies that are to be found scattered here and there in the pages of Holy Writ, The teaching of doctrine, according to the Vicar, lay at the bottom of the divisions of Christendom, but there could be no controversy over the latitude and longitude of the sites mentioned in Scripture.

The landlord, proprietor of the Ship and of Mrs. Susanna Verstage, was a dull, obstinate man, slow of thought and of speech, withal kindly. Like many another dull man, if he did a stupid thing he stuck to it;

and the stupider the thing done, the greater the tenacity with which he held to the consequences. His mind was chiefly occupied with a small farm acquired out of the sand waste, hedged about, dressed and cultivated, and increasing annually in value. In this was his interest and pride; he cared nothing for the tavern, save as an adjunct to the farm. All his energies were devoted to the latter, and he allowed his wife to rule supreme in the inn. Simon Verstage was a well-to-do man. He must have managed very ill had he not made a farm answer for which he paid no rent, save an acknowledgment of 6d. an acre to the lord of the manor. He held the land on a head rent upon the lives of himself, his wife, and his son. The public-house, well frequented by wayfarers, and in good repute among the villagers, supplemented the profits made out of the farm in good years, and made up for deficit in such years as rain and deficiency in sun made bad agriculturally.

The inn stood at a junction of roads, or rather where two lanes fell into the main London and Portsmouth road. It sometimes went in consequence by the name of The Lane End Inn. In situation it was fairly sheltered, a hillock of sand rock sheltered it on the east from the bitter winds that swept the waste between Milford and Thursley, and a growth of huge hollies was its protection against the equally cold blasts from the north.

So long as Iver was a small boy, his father employed him about the farm, to assist him in ploughing, to hoe potatoes, and wield the muck-fork in the cow-house, or, to use the local term, the cow-stall. He kept the lad hard at work from morning rise till set of day.

Iver endured this, not entering with interest and pleasure into the work of the farm. He had no perception of the points of a bullock, and he had a prejudice in favor of ragged hedges.

Iver's neglect of duties, and forgetfulness of what was told him, called forth reprimand and provoked chastisement. They were not due to wilfulness or frivolity, but to preoccupation of the mind. The boy had no natural taste for the labors of the field. He disliked them; for everything else he had eyes, save for that which pertained to the tasks imposed on him.

Throughout early boyhood this lack of interest and inattention had caused much friction, and this friction became aggravated as he grew older, and his natural bent became more marked.

It would be hard to find in one family two persons so utterly dissimilar as Iver and his father. They seemed to have diverse faculties seated in their several organs. They neither saw, heard, nor smelt in the same manner, or rather saw, heard, and smelt so differently as to feel in distinct fashion. What pleased the one was distasteful to the other.

It was not possible for Iver to open his mind to his father, because his father could not understand and appreciate his thoughts.

But if his heart was sealed to Simon Verstage, it was open to his mother, who loved and spoiled him, and took his part invariably, whether the boy were in the right or wrong. In every way possible she humored his fancies; and she, unwisely, condoled with him on what she was pleased to consider as his father's injustice. At length there ensued a rupture so wide, so aggravated by mutual recrimination, that Mrs. Verstage doubted her ability to bridge it over.

This breach was occasioned by Iver one morning climbing to the sign-board and repainting the stern of the vessel, which had long irritated his eye because, whereas the ship was represented sideways, the stern was painted without any attempt at fore-shortening; in fact, full front, if such a term can be applied to a stern.

The laws of perspective were outraged in the original painting; of such laws Iver knew nothing. What he did know was that the picture was wrong. His eye, his natural instinct told him so. The matter had been for long one of controversy between himself and his father. The latter had been unable to understand that if the portholes at the side were visible, the entire stern could not possibly be viewed in full.

"She's got a stern, ain't she?" asked the old man. "If she has, then wot's we to deny it her?"

At length Iver cut the controversy short, and brought the quarrel to a crisis by climbing a ladder with a brush and some paints obtained from the village carpenter, during the temporary absence of his father, and putting the foreshortening to rights to the best of his ability.

When the old man was aware what his son had done on his return from Godalming, whither he had betaken himself to a fair, then he was furious. He stormed at Iver for daring to disfigure the sign-board, and at his wife for suffering him to do it unreproved.

Iver turned stubborn and sulky. He muttered an answer, lacking in that respect due to a parent. The old man became abusive.

Mrs. Verstage intervened ineffectually; and when night arrived the youth made a bundle of his clothes and left the house, with the resolve not to return to it so long as his father lived.

Whither he had gone, for a long time was unknown. His mother wept, so did Mehetabel. The old man put on an assumption of indifference, was short and ungracious to his wife. He was constrained to engage a man to do the farm work hitherto imposed upon Iver, and this further tended to embitter him against his rebellious son. He resented having to expend money when for so long he had enjoyed the work of Iver free of cost.

The boy's pride prevented him from writing home till he had secured himself a position in which he could maintain himself. When he did communicate with Thursley, it was through Mehetabel, because Simon had forbidden any allusion to the truant boy, and Mrs. Verstage was not herself much of a scholar, and did not desire unnecessarily to anger her husband by having letters in his handwriting come to her by the post.

Years passed, during which the landlady's heart ached for her son: and as she might not speak of him to Simon, she made a confidant of Mehetabel.

Thus, the old woman and the girl were drawn closer together, and Mehetabel glowed with the thought that she was loved by the hostess as though she were her own daughter.

To talk about the absent one was the great solace of Susanna Verstage's life. There ever gnawed at her heart the worm of bereavement from the child in whom her best affections, her highest pride, her sole ambitions were placed. It may be questioned whether, without the sympathetic ear and heart of Mehetabel into which to pour her troubles and to which to confide her hopes, the woman would not have deteriorated into a hard-hearted virago.

Her love to Simon, never very hot, had dried up. He had wounded her to the quick in unpardonable fashion in driving her only child out of the house, and all for the sake of a two-penny-ha'penny signboard.

Throughout her work she schemed, she thought for Iver; she toiled and endured in the tavern only to amass a competence for him. She clung to the place only because she trusted some day he would return to it, and because every corner was sweet with recollections of him.

When not at work she dreamed, waking or sleeping, and all her dreams were of him. She built castles in the air—all occupied by him. She had but one hope: to meet her son again. All her activities, all her thoughts, all her aspirations, all her prayers were so many lines focussing on one point, and that her son. To Mehetabel she told her mind, and Mehetabel shared all her hopes; the heart of the girl beat in entire sympathy with that of the hostess. Iver's letters were read and re-read, commented on, and a thousand things read into them by the love of the mother that were not, and could not be there. These letters were ever in the girl's bosom, kept there to be out of reach of old Simon, and to be accessible at all moments to the hungering mother. They heard that Iver had taken to painting, and that he was progressing in his profession; that he gave lessons and sold pictures.

What musings this gave rise to! what imaginations! What expectations!

Mrs. Verstage never wearied of talking of Iver to Mehetabel, and it never wearied the girl to speak with the mother about him.

The girl felt that she was indispensable to the old woman; but that she was only indispensable to her so long as Iver was away never entered into her imagination.

There is a love that is selfish as well as a love that is wholly self-annihilating, and an inexperienced child is incapable of distinguishing one from the other.

There is false perspective in the human heart as well as upon signboards.

CHAPTER VIII. — ONLY A CHARITY GIRL

Simon Verstage sat outside the door of his house, one hot June evening, smoking his pipe.

By his side sat his wife, the hostess of the Ship. Eighteen years have passed since we saw her last, and in these years she has become more plump, a little more set in features, and mottled in complexion, but hardly otherwise older in appearance.

She was one of those women who wear well, till a sickness or a piercing sorrow breaks them down, and then they descend life's ladder with a drop, and not by easy graduation.

Yet Mrs. Verstage had not been devoid of trouble, for the loss of her son, the very apple of her eye, had left an ache in her heart that would have been unendurable, were not the balm of hope dropped into the wound. Mehetabel, or as she was usually called Matabel, had relieved her of the most onerous part of her avocation. Moreover, she was not a woman to fret herself to fiddle-strings; she was resolute and patient. She had formed a determination to have her son home again, even if she had to wait for that till his father was put under ground. She was several years younger than Simon, and in the order of nature might calculate on enjoyment of her widowhood.

Simon and his wife sat in the wide porch. This had been constructed as an accommodation for wayfarers, as an invitation to take shade and shelter in hot weather or Mustering storm; but it also served what was uncontemplated, as an ear to the house. Whatever was uttered there was audible within—a fact very generally forgotten or unsuspected by such as occupied the porch. And, indeed, on the present occasion, this fact was wholly unconsidered by the taverner and his spouse, either because it escaped their minds that the porch was endowed with this peculiarity, or else because the only person then in the house was Mehetabel, and her hearing or not hearing what was said was an indifferent matter.

Had there been customers present, drinking, the two would not have been together when and where they were, nor would the topic of conversation between them have been of a private nature.

The innkeeper had begun with a remark which all the world might hear, and none would controvert, viz., that it was fine hay-making weather, and that next day he purposed carrying the crop.

But Mrs. Verstage was indisposed to discuss a matter so obvious as the weather, and so certain as that it would be utilized for saving the hay. She plunged at once into that which lay near her heart, and said, "Simon, you'll answer that there letter now?"

"Whose? Iver's?"

"Of course, Iver's letter. Now you yourself have heard from him, and what does that mean but he wants all square between you. He has got into a famous business. He sells his pictures and gives lessons in drawing and painting at Guildford. It's but a matter of time and he will be a great man."

"What! as a drawing master? I'd as lief he played the fiddle and taught dancing."

"How can you say that, Simon?"

"Because it is what I feels. Here he had a good farm, a good inn, and a good business—one that don't dwindle but is on the increase, and the land bettering every day—and yet off he went, chucked aside the blessin's of Providence, to take up wi' scribblin' and scrawlin' on paper. If it weren't a thing altogether shameful it would be clear ridic'lous."

Simon sucked in smoke enough to fill his lungs, and then blew it forth leisurely in a long spiral.

"Odds' life," said he, "I don't see why I shu'd concern myself about the hay, nor anythin' else. I've enough to live upon and to enjye myself. What more do I want now?"

"What more?" inquired the landlady, with a sigh and a catch in her voice—a sigh of sorrow, a catch of resentment. "What more—when your son is away?"

"Whose fault is that? Home weren't good enough for he. Even the Old Ship on the sign-board didn't give him satisfaction, and he must alter it. I don't see why I should worrit myself about the hay or any other thing. I'll just put up my feet an enjye myself."

"Simon, I pray you answer Iver's letter. Opportunities be like fleas, to be took sharp, or away they goes, they be terrible long-legged. Opportunities only come now and then, and if not caught are lost past recall. 'Twas so wi' Temperance Noakes, who might a' had the chimbley-sweep if she'd a kissed him when he axed. But she said, Wipe and wash your face fust—and she's an old maid now, and goin' sixty. Consider, Simon. Iver be your son, your only child. It's Providence makes us wot we is; that's why you're a man and not a woman. Iver hadn't a gift to be a farmer, but he had to paintin'. It can't be other—it's Providence orders all, or you might be a mother and nursin' a baby, and I smokin' and goin' after the plough in leggin's."

"That's all gammon," growled the landlord.

"We be gettin' old," pursued Mrs. Verstage. "In the end you'll have to give up work, and who but Iver is to come after you here?"

"Him—Iver!" exclaimed Simon. "Your own self says 'e ain't fit to be a farmer."

"Then he may let the farm and stick to the inn."

"He ain't got the makin' of a publican in him," retorted the man; "he's just about fit for nothin' at all."

"Indeed, but he is, Simon," pleaded the woman, "only not in the way you fancies. What good be you now in a public-house? You do nothing there, it is I who have all the managin'."

"I attend to the farm. Iver can do neither. All the money you and I ha' scraped together he'll chuck away wi' both hands. He'll let the fences down I ha' set up; he'll let weeds overrun the fields I ha' cleared. It shall not be. It never shall be."

"He may marry a thrifty wife, as you have done."

"And live by her labor!" he exclaimed, drawing his pipe from his mouth and in knocking out the ash in his anger breaking the stem. "That a child o' mine should come to that!"

"Iver is your own flesh and blood," persisted the woman, in great excitement. "How can you be so hard on him? It's just like that old fowl as pecked her eggs, and we had to wring her neck. It's like rabbits as eat their own young. Nonsense! You must be reconciled together. What you have you cannot leave to a stranger."

"I can do what I will with my own," retorted Simon. "Look here, Susanna, haven't you had that girl, Matabel, with you in place of a child all these years? Don't she work like a slave? Don't she thoroughly understand the business? Has she ever left the hogs unmeated, or the cow unmilked? If it pleases you to go to market, to be away for a week, a fortni't you know that when you come home again everything will be just as you left it, the house conducted respectable, and every drop o' ale and ounce o' 'backy accounted for."

"I don't deny that Matabel's a good girl. But what has that to do with the matter?"

"What! Why everything. What hinders me leavin' the whole pass'l o' items, farm and Ship to her? She'll marry a stiff man as'll look after the farm, and she'll mind the public-house every mite as well as ever have you, old woman. That's a gal as knows chalk from cheese."

Mrs. Verstage leaned back with a gasp of dismay and a cramp at her heart. She dropped her hands on her lap.

"You ain't speaking serious, Simon?"

"I might do wuss," said he; "and the wust I could do 'ad be to give everythin' to that wastrel, Iver, who don't know the vally of a good farm and of a well-established public-house. I don't want nobody after I'm dead and gone to see rack and ruin where all were plenty and good order both on land and in house, and that's what things would come to wi' Iver here."

"Simon, he is a man now. He was a boy, and what he did as a boy he won't do as a man."

"He's a dauber of paints still."

The taverner stood up. "I'll go and cast an eye over the hay-field," he said. "It makes me all of a rage like to think o' that boy."

He threw away the broken pipe and walked off.

Mrs. Verstage's brain spun like a teetotum; her heart turned cold.

She was startled out of her musings by the voice of Mehetabel, who said, "Mother, it is so hot in the kitchen that I have come out to cool myself. Where is father? I thought I heard him talking with you?"

"He's gone to the hay-field. He won't answer Iver's letter. He's just about as hard as one o' them Hammer Ponds when frozen to the bottom, one solid lump."

"No, mother, he is not hard," said Mehetabel, "but he does not like to seem to give way all at once. You write to Iver and tell him to come here; that were better than for me to write. It will not seem right for him to be invited home by me. The words from home must be penned by you just as though spoke by you. He will return. Then you will see that father will never hold out when he has his own son before his eyes."

"Did you hear all that father and I was sayin'?" asked the hostess, suspiciously.

"I heard him call out against Iver because he altered the signboard; but that was done a long time agone."

"Nuthin' else?"

"And because he would never make a farmer nor an innkeeper."

"It's a dratted noosence is this here porch," muttered the hostess. "It ort to 'a been altered ages agone, but lor', heart-alive, the old man be that stubborn and agin' all change. And you heard no more?"

"I was busy, mother, and didn't give attention to what didn't concern me."

"Oh!" said Mrs. Verstage, "only listened, did you, to what did concern you?"

A fear had come over the hostess lest the girl had caught Simon's words relative to his notion, rather than intention, of bequeathing what he had away from Iver and to the child that had been adopted.

Of course, Simon did not seriously purpose doing anything of the sort. It was foolish, inconsiderate of him to give utterance to such a thought, and that in such a place as the porch, whence every whisper was conveyed throughout the interior of the house.

If Mehetabel had overheard his words, what a Fool's Paradise she might create for herself! How her head might be turned, and what airs she might give herself.

Leave the farm, the inn, everything to a girl with whom they were wholly unconnected, and to the detriment of the son. Hoity-toity! such a thought must not be allowed to settle, to take root, to spring up and fructify.

"Mother," said the girl, "I think that you ought to write to Iver with your own hand, though I know it will cost you trouble. But it need not be in many words. Say he must come himself without delay and see father. If Iver keeps at a distance the breakage will never be mended, the wound will never be healed. Father is a resolute man, but he is tender-hearted under all, and he's ever been wonderful kind to me."

"Oh, yes, so long as he ain't crossed he's right enough with anyone," answered Mrs. Verstage quickly. She did not relish the allusion to the old man's kindness towards Mehetabel, it seemed to her suspicious heart due to anticipation of what had been hinted by him. She considered a moment, and determined to have the whole matter out, and to dash any expectations the girl might have formed at once and for ever. A direct woman Mrs. Verstage had ever been.

"Matabel," she said, and drew her lips together and contracted her brows, "whatever father may scheme about making a will, it's all gammon and nonsense. I don't know whether he's said any tomfoolery about it to you, or may do so in time to come. Don't think nuthin' of it. Why should he make a will? He has but Iver to whom he can leave what he has. If he don't make a will—where's the odds? The law will see to it; that everything goes to Iver, just as it ort."

"You will write to Iver to come?"

"Yes, I will. Matters can't be worse than they be, and they may come to a betterment. O dear life of me! What I have suffered all these years, parted from my only child."

"I have tried to do what I could for you, dear mother."

"Oh, yes"—the bitterness was still oozing up in the woman's heart, engalling her own mind—"that I know well enough. But then you ain't my flesh and blood. You may call me mother, and you may speak of Simon as father, but that don't alter matters, no more nor when Samuel Doit would call the cabbage plants broccaloes did it make 'em grow great flower heads like passon's wigs. Iver is my son, my very own child. You, Matabel, are only—"

"Only what, mother?"

"Only a charity girl."

The words were hardly spoken before a twinge of conscience made Mrs. Verstage aware that she had given pain to the girl who had been to her as a daughter.

Yet she justified herself to herself with the consideration that it was in the end kindest to cut down ruthlessly any springing expectation that might have started to life at the words of Simon Verstage. The hostess cast a glance at Mehetabel, and saw that her face was quivering, that all color had gone out of her cheeks, that her hands were contracted as with the cramp.

"I had no wish to hurt you," said the landlady; "but facks are facks, and you may pull down the blinds over 'em wi'out putting them out o' existence. There's Laura Tickner—got a face like a peony. She sez it's innade modesty; but we all knows it's arrysippelas, and Matthew Maunder tells us his nose comes from indigestion; but it's liquor, as I've the best reason to know. Matabel, I love you well, but always face facks. You can't get rid of facks any more than you can get rid of fleas out o' poultry."

Mrs. Verstage disappeared through the doorway. Mehetabel seated herself on the bench. She could not follow the hostess, for her limbs trembled and threatened to give way.

She folded her arms on her lap, and leaned forward, with her eyes on the ground.

"A charity girl! Only a charity girl!"

She said the words to herself again and again. Her eyes burnt; a spray hung on her eyelids. Her lips were contracted with pain, spasms ran through her breast.

"Only a charity girl! She'd never, never a'sed that had she loved me. She don't." Then came a sob. Mehetabel tried to check it, but could not, and the sound of that sob passed through the house. It was followed by no other.

The girl recovered herself, leaned back against the wall, and looked at the twilight sky.

There was no night now. The season was near midsummer:—

"Barnaby bright,
All day and no night."

Into the luminous blue sky Mehetabel looked steadily, and did battle with her own self in her heart.

That which had been said so shortly was true; had it been wrapped up in filagree—through all disguise the solid unpleasant truth would remain as core. If that were true, then why should she be so stung by the few words that contained the truth?

It was not the words that had hurt her—she had heard them often at school—it was that "Mother" had said them. It was the way in which they had been uttered.

Mrs. Verstage had ever been kind to the girl; more affectionate when she was quite a child than when she became older. Gradually the hostess had come to use her, and using her as a servant, to regard her in that light.

Susanna Verstage was one of those women to whom a baby is almost a necessity, certainly a prime element of happiness. As she philosophically put it, "Men likes 'baccy; wimin likes babies; they was made so;" but the passion for a baby was doubly strong in the heart of the landlady. As long as Mehetabel was entirely dependent, the threads that held her to the heart of the hostess were very strong, and very many, but so soon as she became independent, these threads were relaxed. The good woman had a blunt and peremptory manner, and she at times ruffled the girl by sharpness of rebuke; but never previously had she alluded to her peculiar position and circumstances in such a galling manner.

Why had she done this now? Why gone out of her way to do so?

Mehetabel thought how wonderful it was that she, a stranger, should be in that house, treated almost, though not wholly, as its child, whereas the son of the house was shut out from it,—that against him only was the door fast, which was held open with invitation to every one else.

It was the thought of this contrast, perhaps, that had been working in Mrs. Verstage's mind, and had provoked the impatience and occasioned the cruel words.

"Well," said Mehetabel to herself, "I must face it. I have only the name that Iver gave me in the barn. I have no father, no mother, and no other name than that which I am given in charity." She looked at her gown. "I owe that to charity;" at her hands—"My flesh is nourished out of charity." She wiped her eyes—the very kerchief was a gift to her in charity. "It is so," she said. "I must bear the thought and get accustomed to it. I was given a name in charity, and in charity my father was granted a grave. All I can look to as in some fashion my own—and yet they are not my own—be the headstone in the churchyard to show how my real father was killed, and the gallows on Hind Head, with the chains, to tell where those hung who killed him. 'Tain't every one can show that." She raised her head with a flash of pride. Human Nature must find something on which to plume itself. If nothing else can be found, then a murdered father and a gallows for the murderers served.

Mehetabel was a handsome girl, and she knew it. She could not fail to know it, situated as she was. The men who frequented the public house would not leave a girl long in doubt whether she were comely or the reverse.

But Mehetabel made small account of her appearance. No youth of the neighborhood had won his way into her heart; and she blew away the compliments lavished upon her as the men blew away the froth from their tankards. What mattered it whether she were good-looking or not, so long as she was only Mehetabel, without a surname, without kin, without a penny!

When Iver had run away from home she had done all that lay in her power to comfort the mother. She had relieved the landlady of half of her work; she had stayed up her heart when downcast, despondent. She had talked with her of the absent son, whose name the father would not allow to be mentioned in his hearing; had encouraged her with hopes, and, by her love, had sought to compensate for the loss.

It was due to her that the Ship Inn had a breath of youth and cheerfulness infused into it. But for her, the absence and indifference of the host, and the moroseness of the disappointed hostess, would have driven custom away.

Mrs. Verstage had found her useful, even necessary. She could hardly endure to be for an hour without her, and she had come to rely upon her more and more in the conduct of business, especially such as required sufficient scholarship to do correspondence and keep accounts.

The hostess was proud of the girl's beauty and engaging manner, and took to herself some of the credit of having her adopted daughter regarded as the belle of Thursley. She was pleased to see that the men admired her, not less than the women envied her. There was selfishness in all this. Mrs. Verstage's heart was without sincerity. She had loved Mehetabel as a babe, because the child amused her. She liked her as a girl, because serviceable to her, and because it flattered her vanity to think that her adopted daughter should be so handsome.

Now, however, that the suspicion was engendered that her own son might be set aside in favor of the adopted child, through Simon's partiality, at once her maternal heart took the alarm, and turned against the girl in resolution to protect the rights of Iver, Mehetabel did not understand the workings of Susanna Verstage's mind. She felt that the regard entertained for her was troubled.

She had heard Simon Verstage's remark about constituting her his heir, but had so little considered it as seriously spoken, and as embodying a resolution, that it did not now occur to her as an explanation of the altered conduct of the "mother" towards herself.

Mehetabel felt instinctively that a vein of truer love throbbed in the old host than in his wife; and now, with a hunger for some word of kindness after the rebuff she had sustained, she stood up and walked in the direction of the hayfield to meet Simon Verstage on his return journey.

As she stepped along she heard a footfall behind her. The step was quickened, and a hand was laid on her shoulder. She turned, and exclaimed sharply:

"Bideabout—what do you want?"

"You, Matabel."

A man stayed her: the Broom-Squire.

"What with me?"

"I want you to listen to what I have to say."

"I can spare you a minute, not more. I expect father. He has gone to look at the hay."

Mehetabel disengaged her shoulder from his grasp. She stepped back. She had no liking for the Broom-Squire. Indeed, he inspired her with a faint, undefined repugnance.

Jonas was now a middle-aged man, still occupying his farm in the Punch-Bowl, making brooms, selling holly, cultivating his patch of land, laying by money and still a bachelor.

He had rounded shoulders and a short neck; this made him thrust his head forward in a peering manner, like a beast of prey watching for a victim. His eyes were keen and restless. His hair was short-cut, and his ears projected from the sides of his head like those of a bat. Otherwise he was not a bad-looking man. His features were good, but his expression was unpleasant. The thin lip was curled contemptuously; and he had a trick of thrusting forth his sharp tongue to wet his lips before making a spiteful remark.

He was a frequent visitor at the Ship, and indeed his inclination for liquor was his one weakness.

Of late he had been much oftener at this inn than formerly. Latterly he had been profuse in his compliments to Mehetabel, which she had put aside, much as she brushed empty tankards, and tobacco ash off the table. He was no welcome guest. His bitter tongue was the occasion of strife, and a brawl was no infrequent result of the appearance of the Broom-Squire in the public house. Sometimes he himself became the object of attack, but usually he succeeded in setting others by the ears and in himself escaping unmolested. But on one of the former occasions he had lost two front teeth, and through the gap thus formed he was wont to thrust his tongue.

"I am glad to have caught you," said the Broom-Squire; "and caught you alone—it is hard to find you so—as it's hard to find a treacle cask without flies round it."

"What have you to say?"

"You have always slipped out of my way when I thought I had you."

"I did not know that you had a fancy to catch me alone." She made as if to proceed on her course.

"Stand still," said he imperiously. "It must come out. Do not look at me with that keep-your-distance air. I mean no incivility. I care a deal more for you than for any one else."

"That is not saying much."

"I care for you alone in all the world."

"Except yourself."

"Of course."

He breathed as though relieved of a burden.

"Look here, Mehetabel, I've not been a marrying man. Wife and family cost too much. I've been saving and not spending. But this can't go on forever. All good things come to an end some time. It has come to this, I must have a woman to mind the house. My sister and I have had a tiff. You know her, Sarah

Rocliffe. She won't do as I like, and what I want. So I'll just shut the door in her face and make a long nose at her, and say, 'Got some one else now.'"

"So," exclaimed Mehetabel, the color rushing to her cheeks in anger, "you want me as your housekeeper that you may make a nose at your sister and deny her the house."

"I won't have any other woman in my house but yourself."

"You will have to wait a long time before you get me."

"I mean all fair and honorable," said Jonas. "I didn't say housekeeper, did I? I say wife. If any chap had said to me, Bideabout, you are putting your feet into a rabbit net, and will be caught, and—'" he made a sign as if knocking a rabbit's neck to kill it—"I say, had any one said that, I'd a' laughed at him as a fool."

"You may laugh at him still," said the girl. "No one that I know has set any net for you."

"You have," he sniggered. "Aye, and caught me."

"I!" laughed Mehetabel contemptuously, "I spread a net for you? It is you who pursue and pester me. I never gave you a thought save how to make you keep at arm's length."

"You say that to me." His color went.

"It is ridiculous, it is insulting of you to speak to me of netting and catching. What do I want of you save to be let go my way."

"Come, Mehetabel," said the Broom-Squire caressingly, "we won't quarrel about words. I didn't mean what you have put on me. I want you to come and be my wife. It isn't only that I've had a quarrel with my sister. There's more than that. There is something like a stoat at my heart, biting there, and I have no rest till you say—'I'll have you, Jonas!'"

"The stoat must hang on. I can't say that."

"Why not?"

"I am not obliged to give a reason."

"Will you not have me?"

"No, Bideabout, I will not. How can I take an offer made in this way? When you ask me to enable you to be rude to your sister, when you speak of me as laying traps for you; and when you stay me on my road as if you were a footpad."

Again she made an attempt to go in the direction of the hayfield. Her bosom was heaving with anger, her nostrils were quivering.

Again he arrested her.

"If you will not let me go," said she, "I will call for help. Here comes father. He shall protect me."

"I'll have you yet," said the Broom-Squire with a sneer. "If it ain't you that nets me, then it'll be I net you, Mehetabel."

CHAPTER X. — INTO THE NET

"We must have cake and ale for the hayfield," said Mrs. Verstage. "Of ale there be plenty in the house, but for cake, I must bake. It ort to ha' been done afore. Fresh cakes goes twice as fast as stale, but blessin's on us, the weather have been that changeable I didn't know but I might put it off to anywhen."

This was said on the morrow of the occurrence just described.

Whilst Mrs. Verstage was engaged in the baking she had not time for much talk, but she asked abruptly: "What's that as to Bideabout? Father said he'd come on you and him, and you was both in a sort o' take on."

Mehetabel had no reason for reticence, and she told the hostess of the suit of the Broom-Squire, and of the manner in which he made his proposal. Mrs. Verstage said nothing at the time. She was occupied— too occupied for comments. But when the cake was in the oven, she seated herself at the kitchen table, with a sigh of relief, and beckoned to Mehetabel to do the same.

Mrs. Verstage was warm, both on account of the heat of the morning, but also because she had been hard at work. She fanned herself with a dish, and as she did so looked at the girl.

"So—the Broom-Squire offered himself, did he?"

Mehetabel made a sign in the affirmative.

"Well," continued the hostess, "if he weren't so good a customer here he would be suitable enough. But yet a good wife will soon cure him. A hudger (bachelor) does things as a married man don't allow himself."

Mehetabel looked questioningly at the landlady.

She said: "There must be good stuff in a man, or marriage won't bring it out."

"Who says there ain't good stuff in Bideabout?"

"I have never seen the glint of it."

"You don't see the iron ore as lies under the sand, but there it is, and when wanted it can be worked. I like a man to show his wust side forefront. There's many a man's character is like his wesket, red plush and flowers in front and calico in rags behind hid away under his coat."

Mehetabel was surprised, troubled. She made no response, but color drifted across her face.

"After all," pursued Mrs. Verstage, "he may ha' come here not after liquor, but drawed by you. Then you see he's been alone all these years, and scriptur' saith it ain't good for a man to be that. They goes sour and mouldy—men do if unmarried. I think you'd be fulfillin' your dooty, and actin' accordin' to the word o' God if you took him."

"I—mother! I!" The girl shrank back. "Mother, let him take some one else. I don't want him."

"But he wants you, and he don't want another. Matabel, it's all moonshine about leap year. The time never comes when the woman can ax the man. It's tother way up—and Providence made it so. Bideabout has a good bit o' land, for which he is his own landlord, he has money laid by, so folks tell. You might do worse. It's a great complerment he's paid you. You see he's well off, and you have nothin'. Men generally, nowadays, look out for wives that have a bit o' money to help buy a field, or a cow, or nothin' more than a hog. You see Bideabout's above that sort o' thing. If you can't have butter to your bread, you must put up wi' drippin'."

"I'm not going to take Bideabout," said Mehetabel.

"I don't say you should. But he couldn't a took a fancy to you wi'out Providence ordainin' of it."

"And if I don't like him," threw in the girl, half angry, half in tears, "I suppose that is the doings of Providence too?"

Mrs. Verstage evaded a reply to this. She said: "I do not press you to take him. You are kindly welcome to stay on with us a bit, till you've looked about you and found another. We took you up as a babe and cared for you; but the parish allowance was stopped when you was fourteen. It shan't be said of us that bare we took you in and bare we turn you out. But marry you must. It's ordained o' nature. There's the difference atwixt a slug and a snail. The snail's got her own house to go into. A slug hasn't. When she's uncomfortable she must go underground."

The hostess was silent for awhile. Mehetabel said nothing. Her cheeks burned. She was choking.

Mrs. Verstage went on: "There was Betsy Purvis—she was a bit of a beauty, and gave herself airs. She wouldn't have Farmer James, as his legs was so long, he looked like a spider—and she wouldn't have Odger Kay, as his was too short—he looked like a dachs-dog. It came in the end she married Purvis, who had both his legs shot off in the wars, 'cos and why? she couldn't get another. She'd been too finical in choosin'."

"Are you tired of me?" gasped the girl. "Do you wish to be rid of me?"

"Not at all," answered the landlady. "It's becos we're so fond of you, father and I, that we want to see you well settled."

"And father—does he wish me to take Bideabout?"

Mrs. Verstage hesitated.

"He hasn't said that right out. You see he didn't know for certain Jonas were hoppin' about you. But he'd be tremendous pleased to have you well married."

"And you think I should be well married if I became Bideabout's wife?"

"Of course. He's a great catch for the likes of you, who belong to nobody and to no place, properly. Beggars mustn't be choosers."

Mehetabel sprang to her feet.

"It is so. I am a beggar. I am only a charity girl, nothing else."

She struck her head against the wall. "Let me beat my brains out if I am in your way. Why should I be thrown into the arms of any passer-by?

"You misjudge and misunderstand me," said Mrs. Verstage, hotly. "Because you have been with me so long, and because I love you, I want to see you settled. Because I can't give you a prince in spangles and feathers you fly out against me."

"I don't ask for a prince, only to be let alone. I am happy here, as a girl, working for you and father."

"But we shall not live forever. We are growing old, and shall have to give up. Iver may return any day, and then—"

The hostess became crimson to the temples; she knew how handsome the girl was, doubly handsome she seemed now, in her heat and agitation, and it occurred to Mrs. Verstage that Iver with his artistic appreciation of the beautiful, might also think her handsome, that the old childish fancy for each other might spring to new and to stronger life, and that he might even think of Mehetabel as a wife. That would never, never do. For Iver something better must be found than a girl without means, friends, and name.

"What then?" asked Mehetabel. "Suppose Iver do come here and keep the inn. I can go with you wherever you go, and if you become old, I can attend to you in your old age."

"You are good," said Mrs. Verstage; but although her words were gracious, her manner was chilling. "It is for us to think of you and your future, not you to consider for us. The Broom-Squire—"

"I tell you, mother, I don't like him."

"You must hear me out. You do not love him. Lawk-a-jimmeny! we can't all marry for love. You don't suppose I was in love with Simon when I took him? I was a good-looking wench in my day, and I had many admirers, and were more of tragedy-kings than Simon. But I had sense, and I took him for the sake of the Ship Inn and the farm. We have lived happy together, and if it hadn't been for that matter of Iver, there'd not ha' been a cloud between us. Love grows among married folk, like chickweed in a garden. You can't keep it out. It is thick everywhere, and is never out o' season. I don't say there ain't a ripping of it out one day—but it comes again, twice as thick on the morrow, and much good it does! I don't think I cared for Simon when I took him any more than you care for Jonas, but I took him, and we've fared well enough together." After a pause the hostess said, "Talkin' of marriage, I have a fine scheme in my head. If Iver comes back, as I trust he will, I want him to marry Polly Colpus."

"Polly Colpus, mother!"

"She's James Colpus's only child, and will come in for money. James Colpus is a wonderful thrivin' man."

"But she has a moustache."

"What of that, if she have money?"

"But—Iver—if he couldn't bear an ugly signboard to the house, will he relish an ugly figure-head to his wife within it?"

"She has gold which will gild her moustache."

"I don't know," said Mehetabel; "Iver wouldn't take the business at his father's wish, will he take a wife of his mother's providing?"

"He will know which side his bread is buttered better than some persons I could name."

"I fancy when folk look out for wives, they don't borrow their mother's eyes."

"You cross me in everything to-day," said the hostess, peevishly.

Mehetabel's tears began to flow.

Mrs. Verstage was a woman who did not need much time or much balancing to arrive at a determination, and when she had formed her resolution, she clung to it with the same tenacity as her husband did to his.

Her maternal jealousy had been roused, and the maternal instinct is the strongest that exists in the female nature. Many a woman would allow herself to be cut to bits for her child. But not only will she sacrifice herself without hesitation, but also any one else who in any way hinders the progress of her schemes for the welfare of her child. Mrs. Verstage entertained affection for the girl, an affection very real, yet not to the extent of allowing it to blind her to the true interests of her own son. She was roused to jealousy by the partiality of Simon for his adopted daughter, to the prejudice of Iver. And now she was gravely alarmed lest on the return of Iver, the young affection of the two children for each other should take a new spell of life, assume a new form, and intensify into passion.

Accordingly she was resolved, if possible, to remove the girl from the Ship before the arrival of Iver. The proposal of the Broom-Squire was opportune, and she was anxious to forward his suit as the best means for raising an insuperable barrier between her son and the girl, as well as removing her from Simon, who, with his characteristic wrong-headedness, might actually do what he had proposed.

"I don't see what you're crying about," said Mrs. Verstage, testily. "It ain't no matter to you whether Iver takes Polly Colpus or a Royal Princess."

"I don't want him to be worried, mother, when he comes home with having ugly girls rammed down his throat. If you begin that with him he'll be off again."

"Oh! you know that, do you?"

"I am sure of it."

"I know what this means!" exclaimed the angry woman, losing all command over her tongue. "It means, in plain English, just this—'I'm going to try, by hook or by crook, to get Iver for myself.' That's what you're driving at, hussy! But I'll put you by the shoulders out of the door, or ever Iver comes, that you may be at none of them tricks. Do you think that because he baptized you, that he'll also marry you?"

Mehetabel sprang through the door with a cry of pain, of wounded pride, of resentment at the injustice wherewith she was treated, of love in recoil, and almost ran against the Broom-Squire. Almost without power to think, certainly without power to judge, fevered with passion to be away out of a house where she was so misjudged, she gasped, "Bideabout! will you have me now—even now. Mother turns me out of doors."

"Have you? To be sure I will," said Jonas; then with a laugh out of the side of his mouth, he added in an undertone, "Don't seem to want that I should set a net; she runs right into my hands. Wimen is wimen!"

CHAPTER XI. — A SURNAME AT LAST

When Simon Verstage learned that Mehetabel was to be married to the Broom-Squire, he was not lightly troubled. He loved the girl more dearly than he was himself aware. He was accustomed to see her about the house, to hear her cheerful voice, and to be welcomed with a pleasant smile when he returned from the fields. There was constitutional ungraciousness in his wife. She considered it lowering to her dignity, or unnecessary, to put on an amiable face, and testify to him pleasure at his presence. Little courtesies are dear to the hearts of the most rugged men; Simon received them from Mehetabel, and valued them all the more because withheld from him by his wife. The girl had known how to soothe him when ruffled, she had forestalled many of his little requirements, and had exercised a moderating influence in the house. Mrs. Verstage, in her rough, imperious fashion, had not humored him, and many a domestic storm was allayed by the tact of Mehetabel.

Simon had never been demonstrative in his affection, and it was only now, when he was about to lose her, that he became aware how dear she was to his old heart. But what could he do, now that she had given herself to Jonas Kink? Of the manner in which this had been brought about he knew nothing. Had he been told he would have stormed, and insisted on the engagement coming to an end. But would this have mended matters? Would it not have made Mehetabel's position in the house only more insupportable?

He remained silent and depressed for a week, and when the girl was in the room followed her with his eyes, with a kindly, regretful light in them. When she passed near him, he held out his hand, took hers, squeezed it, and said, "Matabel, we shall miss you:—wun'erful—wun'erful!"

"Dear father!" she would answer, and return the pressure of his hand, whilst her eyes filled.

"I hope you'll be happy," he would say; then add, "I suppose you will. Mother says so, and wimen knows about them sort o' things better nor we."

To his wife Simon said, "Spare nothing. Give her a good outfit, just as if she was our own daughter. She has been a faithful child, and has saved us the expense and worrit of a servant, and I will not have it said—but hang it! what odds to me what is said? I will not have her feel that we begrudge her aught. She has no father and mother other than we, and we must be to her all that we can."

"Leave that to me," said the wife.

Mainly through the instrumentality of Mrs. Verstage the marriage was hastened on; it was to be as soon as the banns had been called thrice.

"Wot's the good o' waitin'?" asked Mrs. Verstage, "where all is pleasant all round, and all agreed?"

Mehetabel was indifferent, even disposed to have the wedding speedily, there was no advantage in postponing the inevitable. If she were not wanted in the Ship, her presence was desired in the Punch-Bowl, if not by all the squatters there, at all events by the one most concerned.

She felt oppression in the house in which she had been at home from infancy, and was even conscious that her adopted mother was impatient to be rid of her. Mehetabel was proud, too proud to withdraw from her engagement, to acknowledge that she had rushed into it without consideration, and had accepted a man whom she did not love. Too proud, in fine, to continue one day longer than need be, eating the bread of charity.

Seamstresses were summoned, and every preparation made that Mehetabel should have abundance of clothing when she left the Ship.

"Look here, Susanna," said Simon, "you'll have made a pocket in them gownds, you mind."

"Yes, Simon, of course."

"Becos I means to put a little purse in for Matabel when she goes from us—somethin' to be her own. I won't have the little wench think we han't provided for her."

"How much?" asked Mrs. Verstage, jealously.

"That I'm just about considerin'," answered the old man cautiously.

"Don't you do nothin' reckless and unraysonable, Simon. What will she want wi' money? Hasn't she got the Broom-Squire to pay for all and everything?"

During the three weeks that intervened between the precipitate and ill-considered engagement and the marriage, Mehetabel hardly came to her senses. Sometimes when occupied with her work in the house a qualm of horror came over her and curdled the blood in her heart; then with a cold sweat suffusing her brow, and with pale lips, she sank on a stool, held her head between her palms, and fought with the thoughts that rose like spectres, and with the despair that rolled in on her soul like a dark and icy tide.

The words spoken by the hostess had made it impossible for her to retrace her steps. She could not understand what had come over Mrs. Verstage to induce her to address her as she had. The after conduct of the hostess was such as showed her that although wishing her well she wished her away, and that though having a kindly feeling towards her, she would not admit a renewal of former relations. They might continue friends, but only on condition of being friends at a distance. Mehetabel racked her brain to find in what manner she had given offence to the old woman, and could find none. She was thrust from the only bosom to which she had clung from infancy, without a reason that she could discover. Meanwhile she drew no nearer to Bideabout. He was delighted at his success, and laid aside for a while his bitterness of speech. But she did not admit him to nearer intimacy. His attempts at familiarity met with a chilling reception; the girl had to exercise self-restraint to prevent the repugnance with which she received his addresses from becoming obvious to him and others.

Happily for her peace of mind, he was a good deal away, engaged in getting his house into order. It needed clearing out, cleansing and repairing. No money had been expended on dilapidations, very little soap and water on purification, since his mother's death.

His sister, Mrs. Rocliffe, some years older than himself, living but a few yards distant, had done for him what was absolutely necessary, and what he had been unable to do for himself; but her interest had naturally been in her own house, not in his.

Now that he announced to her that he was about to marry, Sarah Rocliffe was angry. She had made up her mind that Jonas would continue a "hudger," and that his house and land would fall to her son, after his demise. This was perhaps an unreasonable expectation, especially as her own conduct had precipitated the engagement; but it was natural. She partook of the surly disposition of her brother. She could not exist without somebody or something to fall out with, to scold, to find fault with. Her incessant recrimination had at length aroused in Jonas the resolve to cast her wholly from his dwelling, to have a wife of his own, and to be independent of her service.

Sarah Rocliffe ascertained that she had overstepped the mark in quarrelling with her brother, but instead of blaming herself she turned the fault on the head of the inoffensive girl who was to supplant her. She resolved not to welcome her sister-in-law with even a semblance of cordiality.

Nor were the other colonists of the Bowl favorably disposed. It was a tradition among them that they should inter-marry. This rule had once been broken through with disastrous results. The story shall be told presently.

The squatter families of the Punch-Bowl hung together, and when Sarah Rocliffe took it in dudgeon that her brother was going to marry, then the entire colony of Rocliffes, Boxalls, Nashes, and Snellings adopted her view of the case, and resented the engagement as though it were a slight cast on them.

As if the Bowl could not have provided him with a mate meet for him! Were there no good wenches to be found there, that he must go over the lips to look for a wife? The girls within the Bowl, thanks be, had all surnames and kindred. Matabel had neither.

It was not long before Bideabout saw that his engagement to Mehetabel was viewed with disfavor by him immediate neighbors, but he was not the man to concern himself about their opinions. He threw about his jibes, which did not tend to make things better. The boys in the Bowl had concocted a jingle which they sang under his window, or cast at him from behind a hedge, and then ran away lest he should fall on them with a stick. This was their rhyme:—

"A harnet lived in an 'ollow tree,
A proper spiteful twoad were he.
And he said as married and 'appy he'd be;
But all folks jeered and laughed he-he!"

Mehetabel's cheeks were pale, and her brows were contracted and her lips set as she went to Thursley Church on the wedding-day, accompanied by Mrs. Verstage and some village friends.

Gladly would she have elected to have her marriage performed as quietly as possible, and at an hour and on a day to which none were privy save those most immediately concerned. But this did not suit the pride of the hostess, who was resolved on making a demonstration, of getting to herself the credit of having acted a generous and even lavish part towards the adopted child.

Mehetabel held up her head, not with pride, but with resolution not to give way. Her brain was stunned. Thought would no more flow in it than veins of water through a frozen soil. All the shapes of human beings that passed and circled around her were as phantasms. In church she hardly gathered her senses to know when and what to respond.

She could scarcely see the register through the mist that had formed over her eyes when she was required to sign her Christian name, or collect her thoughts to understand the perplexity of the parson, as to how to enter her, when she was without a surname.

When congratulated with effusion by Mrs. Verstage, with courtesy by the Vicar, and boisterously by the boys and girls who were present, she tried to force a smile, but ineffectually, as her features were set inflexibly.

The bridegroom kissed her cheek. She drew back as if she had been stung, as a sensitive plant shrinks from the hand that grasps it.

The previous day had been one of rain, so also had been the night, with a patter of raindrops on the roof above Mehetabel's attic chamber, and a flow of tears beneath.

During the morning, on the way to church, though there had been no rain, yet the clouds had hung low, and were threatening.

They separated and were brushed aside as the wedding party issued from the porch, and then a flood of scorching sunlight fell over the bride and bridegroom. For the first time Mehetabel raised her head and looked up. The impulse was unconscious—it was to let light shine into her eyes and down into the dark, despairing chambers of her soul filled only with tears.

The villagers in the churchyard murmured admiration; as she issued from the gates they cheered.

Bideabout was elate; he was proud to know that the handsomest girl in the neighborhood was now his. It was rare for a sarcastic curl to leave his lips and the furrow to be smoothed on his brow. Such a rare occasion was the present. And the Broom-Squire had indeed secured one in whom his pride was justifiable.

No one could say of Mehetabel that she had been frivolous and forward. Reserved, even in a tavern: always able to maintain her dignity; respecting herself, she had enforced respect from others. That she was hard-working, shrewd, thrifty, none who visited the Ship could fail to know.

Many a lad had attempted to win her favor, and all had been repulsed. She could keep forward suitors at a distance without wounding their self-esteem, without making them bear her a grudge. She was tall, well-built and firmly knit. There was in her evidence of physical as well as of moral strength.

Though young, Mehetabel seemed older than her years, so fully developed was her frame, so swelling her bosom, so set were her features.

Usually the girl wore a high color, but of late this had faded out of her face, which had been left of an ashen hue. Her pallor, however, only gave greater effect to the lustre and profusion of her dark hair and to the size and to the velvet depth and softness of her hazel eyes.

The girl had finely-moulded eyebrows, which, when she frowned through anger, or contracted them through care, met in one band, and gave a lowering expression to her massive brow.

An urchin in the rear nudged a ploughboy, and said in a low tone, "Jim! The old harnet out o' the 'ollow tree be in luck to-day. Wot'll he do with her, now he's ketched a butterfly?"

"Wot be he like to do?" retorted the bumpkin. "A proper spiteful twoad such as he—why, he'll rumple all the color and booty out o' her wings, and sting her till her blood runs pison."

Then from the tower pealed the bells.

Jonas pressed the arm of Mehetabel, and leering into her face, said: "Come, say a word o' thanks. Better late than never. At the last, through me, you've gotten a surname."

CHAPTER XII. — UNEXPECTED

The wedding party was assembled at the Ship, which for this day concerned itself not with outsiders, but provided only for such as were invited to sit and drink, free of charge, to the health and happiness of bride and bridegroom.

The invitation had been extended to the kinsfolk of Jonas in the Punch-Bowl, as a matter of course; but none had accepted, one had his farm, another his business, and a third could not go unless his wife let him.

Consequently the bridegroom was badly supported. He was not the man to make friends, and such acquaintances of his as appeared did so, not out of friendship, but in expectation of eating and drinking at the landlord's table.

This angered Jonas, who, in church, on looking around, had noticed that his own family had failed to attend, but that they should fail also at the feast was what surprised him.

"It don't matter a rush," scoffed he in Mehetabel's ear, "we can get along without 'em, and if they won't come to eat roast duck and green peas, there are others who will and say 'Thank'y.'"

The announcement of Jonas's engagement had been indeed too bitter a morsel for his sister to swallow. She resented his matrimonial project as a personal wrong, as a robbery committed on the Rocliffes. Her husband was not in good circumstances; in fact, the family had become involved through a marriage, to which allusion has already been made; and had not thereafter been able to recover from it.

She had felt the pressure of debt, and the struggle for existence. It had eaten into her flesh like a canker, and had turned her heart into wormwood. In her pinched circumstances, even the pittance paid by her brother for doing his cooking and washing had been a consideration. This now was to be withdrawn.

Sarah Rocliffe had set her ambition on the acquisition of her brother's estate, by which means alone, as far as she could see, would the family be enabled to shake off the incubus that oppressed it. Content in her own lifetime to drudge and moil, she would have gone on to the end, grumbling and fault-finding, indeed, but satisfied with the prospect that at some time in the future her son would inherit the adjoining farm and be lifted thereby out of the sorry position in which was his father, hampered on all sides, and without cheeriness.

But this hope was now taken from her. Jonas was marrying a young and vigorous wife, and a family was certain to follow.

The woman had not the command over herself to veil her feelings, and put on a semblance of good humor, not even the grace to put in an appearance at the wedding.

The story must now be told which accounts for the embarrassed circumstances of the Rocliffe family.

This shall be done by means of an extract from a periodical of the date of the event which clouded the hitherto flourishing condition of the Rocliffes. The periodical from which the quotation comes is "The Royal Magazine, or Gentleman's Monthly Companion" for 1765.

"A few weeks ago a gentlewoman, about twenty-five years of age, applied to a farmer and broom-maker, near Hadleigh, in Hants [1] for a lodging, telling them that she was the daughter of a nobleman, and forced from her father's house by his ill-treatment. Her manner of relating the story so affected the farmer that he took her in, and kindly entertained her.

[1] Not really in Hants, but in Surrey, adjoining the County demarcation.

"In the course of conversation, she artfully let drop that she had a portion of £90,000, of which she should be possessed as soon as her friends in London knew where she was.

"After some days' stay she told the farmer the best return in her power for this favor would be to marry his son, Thomas (a lad about eighteen), if it was agreeable to him. The poor old man was overjoyed at the proposal, and in a short time they were married; after which she informed her father-in-law she had great, interest at Court, and if he could for the present raise money to equip them in a genteel manner, she could procure a colonel's commission for her husband.

"The credulous farmer thereupon mortgaged his little estate for £100, and everything necessary being bought for the new married couple, they took the rest of the money and set out for London, accompanied by three of the farmer's friends, and got to the Bear Inn, in the Borough, on Christmas eve; where they lived for about ten days in an expensive manner; and she went in a coach every morning to St. James's end of the town, on pretence of soliciting for her husband's commission, and to obtain her own fortune. But it was at length discovered that the woman was an impostor; and the poor country people were obliged to sell their horses by auction towards defraying the expenses of the inn before they could set out on their return home, which they did on foot, last Saturday morning."

If the hundred pounds raised on mortgage had covered all the expenses incurred, the Rocliffes might have been satisfied.

Unhappily they got further involved. They fell into the hands of a lawyer in Portsmouth, who undertook to see them righted, but the only advantage they gained from his intervention was the acquisition of certain information that the woman who had married Thomas had been married before.

Accordingly Thomas was free, and he used his freedom some years later, when of a ripe age, to marry Sarah Kink, the sister of Bideabout.

Rocliffe had never been able to shake himself free of the ridicule that attended to him, after the expedition to London, and what was infinitely more vexatious and worse to endure was the burden of debt that had then been incurred, and which was more than doubled through the activity of the lawyer by whom he had been inveigled into submitting himself and his affairs to him.

As the eating and drinking proceeded, the Broom-Squire drank copiously, became noisy, boastful, and threw out sarcastic remarks calculated to hit those who ate and drank with him, but were mainly directed against those of his own family who had absented themselves, but to whose ears he was confident they would be wafted.

Mehetabel, who saw that he was imbibing more than he could bear without becoming quarrelsome lost her pallor, and a hectic flame kindled in her cheek.

Mrs. Verstage looked on uneasily. She was familiar with the moods of Bideabout, and feared the turn matters would take.

Presently he announced that he would sing a song, and in harsh tones began:—

"A cobbler there was, and he lived in a stall,
But Charlotte, my nymph, had no lodging at all.
And at a Broom-Squire's, in pitiful plight,
Did pray and beseech for a lodging one night,
Derry-down, derry-down.

"She asked for admittance, her story to tell.
Of all her misfortunes, and what her befel,

Of her parentage high,—but so great was her grief,
Shed never a comfort to give her relief,
Derry-down, derry-down. [2]

[2] *This is the beginning of a long ballad based on the incidents above mentioned, which is still current in the neighborhood.*

"Now, look here," said Simon Verstage, interrupting the singer, "We all of us know that there ballet, pretty well. It's vastly long, if I remembers aright, something like fourteen verses; and I think we can do very well wi'out it to-night. I fancy your brother-inlaw, Thomas, mightn't relish it."

"He's not here," said the Broom-Squire.

"But I am here," said the landlord, "and I say that the piece is too long for singing, 'twill make you too hoarse to say purty speeches and soft things to your new missus, and it's a bit stale for our ears."

"It's an ill bird that befouls its own nest," said a young fellow present.

Bideabout overheard the remark. "What do you mean by that? Was that aimed at me?" he shouted and started to his feet.

A brawl would have inevitably ensued, but for a timely interruption.

In the door stood a well-dressed, good-looking young man, surveying the assembled company with a smile.

Silence ensued. Bideabout looked round.

Then, with a cry of joy, mingled with pain, Mrs. Verstage started from her feet.

"It is Iver! my Iver!"

In another moment mother and son were locked in each other's arms.

The guests rose and looked questioningly at their host, before they welcomed the intruder.

Simon Verstage remained seated, with his glass in his hand, gazing sternly into it. His face became mottled, red spots appeared on the temples, and on the cheekbones; elsewhere he was pale.

Mehetabel went to him, placed her hand upon his, and said, in a trembling voice, "Dear father, this is my wedding day. I am about to leave you for good. Do not deny me the one and only request I make. Forgive Iver."

The old man's lips moved, but he did not speak. He looked steadily, somewhat sternly, at the young man and mustered his appearance.

Meanwhile Iver had disengaged himself from his mother's embrace, and he came towards his father with extended hand.

"See," said he cheerily, "I am free to admit, and do it heartily, that I did wrong, in painting over the stern of the vessel, and putting it into perspective as far as my lights went. Father! I can remove the coat of paint that I put on, and expose that outrageous old stern again. I will do more. I will violate all the laws of perspective in heaven and earth, and turn the bows round also, so as to thoroughly show the ship's head, and make that precious vessel look like a dog curling itself up for a nap. Will that satisfy you?"

All the guests were silent, and fixed their eyes anxiously on the taverner.

Iver was frank in speech, had lost all provincial dialect, was quite the gentleman. He had put off the rustic air entirely. He was grown a very handsome fellow, with oval face, full hair on his head, somewhat curling, and his large brown eyes were sparkling with pleasure at being again at home. In his whole bearing there was self-confidence.

"Simon!" pleaded Mrs. Verstage, with tears in her voice, "he's your own flesh and blood!"

He remained unmoved.

"Father!" said Mehetabel, clinging to his hand, "Dear, dear father! for my sake, whom you have loved, and whom you lose out of your house to-day."

"There is my hand," said the old man.

"And you shall have the ship again just as suits your heart," said Iver.

"I doubt," answered the taverner, "it will be easier to get the Old Ship to look what she ort, than it will be to get you to look again like a publican's son."

The reconciliation on the old man's side was without cordiality, yet it was accepted by all present with cheers and handshakings.

It was but too obvious that the modish appearance of his son had offended the old man.

"Heaven bless me!" exclaimed Iver, when this commotion was somewhat allayed. He was looking with undisguised admiration and surprise at Mehetabel.

"Why," asked he, pushing his way towards her, "What is the meaning of all this?"

"That is Matabel, indeed," explained his mother. "And this is her wedding day."

"You married! You, Matabel! And, to-day! The day of my return! Where is the happy man? Show him to me."

His mother indicated the bridegroom. Mehetabel's heart was too full to speak; she was too dazed with the new turn of affairs to know what to do.

Iver looked steadily at Jonas.

"What!" he exclaimed, "Bideabout! Never, surely! I cannot mistake your face nor the look of your eyes. So, you have won the prize—you!"

Still he looked at Jonas. He refrained from extending his hand in congratulation. Whether thoughtlessly or not, he put it behind his back. An expression passed over his face that the bride observed, and it sent the blood flying to her cheek and temples.

"So," said Iver, and now he held out both hands, "Little Matabel, I have returned to lose you!"

He wrung her hands, both,—he would not let them go.

"I wish you all joy. I wish you everything, everything that your heart can desire. But I am surprised. I can't realize it all at once. My little Matabel grown so big, become so handsome—and, hang me, leaving the Old Ship! Poor Old Ship! Bideabout, I ought to have been consulted. I gave Matabel her name. I have certain rights over her, and I won't surrender them all in a hurry. Here, mother, give me a glass, 'tis a strange day on which I come home."

Dissatisfaction appeared in his face, hardly to be expected in one who should have been in cloudless radiance on his return after years of absence, and with his quarrel with the father at an end.

Now old acquaintances crowded about him to ask questions as to how he had lived during his absence, upon what he had been employed, how the world had fared with him, whether he was married, and if so, how many children he had got, and what were their respective ages and sexes, and names and statures.

For a while bride and bridegroom were outside the circle, and Iver was the centre of interest and regard. Iver responded good-humoredly and pleaded for patience. He was hungry, he was thirsty, he was dusty and hot. He must postpone personal details till a more convenient season. Now his mind was taken up with the thought, not of himself, but of his old playmate, his almost sister, his—he might dare to call her, first love—who was stepping out of the house, out of his reach, just as he stepped back into it, strong with the anticipation of finding her there. Then raising his glass, and looking at Matabel, he said: "Here's to you, Matabel, and may you be very happy with the man of your choice."

"Have you no good wish for me?" sneered the Broom-Squire.

"For you, Bideabout," answered Iver, "I do not express a wish. I know for certainty that you, that any man, not may, but must be happy with such a girl, unless he be a cur."

CHAPTER XIII. — HOME

Bideabout was driving his wife home.

Home! There is no word sweeter to him who has created that reality to which the name belongs; but there is no word more full of vague fears to one who has it to create.

Home to Bideabout was a rattle-trap farmhouse built partly of brick, mainly of timber, thatched with heather, at the bottom of the Punch-Bowl.

It was a dwelling that served to cover his head, but was without pleasant or painful associations—a place in which rats raced and mice squeaked; a place in which money might be made and hoarded, but on which little had been spent. It was a place he had known from childhood as the habitation of his parents, and which now was his own. His childhood had been one of drudgery without cheerfulness, and was not looked back on with regret. Home was not likely to be much more to him in the future than it was in the present. More comfortable perhaps, certainly more costly. But it was other with Mehetabel.

She was going to the unknown.

As we shudder at the prospect of passing out of this world into that beyond the veil, so does many a girl shrink at the prospect of the beyond seen through the wedding ring.

She had loved the home at the Ship. Would she learn to love the home in the Punch-Bowl?

She had understood and made allowance for the humors of the landlord and landlady of the tavern; did she know those of her future associate in the farm? To many a maid, the great love that swells her heart and dazzles her brain carries her into the new condition on the wings of hope.

Love banishes fear. Confidence in the beloved blots out all mistrust as to the future.

But in this case there was no love, nothing to inspire confidence; and Mehetabel looked forward with vague alarm, almost with a premonition of evil.

Jonas was in no mood for meditation. He had imbibed freely at the inn, and was heavy, disposed to sleep, and only prevented from dozing by the necessity he was under of keeping the lazy cob in movement.

For if Jonas was in no meditative mood, the old horse was, and he halted at intervals to ponder over the load he was drawing, and ask why on this occasion he had to drag uphill two persons instead of one.

The sun had set before the couple left the Ship.

The road ascended, at first gradually, then at a more rapid incline. The cob could not be induced to trot by word or whip; and the walk of a horse is slower than that of a man.

"It's bostall (a steep ascent, in the Wealden dialect) till we come to the gallows," muttered Jonas; "then we have the drove-road down into the Punch-Bowl."

Mehetabel tightened her shawl about her shoulders and throat. The evening was chilly for the time of the year. Much rain had fallen, and the air was charged with moisture, that settled in cold dew on the cart, on the harness, on Bideabout's glazed hat, on the bride's clothing, bathing her, all things, as in the tears of silent sorrow.

"One of us must get out and walk," said the bridegroom. "Old Clutch—that's the 'oss—is twenty-five, and there's your box and bundle behind."

He made no attempt to dismount, but looked sideways at the bride.

"If you'll pull up I'll get out and walk," she answered. "I shall be glad to do so. The dew falls like rain, and I am chilled to the marrow."

"Right then," assented the Broom-Squire, and drew the rein.

Mehetabel descended from her seat in the cart. In so doing something fell on the road from her bosom. She stooped and picked it up.

"Wots that?" asked Jonas, and pointed to the article with his whip, that was flourished with a favor of white ribbons.

"It is a present father has made me," answered Mehetabel. "I was in a hurry—and not accustomed to pockets, so I just put it into my bosom. I ought to have set it in a safer place, in the new pocket made to my gown. I'll do that now. Its money."

"Money!" repeated Bideabout. "How much may it be?"

"I have not looked."

"Then look at it, once now (at once)."

He switched the whip with its white favor about, but kept his eye on Mehetabel.

"What did he give it you for?"

"As a wedding present."

"Gold, is it?"

"Gold and notes."

"Gold and notes. Hand 'em to me. I can count fast enough."

"The sum is fifteen pounds—dear, kind, old man."

"Fifteen pounds, is it? You might ha' lost it wi' your carelessness."

"I'll not be careless now."

"Good, hand it me."

"I cannot do that, Jonas. It is mine. Father said to me I was to keep it gainst a rainy day."

"Didn't you swear in church to endow me with all your worldly goods?" asked the Broom-Squire.

"No, it was you who did that. I then had nothing."

"Oh, was it so? I don't remember that. If you'd had them fifteen pounds then, and the passon had knowed about it, he'd ha' made you swear to hand it over to me—your lord and master."

"There's nothing about that in the Prayer-book."

"Then there ort to be. Hand me the money. You was nigh on losing the lot, and ain't fit to keep it. Fifteen pounds!"

"I cannot give it to you, Bideabout; father told me it was to be my very own, I was not to let it go out of my hands, not even into yours, but to husband it."

"Ain't I your husband?"

"I do not mean that, to hoard it against an evil day. There is no saying when that may come. And I passed my word it should be so."

He growled and said, "Look here, Matabel. It'll be a bostall road with you an' me, unless there's give on one side and take on the other."

"Is all the give to be on my side, and the take on yours?"

"In coorse. Wot else is matrimony? The sooner you learn that the better for peace."

He whipped the cob, and the brute moved on.

Mehetabel walked forward and outstripped the conveyance. Old Clutch was a specially slow walker. She soon reached that point at which moorland began, without hedge on either side. Trees had ceased to stud the heathy surface.

Before her rose the ridge that culminated where rose the gallows, and stood inky black against the silvery light of declining day behind them.

To the north, in the plain gleamed some ponds.

Curlew were piping sadly.

Mehetabel was immersed in her own thoughts, glad to be by herself. Jonas had not said much to her in the cart, yet his presence had been irksome. She thought of the past, of her childhood along with Iver, of the day when he ran away. How handsome he had become! What an expression of contempt had passed over his countenance when he looked at Bideabout, and learned that he was the bridegroom— the happy man who had won her! How earnestly he had gazed into her eyes, till she was compelled to lower them!

Was Iver going to settle at the Ship? Would he come over to the Punch-Bowl to see her? Would he come often and talk over happy childish days? There had been a little romance between them as children: long forgotten: now reviving.

Her hand trembled as she raised it to her lips to wipe away the dew that had formed there.

She had reached the highest point on the road, and below yawned the great crater-like depression, at the bottom of which lay the squatter settlement. A little higher, at the very summit of the hill, stood the gibbet, and the wind made the chains clank as it trifled with them. The bodies were gone, they had mouldered away, and the bones had fallen and were laid in the earth or sand beneath, but the gallows remained.

Clink! clink! clank! Clank! clink! clink!

There was rhythm and music, as of far-away bells, in the clashing of these chains.

The gibbet was on Mehetabel's left hand; on the right was the abyss.

She looked down into the cauldron, turning with disgust from the gallows, and yet was inspired with an almost equal repugnance at the sight of the dark void below.

She was standing on the very spot where, eighteen years before, she had been found by Iver. He had taken her up, and had given her a name. Now she was taken up by another, and by him a new name was conferred upon her.

"Come!" said Jonas; "it's all downhill, henceforth."

Were the words ominous?

He had arrived near her without her hearing him, so occupied had her mind been. As he spoke she uttered a cry of alarm.

"Afraid?" he asked. "Of what?"

She did not answer. She was trembling. Perhaps her nerves had been overwrought. The Punch-Bowl looked to her like the Bottomless Pit.

"Did you think one of the dead men had got up from under the gallows, and had come down to talk with you?"

She did not speak. She could not.

"It's all a pass'l o' nonsense," he said. "When the dead be turned into dust they never come again except as pertaties or the like. There was Tim Wingerlee growed won'erful fine strawberries; they found out at last he took the soil in which he growed 'em from the churchyard. I don't doubt a few shovelfuls from under them gallows 'ud bring on early pertaties—famous. Now then, get up into the cart."

"I'd rather walk, Jonas. The way down seems critical. It is dark in the Bowl, and the ruts are deep."

"Get up, I say. There is no occasion to be afraid. It won't do to drive among our folk, to our own door, me alone, and you trudgin', totterin' behind. Get up, I say."

Mehetabel obeyed.

There was a fragrance of fern in the night air that she had inhaled while walking. Now by the side of Bideabout she smelt only the beer and stale tobacco that adhered to his clothes.

"I am main glad," said he, "that all the hustle-bustle is over. I'm glad I'm not wed every day. Fust and last time I hopes. The only good got as I can see, is a meal and drink at the landlord's expense. But he'll take it out of me someways, sometime. Folks ain't liberal for nuthin'. 'Tain't in human nature."

"It is very dark in the Punch-Bowl," said Mehetabel. "I do not see a glimmer of a light anywhere."

"That's becos the winders ain't looking this way. You don't suppose it would be a pleasure to have three dead men danglin' in the wind afore their eyes all day long. The winders look downward, or else there's a fold of the hill or trees between. But I know where every house is wi'out seeing 'em. There's the Nashes', there's the Boxalls', there's the Snellings', there's my brother-in-law's, Thomas Rocliffe's, and down there be I."

He pointed with his whip. Mehetabel could distinguish nothing beyond the white favor bound to his whip.

"We're drivin to Paradise," said Jonas. And as to this remark she made no response, he explained— "Married life, you know."

She said nothing.

"It rather looks as if we were going down to the other place," he observed, with a sarcastic laugh. "But there it is, one or the other—all depends on you. It's just as you make it; as likely to be one as the other. Give me that fifteen pounds—and Paradise is the word."

"Indeed, Jonas, do you not understand that I cannot go against father's will and my word?"

The road, or rather track, descended along the steep side of the Punch-Bowl, notched into the sand falling away rapidly on the left hand, on which side sat Mehetabel.

At first she had distinguished nothing below in the blackness, but now something like a dead man's eye looked out of it, and seemed to follow and observe her.

"What is that yonder?" she asked.

"Wot is wot?" he asked in reply.

"That pale white light—that round thing glimmerin' yonder?"

"There's water below," was his explanation of the phenomenon.

In fact that which had attracted her attention and somewhat alarmed her, was one of the patches of water formed in the marshy bottom of the Punch-Bowl by the water that oozes forth in many springs from under the sandstone.

The track now passed under trees.

A glimpse of dull orange light, and old Clutch halted, unbidden.

"Here we be, we two," said Jonas. "This is home. And Paradise, if you will."

CHAPTER XIV. — NOT PARADISE

At the moment that the cart halted, a black dog burst out of the house door, and flew at Mehetabel as she attempted to descend.

"Ha, Tartar!" laughed Jonas. "The rascal seems to know his reign is over. Go back, Tartar. I'll thrash you till the favor off my whip is beat into your hide, if you don't be quiet. Hitherto he has guarded my house, when I have been from home. Now that will be your duty, Matabel. Can't keep a wife and a dog. 'Twould be too extravagant. Tartar! Down! This is your mistress—till I get rid of you."

The dog withdrew reluctantly, continuing to growl and to show his fangs at Mehetabel.

In the doorway stood Sally Rocliffe, the sister of Jonas. Though not so openly resentful of the intrusion as was Tartar, she viewed the bride with ill-disguised bad humor; indeed, without an affectation of cordiality.

"I thought you was never coming," was Sarah's salutation. "Goodness knows, I have enough to do in my own house, and for my own people, not to be kept dancin' all these hours in attendance, because others find time for makin' fools of themselves. Now, I hope I shall not be wanted longer. My man needs his meals as much as others, and if he don't get 'em reglar, who suffers but I? Dooty begins at home. You might have had more consideration, and come earlier, Jonas."

The woman accorded to Mehetabel but a surly greeting. The young bride entered the house. A single tallow dip was burning on the table, with a long dock to it, unsnuffed. The hearth was cold.

"I didn't light a fire," said Mrs. Rocliffe; "you see it wouldn't do. Now you have come as mistress, it's your place to light the fire on the hearth. I've heard tell it's unlucky for any other body to do it. Not as I knows." She shrugged her shoulders. It seemed that this was a mere excuse put forward to disguise her indolence, or to veil her malevolence.

Mehetabel looked around her.

There were no plates. There was nothing to eat prepared on the kitchen table. No cloth; nothing whatever there, save the guttering candle.

"I didn't lay out nuthin'," said Mrs. Rocliffe; "you see, how was I to say you'd want vittles? I suppose you have had as much as is good for you away where you come from—at the Ship. If you are hungry—there's cold rabbit pie in the larder, if it ain't gone bad. This weather has been bad for keepin' meat. There's bread in the larder, if you don't mind the rats and mice havin' been at it. That's not my fault. Jonas, he had some for his break'us, and never covered up the pan, so the varmin have got to it. There's ale, too, in a barrel, I know, but Jonas keeps the key to that lest I should take a sup. He begrudges me that, and expects me to work for him like a galley-slave."

Then the woman was silent, looking moodily down. The floor was strewn with flakes of whitewash as though snow had fallen over it.

"You see," said Mrs. Rocliffe, "Jonas would go to the expense of whitenin' the ceilin', just because you was comin.' It had done plenty well for father and mother, and I don't mind any time it were whitened afore, and I be some years the elder of Jonas. The ceiling was that greasy wi' smoke, that the whitewashin' as it dried 'as pealed off, and came down just about. You look up—the ceilin' is ten times worse than afore. It looks as if it were measly. I wouldn't sweep up the flakes as fell off just to let Jonas see what comes of his foolishness. I told him it would be so, but he wouldn't believe me, and now let him see for himself—there it is."

With a sort of malignant delight the woman observed Mehetabel, and saw how troubled and unhappy she was.

Again a stillness ensued. Mehetabel could hear her heart beat. She could hear no other sound. She looked through the room towards the clock. It was silent.

"Ah, now there," said Sarah Rocliffe. "There be that, to be sure. Runned down is the weight. It wasn't proper for me now to wind up the clock. As you be the new mistress in the house, it is your place and dooty. I suppose you know that."

Then from without Mehetabel heard the grunts of the sow in the stye that adjoined the house, and imparted an undesirable flavor to the atmosphere in it.

"That's the sow in the pen," said Mrs. Rocliffe; "she's wantin' her meat. She hain't been galliwantin', and marryin', and bein' given in marriage. I'm not the mistress, and I've not the dooty to provide randans and crammins for other folks' hogs. She'll be goin' back in her flesh unless fed pretty smart. You'd best do that at once, but not in your weddin' dress. You must get acquainted together, and the sooner the better. She's regular rampagous wi' hunger."

"Would you help me in with my box, Mrs. Rocliffe?" asked Mehetabel. "Jonas set it down by the door, and if I can get that upstairs I'll change my dress at once, and make the fire, clean the floor, wind up the clock, and feed the hog."

"I've such a terrible crick in my back, I dussn't do it," answered Sarah Rocliffe. "Why, how much does that there box weigh? I wonder Jonas had the face to put it in the cart, and expect Clutch to draw it. Clutch didn't like it now, did he?"

"But how can I get my box in and carried up? Jonas is with the horse, I suppose?"

"Oh, yes, he is minding the horse. Clutch must be made comfortable, and given his hay. I'll be bound you and Jonas have been eatin' and drinkin' all day, and never given Clutch a mouthful, nor washed his teeth with a pail o' water."

"I'm sure Joe Filmer looked to the horse at the Ship. He is very attentive to beasts."

"On ordinary days, and when nuthin' is goin' on, I dare say—not when there's weddin's and ducks and green peas goin' for any who axes for 'em."

The report that ducks and green peas were to form an element of the entertainment had been told everywhere before the day of the marriage, and it was bitterness to Mrs. Rocliffe to think that "on principle," as she put it, she had been debarred from eating her share.

"Ducks and green peas!" repeated she. "I s'pose you don't reckon on eating that every day here, no, nor on Sundays, no, not even at Christmas. 'Taint such as we in the Punch-Bowl as can stuff ourselves on ducks and green peas. Green peas and ducks we may grow—but we sells 'em to the quality."

After some consideration Mrs. Rocliffe relented sufficiently to say, "I don't know but what Samuel may be idlin'; he mostly is. I'll go and send my son Samuel to help you with the box."

Then with a surly "Good-night" the woman withdrew.

After a couple of minutes, she returned: "I've come back," she said, "to tell you that if old Clutch is off his meat—and I shouldn't wonder if he was—wi' neglect and wi' drawing such a weight—then you'd best set to work and make him gruel. Jonas can't afford to lose old Clutch, just becos he's got a wife." Then she departed again.

Jonas was indeed in the stable attending to the horse. He had, moreover, to run the cart under shelter. Mehetabel put out a trembling hand to snuff the candle. Her hand was so unsteady that she extinguished the light. Where to find the tinder box she knew not. She felt for a bench, and in the darkness when she had reached it, sank on it, and burst into tears.

Such was the welcome to her new home.

For some time she sat with as little light in her heart as there was without.

She felt some relief in giving way to her surcharged heart. She sobbed and knitted her fingers together, unknitted them, and wove them together again in convulsions of distress—of despair.

What expectation of happiness had she here? She was accustomed at the Ship to have everything about her neat and in good order. The mere look round that she had given to the room, the principal room of the house she had entered, showed how ramshackle it was. To some minds it is essential that there should be propriety, as essential as that the food they consume should be wholesome, the water they drink should be pure. They can no more accommodate themselves to disorder than they can to running on hands and feet like apes.

It was quite true that this house would be given up to Mehetabel to do with it what she liked. But would her husband care to have it other than it was? Would he not resent her attempts to alter everything?

And for what purpose would she strive and toil if he disapproved of her changes?

She had no confidence that in temper, in character, in mind, he and she would agree, or agree to differ. She knew that he was grasping after money, that he commended no man, but had a disparaging word for every one, and envy of all who were prosperous. She had seen in him no sign of generosity of feeling, no spark of honor. No positive evil was said of him; if he were inclined to drink he was not a drunkard; if he stirred up strife in himself he was not quarrelsome. He over-reached in a bargain, but never did anything actually dishonest. He was not credited with any lightness in his moral conduct towards any village maid. That he was frugal, keen witted, was about all the good that was said, and that could be said of him. If he had won no one's love hitherto, was it likely that there was anything lovable in him? Would he secure the affections of his wife?

Thoughts rose and fell, tossed and broke in Mehetabel's brain; her tears fell freely, and as she was alone in the house she was able to sob without restraint.

Jonas had chained up Tartar, and the dog was howling. The pig grunted impatiently. A rat raced across the floor. Cockroaches came out in the darkness and stirred, making a strange rustling like the pattering of fine rain.

Mehetabel could hear the voice of her husband in the yard. He was thrusting the cart under a roof. He would be in the house shortly, and she did not wish that he should find her in tears, that he should learn how weak, how hopeless she was.

She put her hand into her pocket for a kerchief, and drew forth one, with which she staunched the flow from her eyes, and dried her cheeks. She put her knuckle to her lips to stay their quivering. Then, when she had recovered some composure, she drew a long sigh and replaced the sodden kerchief in her pocket.

At that moment she started, sprang to her feet, searched her pocket in the darkness with tremulous alarm, with sickness at her heart.

Then, not finding what she wanted, she stooped and groped along the floor, and found nothing save the flakes of fallen whitewash.

She stood up panting, and put her hand to her heart. Then Jonas entered with a lantern, and saw her as she thus stood, one hand to her brow, thrusting back the hair, the other to her heart; he was surprised, raised his lantern to throw the light on her face, and said:—"Wot's up?"

"I have been robbed! My fifteen pounds have been taken from me."

"Well I—"

"Jonas!" she said, "I know it was you. It was you who robbed me, where those men robbed my father. Just as I got into the cart you robbed me."

He lowered the lantern.

"Look here, Matabel, mind wot I said. In matrimony it's all give and take, and if there ain't give on one side, then there's take, take on the t'other. I ain't going to have this no Paradise if I can help it."

CHAPTER XV. — IVER

Next day was bright; but already some rime lay in the cold and marshy bottom of the Punch-Bowl.

Mehetabel went round the farm with Bideabout, and with some pride he showed her his possessions, his fields, his barn, sheds and outhouses. Amongst these was that into which she had been taken on the night of her father's murder.

She had often heard the story from Iver. She knew how that every door had been shut against her except that of the shed in which the heather and broom steels were kept that belonged to Jonas, and which served as his workshop.

With a strange sense, as though she were in the hands of Fate thrusting her on, she knew not whither, with remorseless cogency, the young wife looked into the dark shed which had received her eighteen years before.

It was wonderful that she should have begun the first chapter of her life there, and that she should return to the same spot to open the second chapter.

She felt relieved when Jonas left her to herself. Then she at once set to work on the house, in which there was much to be done. She was ambitious to get it into order and comfort before Mrs. Verstage came to visit her in her new quarters.

As she worked, her mind reverted to the Ship. Would she be missed there? Would the new maid engaged be as active and attentive as she had been? Her place in the hearts of the old couple was now occupied by Iver. However much the innkeeper might pretend to be hard of reconciliation, yet he must yearn after his own son; he must be proud of him now that Iver was grown so fine and independent, and had carved for himself a place in the world.

When the first feeling of regret over her departure was passed away, then all their thoughts, their aspirations, their pride would be engrossed by Iver.

Mehetabel was scouring a saucepan. She lowered it, and her hands remained inactive. Iver!—she saw him, as he stood before her in the Ship, extending his hands to her. She almost felt his grasp again.

Mehetabel brushed back the hair that had fallen over her face; and as she did so a tear ran down her cheek.

Then she heard her husband's voice; he was speaking with Samuel Rocliffe, his nephew; and it struck her as never before, how harsh, how querulous was his intonation.

During the day, Mrs. Rocliffe came in, looked about inquisitively, and pursed up her lips when she saw the change effected, and conjectured that more was likely to follow.

"I suppose nuthin' is good enough as it was—but you must put everything upside down?"

"On the contrary, I am setting on its feet everything I have found topsy-turvy."

To the great surprise of all, on the following Sunday, Bideabout, in his best suit, accompanied Mehetabel to church. He had never been a church-goer. He begrudged having to pay tithes. He begrudged having to pay something for his seat in addition to tithes to the church, if he went to a dissenting chapel. If religious ministrations weren't voluntary and gratuitous, "then," said Jonas, "he didn't think nuthin' of 'em."

Jonas had been disposed to scoff at religion, and to work on Sundays, though not so openly as on other days of the week. He went to church now because he was proud of his wife; not out of devotion, but vanity.

Some days later arrived a little tax-cart driven by Iver, with Mrs. Verstage in it.

The hostess had already discovered what a difference it made in her establishment to have in it a raw and dull-headed maid in the room of the experienced and intelligent daughter. She did not regret what she had done—she had removed Mehetabel out of the reach of Iver, and had no longer any anxiety as to the disposal of his property by Simon. For her own sake she was sorry, as she plainly saw that her life was likely to run less smoothly in the future in her kitchen and with her guests. Now that Mehetabel was no longer dangerous, her heart unfolded towards her once more.

The young wife received Mrs. Verstage with pleasure. The flush came into her cheeks when she saw her, and for the moment she had no eyes, no thoughts, no welcome for Iver.

The landlady was not so active as of old, and she had to be assisted from her seat. As soon as she reached the ground she was locked in the embrace of her daughter by adoption.

Then Mehetabel conducted the old woman over the house, and showed her the new arrangements she had made, and consulted her on certain projected alterations.

Jonas had come to the door when the vehicle arrived; he was in his most gracious mood, and saluted first the hostess and then her son, with unwonted cordiality.

"Come now, Matabel," said Mrs. Verstage, when both she and the young wife were alone together, "I did well to push this on, eh? You have a decent house, and a good farm. All yours, not rented, so none can turn you out. What more could you desire? I dare be sworn Bideabout has got a pretty nest egg stuck away somewhere, up the chimney or under the hearth. Has he shown you what he has? There was the elder Gilly Cheel was a terrible skinflint. When he died his sons hunted high and low for his money and couldn't find it. And just as they wos goin' to bury him, the nuss said she couldn't make a bootiful corpse of him, he were that puffed in his mouth. What do you think, Matabel? The old chap had stuffed his money into his mouth when he knew he was dyin'. Didn't want nobody to have it but himself. Don't you let Bideabout try any of them games."

"Have you missed me greatly, dear mother?" asked Mehetabel, who had heard the story of Giles Cheel before.

Mrs. Verstage sighed.

"My dear, do you know the iron-stone bowl as belonged to my mother. The girl broke it, and hadn't the honesty to say so, but stuck it together wi' yaller soap, and thought I wouldn't see it. Then one of the customers made her laugh, and she let seven pewters fall, and they be battered outrageous. And she has been chuckin' the heel taps to the hog, and made him as drunk as a Christian. She'll drive me out of my seven senses."

"So you do miss me, mother?"

"My dear—no—I'm not selfish. It is all for your good. There wos Martha Lintott was goin' to a dance, and dropped her bustle. Patty Pickett picked it up, and thinkin' she couldn't have too much of a good thing, clapped it on a top of her own and cut a fine figure wi' it—wonderful. And Martha looked curious all up and down wi'out one. But she took it reasonable, and said, 'What's one woman's loss is another woman's gain.' O, my dear life! If Iver would but settle with Polly Colpus I should die content."

"Is not the match agreed to yet?"

"No!" Mrs. Verstage sighed. "I've got my boy back, but not for long. He talks of remaining here awhile to paint—subjects, he calls 'em, but he don't rise to Polly as I should like. Polly is a good girl. Master Colpus was at your weddin', and was very civil to Iver. I heard him invite the boy to come over and look in on him some evening—Sunday, for instance, and have a bite of supper and a glass. But Iver hasn't been nigh the Colpuses yet; and when I press him to go he shrugs his shoulders and says he has other and better friends he must visit first."

Mrs. Verstage sighed again.

"Well, perhaps he doesn't fancy Polly," said Mehetabel.

"Why should he not fancy her? She will have five hundred pounds, and old James Colpus's land adjoins ours. I don't understand Iver's ways at all."

Mehetabel laughed. "Dear mother, you cannot expect that; he did not think with his father's head when a boy. He will think only with his own head now he is a man."

"Look here, Matabel. I'll leave Iver to you for half-an-hour. Show him the cows. I'll make Bideabout take me to his sister. I want to have it out with her for not coming to the wedding. I'm not the person to let these things pass. Say a word to Iver about Polly, there is a dear. I cannot bring them together, but you may, you are so clever."

Meanwhile Iver and Jonas had been in conversation. The latter had been somewhat contemptuous about the profession of an artist, and was not a little astonished when he heard the prices realized by pictures. Iver told the Broom-Squire that he intended making some paintings of the Punch-Bowl, and that he had a mind to draw Kink's farm.

In that case, said Bideabout, a percentage of the money such a picture fetched would be due to him. He didn't see that anyone had a right to take a portrait of his house and not pay him for it. If Iver were content to draw his house, he must, on no account, include that of the Rocliffes, for there was a mortgage on that, and there might be trouble with the lawyers.

Mrs. Verstage proposed to Bideabout that she should go with him to his sister's house, and he consented.

"Look here, Matabel," said he, "there is Mister Iver thinks he can make a pictur' of the spring, if you'll get a pitcher and stand by it. I dare say if it sells, he'll not forget us."

"I wish I could take Mehetabel and her pitcher off your hands, and not merely the portrait of both," laughed Iver, to cover the confusion of the girl, who reddened with annoyance at the grasping meanness of Jonas.

When Iver was alone with her, as they were on their way to the spring, he said, "Come, this will not do at all. For the first time we are free to chat together, as in the old times when we were inseparable friends. Why are you shy now, Matabel?"

"You must be glad to be home again with the dear father and mother," she said.

"Yes, but I miss you; and I had so reckoned on finding you there."

"You will remain at the Ship now," urged she.

"I don't know that. I have my profession. I have leisure during part of the summer and fall, making studies for pictures—but I take pupils; they pay."

"You must consider the old folk."

"I do. I will visit them occasionally. But art is a mistress, and an imperious one. When one is married one is no longer independent."

"You are married?" asked Mehetabel, with a flush in her cheeks.

"Yes, to my art."

"Oh! to paints and brushes! Tell me true, Iver! Has no girl won your heart whilst you have been from home?"

"I have found many to admire, but my heart is free. I have had no time to think of girls' faces—save as studies. Art is a mistress as jealous as she is exacting."

Mehetabel drew a long breath. There went up a flash of light in her mind, for which she did not attempt to account. "You are free—that is famous, and can take Polly Colpus."

Then she laughed, and Iver laughed.

They laughed long and merrily together.

"This is too much," exclaimed Iver. "At home father is at me to exchange the mahl-stick for an ox-goad, and mother wearies me with laudation of Polly Colpus. I shall revolt and run away, as I did not expect you to lend a hand with Polly."

"You must not run away," said Mehetabel, earnestly. "Iver! I was all those years at the Ship, with mother, after you went, and I have seen how her heart has ached for you. She is growing old. Let her have consolation during the years that remain for the sorrow of those that are past."

"I cannot take to farming, nor turn publican, and I will not have Polly Colpus."

"Here is the spring," said Mehetabel.

She set the pitcher beside the water, leaned back in the hedge, musing, with her finger to her chin, her eyes on the ground, and her feet crossed.

"Stand as you are. That is perfect. Do not stir. I will make a pencil sketch."

The spring gushed from under a bank, in a clear and copious jet. It had washed away the sand, and had buried itself in a nook among ferns and moss. On the top of the bank was a rude shed, open at the side, with a cart at rest in it. Wild parsnips in full flower nodded before the water.

"I could desire nothing better," said Iver, "and that pale blue skirt of yours, the white stockings, the red kerchief round your head—in color as in arrangement everything is admirable."

"You have not your paints with you."

"I will come another day and bring them. Now I will only sketch in the outline."

Presently Iver laughed. "Matabel! If I took Polly she would be of no use to me whatever, not even as a model."

Presently the Broom-Squire returned with Mrs. Verstage, and looked over the shoulder of the artist.

"Not done much," he said.

"I shall have to come again and yet again, to put in the color," said Iver.

"Come when and as often as you like," said Bideabout. Neither of the men noticed the shrinking that affected the entire frame of Mehetabel, as Jonas said these words, but it was observed by Mrs. Verstage, and a shade of anxiety swept over her face.

CHAPTER XVI. — AGAIN-IVER

A few days after this first visit, Iver was again at the Kinks' farm.

The weather was fine, and he protested that he must take advantage of it to proceed with his picture.

Mehetabel was reluctant to stand. She made excuses that were at once put aside.

"If you manage to sell pictures of our place," said Bideabout, "our Punch-Bowl may get a name, and folk come here picnicking from Godalming and Guildford and Portsmouth; and I'll put up a board with Refreshments—Moderate, over the door, and Matabel shall make tea or sell cake, and pick up a trifle towards; housekeeping."

A month was elapsed since Mehetabel's marriage, the month of honey to most—one of empty comb without sweetness to her. She had drawn no nearer to her husband than before. They had no interests, no tastes in common. They saw all objects through a different medium.

It was not a matter of concern to Mehetabel that she was left much alone by Jonas, and that her sister-in-law and the rest of the squatters treated her as an interloper.

As a child, at the Ship, without associates of her own age, after Iver's departure, she had lived much to herself, and now her soul craved for solitude. And yet, when she was alone the thoughts of her heart troubled her.

Jonas was attached, in his fashion, to his beautiful wife; he joked, and was effusive in his expressions of affection. But she did not respond to his jokes, and his demonstrations of affection repelled her. Jonas was too dull, or vain, to perceive this, and he attributed her coldness to modesty, real or affected, probably the latter.

Mehetabel shrank from looking full in the face, the thought that she must spend the rest of her life with this man. She was well aware that she could not love him, could hardly bring herself to like him, the utmost she could hope was that she might arrive at enduring him.

Whilst in this condition of unrest and discouragement, Iver appeared, and his presence lit up the desolation in which she was. The sight of him, the sound of his voice, aroused old recollections, helped to drive away the shadows that environed her, and that clouded her mind. There was no harm in this, and yet she was uneasy. Cheerful as she was when he was present, there was something feverish in this cheerfulness, and it left her more unhappy than before when he was gone, and more conscious of the impossibility of accommodating herself to her lot.

The visit on one fine day was followed by another when the rain fell heavily.

Iver entered the house, shook his wet hat and cloak, and with a laugh, exclaimed—

"Here I am—to continue the picture."

"In such weather?"

"Little woman! When I started the wind was in the right quarter. All at once it veered round and gave me a drenching. What odds? You can stand at the window, and I can proceed with the figure. It was tedious at the Ship. Between you and me and the post, I cannot get along with the fellows who come there to drink. You are the only person in Thursley with whom I can talk and be happy."

"Bideabout is not at home."

"I didn't come through the rain to see Bideabout, but you."

"Will you have anything to eat or drink?"

"Anything that you can give me. But I did not come for that. To tell the truth, I don't think I'll venture on the picture. The light is so bad. It is of no consequence. We can converse. I am sick of public-house talk. I ran away to be with you. We are old chums, are we not, dear Matabel?"

A fire of peat was on the hearth. She threw on skin-turf that flamed up.

Iver was damp. His hands were clammy. His hair ends dripped. His face was running with water. He spread his palms over the flame, and smiled.

"And so you were tired of being at home?" she said, as she put the turves together.

"Home is no home to me, now you are gone," was his answer.

Then, after a pause, during which he chafed his hands over the dancing flame, he added: "I wish you were back in the old Ship. The old Ship! It is no longer the dear old Ship of my recollections, now that you have deserted. Why did you leave? It is strange to me that my mother did not write and tell me that you were going to be married. If she had done that—"

He continued drying his hands, looking dreamily into the flame, and left the sentence incomplete.

"It is queer altogether," he pursued. "When I told her I was at Guildford, and proposed returning, she put me off, till my father was better prepared. She would break the news to him, see how—he took it, and so on. I waited, heard no more, so came unsummoned, for I was impatient at the delay. She knew I wished to hear about you, Mattee, dear old friend and playmate. I asked in my letters about you. You know you ceased to write, and mother labored at the pen herself, finally. She answered that you were well—nothing further. Why did she not tell me of your engagement? Have you any idea, Matabel?"

She bowed over the turf, to hide her fate, but the leaping flame revealed the color that mantled cheek, and throat, and brow. Her heart was beating furiously.

"That marriage seems to me to have been cobbled up precious quickly. Were you so mighty impatient to have the Broom-Squire that you could not wait till you were twenty? A girl of eighteen does not know her own mind. A pretty kettle of fish there will be if you discover, when too late, that you have made a mistake, and married the wrong man, who can never make you happy."

Mehetabel started upright, and went with heaving bosom to the window, then drew back in surprise, for she saw the face of Mrs. Rocliffe at the pane, her nose applied to and flattened against the glass, and looking like a dab of putty.

She was offended at the woman's inquisitiveness, and went to the door to inquire if she needed anything.

"Nuthin' at all," answered Sarah, with a laugh, "except to see whether my brother was home. It's early days beginning this, I call it."

"What do you mean?"

"Oh, nuthin'."

"Iver is here," said Mehetabel, controlling herself. "Will you please to come in?"

"But Jonas is not, is he?"

"No; he has gone to Squire Mellers about a load of stable-brooms."

"I wouldn't come in on no account," said Mrs. Rocliffe. "Two's company, three's none," and she turned and departed.

After she had shut the door Mehetabel went hastily through the kitchen into the scullery at the back. Her face was crimson, and she trembled in all her joints.

Iver called to her; she answered hastily that she was engaged, and presently, after she had put bread and cake and butter on the table, she fled to her own room upstairs, seated herself on a chair, and hid her burning face in her apron.

The voice of her husband below afforded sensible relief to her in her mortification. He was speaking with Iver; cursing the weather and his bad luck. His long tramp in the rain had been to no purpose. The Squire, to whose house he had been, was out. She washed her face, combed and smoothed her hair, and slowly descended the stairs.

On seeing her Jonas launched forth in complaints, and showed himself to be in an evil temper. He must have ale, not wish-wash tea, fit only for old women. He would not stuff himself with cake like a school child. He must have ham fried for him at once.

He was in an irritable mood, and found fault with his wife about trifles, or threw out sarcastic remarks that wounded, and made Iver boil with indignation. Jonas did not seem to bear the young artist a grudge; he was, in fact, pleased to see him, and proposed to him to stay the evening and have a game of cards.

It was distressing to Mehetabel to be rebuked in public, but she made no rejoinder. Jonas had seized on the opportunity to let his visitor see that he was not tied to his wife's apron string, but was absolute master in his own house. The blood mounted to Iver's brow, and he clenched his hands under the table.

To relieve the irksomeness of the situation Iver proceeded to undo a case of his colored sketches that he had brought with him.

These water-colors were charming in their style, a style much affected at that period; the tints were stippled in, and every detail given with minute fidelity. The revolution in favor of blottesque had not yet set in, and the period was happily far removed from that of the impressionist, who veils his incapacity under a term—an impression, and calls a daub a picture. Nature never daubs, never strains after effects. She is painstaking, delicate in her work, and reticent.

Whilst Mehetabel was engaged frying ham, Iver showed his drawings to the Broom-Squire, who treated them without perception of their beauty, and valued them solely as merchandise. But when supper was ready, and whilst Jonas was eating, he had a more interested and appreciative observer in Mehetabel, to whom the drawings afforded unfeigned pleasure. In her delight she sat close to Iver; her warm breath played over his cheek, as he held up the sketches to the light, and pointed out the details of interest.

Once when these were minute, and she had to look closely to observe them, in the poor light afforded by the candle, without thinking what he was about, Iver put his hand on her neck. She started, and he withdrew it. The action was unobserved by Bideabout, who was engrossed in his rasher.

When Jonas had finished his meal, he thrust his plate away, produced a pack of cards, and said—

"Here, Mr. Iver, are pictures worth all of yours. Will you come and try your luck or skill against me? We'll have a sup of brandy together. Matabel, bring glasses and hot-water."

Iver went to the door and looked out. The rain descended in streams; so he returned to the table, drew up his chair and took a hand.

When Mehetabel had washed the plates and dishes used at the meal, she seated herself where she could see by the candle-light, took up her needlework, and was prepared to snuff the wick as was required.

Iver found that he could not fix his attention on the game. Whenever Mehetabel raised her hand for the snuffers, he made a movement to forestall her, then sometimes their eyes met, and she lowered hers in confusion.

The artistic nature of Iver took pleasure in the beautiful; and the features, coloring, grace of the young Broom-Squiress, were such as pleased him and engaged his attention. He made no attempt to analyze his feelings towards her. He was not one to probe his own heart, nor had he the resolution to break away from temptation, even when recognized as such. Easy-going, good-natured, impulsive, with a spice of his mother's selfishness in his nature, he allowed himself to follow his inclinations without consideration whither they might lead him, and how they might affect others.

Iver's eyes, thoughts, were distracted from the game. He lost money—five shillings, and Jonas urged him to play for higher stakes.

Then Mehetabel laid her needlework in her lap, and said—

"No, Iver, do not. You have played sufficiently, and have lost enough. Go home."

Jonas swore at her.

"What is that to you? We may amuse ourselves without your meddling. What odds to you if he loses, so long as I win. I am your husband and not he."

But Iver rose, and laughingly said:—

"Better go home with a wet jacket than with all the money run out of my pocket. Good-night, Bideabout."

"Have another shot?"

"Not another."

"She put you up to this," with a spiteful glance at Mehetabel.

"Not a bit, Jonas. Don't you think a chap feels he's losing blood, without being told he is getting white about the gills."

The Broom-Squire sulkily began to gather up the cards.

"What sort of a night is it, Mehetabel? Go to the door and see," said he.

The girl rose and opened the door.

Without, the night was black as pitch, and in the light that issued the raindrops glittered as they fell. In the trees, in the bushes, on the grass, was the rustle of descending rain.

"By Jove, it's worse than ever," said Iver: "lend me a lantern, or I shall never reach home."

"I haven't one to spare," replied Bideabout; "the hogs and calves must be tended, and the horse, Old Clutch, littered down. Best way that you have another game with me, and you shall stay the night. We have a spare room and bed."

"I accept with readiness," said Iver.

"Go—get all ready, Matabel. Now, then! you cut, I deal."

CHAPTER XVII. — DREAMS

Iver remained the night in the little farm-house. He thought nothing as he lay in bed of the additional shillings he had lost to Jonas, but of the inestimable loss he had sustained in Mehetabel.

The old childish liking he had entertained for her revived. It did more than revive, it acquired strength and heat. As a boy he had felt some pride and self-consequence because of the child whom he had introduced into the Christian Church, and to whom he had given a name. Now he was elated to think that she was the most beautiful woman he had seen, and angry with the consciousness that she was snatched from him.

Why had he not returned to Thursley a day, half a day, earlier? Why had Fate played such a cruel game with him? What a man this Jonas Kink was who had won the prize. Was he worthy of it? Did he value

Mehetabel as he should? A fellow who could not perceive beauty in a landscape and see the art in his drawings was not one to know that his wife was lovely, or if he knew it did so in a stupid, unappreciative manner. Did he treat Mehetabel kindly; with ordinary civility? Iver remembered the rebukes, the slights put on her in his own presence.

Iver's bedroom was neat, everything in it clean. The bed was one of those great tented four-posters which were at the time much affected in Surrey, composed of covering and curtains of striped—or pranked—cotton, blue and white. Mehetabel, in the short while she had been in the Punch-Bowl, had put the spare room in order. She had found it used as a place for lumber, every article of furniture deep in dust, and every curtain rent. The corners of the room had been given over for twenty years as the happy hunting-ground of spiders. Although Bideabout had taken some pains to put his house in order before his marriage, repairs had been executed only on what was necessary, and in a parsimonious spirit. The spare room had been passed over, as not likely to be needed. To that as to every other portion of the house, Mehetabel had turned her attention, and it was now in as good condition to receive a guest as the bedrooms in the Ship Inn.

Presently Iver went to sleep, lulled by the patter of the rain on the roof, on the leaves, and the sobbing of the moist wind through the ill-adjusted casement.

As he slept he had a dream.

He thought that he heard Thursley Church bells ringing. He believed he had been to church to be married. He was in his holiday attire, and was holding his bride by the hand. He turned about to see who was his partner, and recognized Mehetabel. She was in white, but whiter than her dress and veil was her bloodless face, and her dark brows and hair marked it as with mourning.

There was this strange element in his dream, that he could not leave the churchyard.

He endeavored to follow the path to the gate, outside which the villagers were awaiting them with flowers and ready to cheer; but he was unable to reach it. The path winded in and out among the gravestones, and round and round the church, till at length it reached the tomb of the murdered sailor.

All the while the ringers were endeavoring to give the young bridal pair a merry peal, and failed. The ropes slid from their hands, and only the sexton succeeded in securing one, and with that he tolled. Distinctly Iver saw the familiar carving of the three murderers robbing and killing their victim. He had often laughed over the bad drawing of the figures—he laughed now, in sleep.

Then he thought that he heard Mehetabel reproach him for having returned, to be her woe. And that between each sentence she sobbed.

Thereupon he again looked at her.

She was beautiful, more beautiful than ever—a beauty sublimated, rendered almost transparent. As he looked she became paler, and the hand he held grew colder. Now ensued a strange phenomenon.

She was sinking. Her feet disappeared in the spongy turf that oozed with water after the long rain. Her large dark eyes were fixed on him entreatingly, reproachfully.

Then she was enveloped to her knees, and as she went down, the stain of the wet grass and the soil of the graveyard clay rose an inch up her pure white garment.

She held his hand tenaciously, as the only thing to which she could cling to save her from being wholly engulfed.

Then she was swallowed up to her waist, and he became aware that if he continued to clasp her hand, she would drag him under the earth. In his dream he reasoned with her. He pointed out to her that it was impossible for him to be of any service to her, and that he was jeopardizing his own self, unless he disengaged himself from her.

He endeavored to release his hand. She clung the more obstinately, her fingers were deadly cold and numbed him, yet he was resolute in self-defence, and finally freed his hand. Then she sank more rapidly, with despair in the upturned face. He tried to escape her eyes, he could not. It was a satisfaction to him when the rank grass closed over them and got between the lips that were opened in appeal for help. Then ensued a gulp. The earth had swallowed her up, and in dream, he was running for his pallet and canvas to make a study of the spot where she had sunk, in a peculiarly favorable light. He woke, shivering, and saw that the gray morning was looking in at his window between the white curtains.

His hand, that had felt so chill, was out of the bed, and the coverlet had slid off him, and was heaped on the floor.

The wind had shifted, and now pressed the clouds together, rolled them up and swept them into the lumber-house of clouds below the horizon. He dressed leisurely, shook himself, to shake off the impression produced by his dream, and laughed at himself for having been disturbed by it.

When he came downstairs he found that both Mehetabel and Jonas were already on their feet, and that the former was preparing breakfast. Her eyes were red, as if she had been crying.

"How did you sleep?" she asked, with faint smile—"and what were your dreams?"

"They say that the first dream in new quarters comes true," threw in the Broom-Squire; "but this is the idle chatter of old wives. I make no count of it."

Mehetabel observed that Iver started and seemed disconcerted at this question relative to his dream. He evaded an answer, and she saw that the topic was unpleasant, and to reply inconvenient. She said no more; and Jonas had other matters to think about more substantial than dreams. Yet Mehetabel could not fail to perceive that their guest was out of tune. Was he annoyed at having lost money, or was he in reality troubled by something that had occurred during the night? An hour later Iver prepared to leave.

"Come with me a little way," he pleaded with the hostess, "see me safe off the premises."

She did as was desired, though not without inner reluctance. And yet, at the same time she felt that with his departure a something would be gone that could not be replaced, a light out of her sky, a strain of music out of her soul.

The white fog lay like curd at the bottom of the Punch-Bowl. Here and there a tree-top stood above the vapor, but only as a bosky islet in the surface of mist, dense and chill. The smoke from the chimneys of the squatter houses rose like steaming springs, but the brick chimneys were submerged. So dense was the fog that it muffled all sound, impeded the breath, struck cold to the marrow. It smelt, for the savors of hog-pen and cow-stall were caught and not allowed to dissipate.

A step, and those ascending the side of the great basin were out of the mist, and in sunshine, but it still held their feet to the knees; another step and they were clear, and then their shadows were cast, gigantic, upon the white surface below, and about each head was a halo of light and rainbow tints.

Every bush was twinkling as hung with diamonds of the purest water. Larks were trilling, pouring forth in song the ecstasy that swelled their hearts. The sky was blue as a nemophyla, and cloudless.

As soon as Iver and Mehetabel had issued from the fog and were upon the heath, and in the sunshine, she stayed her feet.

"I will go no further," she said.

"Look," said he, "how the fog lies below at the bottom of the Punch-Bowl, as though it were snow. Above, on the downs all is sunshine."

"Yes, you go up into the light and warmth," answered she. "I must back and down into the cold vapors, cold as death."

He thought of his dream. There was despondency in her tone.

"The sun will pierce and scatter the vapors and shine over and warm you below."

She shook her head.

"Iver," she said, "you may tell me now we are alone. What was your dream?"

Again he appeared disconcerted.

"Of what, of whom did you dream?"

"Of whom else could I dream but you—when under your roof," said he with a laugh.

"Oh, Iver! and what did you dream about me?"

"Arrant nonsense. Dreams go by contraries."

"Then what about me?"

"I dreamt of your marriage."

"Then that means death."

He caught her to him, and kissed her lips.

"We are brother and sister," he said, in self-exculpation. "Where is the harm?"

She disengaged herself hastily.

She heard a cough and looked round, to see the mocking face of Sarah Rocliffe, who had followed and had just emerged from the curdling fog below.

CHAPTER XVIII. — REALITIES

Iver was gone.

The light that had sparkled in Mehetabel's eyes, the flush, like a carnation in her cheek, faded at once. She was uneasy that Mrs. Rocliffe had surprised her and Iver, whilst he gave her that ill-considered though innocent parting salute.

What mischief she might make of it! How she might sow suspicion of her in the heart of Jonas, and Iver would be denied the house! Iver denied the house! Then she would see him no more, have no more pleasant conversations with him. Indeed, then the cold, clammy fog into which she descended was a figure of the life hers would be, and it was one that no sun's rays could dissipate.

After she had returned to the house she sank in a dark comer like one weary after hard labor, and looked dreamily before her at the floor. Her hands and her feet were motionless.

A smile that every moment became more bitter sat on her lips. The muscles of her face became more rigid.

What if through jealousy, open discord broke out between her and Jonas? Would it make her condition more miserable, her outlook more desperate? She revolved in thought the events that were past. She ranged them in their order—the proposal of Jonas, her refusal, the humiliation to which she had been subjected by Mrs. Verstage which had driven her to accept the man she had just rejected, the precipitation with which the marriage had been hurried on, then the appearance of Iver on her wedding day.

She recalled the look that passed over his face when informed that she was a bride, the clasp of his hands, and now—now—his kiss burned on her lips, nay, had sunk in as a drop of liquid fire, and was consuming her heart with anguish and sweetness combined.

Was the kiss that of a brother to a sister? Was there in it, as Iver said, no harm, no danger to herself? She thought of the journey home from the Ship on her wedding evening, of the fifteen pounds of which she had been robbed by her husband, the money given her by "father" against the evil day. She had been deceived, defrauded by the man she had sworn to honor, love, and obey. She had not acquired love for him. Had he not by this act forfeited all claim to both love and honor?

She thought again of Iver, of his brown, agate-like eyes, but eyes in which there was none of the hardness of a stone. She contrasted him with Jonas. How mean, how despicable, how narrow in mind and in heart was the latter compared with the companion of her youth.

Mehetabel's face was bathed in perspiration. She slid to her knees to pray; she folded her hands, and found herself repeating. "Genesis, fifty chapters; Exodus, forty; Leviticus, twenty-seven; Numbers, thirty-six; Deuteronomy, thirty-four; these are the books that constitute the Pentateuch. The Book of Joshua—"

Then she checked herself. In her distress, her necessity, she was repeating the lesson last acquired in Sunday-school, which had gained her a prize. This was not prayer. It brought her no consolation, it afforded her no strength. She tried to find something to which to cling, to stay her from the despair into which she had slipped, and could only clearly figure to herself that "the country of the Gergesenes lay to the southeast of the Sea of Tiberias and that a shekel weighed ten hundred-weights and ninety-two grains, Troy weight, equal to in avoirdupois—" her brain whirled. She could not work out the sum. She could not pray. She could recall no prayer. She could look to nothing beyond the country of the Gergesenes. And yet, never in her life had she so needed prayer, strength, as now, when this new guilty passion was waking in her heart.

Shuddering at the thought of revolt against her duty, unable altogether to abandon the hope, the longing to see Iver again, filled with vague terror of what the future might bring forth, she remained as struck with paralysis, kneeling, speechless, with head bowed, hands fallen at her side, seeing, hearing, knowing nothing; and was roused with a start by the voice of Jonas who entered, and asked—,

"Wot's up now?"

She could not answer him. She sprang to her feet and eagerly flew to the execution of her domestic duties.

Iver returned from his visit to the Punch-Bowl with a mind occupied and ill at ease.

He had allowed himself, without a struggle, to give way to the impression produced on him by the beauty of Mehetabel. He enjoyed her society—found pleasure in talking of the past. Her mind was fresh; she was intelligent, and receptive of new ideas. She alone of all the people of Thursley, whom he had encountered, was endowed with artistic sense—was able to set the ideal above what was material. He did not ask himself whether he loved her. He knew that he did, but the knowledge did not trouble him. After a fashion, Mehetabel belonged to him as to none other. She was associated with his earliest and sunniest recollections.

Mehetabel could sympathize with him in his love for the beautiful in Nature. She had ever been linked with his mother in love for him. She had been the vehicle of communication between him and his mother till almost the last moment; it was through her that all tidings of home had reached him.

When his father had refused to allow Iver's name to be mentioned in his presence, for hours daily the thoughts of him had been in the hearts of his mother and this girl. With united pity and love, they had followed his struggles to make his way.

There was much obstinacy in Iver.

Resolution to have his own way had made him leave home to follow an artistic career, regardless of the heartache he would cause his mother, and the resentment he would breed in his father.

Thus, without consideration of the consequences to himself, to Mehetabel, to Jonas, he allowed his glowing affection for the young wife to gather heat, without attempt to master or extinguish it.

There is a certain careless happiness in the artistic soul that is satisfied with the present, and does not look into the future. The enjoyment of the hour, the banquet off the decked table, the crown of roses freshly blown, suffice the artist's soul. It has no prevision of the morrow—makes no provision for the winter.

That the marriage of Mehetabel with Jonas had raised barriers between them was hardly considered. That the Broom-Squire might resent having him hover round his young flower, did not enter into Iver's calculations; least of all did it concern him that he was breaking the girl's heart, and forever making it impossible for her to reconcile herself to her position.

As Iver walked home over the common, and enjoyed the warmth and brilliancy of the sun, he asked himself again, why his mother had not prepared him for the marriage of Mehetabel.

Mehetabel had certainly not taken Jonas because she loved him. She was above sordid considerations. What, then, had induced her to take the man? She had been happy and contented at the Ship; why, then, did she leave it?

On reaching home, he put the question to his mother. "It is a puzzle to me, which I cannot unravel, why has Matabel become Bideabout's wife?"

"Why should she not?" asked his mother in return. "It was a catch for such as she—a girl without a name, and bare of a dower. She has every reason to thank me for having pushed the marriage on."

Iver looked at his mother with surprise.

"Then you had something to do with it?"

"Of course I had," answered she. "I did my duty. I am not so young as I was. I had to think for Matabel's future. She is no child of mine. She can expect nothing from your father nor from me. When a good offer came, then I told her to accept and be thankful. She is a good girl, and has been useful in the house, and some people think her handsome. But young men don't court a girl who has no name, and has had three men hanged because of her."

"Mother! what nonsense! The men were executed because they murdered her father."

"It is all one. She is marked with the gallows. Ill-luck attaches to her. There has been a blight on her from the beginning. I mind when her father chucked her down all among the fly-poison. Now she has got the Broom-Squire, she may count herself lucky, and thank me for it."

"Good heavens!" exclaimed Iver. "Then this marriage is your doing?"

"Yes—I told her that, before you came here, I must have her clear out of the house."

"Why?"

A silence ensued. Mrs. Verstage looked at her son—into his great, brown eyes—and what she saw there alarmed her. Her lips moved to speak, but she could utter no words. She had let out her motive without consideration in the frankness that was natural to her.

"I ask, mother, why did you stop Matabel from writing, and take up the correspondence yourself at last; and then, when you did write to me at Guildford, you said not one word about Mehetabel being promised to the Broom-Squire?"

"I could not put all the news of the parish into my letter. How should I know that this concerned you?"

"We were together as children. If ever there were friends in the world, it was we."

"I am a bad writer. It takes me five minutes over one word, just about. I said what I had to say, and no more, and I were a couple o' days over that."

"Why did you ask me to postpone my coming home?—why seek to keep me away till after Mehetabel's marriage?"

"There was a lot to do in the house, preparation for the weddin'—her gownds—I couldn't have you here whilst all the rout was on. I wanted to have you come when all was quiet again, and I could think of you. What wi' preparations and schemin' my head was full."

"Was that the only reason, mother?"

She did not answer. Her eyes fell.

Iver threw his hat on the table, and went to his room. He was incensed against his mother. He guessed the reason why she had urged on the marriage, why she had kept him in ignorance of the engagement, why she had delayed his return to Thursley.

She had made her plans. She wished to marry him to Polly Colpus, and she dreaded his association with Mehetabel as likely to be prejudicial to the success of her cherished scheme, now that the girl was in the ripeness of her beauty and to Iver invested with the halo of young associations, of boy romance.

If his mother had told him! If she had not bidden him postpone his coming home! Then all would have turned out well. Mehetabel would not have been linked to an undesirable man, whom she could not love; and he would have been free to make her his own.

His heart was bitter as wormwood.

Mrs. Verstage saw but too plainly that her son was estranged from her; and she could form a rough estimate of the reason. He addressed her indeed with a semblance of love and showed her filial attention, but her maternal instinct assured her that something stood between them, something which took the reality and spontaneity out of his demonstrations of affection.

Iver occupied himself with the picture of Mehetabel at the fountain. It was his great pleasure to work thereon. If he was not engaged at his canvas in the tavern, he was wandering in the direction of the

Punch-Bowl to make studies for pictures, so he said. His mother saw that there was no prospect of retaining her son at the Ship for long. What held him there was not love for her, desire to recover lost ground with his father, not a clinging to his old home, not a desire to settle and take up his father's work; it was something else—she feared to give utterance to the thought haunting her mind.

"You are a fool, old woman," said her husband to her one night. "You and I might have been easy and happy in our old age had you not meddled and made mischief. You always was a great person for lecturin' about Providence, and it's just about the one thing you won't let alone."

"What do you mean, Simon?" she asked, and her heart beat fast with presage of what he would say.

"Why, Susan, if you had not thrust Mehetabel into the Broom-Squire's arms when she didn't want to be there no more nor among brimbles, then Iver would have taken her and all would have been peace."

"What makes you say that?" she asked, in a flutter of terror.

"Oh, I'll be bound it would have been so. Iver has been asking all manner of questions about Matabel, and why she took Jonas. I sed it was agin my wishes, but that you would have it, so Matabel had to give in."

"Simon, why did you say that? You set the boy against me."

"I don't see that, Sanna. It is you who have put the fat in the fire. If you try to turn a stream to run uphill, you will souse your own field, and won't get the water to go where you drive it. It's my belief that all the while he has been away, Iver has had his mind set upon Matabel. I'm not surprised. You may go through Surrey, and won't find her match. Now he comes home and finds that you have spoiled his chance, with your meddlesomeness—and there'll be the devil to pay, yet. That's my opinion."

The old man turned on his side and was asleep, but self-reproach for what was past and doubt as to the future kept his wife awake all night.

CHAPTER XIX. — BACK AGAIN

Fever boiled in the heart of Mehetabel. A mill-race of ideas rushed through her brain.

She found no rest in her household work, for it was not possible for her to keep her mind upon it. Nor was there sufficient employment to be found in the house to engage all her time.

Do what she would, make for herself occupation, there was still space in which to muse and to torment herself with her thoughts. Whilst her hands were engaged she craved for leisure in which to think; when unemployed, the ferment within rendered idleness intolerable.

When the work of the house was accomplished, she went to the fountain where she had been drawn by Iver, and there saw again the glowing brown of his eyes fixed on her, and reheard the tones of his voice addressing her. Then she would start as though stung by a wasp and go along the track up the Punch-Bowl, recalling every detail of her walk with Iver, and feeling again his kiss upon her lips. She tried to forget him; with a resolution of which she was capable she shut against his entry every door of her heart. But she found it was impossible to exclude the thoughts of him. Had she not looked up to him from early childhood, and idolized him? She had been accustomed to think of him, to talk of him daily to his mother, after he had left the Ship. That mother who had forcibly separated her from him had herself ingrafted Iver into her inmost thoughts, made of him an integral portion of her mind. She had been taught by Mrs. Verstage to bring him into all her dreams of the future, as a factor without which that future would be void and valueless, She had, indeed, never dreamed of him as a lover, a husband; nevertheless to Mehetabel the future had always been associated in a vague, yet very real, manner with Iver. His return was to inaugurate the epoch of a new and joyous existence. It was not practicable for her to pluck out of her heart this idea, which had thrust its fibres through every layer and into every corner of her mind. Those fibres were now thrilling with vitality, asserting a vigorous life.

She asked herself the same question that had presented itself to his mind, what if Iver had returned one day, one hour, before he actually did? Then her marriage with Jonas would have been made impossible. The look into his eyes, the pressure of his hand would have bound her to him for evermore.

"Why, why, and oh why!" with a cry of pain, "had he not returned in time to save her?"

"Why, why, and oh why!" with blood from her heart, "did he return at all when too late to save her?"

Mehetabel had a clear and sound understanding. She was not one to play tricks with her conscience, and to reason herself into allowing what she was well aware was wrong. She nourished herself in no delusion that her marriage with Jonas was formal and devoid of the sanction of a spiritual bond.

She took her Prayer Book, opened the marriage service, and re-read the vows she had made.

She had been asked, "Wilt thou have this man, Jonas, to thy wedded husband, to live together after God's ordinance . . . and forsaking all other keep thee only unto him, so long as ye both shall live?" and thereto, in the sight of God and of the congregation, she had promised. There was no escape from this.

She had said—"I, Mehetabel, take thee, Jonas, to be my wedded husband, to have and to hold, from this day forward, for better, for worse, for richer, for poorer, in sickness and in health, to love, cherish and obey, till death us do part, according to God's holy ordinance, and thereto I give thee my troth."

There was no proviso inserted, as a means of escape; nothing like: I will be true to thee unless Iver return; unless, thou, Bideabout, prove unworthy of my love and obedience; unless there be incompatibility of temper; unless I get tired of thee, and change my mind.

Mehetabel knew what the words meant, knew that she had been sincere in intent when she said them. She knew that she was bound, without proviso of any kind.

She knew that she could not love Iver and be guiltless. But she was aware also, now, when too late, that she had undertaken towards Jonas what was, in a measure, impossible.

Loyal to Jonas as far as outward conduct could make her, that she was confident she would remain, but her heart had slipped beyond her control, and her thoughts were winged and refused to be caged.

"I say, Matabel!"

The young wife started, and her bosom contracted. Her husband spoke. He had come on her at a moment when, lost in day-dreams, she least expected, desired, his presence.

"What do you want with me, Jonas?" she asked as she recovered her composure.

"I want you to go to the Ship. The old woman there has fallen out with the maid, and there are three gentlemen come for the shooting, and want to be attended to. The old woman asked if you would help a bit. I said 'Dun know:' but after a bit we agreed for a shilling a day."

"Never!" gasped Mehetabel.

"I tried to screw more out of her necessity, but could not. Besides, if you do well, you'll get half a crown from each of the gents, and that'll be seven and six; and say three days at the Inn, half-a-guinea all in all. I can spare you for that."

"Jonas, I do not wish to go."

"But I choose that you shall."

"I pray you allow me to remain here."

"There's Mr. Iver leaves to-day for his shop at Guildford, and I reckon the old woman is put about over that, too."

After some hesitation Mehetabel yielded. The thought that Iver would not be at the Ship alone induced her to consent.

She was hurt and angry that her husband had stipulated for payment for her services. After the kindness, the generosity with which she had been treated, this seemed ungracious in the extreme. She said as much.

"I don't see it," answered Jonas. "When you wos a baby she made the parish pay her for taking you. Now she wants you, it is her turn to pay."

Bideabout did not allow his wife much time in which to make her preparations. He had business in Godalming with a lawyer, and was going to drive old Clutch thither. He would take Mehetabel with him as far as Thursley.

On reaching the tavern Mrs. Verstage met her with effusion, and Iver, hearing his mother's exclamation, ran out.

Mehetabel was surprised and confused at seeing him. He caught her by the hand, helped her to descend from the cart, and retained his hold of her fingers for a minute after it was necessary.

He had told his mother that he must return to Guildford that day; and when she had asked for Mehetabel's help she had calculated on the absence of her son, who had been packing up his canvas and paints. To him she had not breathed a word of the likelihood that Mehetabel would be coming to her aid.

"I daresay Bideabout will give you a lift, Iver," she said.

"I don't know that I can," said Jonas. "I've promised to pick up Lintott, and there ain't room in the trap for more than two."

Then the Broom-Squire drove away.

"See, Matabel," said Iver, pointing to the signboard, "I've redaubed the Old Ship, quite to my father's satisfaction. By Jove, I told mother I should return to Guildford to-day—but now, hang me, if I do not defer my departure for a day or two."

Mrs. Verstage looked reproachfully at her son.

"Mother," said he in self-exculpation. "I shall take in ideas, a model costs me from a shilling to half-acrown an hour, and here is Matabel, a princess of models, will sit for nothing."

"I shall be otherwise employed," said the girl, in confusion.

"Indeed, I shan't spare her for any of that nonsense," said Mrs. Verstage.

The hostess was much perplexed. She had reckoned on her son's departure before Mehetabel arrived. She would not have asked for her assistance if she had not been convinced that he would take himself off.

She expostulated. Iver must not neglect his business, slight his engagements. He had resolved to go, and had no right to shilly-shally, and change his mind. She required his room. He would be in the way with the guests.

To all these objections Iver had an answer. In fine, said he, with Mehetabel in the house he could not and he would not go.

What was Mehetabel to do? Jonas had locked up his house and had carried away the key with him; moreover, to return now was a confession of weakness. What was Mrs. Verstage to do? She had three visitors, real gentlemen, in the house. They must be made comfortable; and the new servant, Polly, according to her notion, was a hopeless creature, slatternly, forgetful, impudent.

There was no one on whom the landlady could fall back, except Mehetabel, who understood her ways, and was certain to give satisfaction. Mrs. Verstage was not what she had once been, old age, and more than that, an internal complaint, against which she had fought, in which she had refused to believe, had quite recently asserted itself, and she was breaking down.

There was consequently no help for it. She resolved to keep a sharp lookout on the young people, and employ Mehetabel unremittingly. But of one thing she was confident. Mehetabel was not a person to forget her duty and self-respect.

The agitation produced by finding that Iver purposed remaining in the house passed away, and Mehetabel faced the inevitable.

Wherever her eye rested, memories of a happy girlhood welled up in her soft and suffering breast. The geraniums in the window she had watered daily. The canary—she had fed it with groundsel. The brass skillets on the mantelshelf—they had been burnished by her hand. The cushion on "father's" chair was of her work. Everything spoke to her of the past, and of a happy past, without sharp sorrows, without carking cares.

Old Simon was rejoiced to see Mehetabel again in the house. He made her sit beside him. He took her hand in his, and patted it. A pleasant smile, like a sunbeam, lit up his commonplace features.

"Mother and I have had a deal to suffer since you've been gone," said Simon. "The girl Polly be that stupid and foreright (awkward) we shall be drove mad, both of us, somewhen."

"Do you see that window-pane?" he asked, pointing to a gap in the casement. "Polly put her broom handle through. There was not one pane broke all the time you was with us, and now there be three gone, and no glazier in the village to put 'em to rights. You mind the blue pranked (striped) chiney taypot? Mother set great store on that. Polly's gone and knocked the spout off. Mother's put about terrible over that taypot. As for the best sheets, Polly's burnt a hole through one, let a cinder fly out on it, when airing. Mother's in a pretty way over that sheet. I don't know what there'll be to eat, Polly left the larder open, and the dog has carried off a leg of mutton. It has been all cross and contrary ever since you went."

Simon mused a while, holding Mehetabel's hand, and said after a pause, "It never ort to a' been. You was well placed here and never ort to a' left. It was all mother's doing. She drove you into weddin' that there Broom-Squire. Women can't be easy unless they be hatchin' weddin's; just like as broody hens must be sittin' on somethin'. If that had never been brought about, then the taypot spout would not have been knocked off, nor the winder-pane broken, nor the sheet riddled wi' a cinder, nor the dog gone off wi' the leg o' mutton."

Mehetabel was unable to suppress a sigh.

"Winter be comin' on," pursued the old man, "and mother's gettin' infirm, and a bit contrary. When Polly worrits her, then I ketches it. That always wos her way. I don't look forward to winter. I don't look forward to nuthin' now—" He became sorrowful. "All be gone to sixes and sevens, now that you be gone, Matabel. What will happen I dun' know, I dun' know."

"What may happen," said Mehetabel, "is not always what we expect. But one thing is certain—lost happiness is past recovery."

CHAPTER XX. — GONE

During the evening Iver was hardly able to take his eyes off Mehetabel, as she passed to and fro in the kitchen.

She knew where was every article that was needed for the gentlemen. She moved noiselessly, did everything without fuss, without haste.

He thought over the words she had uttered, and he had overheard: Lost happiness is past recovery. Not only was she bereft of happiness, but so was he. His father and mother, when too late, had found that they also had parted with theirs when they had let Mehetabel leave the house.

She moved gracefully. She was slender, her every motion merited to be sketched. Iver's artistic sense was excited to admiration. What a girl she was! What a model! Oh, that he had her as his own!

Mehetabel knew that she was watched, and it disconcerted her. She was constrained to exercise great self-control; not to let slip what she carried, not to forget what tasks had to be discharged.

In her heart she glowed with pride at the thought that Iver loved her—that he, the prince, the idol of her childhood, should have retained a warm place in his heart for her. And yet, the thought, though sweet, was bitter as well, fraught with foreshadowings of danger.

Mrs. Verstage also watched Mehetabel, and her son likewise, with anxious eyes.

The old man left the house to attend to his cattle; and one of the gentlemen came to the kitchen-door to invite Iver, whose acquaintance he had made during the day, to join him and his companions over a bowl of punch.

The young man was unable to refuse, but left with reluctance manifest enough to his mother and Mehetabel.

Then, when the hostess was alone with the girl, she drew her to her side, and said, "There is now nothing to occupy you. Sit by me and tell me about yourself and how you get on with Bideabout. You have no notion how pleased I am to have you here again."

Mehetabel kissed the old woman, and a tear from her eye fell on the withering cheek of the landlady.

"I dare be bound you find it lonely in the new home," said Mrs. Verstage. "Here, in an inn, there is plenty of life; but in the farm you are out of the world. How does the Broom-Squire treat you?"

She awaited an answer with anxiety, which she was unable to disguise.

After a pause Mehetabel replied, with heightened color, "Jonas is not unkind."

"You can't expect love-making every day," said the hostess. "It's the way of men to promise the sun, moon, and planets, till you are theirs, and after that, then poor women must be content to be given a spark off a fallen star. There was Jamaica Cheel runn'd away with his Betsy because he thought the law wouldn't let him have her; she was the wife of another, you know. Then he found she never had been proper married to the other chap, and when he discovered he was fast tied to Betsy he'd a run away from her only the law wouldn't let him. Jonas ain't beautiful and young, that I allow."

"I knew what he was when I married him," answered Mehetabel. "I cannot say I find him other than what I expected."

"But is he kind to you?"

"I said he was not unkind."

Mrs. Verstage looked questioningly at her adopted child. "I don't know," she said, with quivering lips. "I suppose I was right. I acted for the best. God knows I sought your happiness. Do not tell me that you are unhappy."

"Who is happy?" asked Mehetabel, and turned her eyes on the hostess, to read alarm and distress in her face. "Do not trouble yourself about me, mother. I knew what I was doing when I took Jonas. I had no expectation of finding the Punch-Bowl to be Paradise. It takes a girl some time to get settled into fresh quarters, and to feel comfortable among strangers. That is mainly my case. I was perhaps spoiled when here, you were so kind to me. I thank you, mother, that you have not forgotten me in your great joy at getting Iver home again."

"There was Thomasine French bought two penn'orth o' shrimps, and as her husband weren't at home thought to enjoy herself prodigious. But she came out red as a biled lobster. With the best intentions things don't always turn out as expected," said Mrs. Verstage, "and the irritation was like sting nettles and—wuss." Then, after a pause, "I don't know how it is, all my life I have wished to have Iver by me. He went away because he wanted to be a painter; he has come back, after many years, and is not all I desire. Now he is goyn away. I could endure that if I were sure he loved me. But I don't think he does. He cares more for his father, who sent him packin' than he does for me, who never crossed him. I don't understand him. He is not the same as he was."

"Iver is a child no longer," said Mehetabel. "You must not expect of him more than he can give. What you said to me about a husband is true also of a child. Of course, he loves you, but he does not show it as fully as you desire. He has something else now to fill his heart beside a mother."

"What is that?" asked Mrs. Verstage, nervously.

"His art," answered Mehetabel.

"Oh, that!" The landlady was not wholly satisfied, she stood up and said with a sigh, "I fancy life be much like one o' them bran pies at a bazaar. Some pulls out a pair of braces as don't wear trousers, and others pull out garters as wears nuthin' but socks. 'Tis a chance if you get wot's worth havin. Well, I must go look out another sheet in place of that Polly has burnt."

"Let me do that, mother."

"No, as you may remember, I have always managed the linen myself."

A few minutes later, after she had left the room, Iver returned. He had escaped from the visitors on some excuse.

His heart was a prey to vague yearnings and doubts.

With pleasure he observed that his mother was no longer in the kitchen. He saw Mehetabel hastily dry her eyes. He knew that she had been crying, and he thought he could divine the cause.

"You are going to Guildford to-morrow morning, are you not?" she asked hastily.

"I don't know."

Iver planted himself on a stool before the fire, where he could look up into Mehetabel's face, as she sat in the settle.

"You have your profession to attend to," she said. "You do not know your own mind. You are changeful as a girl."

"How can I go—with you here?" he exclaimed, vehemently.

She turned her head away. He was looking at her with burning eyes.

"Iver," she said, "I pray you be more loving to your mother. You have made her heart ache. It is cruel not to do all you can now to make amends to her for the past. She thinks that you do not love her. She is failing in health, and you must not drip drops of fresh sorrow into her heart during her last years."

Iver made a motion of impatience.

"I love my mother. Of course I love her."

"Not as truly as you should, Iver," answered Mehetabel. "You do not consider the long ache—"

"And I, had not I a long ache when away from home?"

"You had your art to sustain you. She had but one thought—and that of you."

"She has done me a cruel wrong," said he, irritably.

"She has never done anything to you but good, and out of love," answered the girl vehemently.

"To me; that is not it."

Mehetabel raised her eyes and looked at him. He was gazing moodily at the fire.

"She has stabbed me through you," exclaimed Iver, with a sudden outburst of passion. "Why do you plead my mother's cause, when it was she—I know it was she, and none but she—who thrust you into this hateful, this accursed marriage."

"No, Iver, no!" cried Mehetabel in alarm. "Do not say this. Iver! talk of something else."

"Of what?"

"Of anything."

"Very well," said he, relapsing into his dissatisfied mood. "You asked me once what my dream had been, that I dreamt that first night under your roof. I will tell you this now. I thought that you and I had been married, not you and Jonas, you and I, as it should have been. And I thought that I looked at you, and your face was deadly pale, and the hand I held was clay cold."

A chill ran through Mehetabel's veins. She said, "There is some truth in it, Iver. You hold a dead girl by the hand. To you, I am, I must be, forever—dead."

"Nonsense. All will come right somehow."

"Yes, Iver," she said; "it will so. You are free and will go about, and will see and love and marry a girl worthy of you in every way. As for me, my lot is cast in the Punch-Bowl. No power on earth can separate me from Bideabout. I have made my bed and must lie on it, though it be one of thorns. There is but one thing for us both—we must part and meet no more."

"Matabel," he put forth his hand in protest.

"I have spoken plainly," she said, "because there is no good in not doing so. Do not make my part more difficult. Be a man—go."

"Matabel! It shall not be, it cannot be! My love! My only one."

He tried to grasp her.

She sprang from the settle. A mist formed before her eyes. She groped for something by which to stay herself.

He seized her by the waist. She wrenched herself free.

"Let me go!" she cried. "Let me go!"

She spoke hoarsely. Her eyes were staring as if she saw a spirit. She staggered back beyond his reach, touched the jambs of the door, grasped them with a grasp of relief. Then, actuated by a sudden thought, turned and fled from the room, from the house.

Iver stood for a minute bewildered. Her action had been so unexpected that he did not know what to think, what to do.

He went to the porch and looked up the road, then down it, and did not see her.

Mrs. Verstage, came out. "Where is Matabel?" she asked, uneasily.

"Gone!" said Iver. "Mother—gone!"

CHAPTER XXI. — THOR'S STONE

Mehetabel ran, neither along the way that led in the direction of Portsmouth, nor along that to Godalming, but to the Moor.

"The Moor," is the marsh land that lies at the roots of the sandstone heights that culminate in Hind Head, Leith Hill, and the Devil's Jumps. As already said, the great mass of Bagshot sand lies upon a substratum of clay. The sand drinks in every drop of rain that falls on the surface. This percolates through it till it reaches the clay, which refuses to absorb it, or let it sink through to other beds. Thereupon the accumulated water breaks forth in springs at the base of the hills, and forms a wide tract of morass, interspersed with lagoons that teem with fish and wild fowl. This region is locally known as "Moor," in contradistinction to the commons or downs, which are the dry sandy upland.

"The Moor" is in many places impassable, but the blown sand has fallen upon it, and has formed slight elevations, has drifted into undulations, and these strips of rising ground, kept moist by the water they absorb, have become covered with vegetation. It is, moreover, possible by their means to penetrate to the heart of, and even thread, the intricacies, and traverse the entire region of the Moor.

But it is, at best, a wild and lonesome district, to be explored with caution, a labyrinth, the way through which is known only to the natives of the sandhills that dominate the marshy plain.

About thirty years ago a benevolent and beneficent landlord, in a time of agricultural distress, gave employment to a large number of men out of work in the construction of a causeway across the Thursley "Moor."

But the work was of no real utility, and it is now overgrown with weeds, and only trodden by the sportsman in pursuit of game and the naturalist in quest of rare insects and water plants.

A considerable lake, Pudmere, or Pug—Puckmere, lies in the Thursley marsh land, surrounded with dwarf willows and scattered pines. These latter have sprung from the wind-blown seeds of the plantations on higher ground. Throughout this part of the country an autumn gale always results in the upspringing of a forest of young pines, next year, to leeward of a clump of cone-bearing trees. In the Moor such self-sown woods come to no ripeness. The pines are unhealthy and stunted, hung with gray moss, and eaten out with canker. The excessive moisture and the impenetrable subsoil, and the shallowness of the congenial sand that encouraged them to root make the young trees decay in adolescence.

An abundant and varied insect world has its home in the Moor. The large brown hawkmoth darts about like an arrow. Dragon flies of metallic blue, or striped yellow and brown, hover above the lanes of water, lost in admiration of their own gorgeous selves reflected in the still surface. The great water-beetle booms against the head of the intruder, and then drops as a stone into the pool at his feet. Effets, saffron yellow bellied, with striped backs, swim in the ponds or crawl at their bottom. The natterjack, so rare elsewhere, differing from a toad in that it has a yellow band down its back, has here a paradise. It may be seen at eve perched on a stock of willow herb, or running—it does not hop—round the sundew, clearing the glutinous stamens of the flies that have been caught by them, and calling in a tone like the warning note of the nightingale. Sleeping on the surface the carp lies, and will not be scared save by a stone thrown into the still water in which it dreams away its life.

The sandy elevations are golden with tormintilla; a richer gold is that which lies below, where the marsh glows with bog asphodel. The flowering rush spreads its pale pink blossoms; a deeper crimson is the marsh orchis showing its spires among the drooping clusters of the waxy-pink, cross-leaved heath, and the green or pale and rosy-tinted bog-mosses.

Near Pudmoor Pool stands a gray block of ironstone, a solitary portion of the superincumbent bed that has been washed away. It resembles a gigantic anvil, and it goes by the name of Thor's Stone. The slopes that dip towards it are the Thor's-lea, and give their name to the parish that includes it and them.

At one time there was a similar mass of iron at the summit of Borough Hill, that looks down upon the morasses.

To this many went who were in trouble or necessity, and knocking on the stone made known their requirements to the Pucksies, and it was asserted, and generally believed, that such applicants had not gone away unanswered, nor unrelieved.

It was told of a certain woman who one evening sought to be freed by this means from the husband who had made her life unendurable, that that same night—so ran the tale—he was returning from the tavern, drunk, and stumbling over the edge of a quarry fell and broke his neck. Thereupon certain high moralists and busybodies had the mass of stone broken up and carted away to mend the roads, with the expectation thereby of putting an end to what they were pleased to term "a degrading superstition."

To some extent the destruction of the Wishing Block did check the practice. But there continued to be persons in distress, and women plagued with drunken husbands, and men afflicted with scolding wives. And when the pilgrimage of such to Borough Hill ceased, because of the destruction of the stone on it, then was it diverted, and the current flowed instead to Thor's Stone—a stone that had long been regarded with awe, and which now became an object of resort, as it was held to have acquired the merits of the block so wantonly demolished on Borough Hill.

Nevertheless, the object of the high moralists and busybodies was partially attained, inasmuch as the difficulties and dangers attending a visit to Thor's Stone reduced the number of those seeking superhuman assistance in their difficulties. Courage was requisite in one who ventured to the Moor at night, and made a way to the iron-stone block, over tracts of spongy morass, among lines of stagnant ooze, through coppices of water-loving willows and straggling brier. This, which was difficult by day, was dangerous in a threefold degree at night. Moreover, the Moor was reputed to be haunted by spirits, shadows that ran and leaped, and peered and jabbered; and Puck wi' the lantern flickered over the surface of the festering bog.

If, then, the visits to Thor's Stone were not so many as to the stone on Borough Hill, this was due less to the waning of superstition than to the difficulties attending an expedition to the former. Without considering what she was doing, moved by a blind impulse, Mehetabel ran in the direction of Puck's Moor.

And yet the impulse was explicable. She had often thought over the tales told of visits to the habitation of the "Good Folk" on Borough Hill, and the transfer of the pilgrimage to Thor's Stone. She had, of late, repeatedly asked herself whether, by a visit thither, she might not gain what lay at her heart—an innocent desire—none other than that Iver should depart.

Now that he had made open show of his passion, that all concealment was over between them, every veil and disguise plucked away—now she felt that her strength was failing her, and it would fail completely if subjected to further trial.

One idea, like a spark of fire shooting through her brain, alone possessed her at this moment. Her safety depended on one thing—the removal of Iver. Let him go! Let him go! then she could bear her lot. Let her see him no more! then she would be able to bring her truant heart under discipline. Otherwise her life would be unendurable, her tortured brain would give way, her overtaxed heart would break.

She found no stay for her soul in the knowledge where was situated the country of the Gergesenes, no succor in being well drilled in the number of chapters in Genesis. She turned desperately, in her necessity, to Thor's Stone, to the spirits—what they were she knew not—who aided those in need, and answered petitions addressed to them.

The night had already set in, but a full golden moon hung in the sky, and the night was in no way dark and dreadful.

When she reached the Moor, Mehetabel ran among sheets of gold, leaped ribbons of shining metal, danced among golden filagree—the reflection of the orb in the patches, channels, frets of water. She sprang from one dark tuft of rushes to another; she ran along the ridges of the sand. She skipped where the surface was treacherous. What mattered it to her if she missed her footing, sank, and the ooze closed over her? As well end so a life that could never be other than long drawn agony.

Before leaving the heath, she had stooped and picked up a stone. It was a piece of hematite iron, such as frequently occurs in the sand, liver-shaped, and of the color of liver.

She required a hammer, wherewith to knock on Thor's anvil, and make her necessities known, and this piece of iron would serve her purpose.

Frogs were croaking, a thousand natterjacks were whirring like the nightjar. Strange birds screamed and rushed out of the trees as she sped along. White moths, ghostlike, wavered about her, mosquitoes piped. Water-rats plunged into the pools.

As a child she had been familiar with Pudmoor, and instinctively she walked, ran, only where her foot could rest securely.

A special Providence, it is thought, watches over children and drunkards. It watches also over such as are drunk with trouble, it holds them up when unable to think for themselves, it holds them back when they court destruction.

To this morass, Mehetabel had come frequently with Iver, in days long gone by, to hunt the natterjack and the dragon-fly, to look for the eggs of water fowl, and to pick marsh flowers.

As she pushed on, a thin mist spread over portions of the "Moor." It did not lie everywhere, it spared the sand, it lay above the water, but in so delicate a film as to be all but imperceptible. It served to diffuse the moonlight, to make a halo of silver about the face of the orb, when looked up to by one within the haze, otherwise it was scarcely noticeable.

Mehetabel ran with heart bounding and with fevered brain, and yet with her mind holding tenaciously to one idea.

After a while, and after deviations from the direct course, rendered necessary by the nature of the country she traversed, Mehetabel reached Thor's Stone, that gleamed white in the moonbeam beside a sheet of water, the Mere of the Pucksies. This mere had the mist lying on it more dense than elsewhere. The vapor rested on the surface as a fine gossamer veil, not raised above a couple of feet, hardly ruffled by a passing sigh of air. A large bird floated over it on expanded wings, it looked white as a swan in the moonlight, but cast a shadow black as pitch on the vaporous sheet that covered the face of the pool.

It was as though, like Dinorah, this bird were dancing to its own shadow. But unlike Dinorah, it was silent. It uttered no song, there was even no sound of the rush of air from its broad wings. When Mehetabel reached the stone she stood for a moment palpitating, gasping for breath, and her breath passing from her lips in white puffs of steam.

The haze from the mere seemed to rise and fling its long streamers about her head and blindfold her eyes, so that she could see neither the lake nor the trees, not even the anvil-stone. Only was there about her a general silvery glitter, and a sense of oppression lay upon her.

Mehetabel had escaped from the inn, as she was, with bare arms, her skirt looped up.

She stood thus, with the lump of ironstone resting on the block, the full flood of moonlight upon her, blinding her eyes, but revealing her against a background of foliage, like a statue of alabaster. Startled by a rustle in the bulrushes and willow growth behind her, Mehetabel turned and looked, but her eyes were not clear enough for her to discern anything, and as the sound ceased, she recovered from her momentary alarm.

She had heard that a deer was in Pudmoor that was supposed to have escaped from the park at Peperharow. Possibly the creature was there. It was harmless. There were no noxious beasts there. It was too damp for vipers, nothing in Pudmoor was hurtful save the gnats that there abounded. Then, with her face turned to the north, away from the dazzling glory of the moon, Mehetabel swung the lump of kidney iron she had taken as hammer, once from east to west, and once from west to east. With a third sweep she brought it down upon Thor's Stone and cried:

"Take him away! Take him away!"

CHAPTER XXII. — IVER! COME

She paused, drew a long breath.

Again she swung the hammer-stone. And now she turned round, and passed the piece of iron into her left hand. She raised it and struck on the anvil, and cried: "Save me from him. Take him away." A rush, all the leaves of the trees behind seemed to be stirring, and all the foliage falling about her.

A hand was laid on her shoulder roughly, and the stone dropped from her fingers on the anvil. Mehetabel shrank, froze, as struck with a sudden icy blast, and cried out with fear.

Then said a voice: "So! you seek the Devil's aid to rid you of me."

At once she knew that she was in the presence of her husband, but so dazzled was she that she could not discern him.

His fingers closed on her arm, as though each were an iron screw.

"So!" said he, in a low tone, his voice quivering with rage, "like Karon Wyeth, you ask the Devil to break my neck."

"No," gasped Mehetabel.

"Yes, Matabel. I heard you. 'Save me from him. Take him away.'"

"No—no—Jonas."

She could not speak more in her alarm and confusion.

"Take him away. Snap his spine—send a bullet through his skull; cast him into Pug's mere and drown him; do what you will, only rid me of Bideabout Kink, whom I swore to love, honor, and to obey."

He spoke with bitterness and wrath, sprinkled over, nay, permeated, with fear; for, with all his professed rationalism, Jonas entertained some ancestral superstitions—and belief in the efficacy of the spirits that haunted Thor's Stone was one.

"No, Jonas, no. I did not ask it."

"I heard you."

"Not you."

"What," sneered he; "are not these ears mine?"

"I mean—I did not ask to have you taken away."

"Then whom?"

She was silent. She trembled. She could not answer his question.

If her husband had been at all other than he was, Mehetabel would have taken him into her confidence. But there are certain persons to whom to commit a confidence is to expose yourself to insult and outrage. Mehetabel knew this. Such a confidence as she would have given would be turned by him into a means of torture and humiliation.

"Now listen to me," said Jonas, in quivering tones of a voice that was suppressed. "I know all now. I did not. I trusted you. I was perhaps a fool. I believed in you. But Sarah has told me all—how he—that painting ape—has been at my house, meeting you, befooling you, pouring his love-tales into your ears, and watching till my back was turned to kiss you."

She was unable to speak. Her knees smote together.

"You cannot answer," he continued. "You are unable to deny that it was so. Sarah has kept an eye on you both. She should have spoken before. I am sorry she did not. But better late than never. You encouraged him to come to you. You drew him to the house."

"No, Jonas, no. It was you who invited him."

"Ah! for me he would not come. Little he cared for my society. The picture-making was but an excuse, and you all have been in a league against me."

"Who—Jonas?"

"Who? Why, Sanna Verstage and all. Did not she ask to have you at the Ship, and say that the painting fellow was going or gone? And is he not there still? She said it to get you and him together there, away from me, out of the reach of Sarah's eyes."

"It is false, Jonas!" exclaimed Mehetabel with indignation, that for a while overcame her fear.

"False!" cried Bideabout. "Who is false but you? What is false but every word you speak? False in heart, false in word, and false in act." He had laid hold of the bit of ironstone, and he struck the anvil with it at every charge of falsehood.

"Jonas," said Mehetabel, recovering self-control under the resentment she felt at being misunderstood, and her action misinterpreted. "Jonas, I have done you no injury. I was weak. God in heaven knows my integrity. I have never wronged you; but I was weak, and in deadly fear."

"In fear of whom?"

"Of myself—my own weakness."

"You weak!" he sneered. "You—strong as any woman."

"I do not speak of my arms, Jonas—my heart—my spirit—"

"Weak!" he scoffed. "A woman with a weak and timorous soul would not come to Thor's Stone at night. No—strong you are—in evil, in wickedness, from which no tears will withhold you. And—that fellow— that daub-paint—"

Mehetabel did not speak. She was trembling.

"I ask—what of him? Was not he in your thoughts when you asked the Devil to rid you of me—your husband?"

"I did not ask that, Jonas."

"What of him? He has not gone away. He has been with you. You knew he was not going. You wanted to be with him. Where is he—this dauber of canvas—now?"

Then, through the fine gauze of condensing haze, came a call from a distance—"Matabel! Where are you?"

"Oh, ho!" exclaimed the Broom-Squire. "Here he comes. By appointment you meet him here, where you least expected that I would be."

"It is false, Jonas. I came here to escape."

"And pray for my death?"

"No, Jonas, to be rid of him."

Bideabout chuckled, with a sarcastic sneer in the side of his face.

"Come now," said he; "I should dearly like to witness this meeting. If true to me, as you pretend, then obey me, summon him here, and let me be present, unobserved, when you meet. If your wish be, as you say, to be rid of him, I will help you to its fulfilment."

"Jonas!"

"I will it. So alone can you convince me."

She hesitated. She had not the power to gather her thoughts together, to judge what she should do, what under the circumstances would be best to be done.

"Come now," repeated Jonas. "If you are true and honest, as you say, call him."

She put her trembling hand to her head, wiped the drops from her brow, the tears from her eyes, the dew from her quivering lips.

Her brain was reeling, her power of will was paralyzed.

"Come, now," said Jonas once more, "answer him—here am I."

Then Mehetabel cried, "Iver, here am I!"

"Where are you, Mehetabel?" came the question through the silvery haze and the twinkling willow-shoots.

"Answer him, by Thor's Stone," said Jonas.

Again she hesitated and passed her hand over her face.

"Answer him," whispered Jonas. "If you are true, do as I say. If false, be silent."

"By Thor's Stone," called Mehetabel.

Then all the sound heard was that of the young man brushing his way through the rushes and willow boughs.

In the terror, the agony overmastering her, she had lost all independent power of will. She was as a piece of mechanism in the hands of Jonas. His strong, masterful mind dominated her, beat down for a time all opposition. She knew that to summon Iver was to call him to a fearful struggle, perhaps to his death, and yet the faculty of resistance was momentarily gone from her. She tried to collect her thoughts. She could not. She strove to think what she ought to do, she was unable to frame a thought in her mind that whirled and reeled.

Bideabout stooped and picked up a gun he had been carrying, and had dropped on the turf when he laid hold of his wife.

Now he placed the barrel across the anvil stone, with the muzzle directed whence came the sound of the advance of Iver.

Jonas went behind the stone and bent one knee to the ground.

Mehetabel heard the click as he spanned the trigger.

"Stand on one side," said Jonas, in a low tone, in which were mingled rage and exultation. "Call him again."

She was silent. Lest she should speak she pressed both her hands to her mouth.

"Call him again," said Jonas. "I will receive him with a dab of lead in his heart."

She would not call.

"On your obedience and truth, of which you vaunt," persisted Jonas.

Should she utter a cry of warning? Would he comprehend? Would that arrest him, make him retrace his steps, escape what menaced?

Whether she cried or not he would come on. He knew Thor's Stone as well as she. They had often visited it together as children.

"If false, keep silence," said Jonas, looking up at her from where he knelt. "If true, bid him come—to his death, that I may carry out your wish, and rid you of him. If the spirits won't help you, I will."

Then she shrilly cried, "Iver, come!"

CHAPTER XXIII. — A SHOT

After Bideabout had done his business in Godalming he had returned to the Punch-Bowl.

The news had reached his ears that a deer had been seen on the Moor, and he knew that on the following day many guns would be out, as every man in Thursley was a sportsman. With characteristic cunning he resolved to forestall his fellows, go forth at night, which he might well do when the moon was full, and secure the deer for himself.

As he left the house, he encountered his sister.

"Where are you going off to?" she inquired. "And got a gun too."

He informed her of his intention.

"Ah! you'll give us some of the venison," said she.

"I'm not so sure of that," answered the Broom-Squire, churlishly.

"So you are going stag-hunting? That's purely," laughed she.

"Why not?"

"I should have thought you'd best a' gone after your own wife, and brought her home."

"She is all right—at the Ship."

"I know she is at the Ship—just where she ought not to be; just where you should not let her be."

"She'll earn a little money."

"Oh, money!" scoffed Sarah Rocliffe. "What fools men be, and set themselves up as wiser than all the world of women. You've had Iver Verstage here; you've invited him over to paint your Matabel; and here he has been, admiring her, saying soft things to her, and turnin' her head. Sometimes you've been present. Most times you've been away. And now you've sent her to the Ship, and you are off stag huntin'." Then with strident voice, the woman sang, and looked maliciously at her brother.

"Oh, it blew a pleasant gale,
As a frite under sail,
Came a-bearing to the south along the strand.
With her swelling canvas spread.
But without an ounce of lead,
And a signalling, alack t she was ill-manned."

With a laugh, and a snap of her fingers in Bideabout's face, she repeated tauntingly:—

"And a-signalling, alack! she was ill-manned."

Then she burst forth again:—

"She was named the Virgin Dove,
With a lading, all of love.
And she signalled, that for Venus (Venice) she was bound.
But a pilot who could steer.
She required, for sore her fear,
Lest without one she should chance to run aground."

"Be silent, you croaking raven," shouted the Broom-Squire. "If you think to mock me, you are wrong. I know well enough what I am about. As for that painting chap, he is gone—gone to Guildford."

"How do you know that?"

"Because the landlady said as much."

"What—to you?"

"Yes, to me."

Mrs. Rocliffe laughed mockingly.

"Oh, Bideabout," she said, "did not that open your eyes? What did Sanna Verstage mean when she asked you to allow your wife to go to the inn! What did she mean but this?" she mimicked the mistress, "'Please, Master Bideabout, may Matabel come to me for a day or two—that naughty boy of mine is away now. So don't be frightened. I know very well that if he were at the Ship you might hesitate to send Matabel there.'" Then in her own tones Sarah Rocliffe said. "That is the meaning of it. But I don't believe that he is gone."

"Sanna Verstage don't tell lies."

"If he were gone, Matabel would not be so keen to go there."

"Matabel was not keen. She did not wish to go."

"She did wish it; but she made a pretence before you that she did not."

"Hold your slanderous tongue," shouted Jonas. "I'll not hear another word."

"Then you must shut your ears to what all the parish is saying."

Thereupon she told him what she had seen, with amplifications of her own. She was glad to have the opportunity of angering or wounding her brother; of sowing discord between him and his wife.

When he parted from her, she cast after him the remark—"I believe he is still at the Ship."

In a mood the reverse of cheerful, angry with Mehetabel, raging against Iver, cursing himself, and overflowing with spite against his sister Jonas went to the Moor in quest of the strayed deer. He knew very well that his sister bore Mehetabel a grudge; he was sufficiently acquainted with her rancorous humor and unscrupulous tongue to know that what she said was not to be relied on, yet discount as he might what she had told him, he was assured that a substratum of truth lay at the bottom.

Before entering the morass Jonas halted, and leaning on his gun, considered whether he should not go to the tavern, reclaim his wife and reconduct her home, instead of going after game. But he thought that such a proceeding might be animadverted upon; he relied upon Mrs. Verstage's words, that Iver was departing to his professional work, and he was eager to secure the game for himself.

Accordingly he directed his course to the Moor, and stole along softly, listening for the least sound of the deer, and keeping his eye on the alert to observe her.

He had been crouching in a bush near the pool when he was startled by the apparition of Mehetabel.

At first he had supposed that the sound of steps proceeded from the advancing deer, for which he was on the watch, and he lay close, with his barrel loaded, and his finger on the trigger. But in place of the deer his own wife approached, indistinctly seen in the moonlight, so that he did not recognize her. And his heart stood still, numbed by panic, for he thought he saw a spirit. But as the form drew near he knew Mehetabel.

Perplexed, he remained still, to observe her further movements. Then he saw her approach the stone of Thor, strike on it with an extemporized hammer, and cry, "Save me from him! Take him away!"

Perhaps it was not unreasonable that he at once concluded that she referred to himself.

He knew that she did not love him. Instead of each day of married life drawing more closely the bonds that bound them together, it really seemed to relax such as did exist. She became colder, withdrew more into herself, shrank from his clumsy amiabilities, and kept the door of her heart resolutely shut against all intrusion. She went through her household duties perfunctorily, as might a slave for a hated master.

If she did not love him, if her married life was becoming intolerable, then it was obvious that she sought relief from it, and the only means of relief open to her lay through his death.

But there was something more that urged her on to desire this. She not merely disliked him, but loved another, and over his coffin she would leap into that other man's arms. As Karon Wyeth had aimed at and secured the death of her husband, so did Mehetabel seek deliverance from him.

Bideabout sprang from his lurking-place to check her in the midst of her invocation, and to avert the danger that menaced himself. And now he saw the very man draw nigh who had withdrawn the heart of his wife from him, and had made his home miserable; the man on behalf of whom Mehetabel had summoned supernatural aid to rid her of himself.

Kneeling behind Thor's Stone, with the steel barrel of his gun laid on the anvil, and pointed in the direction whence came Iver's voice, he waited till his rival should appear, and draw within range, that he might shoot him through the heart.

"Summon him again," he whispered.

"Iver come!" called Mehetabel.

Then through the illuminated haze, like an atmosphere of glow-worm's light, himself black against a background of shining water, appeared the young man.

Jonas had his teeth clenched; his breath hissed like the threat of a serpent, as he drew a long inspiration through them.

"You are there!" shouted Iver, joyously, and ran forward.

She felt a thrill run through the barrel, on which she had laid her hand; she saw a movement of the shoulder of Jonas, and was aware that he was preparing to fire.

Instantly she snatched the gun to her, laid the muzzle against her own side, and said: "Fire!" She spoke again. "So all will be well."

Then she cried in piercing tones, "Iver! run! run! he is here, and he seeks to kill you."

Jonas sprang to his feet with a curse, and endeavored to wrest the gun from Mehetabel's hand. But she held it fast. She clung to it with tenacity, with the whole of her strength, so that he was unable to pluck it away.

And still she cried, "Run, Iver, run; he will kill you!"

"Let go!" yelled Bideabout. He set his foot against Thor's Stone; he twisted the gun about, he turned it this way, that way, to wrench it out of her hands.

"I will not!" she gasped.

"It is loaded! It will go off!"

"I care not."

"Oh, no! so long as it shoots me."

"Send the lead into my heart!"

"Then let go. But no! the bullet is not for you. Let go, I say, or I will brain you with the butt end, and then shoot him!"

"I will not! Kill me if you will!"

Strong, athletic, lithe in her movements, Mehetabel was a match for the small muscular Jonas. If he succeeded for a moment in twisting the gun out of her hands it was but for an instant. She had caught the barrel again at another point.

He strove to beat her knuckles against Thor's Stone, but she was too dexterous for him. By a twist she brought his hand against the block instead of her own.

With an oath he cast himself upon her, by the impact, by the weight, to throw her down. Under the burden she fell on her knees, but did not relinquish her hold on the gun. On the contrary she obtained greater power over it, and held the barrel athwart her bosom, and wove her arms around it.

Iver was hastening to her assistance. He saw that some contest was going on, but was not able to discern either with whom Mehetabel was grappling nor what was the meaning of the struggle.

In his attempt to approach, Iver was regardless where he trod. He sank over his knees in the mire, and was obliged to extricate himself before he could advance.

With difficulty, by means of oziers, he succeeded in reaching firm soil, and then, with more circumspection, he sought a way by which he might come to the help of Mehetabel.

Meanwhile, regardless of the contest of human passion, raging close by, the great bird swung like a pendulum above the mere, and its shadow swayed below it.

"Let go! I will murder you, if you do not!" hissed Jonas. "You think I will kill him. So I will, but I will kill you first."

"Iver! help!" cried Mehetabel; her strength was abandoning her.

The Broom-Squire dragged his kneeling wife forward, and then thrust her back. He held the gun by the stock and the end of the barrel. The rest was grappled by her, close to her bosom.

He sought to throw her on her face, then on her back. So only could he wrench the gun away.

"Ah, ah!" with a shout of triumph.

He had disengaged the barrel from her arm. He turned it sharply upward, to twist it out of her hold she had with the other arm.

Then—suddenly—an explosion, a flash, a report, a cry; and Bideabout staggered back and fell.

A rush of wings.

The large bird that had vibrated above the water had been alarmed, and now flew away.

CHAPTER XXIV. — THE IRON-STONE HAMMER

For a couple of minutes complete, death-like silence ensued.

Mehetabel, panting, everything swimming, turning before her eyes, remained motionless on her knees, but rested her hands on Thor's Stone, to save herself from falling on her face.

What had happened she hardly knew. The gun had been discharged, and then had fallen before her knees. Whom had it injured? What was the injury done?

She was unable to see, through the veil of tears that covered her eyes. She had not voice wherewith to speak.

Iver, moreover, stood motionless, holding to a willow. He also was ignorant of what had occurred. Was the shot aimed at him, or at Mehetabel? Who had fired?

Crouching against a bush, into which he had staggered and then collapsed, was the Broom-Squire. A sudden spasm of pain had shot through him at the flash of the gun. That he was struck he knew, to what extent injured he could not guess.

As he endeavored to raise one hand, the left, in which was the seat of pain, he became aware that his arm was stiff and powerless. He could not move his fingers.

The blood was coursing over his hand in a warm stream.

A horrible thought rushed through his brain. He was at the mercy of that woman who had invoked the Devil against him, and of the lover on whose account she had desired his death. She had called, and in part had been answered. He was wounded, and incapable of defending himself. This guilty pair would complete the work, kill him; blow out his brains, beat his head with the stock of the gun, and cast his body into the marsh.

Who would know how he came by his death? His sister was aware that he had gone to the moor to stalk deer. What evidence would be producible against this couple should they complete the work and dispose of him?

Strangely unaccountable as it may seem, yet it was so, that at the moment, rage at the thought that, should they kill him, Mehetabel and Iver would escape punishment, was the prevailing thought and predominant passion in Jonas's mind, and not by any means fear for himself. This made him disregard his pain, indifferent to his fate.

"I have still my right hand and my teeth," he said. "I will beat and tear that they may bear marks that shall awake suspicion."

But his head swam, he turned sick and faint, and became insensible.

When Jonas recovered consciousness he lay on his back, and saw faces bowed over him—that of his wife and that of Iver, the two he hated most cordially in the world, the two at least he hated to see together.

He struggled to rise and bite, like a wild beast, but was held down by Iver.

"Curse you! will you kill me so?" he yelled, snapping with his great jaws, trying to reach and rend the hands that restrained him.

"Lie still, Bideabout," said the young painter, "are you crazed? We will do you no harm. Mehetabel is binding up your arm. As far as I can make out the shot has run up it and is lodged in the shoulder."

"I care not. Let me go. You will murder me." Mehetabel had torn a strip from her skirt and was making a bandage of it.

"Jonas," she said, "pray lie quiet, or sit up and be reasonable. I must do what I can to stay the blood."

As he began to realize that he was being attended to, and that Iver and Mehetabel had no intention to hurt him, the Broom-Squire became more composed and patient.

His brows were knit and his teeth set. He avoided looking into the faces of those who attended to him.

Presently the young painter helped him to rise, and offered his arm. This Jonas refused.

"I can walk by myself," said he, churlishly; then turning to Mehetabel, he said, with a sneer, "The devil never does aught but by halves."

"What do you mean?"

"The bullet has entered my arm and not my heart, as you desired."

"Go," she said to the young artist; "I pray you go and leave me with him. I will take him home."

Iver demurred.

"I entreat you to go," she urged. "Go to your mother. Tell her that my husband has met with an accident, and that I am called away to attend him. That is to serve as an excuse. I must, I verily must go with him. Do not say more. Do not say where this happened."

"Why not?"

She did not answer. He considered for a moment and then dimly saw that she was right.

"Iver," she said in a low tone, so that Jonas might not hear, "you should not have followed me; then this would never have happened."

"If I had not followed you he would have been your murderer, Matabel."

Then, reluctantly, he went. But ever and anon turned to listen or to look.

When he was out of sight, then Mehetabel said to her husband, "Lean on me, and let me help you along."

"I can go by myself," he said bitterly. "I would not have his arm. I will have none of yours. Give me my gun."

"No, Jonas, I will carry that for you."

Then he put forth his uninjured right hand, and took the kidney-iron stone from the anvil block, on which Mehetabel had left it.

"What do you want with that?" she asked.

"I may have to knock also," he answered. "Is it you alone who are allowed to have wishes?"

She said no more, but stepped along, not swiftly, cautiously, and turning at every step, to see that he was following, and that he had put his foot on substance that would support his weight.

"Why do you look at me?" he asked captiously.

"Jonas, you are in pain, and giddy with pain. You may lose your footing, and go into the water."

"So—that now is your desire?"

"I pray you," she answered, in distress, "Jonas, do not entertain such evil thoughts."

They attained a ridge of sand. She fell back and paced at his side.

Bideabout observed her out of the corners of his eyes. By the moonlight he could see how finely, nobly cut was her profile; he could see the glancing of the moon in the tears that suffused her cheeks.

"You know who shot me?" he inquired, in a low tone.

"I know nothing, Jonas, but that there was a struggle, and that during this struggle, by accident—"

"You did it."

"No, Jonas. I cannot think it."

"It was so. You touched the trigger. You knew that the piece was on full cock."

"It was altogether an accident. I knew nothing. I was conscious of nothing, save that I was trying to prevent you from committing a great crime."

"A great crime!" jeered he. "You thought only how you might save the life of your love."

Mehetabel stood still and turned to him.

"Jonas, do not say that. You cruelly, you wrongfully misjudge me I will tell you all, if you will I never would have hidden anything from you if I had not known how you would take and use what I said. Iver and I were child friends, almost brother and sister. I always cared for him, and I think he liked me. He went away and I saw nothing of him. Then, at our wedding, he returned home; and since then I have seen him a good many times—you, yourself asked him to the Punch-Bowl, and bade me stand for him to paint. I cannot deny that I care for him, and that he likes me."

"As brother and sister?"

"No—not as brother and sister. We are children no longer. But, Jonas, I have no wish, no thought other than that he should leave Thursley, and that I should never, never, never see his face again. Of thought, of word, of act against my duty to you I am guiltless. Of thoughts, as far as I have been able to hold my thoughts in chains, of words, of acts I have nothing to reproach myself with, there have been none but what might be known to you, in a light clearer than that poured down by this moon. You will believe me, Jonas."

He looked searchingly into her beautiful, pale face—now white as snow in the moonlight. After a long pause, he answered, "I do not believe you."

"I can say no more," she spoke and sighed, and went forward.

He now lagged behind.

They stepped off the sand ridge, and were again in treacherous soil, neither land nor water, but land and water tossed together in strips and tags and tatters.

"Go on," he said. "I will step after you."

Presently she looked behind her, and saw him swinging his right hand, in which was the lump of ironstone.

"Why do you turn your head?" he asked.

"I look for you."

"Are you afraid of me?"

"I am sorry for you, Jonas."

"Sorry—because of my arm?"

"Because you are unable to believe a true woman's word."

"I do not understand you."

"No—I do not suppose you can."

Then he screamed, "No, I do not believe." He leaped forward, and struck her on the head with the nodule of iron, and felled her at his feet.

"There," said he; "with this stone you sought my death, and with it I cause yours."

Then he knelt where she lay motionless, extended, in the marsh, half out of the water, half submerged.

He gripped her by the throat, and by sheer force, with his one available arm, thrust her head under water.

The moonlight played in the ripples as they closed over her face; it surely was not water, but liquid silver, fluid diamond.

He endeavored to hold her head under the surface. She did not struggle. She did not even move. But suddenly a pang shot through him, as though he had been pierced by another bullet. The bandage about his wound gave way, and the hot blood broke forth again.

Jonas reeled back in terror, lest his consciousness should desert him, and he sank for an instant insensible, face foremost, into the water.

As it was, where he knelt, among the water-plants, they were yielding under his weight.

He scrambled away, and clung to a distorted pine on the summit of a sand-knoll.

Giddy and faint, he laid his head against the bush, and inhaled the invigorating odor of the turpentine. Gradually he recovered, and was able to stand unsupported.

Then he looked in the direction where Mehetabel lay. She had not stirred. The bare white arms were exposed and gleaming in the moonlight. The face he did not see. He shrank from looking towards it.

Then he slunk away, homewards.

CHAPTER XXV. — AN APPARITION

When Bideabout arrived in the Punch-Bowl, as he passed the house of the Rocliffes, he saw his sister, with a pail, coming from the cow-house. One of the cattle was ill, and she had been carrying it a bran-mash.

He went to her, and said, "Sally!"

"Here I be, Jonas, what now?"

"I want you badly at my place. There's been an accident."

"What? To whom? Not to old Clutch?"

"Old Clutch be bothered. It is I be hurted terr'ble bad. In my arm. If it weren't dark here, under the trees, you'd see the blood."

"I'll come direct. That's just about it. When she's wanted, your wife is elsewhere. When she ain't, she's all over the shop. I'll clap down the pail inside. You go on and I'll follow."

Jonas unlocked his house, and entered. He groped about for the tinder-box, but when he had found it was unable to strike a light with one hand only. He seated himself in the dark, and fell into a cold sweat.

Not only was he in great pain, but his mind was ill at ease, full of vague terrors. There was something in the corner that he could see, slightly stirring. A little moonlight entered, and a fold flickered in the ray, then disappeared again. Again something came within the light. Was it a foot? Was it the bottom of a skirt? He shrank back against the wall, as far as possible from this mysterious, restless form.

He looked round to see that the scullery door was open, through which to escape, should this thing move towards him.

The sow was grunting and squealing in her stye, Jonas hailed the sound; there was nothing alarming in that. Had all been still in and about the house, there might have come from that undefined shadow in the comer a voice, a groan, a sigh—he knew not what. With an exclamation of relief he saw the flash of Sally Rocliffe's lantern pass the window.

Next moment she stood in the doorway.

"Where are you, Jonas?"

"I am here. Hold up the lantern, Sarah. What's that in the corner there, movin'?"

"Where, Jonas?"

"There—you are almost touchin it. Turn the light."

"That," said his sister; "why don'ty know your own old oilcloth overcoat as was father's, don'ty know that when you see it?"

"I didn't see it, but indistinct like," answered Jonas.

His courage, his strength, his insolence were gone out of him.

"Now, what's up?" asked Sarah. "How have you been hurted?"

Jonas told a rambling story. He had been in the Marsh. He had seen the deer, but in his haste to get within range he had run, caught his foot in a bramble, had stumbled, and the gun had been discharged, and the bullet had entered his arm.

Mrs. Rocliffe at once came to him to examine the wound.

"Why, Jonas, you never did this up yourself. There's some one been at your arm already. Here's this band be off Matabel's petticoat. How came you by that?"

He was confounded, and remained silent.

"And where is the gun, Jonas?"

"The gun!"

He had forgotten all about it in his panic. Mehetabel had been carrying it when he beat her down. He had thought of it no more. He had thought of nothing after the deed, but how to escape from the spot as speedily as possible.

"I suppose I've lost it," he said. "Somewhere in the Moor. You see when I was wounded, I hadn't the head to think of anything else."

Mrs. Rocliffe was examining his arm. The sleeve of his coat had been cut.

"I don't understand your tale a scrap, Jonas," she said. "Who used his knife to slit up your sleeve? And how comes your arm to be bandaged with this bit of Matabel's dress?"

Bideabout was uneasy. The tale he had told was untenable. There was a necessity for it to be supplemented. But his condition of alarm and pain made him unable readily to frame a story that would account for all, and satisfy his sister.

"Jonas," said Sarah, "I'm sure you have seen Matabel, and she did this for you. Where is she?"

Bideabout trembled. He thrust his sister from him, saying, irritably, "Why do you worrit me with questions? My arm wants attendin' to."

"I can't do much to that," answered the woman. "A doctor should look to that. I'll go and call Samuel, and bid him ride away after one."

"I won't be left alone!" exclaimed the Broom-Squire, in a sudden access of terror.

Sarah Rocliffe deliberately took the lantern and held it to his face.

"Jonas," she said, "I'll do nuthin' more for you till I know the whole truth. You've seen your wife and there's somethin' passed between you. I see by your manner that all is not right. Where is Matabel? You haven't been after the deer on the Moor. You have been to the Ship."

"That is a lie," answered Bideabout. "I have been on the Moor. 'Tis there I got shot, and, if you will have it all out, it was Matabel who shot me."

"Matabel shot you?"

"Yes, it was. She shot me to prevent me from killin' him."

"Whom?"

"You know—that painter fellow."

"So that is the truth? Then where is she?"

The Broom-Squire hesitated and moved his feet uneasily.

"Jonas," said his sister, "I will know all."

"Then know it," he answered angrily. "Somehow, as she was helpin' me along, her foot slipped and she fell into the water. I had but one arm, and I were stiff wi' pains. What could I do? I did what I could, but that weren't much. I couldn't draw her out o' the mire. That would take a man wi' two good arms, and she was able to scramble out if she liked. But she's that perverse, there's no knowing, she might drown herself just to spite me."

"Why did you not speak of that at once?"

"Arn't I hurted terr'ble bad? Arn't I got a broken arm or somethin' like it? When a chap is in racks o' pain he han't got all his wits about him. I know I wanted help, for myself, first, and next, for her; and now I've told you that she's in the Moor somewhere. She may ha' crawled out, or she may be lyin' there. I run on, so fast as possible, in my condition, to call for help."

"Where is she? Where did you leave her?"

"Right along between here and Thor's Stone. There's an old twisted Scotch pine with magpies' nests in it—I reckon more nests than there be green stuff on the tree. It's just about there."

"Jonas," said the sister, who had turned deadly white, and who lowered the lantern, unable longer to hold it to her brother's face with steady hand, "Jonas, you never ort to ha' married into a gallus family; you've ketched the complaint. It's bad enough to have men hanged on top o' Hind Head. We don't want another gibbet down at the bottom of the Punch-Bowl, and that for one of ourselves."

Then voices were audible outside, and a light flickered through the window.

In abject terror the Broom-Squire screamed "Sally, save me, hide me; it's the constables!"

He cowered into a corner, then darted into the back kitchen, and groped for some place of concealment.

He heard thence the voices more distinctly. There was a tramp of feet in his kitchen; a flare of fuller light than that afforded by Mrs. Rocliffe's lantern ran in through the door he had left ajar.

The sweat poured over his face and blinded his eyes.

Bideabout's anxiety was by no means diminished when he recognized one of the voices in his front kitchen as that of Iver.

Had Iver watched him instead of returning to the Ship? Had he followed in his track, spying what he did? Had he seen what had taken place by the twisted pine with the magpies' nests in it? And if so, had he hasted to Thursley to call out the constable, and to arrest him as the murderer of his wife.

Trembling, gnawing the nails of his right hand, cowering behind the copper, he waited, not knowing whither to fly.

Then the door was thrust open, and Sally Rocliffe came in and called to him: "Jonas! here is Master Iver Verstage—very good he is to you—he has brought a doctor to attend to your arm."

The wretched man grasped his sister by the wrist, drew her to him, and whispered—"That is not true; it is the constable."

"No, Jonas. Do not be a fool. Do not make folk suspect evil," she answered in an undertone. "There is a surgeon staying at the Ship, and this is the gentleman who has come to assist you."

Mistrustfully, reluctantly, Jonas crept from his hiding place, and came behind his sister to the doorway, where he touched his forelock, looked about him suspiciously, and said—"Your servant, gentlemen. Sorry to trouble you; but I've met with an accident. The gun went off and sent a bullet into my arm. Be you a doctor, sir?" he asked, eyeing a stranger, who accompanied Iver.

"I am a surgeon; happily, now lodging at the Ship, and Mr. Verstage informed me of what had occurred, so I have come to offer my assistance."

Jonas was somewhat reassured, but his cunning eyes fixed on Iver observed that the young painter was looking around, in quest, doubtless, of Mehetabel.

"I must have hot water. Who will attend to me?" asked the surgeon.

"I will do what is necessary," said Mrs. Rocliffe.

"Will you go to bed?" asked the surgeon, "I can best look to you then."

Jonas shook his head. He would have the wound examined there, as he sat in his arm-chair.

Then came the inquiry from Iver—"Where is your wife, Jonas? I thought she had returned with you."

"My wife? She has lagged behind."

"Not possible. She was to assist you home."

"I needed no assistance."

"She ought to be here to receive instructions from the doctor."

"These can be given to my sister."

"But, Bideabout, where is she?"

Jonas was silent, confused, alarmed.

Iver became uneasy.

"Bideabout, where is Matabel. She must be summoned."

"It's nort to you where she be," answered the Broom-Squire savagely.

Then Mrs. Rocliffe stepped forward.

"I will tell you," she said. "My brother is that mad wi' pain, he don't know what to think, and say, and do. As they was coming along together, loving-like, as man and wife, she chanced to slip and fall into the water, and Jonas, having his arm bad, couldn't help her out, as he was a-minded, and he runned accordin' here, to tell me, and I was just about sendin' my Samuel to find and help her."

"Matabel in the water—drowned!"

"Jonas did not say that. She falled in."

"Matabel—fell in!"

Iver looked from Mrs. Rocliffe towards Jonas. There was something in the Broom-Squire's look that did not satisfy him. It was not pain alone that so disturbed his face, and gave it such ghastly whiteness.

"Bideabout," said he, gravely, "I must and will have a proper explanation. I cannot take your sister's story. Speak to me yourself. After what I had seen between you and Matabel, I must necessarily feel uneasy. I must have a plain explanation from your own lips."

Jonas was silent; he looked furtively from side to side.

"I will be answered," said Iver, with vehemence.

"Who is to force me to speak?" asked the Broom-Squire, surlily.

"If I cannot, I shall fetch the constable. I say—where did you leave Mehetabel?"

"My sister told you—under the tree."

"What—not in the water?"

"She may have fallen in. I had but one arm, and that hurting terrible."

"Good heavens!" exclaimed Iver. "You came home whining over your arm—leaving her in the marsh!"

"You don't suppose I threw her in?" sneered Jonas. "Me—bad of an arm."

"I don't know what to think," retorted Iver. "But I will know where Mehetabel is."

In the doorway, with her back to the moonlight, stood a female figure.

The first to see it was Jonas, and he uttered a gasp—he thought he saw a spirit.

The figure entered, without a word, and all saw that it was Mehetabel.

CHAPTER XXVI. — A SECRET

It was indeed Mehetabel.

She entered quietly, without a word, carrying Bideabout's gun, which she placed in the corner, by the fireplace.

Jonas and his sister looked at her, at first terror-struck, as though they beheld a ghost, then with unrest, for they knew not what she would say.

She said nothing.

She was deadly pale, and Iver, looking at her, was reminded of the Mehetabel he had seen in his dream.

At once she recognized that her husband's arm was being dressed, and leisurely, composedly, she came forward to hold the basin of water, and do whatever was required of her by the surgeon.

The first to speak was Iver, who said, "Matabel! We have just been told you had fallen into the water."

"Yes. My dress is soaked."

"And you managed to get out?"

"Yes, when I fell I had hold of my husband's gun and that was caught in a bush; it held me up."

"But how came you to fall?"

"I believe I was unconscious perhaps a faint."

Nothing further could be elicited from her, then or later. Had she any suspicion that she had been struck down? This was a question that, later, Jonas asked himself. But he never knew till—, but we must not anticipate.

A day or two after that eventful night he made some allusion to a blow on her head, when she appeared with a bandage round it.

"Yes," she said: "I fell, and hurt myself."

For some days Bideabout was in much pain and discomfort. His left shoulder had been injured by the ball that had lodged in it, and it was probable that he would always be stiff in that arm, and be unable to raise it above the breast. He was irritable and morose.

He watched Mehetabel suspiciously and with mistrust of her intentions. What did she know? What did she surmise? If she thought that he had attempted to put an end to her life, would she retaliate? In his suspicion he preferred to have his sister attend to him, and Sarah consented to do for him, in his sickness, what he required, not out of fraternal affection, but as a means of slighting the young wife, and of observing the relations that subsisted between her and Jonas.

Sarah Rocliffe was much puzzled by what had taken place. Her brother's manner had roused her alarm. She knew that he had gone forth with his jealousy lashed to fury. She had herself kindled the fire. Then he had come upon Mehetabel and Iver on the Moor, she could not doubt. How otherwise explain the knowledge of the accident which led Iver to bring the surgeon to the assistance of her brother?

But the manner in which the accident had occurred and the occasion of it, all of this was dark to her. Then the arrival of Jonas alone, and his reticence relative to his wife, till she had asked about her; also his extraordinary statement, his manifest terror; and the silence of Mehetabel on her reappearance, all this proved a mystery involving the events of the night, that Sarah Rocliffe was desirous to unravel.

She found that her every effort met with a rebuff from Jonas, and elicited nothing from Mehetabel, who left her in the same uncertainty as was Bideabout, whether she knew anything, or suspected anything beyond the fact that she had fallen insensible into the water. She had fallen grasping the gun, which had become entangled in some bushes, and this together with the water weeds had sustained her. When she recovered consciousness she had drawn herself out of the marsh by means of the gun, and had seated herself under an old pine tree, till her senses were sufficiently clear. Thereupon she had made the best of her way homeward.

What did she think of Jonas for having left her in the water? asked Mrs. Rocliffe.

Mehetabel answered, simply, that she had not thought about it. Wet, cold, and faint, she had possessed no idea save how to reach home.

There was much talk in the Punch-Bowl as well as throughout the neighborhood relative to what had taken place, and many forms were assumed by the rumor as it circulated. Most men understood well enough that Jonas had gone after the Peperharow deer, and was attempting to forestall others—therefore, serve him right, was their judgment, however he came by his accident.

Iver left Thursley on the day following and returned to Guildford. The surgeon staying at the Ship Inn continued his visits to the Punch-Bowl, as long as he was there, and then handed his patient over to the local practitioner.

Mrs. Verstage was little better informed than the rest of the inhabitants of Thursley, for her son had not told her anything about the accident to Jonas, more than was absolutely necessary; and to all her inquiries returned a laughing answer that as he had not shot the Broom-Squire he could not inform her how the thing was done.

She was too much engaged so long as the visitors were in the house, to be able to leave it; and Mehetabel did not come near her.

As soon, however, as she was more free, she started in her little trap for the Punch-Bowl, and arrived at a time when Jonas was not at home.

This exactly suited her. She had Mehetabel to herself, and could ask her any questions she liked without restraint.

"My dear Matabel," she said, "I've had a trying time of it, with the house full, and only Polly to look to for everything. Will you believe me—on Sunday I said I would give the gentlemen a little plum-pudding. I mixed it myself, and told Polly to boil it, whilst I went to church. Of course, I supposed she would do it properly, but with those kind of people one must take nothing for granted."

"Did she spoil the pudding, mother?"

"Oh, no—the pudding was all right."

"Then what harm was done?"

"She spoiled my best nightcap."

"How so?"

"Boiled the puddin' in it, because she couldn't find a bag. I'll never get it proper white again, nor the frills starched and made up. And there is the canary bird, too."

"What of that, mother?"

"My dear, I told Polly to clean out the cage."

"And did she not do it?"

"Oh, yes—only too well. She dipped it in a pan of hot water and soda—and the bird in it."

"What—the canary—is it dead?"

"Of course it is, and bleached white too. That girl makes the water so thick wi' soda you could stand a spoon up in it. She used five pounds in two days."

"Oh, the poor canary!" Mehetabel was greatly troubled for her pet.

"I don't quite understand the ways o' Providence," said Mrs. Verstage. "I don't suppose I shall till the veil be lifted. I understand right enough why oysters ain't given eyes—lest they should see those who are opening their mouths to eat 'em. And if geese were given wings like swallows, they wouldn't bide with us over Michaelmas. But why Providence should ha' denied domestic servants the gift of intelligence wherewith we, their masters and mistresses, be so largely endowed—that beats me. Well," in a tone of resignation, "one will know that some day, doubtless."

After a bit of conversation about the progress of Jonas to convalescence, and the chance of his being able to use his arm, Mrs. Verstage approached the topic uppermost in her mind.

"I should like to hear all about it, from your own mouth, Matabel. There is such a number of wonderful tales going round, all contradictory, and so, of course, all can't be true. Some even tell that you fired the gun and wounded Jonas. But that is ridiculous, as I said to Maria Entiknap. And actually one story is that my Iver was in it somehow. Of course, I knew he heard there was an accident. You told him when you was fetched away. Who fetched you from the Ship? I left you in the kitchen."

"Oh, mother," said Mehetabel, "all the events of that terrible night are confused in my head, and I don't know where to begin—nor what is true and what fancy, so I'd as lief say nothing about it."

"If you can't trust me—" said Mrs. Verstage, somewhat offended.

"I could trust you with anything," answered Mehetabel hastily. "Indeed, it is not that, but somehow I fell, and I suppose with fright, and a blow I got in falling, every event got so mixed with fancies and follies that I don't know where truth begins and fancy ends. For that reason I do not wish to speak."

"Now look here," said Mrs. Verstage, "I've brought you a present such as I wouldn't give to any one. It's a cookery book, as was given me. See what I have wrote, or got Simon to write for me, on the fly-leaf.

"'Susanna Verstage, her book,
Give me grace therein to look.
Not only to look, but to understand,
For learning is better than houses and land.
When land is gone, and money is spent,
Then learning is most excellent.'

"And the reason why I part with this Matabel, is because of that little conversation we had together the other day at the Ship. I don't believe as how you and Bideabout get along together first rate. Now I know men, their ins and outs, pretty completely, and I know that the royal road to their affections is through their stomachs. You use this book of receipts, they're not extravagant ones, but they are all good, and in six months Jonas will just about worship you."

"Mother," said Mehetabel, after thanking her, "you are very kind."

"Not at all. I've had experience in husbands, and you're, so to speak, raw to it. They are humorous persons, are men, you have to give in a little here and take a good slice there. If you give up to them there's an end to all peace and quietness. If you don't give in enough the result is the same. What all men want is to make their wives their slaves. You know, I suppose, how Gilly Cheel, the younger, got his name of Jamaica?"

"I do not think I do."

"Why he and his Bessy are always quarrelling! Neither will yield to the other. At last, by some means, Gilly got wind that in West Indies, there are slaves, and he thought, if he could only get out there with Bess that he'd be able to enslave her and make her do what he wished. So he pretended that he'd got a little money left him in Jamaica, and must needs go out there and settle. She said she wouldn't go, and he had no call to go there, except just for the sake of getting her under control. Then he talked big of the beautiful climate, and all the cooking done by the sun, and no washing needed, because clothing are unnecessary, and not only no washing, but no mending neither, no stockings to knit, no buttons to put on—a Paradise for wimen, said Gilly—but still he couldn't get Bessy to hear of going out to the West Indies. At last, how it was, I can't say, but she got wind of the institootion of slavery there, and then she guessed at once what was working in Gilly's mind. Since that day he's always gone by the name of

Jamaica, and fellows that want to tease him shout, 'Taken your passage yet for you and Bessy to Jamaica?'"

"My dear mother," said Mehetabel, "I should not mind being a slave in my husband's house, and to him, if there were love to beautify and sanctify it. But it would not be slavery then, and now I am afraid that you, mother, have perhaps took it unkind that I did not tell you more about that shot. If so, let me make all good again between us by telling you a real secret. There's no one else knows it."

"What is that?" asked the hostess eagerly.

Mehetabel was nervous and colored.

"May I tell you in your ear?"

Mrs. Verstage extended an ear to her, she would have applied both to Mehetabel's mouth had that been feasible.

The young wife, with diffidence, whispered something.

A beam of satisfaction lit up the old woman's face.

"That's famous. That's just as it ort. With that and with the cookery book, Jonas'll just adore you. There's nuthin' like that for makin' a home homely."

"And you'll come to me?"

"My dear, if alive and well, without fail."

CHAPTER XXVII. — POISON

The Broom-Squire did not recover from his wound with the rapidity that might have been expected. His blood was fevered, his head in a whirl. He could not forget what his sister had said to him relative to Mehetabel and Iver. Jealousy gnawed in his heart like a worm. That the painter should admire her for her beauty—that was nothing—who did not admire her? Had she not been an object of wonder and praise ever since she had bloomed into womanhood at the Ship? That he was envied his beautiful wife did not surprise him. He valued her because begrudged him by others.

He looked at himself in a broken glass he had, and sneered and laughed when he saw his own haggard face, and contrasted it with that of the artist. It was true that he had seen nothing to render him suspicious, when Iver came to his house, but he had not always been present. He had actually forced his wife against her wishes to go to the tavern where Iver was, had thrust her, so to speak, into his arms.

He remembered her call in the Marsh to the spirits to rid her of some one, and he could not believe her explanation. He remembered how that to save Iver, she had thrust the muzzle of the gun against her own side, and had done battle with him for mastery over the weapon. Incapable of conceiving of honor, right feeling, in any breast, he attributed the worst motives to Mehetabel—he held her to be sly, treacherous, and false.

Jonas had never suffered from any illness, and he made a bad patient now. He was irritable, and he spared neither his wife, who attended to him with self-denying patience, nor his sister, who came in occasionally. Mehetabel hoped that his pain and dependence on her might soften his rancorous spirit, and break down his antagonism towards her and every one. The longer his recovery was delayed, the more unrestrained became his temper. He spared no one. It seemed as though his wife's patience and attention provoked into virulent activity all that was most venomous and vicious in his nature. Possibly he was aware that he was unworthy of her, but could not or would not admit this to himself. His hatred of Iver grew to frenzy. He felt that he was morally the inferior of both the artist and of his own wife. When he was at their mercy they had spared his life, and that life of his lay between them and happiness. Had he not sought both theirs? Would he have scrupled to kill either had one of them been in the same helpless position at his feet?

He had come forth in sorry plight from that struggle, and now he was weakened by his accident, and unable to watch Mehetabel as fully as he would have wished.

The caution spoken by the surgeon that he should not retard his recovery by impatience and restlessness was unheeded.

He was wakeful at night, tossing on his bed from side to side. He complained of this to the surgeon, who, on his next visit, brought him a bottle of laudanum.

"Now look here," said he; "I will not put this in your hands. You are too hasty and unreliable to be entrusted with it. Your wife shall have it. It is useful, if taken in small quantities, just a drop or two, but if too much be taken by accident, then you will fall into a sleep from which there is no awaking. I can quite fancy that you in your irritable mood, because you could not sleep, would give yourself an overdose, and then—there would be the deuce to pay."

"And suppose that my wife were to overdose me?" asked the sick man suspiciously.

"That is not a suspicion I can entertain," said the surgeon, with a bow of his head in the direction of Mehetabel, "I have found her thoughtful, exact, and trustworthy. And so you have found her, I will swear, Mr. Kink, in all your domestic life?"

The Broom-Squire muttered something unintelligible, and turned a way.

When the laudanum arrived, he took the bottle and examined it. A death's head and crossbones were on the label. He took out the cork, and smelt the contents of the phial.

Though worn out with want of sleep he refused to touch any of the sedative. He was afraid to trust Mehetabel with the bottle, and afraid to mix his own portion lest in his nervous excitement he might overdo the dose.

Neither would he suffer the laudanum to be administered to him by his sister. As he said to her with a sneer, "A drop too much would give you a chance of my farm, which you won't have so long as I live."

"How can you talk like that?" said Sally. "Haven't you got a wife? Wouldn't the land go to her?"

The land, the house—to Mehetabel, and with his removal, then the way would be opened for Iver as well.

The thought was too much for Jonas. He left his bed, and carried the phial of opium to a little cupboard he had in the wall, that he kept constantly locked. This he now opened, and within it he placed the bottle. "Better endure my sleepless nights than be rocked to sleep by those who have no wish to bid me a good morrow."

Seeing that Mehetabel observed him he said, "The key I never let from my hands."

He would not empty the phial out of the window, because—he thought on the next visit of the surgeon he might get him to administer the dose himself, and he would have to pay for the laudanum, consequently to waste it would be to throw away two shillings.

It chanced one day, when the Broom-Squire was somewhat better, and had begun to go about, that old Clutch was taken ill. The venerable horse was off his feed, and breathed heavily. He stood with head down, looking sulky.

Bideabout was uneasy. He was attached to the horse, even though he beat it without mercy. Perhaps this attachment was mainly selfish. He knew that if old Clutch died he would have to replace him, and the purchase of a horse would be a serious expense. Accordingly he did all in his power to recover his steed, short of sending for a veterinary surgeon. He hastened to his cupboard in the upper chamber, and unlocked it, to find a draught that he might administer. When he had got the bottle, in his haste, being one-handed, he forgot to re-lock and remove the key. Possibly he did not observe that his wife was seated in the window, engaged in needlework. Indeed, for some time she had been very busily engaged in the making of certain garments, not intended for herself nor for her husband. She worked at these in the upper chamber, where there was more light than below in the kitchen, where, owing to the shade of the trees, the room was somewhat dark, and where, moreover, she was open to interruption.

When Bideabout left the room, Mehetabel looked up, and saw that he had not fastened the cupboard. The door swung open, and exposed the contents. She rose, laid the linen she was hemming on the chair, and went to the open press, not out of inquisitiveness, but in order to fasten the door.

She stood before the place where he kept his articles of value, and mustered them, without much interest. There were bottles of drenches for cattle, and pots of ointment for rubbing on sprains, and some account books. That was all.

But among the bottles was one that was small, of dark color, with an orange label on it marked with a boldly drawn skull and crossbones, and the letters printed on it, "Poison."

This was the phial containing the medicine, the name of which she could not recall, that the doctor had given to her husband to take in the event of his sleeplessness continuing to trouble him. The word "poison" was frightening, and the death's head still more so. But she recalled what the surgeon had said, that the result of taking a small dose would be to encourage sleep, and of an overdose to send into a sleep from which there would be no awaking.

Mehetabel could hardly repress a smile, though it was a sad one, as she thought of her husband's suspicions lest she should misuse the draught on him. But her bosom heaved, and her heart beat as she continued to look at it.

She needed but to extend her hand and she had the means whereby all her sorrows and aches of heart would be brought to an end. It was not as if there were any prospect before her of better times. If sickness had failed to soften and sweeten the temper of the Broom-Squire, then nothing would do it. Before her lay a hideous future of self-abnegation, or daily, hourly misery, under his ill-nature; of continuous torture caused by his cruel tongue. And her heart was not whole. She still thought of Iver, recalled his words, his look, the clasp of his arm, his kiss on her lips.

Would the time ever arrive when she could think of him without her pulse bounding, and a film forming over her eyes?

Would it not be well to end this now? She had but to sip a few drops from this bottle and then lay her weary head, and still more weary heart, on the bed, and sleep away into the vast oblivion!

She uncorked the bottle and smelt the laudanum. The odor was peculiar, it was unlike any other with which she was acquainted. She even touched the cork with her tongue. The taste was not unpleasant.

Not a single drop had been taken from the phial. It was precisely in the condition in which it had arrived.

If she did not yield to the temptation, what was it that stayed her? Not the knowledge that the country of the Gergesenes lay southeast of the Lake of Tiberias, otherwise called the Sea of Galilee; nor that the "lily of the field" was the Scarlet Martagon; nor that the latitude and longitude of Jerusalem were 31 deg. 47 min. by 53 deg. 15 min., all which facts had been acquired by her in the Sunday-school; but that which arrested her hand and made her replace the cork and bottle was the sight of a little white garment lying on the chair from which she had risen.

Just then she heard her husband's voice, and startled and confused by what had passed through her mind, she locked the cupboard, and without consideration slipped the key into her pocket. Then gathering up the little garment she went into another room.

Bideabout did not miss the key, or remember that he had not locked up the cupboard, for three days. The bottle with drench he had retained in the stable.

When the old horse recovered, or showed signs of convalescence, then Bideabout took the bottle, went to his room, and thrust his hand into his pocket for the key that he might open the closet and replace the drench.

Then, for the first time, did he discover his loss. He made no great disturbance about it when he found out that the key was gone, as he took for granted that it had slipped from his pocket in the stable, or on his way through the yard to it. In fact, he discovered that there was a hole in his pocket, through which it might easily have worked its way.

As he was unable to find any other key that would fit the lock, he set to work to file an odd key down and adapt it to his purpose. Living as did the squatters, away from a town, or even a large village, they had learned to be independent of tradesmen, and to do most things for themselves.

Nor did Mehetabel discover that she was in possession of the key till after her husband had made another that would fit. She had entirely forgotten having pocketed the original key. Indeed she never was conscious that she had done it. It was only when she saw him unlock the closet to put away the bottle of horse medicine that she asked herself what had been done with the key. Then she hastily put her hand into her pocket and found it.

As Jonas had another, she did not think it necessary for her to produce the original and call down thereby on herself a torrent of abuse.

She retained it, and thus access to the poison was possible to those two individuals under one roof.

CHAPTER XXVIII. — A THREAT

One Sunday, the first snow had fallen in large flakes, and as there had been no wind it had covered all things pretty evenly—it had laden the trees, many of which had not as yet shed their leaves. Mehetabel had not gone to church because of this snow; and Jonas had been detained at home for the same reason, though not from church. If he had gone anywhere it would have been to look for holly trees full of berries which he might cut for the Christmas sale of evergreens.

Towards noon the sun suddenly broke out and revealed a world of marvellous beauty. Every bush and tree twinkled, and as the rays melted the snow the boughs stooped and shed their burdens in shining avalanches.

Blackbirds were hopping in the snow, and the track of hares was distinguishable everywhere.

As the sun burst in at the little window it illumined the beautiful face of Mehetabel and showed the delicate rose in her cheeks, and shone in her rich dark hair, bringing out a chestnut glow not usually visible in it.

Jonas, who had been sitting at his table working at his accounts, looked up and saw his wife at the window contemplating the beauty of the scene. She had her hands clasped, and her thoughts seemed to be far away, though her eyes rested on the twinkling white world before her.

Jonas, though ill-natured and captious, was fond of his wife, in his low, animal fashion, and had a coarse appreciation of her beauty. He was so far recovered from his accident that he could sleep and eat heartily, and his blood coursed as usual through his veins.

The very jealousy that worked in him, and his hatred of Iver, and envy of his advantages of youth, good looks, and ease of manner, made him eager to assert his proprietorship over his wife.

He stepped up to her, without her noticing his approach, put his right arm round her waist and kissed her.

She started, and thrust him back. She was far away in thought, and the action was unintentional. In very truth she had been dreaming of Iver, and the embrace chimed in with her dream, and the action of shrinking and repulsion was occasioned by the recoil of her moral nature from any undue familiarity attempted by Iver.

But the Broom-Squire entirely misconceived her action. With quivering voice and flashing eyes, he said—

"Oh, if this had been Iver, the daub-paint, you would not have pushed me away."

Her eyebrows contracted, and a slight start did not pass unnoticed.

"I know very well," he said, "of whom you were thinking. Deny it if you can? Your mind was with Iver Verstage."

She was silent. The blood rushed foaming through her head; but she looked Bideabout steadily in the face.

"It is guilt which keeps you silent," he said, bitterly.

"If you are so sure that I thought of him, why did you ask?" she replied, and now the color faded out of her face.

Jonas laughed mockingly.

"It serves me right," he said in a tone of resentment against himself. "I always knew what women were; that they were treacherous and untrue; and the worst of all are those who think themselves handsome; and the most false and vicious of all are such as have been reared in public-houses, the toast of drunken sots."

"Why, then, did you take me?"

"Because I was a fool. Every man commits a folly once in his life. Even Solomon, the wisest of men, committed that folly; aye, and many a time, too, for of wives he had plenty. But then he was a king, and folly such as that mattered not to him. He could cut off the head of, or shoot down any man who even looked at or spoke a word to any of his wives. And if one of these were untrue to him, he would put her in a sack and sink her in the Dead Sea, and—served her right. To think that I—that I—the shrewd Broom-Squire, should have been so bewitched and bedeviled as to be led into the bog of marriage! Now I suffer for it." He turned savagely on his wife, and said: "Have you forgotten that you vowed fidelity to me?"

"And you did you not swear to show me love?"

He broke into a harsh laugh.

"Love! That is purely! And just now, when I attempted to snatch a kiss, you struck me and thrust me off, because I was Jonas Kink, and not the lover you looked for?"

"Jonas!" said Mehetabel, and a flame of indignation started into her cheek, and burnt there on each cheek-bone. "Jonas, you are unjust. I swore to love you, and Heaven can answer for me that I have striven hard to force the love to come where it does not exist naturally. Can you sink a well in the sandhill, and compel the water to bubble up? Can you drain away the moor and bid it blossom like a garden? I cannot love you—when you do everything to make me shrink from you. You esteem nothing, no one, that is good. You sneer at everything that is holy; you disbelieve in everything that is honest; you value not the true, and you have no respect for suffering. I do not deny that I have no love for you—that there is much in you that makes me draw away—as from something hideous. Why do not you try on your part to seek my love? Instead of that, you take an ingenious pleasure in stamping out every spark of affection, in driving away every atom of regard, that I am trying so hard to acquire for you. Is all the strivin' to be on my side?—all the thought and care to be with me? A very little pains on your part, some small self-control, and we should get to find common ground on which we could meet and be happy. As to Iver Verstage, both he and I know well enough that we can never belong to each other."

"Oh, I stand between you?"

"Yes you and my duty."

"Much you value either."

"I know my duty and will do it. Iver Verstage and I can never belong to each other. We know it, and we have parted forever. I have not desired to be untrue to you in heart; but I did not know what was possible and what impossible in this poor, unhappy heart of mine when I promised to love you. I did not know what love meant at the time. Mother told me it grew as a matter of course in married life, like chickweed in a garden."

"Am I gone crazed, or have you?" exclaimed Bideabout, snorting with passion. "You have parted with Iver quite so but only till after my death, which you will compass between you. I know that well enough. It was because I knew that, that I would not suffer you to give me doses of laudanum. A couple of drops, where one would suffice, and this obstruction to your loves was removed."

"No, never!" exclaimed Mehetabel, with flashing eye.

"You women are like the glassy pools in the Moor. There is a smooth face, and fair flowers floating thereon, and underneath the toad and the effect, the water-rat and festering poison. I shall know how to drive out of you the devil that possesses you this spirit of rebellion and passion for Iver Verstage."

"You may do that," said Mehetabel, recovering her self-mastery, "if you will be kind, forbearing, and gentle."

"It is not with kindness and gentleness that I shall do it," scoffed the Broom-Squire. "The woman that will not bend must be broken. It is not I who will have to yield in this house I, who have been master here these twenty years. I shall know how to bring you to your senses."

He was in foaming fury. He shook his fist, and his short hair bristled.

Mehetabel shrank from him as from a maniac.

"You have no need to threaten," she said, with sadness in her tone. "I am prepared for anything. Life is not so precious to me that I care for it."

"Then why did you crawl out of the marsh?"

She looked at him with wide-open eyes.

"Make an end of my wretchedness if you will. Take a knife, and drive it into my heart. Go to your closet, and bring me that poison you have there, and pour it between my lips. Thrust me, if you will, into the Marsh. It is all one to me. I cannot love you unless you change your manners of thought and act and speech altogether."

"Bah!" sneered he, "I shall not kill you. But I shall make you understand to fear me, if you cannot love me." He gripped her wrist. "Whether alive or dead, there will be no escape from me. I will follow you, track you in all you do, and if I go underground shall fasten on you, in spirit, and drag you underground as well. When you married me you became mine forever."

A little noise made both turn.

At the door was Sally Rocliffe, her malevolent face on the watch, observing all that passed.

"What do you want here?" asked the Broom-Squire.

"Nuthin', Jonas, but to know what time it is. Our clock is all wrong when it does go, and now, with the cold and snow, I suppose, it has stopped altogether."

Sally looked at the clock that stood in the comer, Jonas turned sharply on his heel, took his hat, and went forth into the backyard of his farm.

"So," said Mrs. Rocliffe, "my brother is in fear of his life of you. I know very well how he got the shot in his elbow. It was not your fault that it did not lodge in his head. And now he dare not take his medicine from your hands lest you should put poison into it. That comes of marrying into a gallows family."

Then slowly she walked away.

Mehetabel sank into the window seat.

However glorious the snow-clad, sunlit world might be without it was nothing to her. Within her was darkness and despair.

She looked at her wrist, marked with the pressure of her husband's fingers. No tears quenched the fire in her eyes. She sat and gazed stonily before her, and thought on nothing. It was as though her heart was frozen and buried under snow; as though her eyes looked over the moor, also frozen and white, but without the sun flooding it. Above hung gray and threatening clouds.

Thus she sat for many minutes, almost without breathing, almost without pulsation.

Then she sprang to her feet with a sob in her throat, and hastened about the house to her work. There was, as it were, a dark sea tumbling, foaming, clashing within her, and horrible thoughts rose up out of this sea and looked at her in ghostly fashion and filled her with terror. Chief among these was the thought that the death of Jonas could and would free her from this hopeless wretchedness. Had the bullet indeed entered his head then now she would have been enduring none of this insult, none of these indignities, none of this daily torture springing out of his jealousy, his suspicion, and his resentfulness.

And at the same time appeared the vision of Iver Verstage. She could measure Jonas by him. How infinitely inferior in every particular was Jonas to the young painter, the friend of her childhood.

But Mehetabel knew that such thoughts could but breed mischief. They were poison germs that would infect her own life, and make her not only infinitely wretched but degrade her in her own eyes. She fought against them. She beat them down as though she were battling with serpents that rose up out of the dust to lash themselves around her and sting her. The look at them had an almost paralyzing effect. If she did not use great effort they would fascinate her, and draw her on till they filled her whole mind and lured her from thought to act.

She had not been instructed in much that was of spiritual advantage when a child in the Sunday-school. The Rector, as has already been intimated, had been an excellent and kindly man, who desired to stand well with everybody, and who was always taking up one nostrum after another as a panacea for every spiritual ill. And at the time when Matabel was under instruction the nostrum was the physical geography of the Holy Land. The only thing the parson did not teach was a definite Christian belief, because he had entered into a compromise with a couple of Dissenting farmers not to do so, and to confine the instruction to such matters as could not be disputed. Moreover, he was, himself, mentally averse to everything that savored of dogma in religion. He would not give his parishioners the Bread of Life, but would supply them with any amount of stones geographically tabulated according to their strata.

However, Matabel had acquired a clear sense of right and wrong, at a little dame's school she had attended, as also from Mrs. Verstage; and now this definite knowledge of right and wrong stood her in good stead. She saw that the harboring of such thoughts was wrong, and she therefore resolutely resisted them. "He said," she sighed, when the battle was over, "that he would follow me through life and death, and finally drag me underground. But, can he be as bad as his word?"

CHAPTER XXIX. — A HERALD OF STRIFE

The winter passed without any change in the situation. Iver did not come home for Christmas, although he heard that his mother was failing in health and strength. There was much amusement in Guildford, and he reasoned that it would be advantageous to his business to take part in all the entertainments, and accept every invitation made him to the house of a pupil. Thursley was not so remote but that he could go there at any time. He was establishing himself in the place, and must strike root on all sides.

This was a disappointment to Mrs. Verstage. Reluctantly she admitted that her health was breaking down, and that, moreover, whilst Simon remained tough and unshaken. The long-expected and hoped for time when Iver should become a permanent inmate of the house, and she would spend her declining years in love and admiration, had vanished to the region of hopes impossible of fulfilment.

Simon Verstage took the decline of his wife's powers very philosophically. He had been so accustomed to her prognostications of evil, and harangues on her difficulties, that he was case-hardened, and did not realize that there was actual imminence of a separation by death.

"It's all her talk," he would say to a confidential friend; "she's eighteen years younger nor me, and so has eighteen to live after I'm gone. There ain't been much took out of her: she's not one as has had a large family. There was Iver, no more; and women are longer-lived than men. She talks, but it's all along of Polly that worrits her. Let Polly alone and she'll get into the ways of the house in time; but Sanna be always at her about this and about that, and it kinder bewilders the wench, and she don't know whether to think wi' her toes, and walk wi' her head."

In the Punch-Bowl the relations that subsisted between the Broom-Squire and his wife were not more cordial than before. They lived in separate worlds. He was greatly occupied with his solicitor in Godalming, to whom he was constantly driving over. He saw little of Mehetabel, save at his meals, and then conversation was limited on his part to recrimination and sarcastic remarks that cut as a razor. She made no reply, and spoke only of matters necessary. To his abusive remarks she had no answer, a deepening color, a clouding eye showed that she felt what he said. And it irritated the man that she bore his insolence meekly. He would have preferred that she should have retorted. As it was, so quiet was the house that Sally Rocliffe sneered at her brother for living in it with Mehetabel, "just like two turtle doves,—never heard in the Punch-Bowl of such a tender couple. Since that little visit to the Moor you've been doin' nothin' but billin and cooin'." Then she burst into a verse of an old folks song, singing in harsh tones—

"A woman that hath a bad husband, I find
By scolding won't make him the better.
So let him be easy, contented in mind,
Nor suffer his foibles to fret her.
Let every good woman her husband adore,
Then happy her lot, though t be humble and poor.
We live like two turtles, no sorrows we know,
And, fair girl! mind this when you marry."

"What happens, in my house is no concern of yours, Sally," Jonas would answer sharply. "If some folk would mind their own affairs they wouldn't be all to sixes and sevens. You look out that you don't get into trouble yet over that foolish affair of Thomas and the Countess. I don't fancy you've come to the end of that yet."

So the winter passed, and spring as well, and then came summer, and just before the scythe cut the green swath, for the hay harvest, Mehetabel became a mother.

The child that was born to her was small and delicate, it lacked the sturdiness of its father and of the mother. So frail, indeed, did the little life seem at first, that grave doubts were entertained whether the babe would live to be taken to church to be baptized.

Mehetabel did not have the comfort of the presence of Mrs. Verstage.

During the winter that good woman's malady advanced with rapid strides, and by summer she was confined to her room, and very generally to her bed.

To Mehetabel it was not only a grief that she was deprived of the assistance of her "mother," but also that, owing to her own condition, she was unable to attend on the failing woman. Deprived of the help of Mrs. Verstage, Mehetabel was thrown on that of her sister-in-law, Sally Rocliffe. Occasions of this sort call forth all that is good and tender in woman, and Sally was not at bottom either a bad or heartless woman. She had been embittered by a struggle with poverty that had been incessant, and had been allowed free use of her tongue by a husband, all whose self-esteem had been taken out of him by his adventure with the "Countess Charlotte," and the derision which had rained on him since. She was an envious and a spiteful woman, and bore a bitter grudge against Mehetabel for disappointing her ambition of getting her brother's farm for her own son Samuel. But on the occasion when called to the assistance of her sister-in-law, she laid aside her malevolence, and the true humanity in the depths of her nature woke up. She showed Mehetabel kindness, though in ungracious manner.

Jonas exhibited no interest in the accession to his family, he would hardly look at the babe, and refused to kiss it.

At Mehetabel's request he came up to see her, in her room; he stood aloof, and showed no token of kindliness and consideration. Sarah went downstairs.

"Jonas," said the young mother, "I have wished to have a word with you. You have been very much engaged, I suppose, and could not well spare time to see me before."

"Well, what have you to say? Come to the point."

"That is easily done. Let all be well between us. Let the past be forgotten, with its differences and misunderstandings. And now that this little baby is given to us, let it be a bond of love and reconciliation, and a promise of happiness to us both."

The Broom-Squire looked sideways at his wife, and said, sulkily, "You remind one of Sanna Verstage's story of Gilly Cheel. He'd been drinking and making a racket in the house, and was so troublesome that she had to turn him out into the street by the shoulders. What did he do, but set his back to the door, and kick with his heels till he'd stove in some of the panels. Then he went to the windows, and beat in the panes, and when he'd made a fine wreck of it all, he stuck in his head, and said, 'This is to tell you, Sanna Verstage, as how I forgive you in a Christian spirit.'"

"Bideabout! What has that to do with me?"

"Everything. Have you not wronged me, sought to compass my death, given your love away from me to another, crossed me in all my wishes?"

"No, Jonas; I have done none of this. I never sought your death, only the removal of one who made happiness to me in my home impossible. It was for you, because of you, that I desired his removal. As for my love, I have tried to give it all to you, but you must not forget that already from infancy, from the first moment that I can remember anything, Iver was my companion, that I was taught to look up to him, and to love him. But, indeed, I needed no teachin' in that. It came naturally, just as the buttercups in the meadow in spring, and the blush on the heather in July. I had not seen him for many years, and I did not forget him for all that. But I never had a thought of him other than as an old playmate. He returned home, the very day we were married, Jonas, as you remember. And since then, he often came to the

Punch-Bowl. You had nothin' against that. I began to feel like the meadow when the fresh spring sun shines on it, that all the dead or sleepin' roots woke up, and are strong again, or as the heather, that seemed dry and lifeless, the buds come once more. But I knew it must not be, and I fought against it; and I went to Thor's Stone for that reason, and for none other."

"A likely tale," sneered Jonas.

"Yes, Bideabout, it is a likely tale; it is the only tale at all likely concerning an honest heart such as mine. If there be truth and uprightness in you, you will believe me. That I have gone through a great fight I do not deny. That I have been driven almost to despair, is also true. That I have cried out for help—that you know, for you heard me, and I was heard."

"Yes—in that a lump of lead was sent into my shoulder."

"No, Jonas, in that this little innocent was given to my arms. You need doubt me no more: you need fear for me and yourself no longer. I have no mistrust in myself at all now that I have this." Lovingly, with full eyes, the mother held up the child, then clasped it to her bosom, and covered the little head and tiny hands with kisses.

"What has that to do with all that has been between us?" asked Bideabout, sneeringly.

"It has everything to do," answered Mehetabel. "It is a little physician to heal all our wounds with its gentle hand. It is a tiny sower to strew love and the seeds of happiness in our united lives. It is a little herald angel that appears to announce to us peace and goodwill."

"I dun know," muttered Jonas. "It don't seem like to be any of that."

"You have not looked in the little face, felt the little hands, as I have. Why, if I had any ache and pain, those wee fingers would with their touch drive all away. But indeed, Jonas, since it came I have had no ache, no pain at all. All looks to me like sunshine and sweet summer weather. Do you know what mother said to me, many months ago, when first I told her what I was expecting?"

"Dun know that I care to hear."

"She gave me a cookery book, and she said to me that when the little golden beam shone into this dark house it would fill it with light, and that, with the baby and me—cooking you nice things to eat, as wouldn't cost much, but still nice, then all would be right and happy, and after all—Paradise, Jonas."

"It seems to me as Sanna Verstage knows nuthin about it."

"Jonas," pleaded Mehetabel, "give the little one a kiss. Take it in your arms."

He turned away.

"Jonas," she said, in a tone of discouragement, after a pause, and after having held out the child to him in vain, and then taken it back to her bosom, "what are you stampin' for?"

He was beating his foot on the flooring.

"I want Sally to come up. I thought you had something to say, and it seems there is nuthin'."

"Nothing, Jonas? Do not go. Do not leave me thus. This is the first time you have been here since this little herald of goodwill appeared in my sky. Do not go! Come to me. Put your hand in mine, say that all is love and peace between us, and there will be no more mistrust and hard words. I will do my duty by you to the very best of my power, but, oh, Jonas, this will be a light thing to accomplish if there be love. Without—it will be heavy indeed."

He continued stamping. "Will Sally never come?"

"Jonas! there is one thing more I desired to say, What is the name to be given to the little fellow? It is right you should give him one."

"I!" exclaimed the Broom-Squire, making for the stairs. "I! Call him any name you will, but not mine. Call him," he turned his mean face round, full of rancor, and with his lip drawn up on one side, "as you like— call him, if it please you—Iver."

He went down the stairs muttering. What words more he said were lost in the noise of his feet.

"Oh, my babe! my babe!" sobbed Mehetabel; "a herald not of goodwill but of wicked strife!"

CHAPTER XXX. — A BEQUEST

As Mehetabel became strong, the better feeling towards her in the heart of Sally Rocliffe sank out of sight, and the old ill-humor and jealousy took the upper hand once more. It was but too obvious to the young mother that the woman would have been well content had the feeble flame of life in the child been extinguished. This little life stood between her son Samuel and the inheritance of the Kink's farm.

Whatever was necessary for the child was done, but done grudgingly, and Mehetabel soon learned that the little being that clung to her, and drew the milk of life from her bosom, was without a friend except herself, in the Punch-Bowl. Jonas maintained a cold estrangement from both her and the babe, its aunt would have welcomed its death.

The knowledge of this rendered her infant only more dear to Mehetabel. Hers was a loving nature, one that hungered and panted for love. She had clung as much as was allowed to the hostess at the inn. She had been prepared with all her heart to love the man to whom she had promised love. But this had been rendered difficult, if not impossible, by his conduct. She would have forgiven whatever wrong he had done her, had he shown the smallest token of affection for his child. Now that he refused the poor, helpless creature the least particle of the love that was its due, her heart that had expanded towards him, turned away and poured all its warmth on the child.

And in love for it she was satisfied. She could dispense with the love of others. She thought, cared for, lived but for this one little object which engrossed her entire horizon, filled every corner of her heart.

Marvellous is maternal love above every other love on earth, the most complete reflex of the love of the Creator for His creatures. In connubial love there is something selfish. It insists on reciprocity. In filial love there is an admixture of gratitude for treatment in the past. In maternal love there is nothing self-seeking, it is pure benevolence, giving, continuous giving, of time, of thought, of body labor, of sleep, of everything. It asks for nothing in return, it expects nothing.

Under the power of this mighty love Mehetabel rapidly became strong, and bloomed. The color returned to her cheek, the brightness to her eye, the smile to her lips, and mirth to her heart.

Whatever seeds of love for Iver had sprung up in her were smothered under the luxuriance of this new love that left in her soul no space for any other. She thought no more of Iver, for she had no thought for any one other than her child.

She who had never had any one of her own round whom to throw her arms, and to clasp to her heart, had now this frail infant; and the love that might have been dispersed among many recipients was given entire to the child—a love without stint, a love without bounds, a love infinitely pure and holy as the love that reigns in Heaven. So completely absorbed was Mehetabel in her love of the child, that the ill-humors of Sarah Rocliffe affected her not, nor did the callousness of her husband deeply wound her. So absorbed was she, that she hardly gave a thought to Simon Verstage and Susanna, and it was with a pang of self-reproach that she received an urgent appeal from the latter to visit her, sent through a messenger, along with a request that she would bring her infant with her in the conveyance sent from the Ship Inn for the purpose.

With readiness and at once Mehetabel obeyed the summons. There was a bright flush of pleasure in her cheek as she mounted to her place in the little cart, assisted by Joe Filmer, the ostler at the Ship, and folded her shawl about the living morsel that was all the world to her.

"Well, upon my word," said Joe, "I think, Matabel, you've grown prettier than ever, and if Bideabout bain't a happy man, he's different constituted from most of us."

Joe might well express his admiration. The young mother was singularly lovely now, with sufficient of the delicacy of her late confinement still on her, and with the glow of love and pride glorifying her face.

She was very pleased to go to the Ship, not so much because she wanted to see the hostess, as because she desired to show her the babe.

"How is mother?" she asked of Joe Filmer.

The ostler shook his head.

"I should say she hain't long to live. She changed terrible last week. If it weren't for her stories about Gilly Cheel, and one or another, one wouldn't believe it was the same woman. And the master, he is that composed over it all—it is wonderful, wonderful."

Mehetabel was shocked. She was not prepared for this news, and the brightness went out of her face. She was even more alarmed and troubled when she saw Mrs. Verstage, on whose countenance the shadow of approaching death was plainly lying.

But the hostess had lost none of the energy and directness of her character.

"My dear Matabel," she said, "it's no use you wishin' an' hopin'. Wishin' an' hopin' never made puff paste without lard. I haven't got in me the one thing which could raise me up again—the power to shake off my complaint. That is gone from me. I thought for long I could fight it, and by not givin' way tire it out. You can do that with a stubborn horse, but not with a complaint such as mine. But there—no more about me, show me the young Broom-Squire."

After the usual scene incident on the exhibition of a babe that is its mother's pride, a scene that every woman can fill in for herself, and which every man would ask to be excused to witness, Mrs. Verstage said: "Matabel, let there be no disguise between us. How do you and your husband stand to each other now?"

"I would rather you did not ask me," was the young wife's answer, after some hesitation.

"That tells me all," said the hostess. "I did hope that the birth of a little son or daughter would have made all right, assisted by the cookery book, but I see plainly that it has not. I have heard some sort of talks about it. Matabel, now that I stand, not with one, but with two feet on the brink of my grave, I view matters in a very different light from what I did before, and I do not mind tellin' you that I have come to the conclusion that I did a wrong thing in persuadin' you to take Bideabout. I have had this troublin' me for a long time, and it has not allowed me rest. I have not had much sleep of late, because of the pain, and because I always have been an active woman, and it puts me out to be a prisoner in my own room, and not able to get about. Well, Matabel, I have fretted a good deal over this, and have not been able to set my conscience at ease. When Polly knocked off the spout of my china teapot, I said to her, 'You must buy me another out of your wages.' She got one, but 'twasn't the same. It couldn't be the same. The fashion is gone out, and they don't make 'em as they did. It is the same with your marriage with Bideabout. The thing is done and can't be undone. So I need only consider how I can make it up in some other way."

"Mother, pray say nothing more about this. God has given me my baby, and I am happy."

"God has given you that," said Mrs. Verstage, "but I have given you nothing. I have done nothin' to make amends for the great wrong I did you, and which was the spoiling of your life. It is not much I can do, but do somethin' I must, and I will, or I shall not die happy. Now, my plan is this. I have saved some money. I have for many years been puttin' away for Iver, but he does not want it greatly. I intend to leave to you a hundred pounds."

"Mother, I pray you do nothing of the kind.

"I must do it, Matabel, to ease my mind."

"Mother, it will make me miserable."

"Why so?"

Mehetabel did not answer.

"I intend this hundred pounds to be your own, and I shall so leave it that it shall be yours, and yours only."

"Mother, it will make matters worse." After some hesitation, and with a heightened color, she told Mrs. Verstage about the fifteen pounds given her on the wedding day by Simon. She told it in such a manner as to screen her husband to the utmost. "You know, mother, Jonas has high notions about duty, and thinks it not well that we should have separate purses. Of course he must judge in these matters, and he is, no doubt, right, whereas I am wrong. But, as he does hold this opinion, it would anger him were I to have this money, and I know what the end would be, that I should have to give it all up to him, so that there might be peace between us. I dare say he is right."

"I have heard folks say that man should do the courtin' before marriage, and the woman after, but I don't hold with it. You may give way to them too much. There was Betsy Chivers was that mild and humoring to her husband that at last he made her do everything, even clean his teeth for him. The hundred pounds is for you, whether you wish to have it or not. It is of no use your sayin' another word."

"Do you mind, if it were given instead to the baby? May it be left to him instead of me? Then there would not be the same difficulty?"

"Certainly, if you like it; but you don't want me to leave him the use of it in his present condition. Why, he'd put it into his mouth for certain. There must be some one to look after it for him till he come of age, and take it upon himself, as the baptism service says."

"There must, of course," said Mehetabel, meditatively.

"Money, edged tools, and fire—these are the three things children mustn't meddle with. But it isn't children only as must be kept off money. Men are just as bad. They have a way of getting rid of it is just astonishin' to us females. They be just like jackdaws. I know them creeturs—I mean jackdaws, not men, come in at the winder and pull all the pins out of the cushion, and carry 'em off to line their nest with 'em. And men—they are terrible secretive with money. They can't leave a lump sum alone, but must be pickin at it, for all the world like Polly and currant cake, or raisin puddin'. As for men, they've exactly the same itchin after money. If I leave the hundred pounds to your little mite, and I'm willin' to do it, I must make some one trustee, and I don't fancy putting that upon Bideabout."

"Of course Jonas would look to his own child's interests, yet—"

"I know. There's a complaint some folks have, they're always eatin' and you can never see as their food has profited them. It's so with Bideabout—he is ever picking up money, but it don't seem to do him a scrap of good. What has he done with his money that he has saved?"

"I do not know."

"And I don't suppose he does himself. No, if you wish me to leave the hundred pounds to the child instead of to yourself then I will do so, heartily, and look about for some one in whom I can place confidence to undertake to be trustee. Simon is too old and he is getting foolish. My word, if, after I'm dead and gone, Simon should take it into his stupid head to marry Polly—I'd rise out of my grave to forbid the banns."

"You need have no fear of that, mother."

"If you had been in the house you could have kept an eye on him. There, again, my wrong deed finds me out. Matabel, it's my solemn conviction that there's no foolishness men won't be up to, especially widowers. They've been kept in order so long that they break out when their wives are dead. Have you ever seen a horse as has been clipped and kept all winter on hay in the stables when he chances to get out into a meadow, up go his heels, he turns frisky, gallops about, and there's no catching him again— not even with oats. He prefers the fresh grass and his freedom. That's just like widowers; or they're ginger beer bottles, very much up, wi' their corks out. What a pity it is Providence has given men so little common sense! Well, I'll see to that matter of the trusteeship, and the little man shall have a hundred pounds as a stand-by in the chance his father may have fooled away his own money."

CHAPTER XXXI. — SURPRISES

Jonas Kink not only raised no objection to having an entertainment at the baptism of his child, but he expressed his hearty desire that nothing should be spared to repay the gossips for what they had done to assist the infant into the Christian Church, by feeding them well, and giving them what they valued more highly, something to drink.

Mehetabel was gratified, and hoped that this was a token that, rude as his manner was, he would gradually unbend and become amiable. On the day of the christening, Bideabout was in a bustle, he passed from one room to another to see that all was in order; he rubbed his palms and laughed to himself. Occasionally his eyes rested on Sally Rocliffe, and then there was a malicious twinkle in them. There was little affection lost between the two. Neither took pains to conciliate the other. Each commented freely on those characteristics of the other which were in fact common to both.

In his ambition to make a man of comparative substance of his son Jonas, the father had not dealt liberally by his daughter, and this had rankled in Sarah's heart. She had irritated her brother by continually raking up this grievance, and assuring him that a brother with natural feeling would, out of generosity of his heart, make amends for the injustice of the father.

Jonas had not the slightest intention of doing anything of the sort, and this he conveyed to Sarah in the most bald and offensive manner possible. For twenty years, ever since the father's death, these miserable bickerings had gone on. Sally had not the sense to desist, where the pursuit of the topic could avail nothing, nor Jonas the kindliness to make her a present which might moderate her sense of having been unjustly treated.

He had been obliged to employ his sister, and yet he suspected, not without cause, that she took away from his house such scraps of food and pots and pipkins as were not likely to be missed. The woman justified her conduct to herself by the argument that she was inadequately paid in coin, and that she was forced to pilfer in order to recoup herself for the outlay of time and muscle in her brother's habitation. Thomas Rocliffe was a quiet, harmless old man, crushed not only by the derision which had clung to him like a robe of Nessus ever since his escapade with the Countess Charlotte, but also by the weight of his wife's tongue. He had sought peace by non-resistance, and this had encouraged her to violence, and had removed the only possible check to her temper. He was not a clever man. Most people thought him soft. His son Samuel was stupid and sullen, rendered both by his mother's treatment from infancy. Thomas had not sufficient intelligence and spontaneity to make a struggle to overcome his embarrassments, and force himself a way out of his difficulties. Instead of the debt that hampered him being gradually reduced, as it might have been by a man with energy, it had increased. Nothing had been spent on the house since the debt had been first contracted, and it was not water-tight. Nothing had been done to the land to dress it, to increase the stock, to open up another spring of revenue. When a bad year came the family fell into actual distress. When a good year ensued no margin was left to serve as a provision for one less favorable.

Mehetabel, pleased that her husband had put no hindrance in the way of a christening feast, had begrudged none of the necessary expense, was active and skilful in the preparation of cakes and pies.

To the church she had to go, so as to be churched immediately before the baptism, and Jonas remained at home, as he said, to see that no one broke in and carried off the good things. Never, within the memory of the oldest inhabitant of the Punch-Bowl; never, it may safely be asserted, since the Punch-Bowl had been formed, had there been seen a table so spread as that in the Kink's farmhouse on the day of the christening, and whilst the party was at the church. In the first place the table had on it a clean linen cover, not riddled with holes nor spotted with iron mould. It was exceptional for any table in the Punch-Bowl to be spread with linen. There stood on it plated and red earthenware dishes, and on the latter many good things. At one end was a cold rabbit pie. Rabbits were, indeed, a glut in Thursley, but such a pie was a phenomenon.

Bideabout's mind was exercised over it. He was curious to know whether the interior corresponded to the promise without. He inserted a knife and lifted the crust just sufficiently to allow him to project his nose to the edge of the dish and inhale the savor of the contents. "My word!" said he, "there's stuffin'. Rabbit and stuffin'. Wot next—and egg. I can see the glimmer of the white and yaller."

He rose from his stooping posture and saw Samuel Rocliffe at the window.

He beckoned to him to enter, and then showed him the table. "Did you ever see the likes?" he asked. "You ain't invited, Sam, but you can look over it all. There's a posy of flowers in the middle of the table, genteel like, as if it were a public house dinner to a club, and look at this pie. Do you see how crinkled it is all round, like the frill of your mother's nightcap? That was done with the scissors, and there's a gloss over the top. That were effected with white o' egg. Just think of that! using white o' egg when eggs is eighteen a shilling, for making the pie shine like your face o' Sundays after you've yaller-soaped it. There's stuffin' inside."

"I wish there were in my inside," said Samuel, surlily.

"You ain't invited. Do you see that thing all of a trimble over there, a sort of pale ornamental cooriosity? That's called a blue-mange. It's made of isinglass and milk and rice flour. It's not for ornament, but to be eaten, by such as is invited. There they come! You cut away. If you was a few years older, we might have invited you. But there ain't room for boys."

The unfortunate Samuel sulkily retired, casting envious eyes at the more favored denizens of the Punch-Bowl who were arriving to partake of the viands only shown to him.

The guests streamed in and took their places. They enjoyed the feast prepared, and passed encomiums on their hostess for her cookery. All fought shy at first of the blanc-mange. None had seen such a confection previously, and each desired that his fellow should taste before committing himself to a helping.

Mrs. Verstage had sent a present of half-a-dozen bottles of currant wine, and these were attacked without any hesitation.

All the males at the table were in their shirt-sleeves. No man thought of risking his Sunday coat by wearing it, even though the viands were cold.

Jonas seemed to thoroughly enjoy himself. He looked about and laughed, and rubbed his hands together under the table.

"Beware!" whispered Sally to her husband. "I can't understand Bideabout. There's some joke as tickles his in'ards tremendous. Wot it is, I don't see."

"He'll let it out presently," said Thomas.

As soon as every appetite was satisfied, and the guests had thrust their plates from them into the midst of the table, Giles Cheel stood up, and looking round cleared his throat, and said, "Ladies and gem'men, neighbors all. I s'pose on such an occasion as this, and after such a feed, it's the dooty of one of us to make a speech. And as I'm the oldest and most respected of the Broom-Squires of the Bowl, I think it proves as I should express the gen'ral feelin' of satisfaction we all have. That there rabbit pie might ha' been proud to call itself hare. The currant wine was comfortin', especially to such as, like myself, has a touch of a chill below the ribs, and it helps digestion. There be some new-fangled notions comin' up about taytotallin. I don't hold by 'em. The world was once drownded with water, and I don't see why we should have Noah's Floods in our insides. The world had quite enough taytotallin' then."

Giles was pulled backwards by the hand of his wife, which grasped the strap of his waistcoat.

"Sit down, you're ramblin' from the p'int."

"Betsy, let go. I be ramblin' up to it."

"Sit down, they've had enough o' yer."

"They've hardly had a taste."

"Everyone be laughin' at yer."

"I'm just about bringin' tears into their eyes."

"If you go on, I'll clap my hand over yer mouth."

"And then I'll punch yer head."

The daily broil in the Cheel house was about to be produced in public. It was stopped by Jonas, who rose to his feet, and with a leer and chuckle round, he said, "Neighbors and friends and all. Very much obliged for the complerment. But don't think it is all about a baby. Nothin' of the kind. It is becos I wanted all, neighbors and friends, to be together whilst I made an announcement which will be pleasant hearin' to some parties, and astonishin' to all. I ain't goin' to detain you very long, for what I've got to say might be packed in a nutshell and carried away in the stomick of a tomtit. You all of you know, neighbors and friends all, as how my brother-in-law made a fool of himself, and was made a fool of through the Countess Charlotte. And how that his farm got mortgaged; and since then, with lawyers, got more charged; and the family have led a strugglin' life since to keep their heads above water. Well, I've got all their mortgage and debts into my hands, and intend—"

He looked round with a malicious laugh. He saw a flutter of expectation in his sister's eyes.

"No, Sally. I ain't going to give 'em up. I hold em, and ain't goin' to stand no shilly-shally about payments when due. You may be sure of that. And wot is more, I won't stand no nonsense from you or Thomas or Samuel, but I expect you to be my very humble servants, or I'll sell you up."

A look of blank consternation fell on the faces of the Rocliffes. Others looked uneasy. Not the Rocliffes only were partially submerged.

"I've somethin' also to say to Gilly Cheel. I ain't goin' to have the Punch-Bowl made a Devil's cauldron of wi' his quarrels—"

"Hear, hear," from Betsy Cheel.

"And unless he lives peaceable, and don't trouble me wi' his noise and she wi' her cattewawlin'."

"That's for you," said Jamaica, and nudged his wife.

"I'll turn 'em both out," proceeded Jonas. "For I've been gettin' his papers into my hands also. And then, as to the Boxalls—"

The members of that clan now looked blank. Consternation was spreading to all at table.

"As to the Boxalls," continued Jonas, "if their time hasn't come just yet, it's comin'. I hope, neighbors and friends all, you've enjyed the dessert."

A dead silence ensued. Every one felt that it would be better to be in the power of a lawyer than of Bideabout.

Tears of mortification and resentment rose in the eyes of Sally Rocliffe. Mehetabel hung her head in shame.

Then Thomas, stolid and surly, flung a letter across the table to the Broom-Squire. "Take that," he said, "I don't wan't to be burdened with nothin' of your'n. 'Tis a letter been lyin' at the post for you, and Mistress Chivers gave it me. Wish I wos rid of everything atwixt us as I be of that there letter now."

Jonas took the missive, turned it about, then carelessly opened it.

As he read his color faded, and he had hardly read to the end before he sank back in his chair with a cry of rage and despair; "The Wealden bank be broke. I'm a ruined man."

CHAPTER XXXII. — ANOTHER SURPRISE

Among those present the only one who came to the assistance of Jonas Kink was his brother-in-law, Thomas Rocliffe, who, thinking that Bideabout was going to have a fit, ran to him and unloosed his black satin cravat.

The revulsion of feeling in the rest was so sudden that it produced a laugh. He who had been exulting in having put their necks under his foot had been himself struck down in the moment of his triumph. He had sought to humble them in a manner peculiarly mean, and no compassion was felt for him now in his distress.

The guests filed out without a word of thanks for the meal of which they had partaken, or an expression of pity for the downcast man.

For some while Bideabout remained motionless, looking at the letter before him on the table. Mehetabel did not venture to approach or address him. She watched him with anxiety, not knowing in which direction the brooding rage within him would break forth. He was now like a thunder-cloud charged with electricity and threatening all with whom he came in contact.

Hearing the wail of her child, she was glad noiselessly to leave the room and hasten to comfort it. Presently Jonas rose, and in a half stupefied condition went to the stable and saddled old Clutch that he might ride to Godalming and learn whether things were as bad as represented.

In his impatience to announce to his guests that he had them under his control he had been somewhat premature. It was true that the negotiations were complete whereby their mortgages and obligations were transferred to him, but the money that he was to pay therefor had not been made over. Now it would not be possible for him to complete the transaction. Not only so, but he had incurred expenses by his employment of a solicitor to carry out his design which it would be extremely difficult for him to meet, if the bank had actually failed.

He alone of all the squires in the Punch-Bowl had put his savings into a bank, and he had done this because he was so frequently and so long from home that he did not dare to leave them anywhere in his house, lest it should be broken into during his absence.

As the Broom-Squire approached Thursley village his horse cast a shoe, and he was obliged to stop at the farrier's to have old Clutch shod.

"How do'y do, Squire?" said the blacksmith. "Been christenin' your baby, I hear."

Bideabout grunted in reply.

"One comes and another goes," said the farrier. "S'pose you've heard the news?"

"Think I have," retorted Jonas, irritably. "It's them banks is broke."

"I don't mean no banks," said the blacksmith. "But Susanna Verstage. I s'pose you've heard she's gone?"

"Gone, where to?"

"That's not for me to say. She's been ailin' some time and now has gone off, sudden like. O' course we knowed it must come, but nobody didn't think it would ha' come so sudden—and she seemed such a hearty woman, only a few months ago. Well, I s'pose it's ordained."

The Broom-Squire did not ask questions. He took very little interest in the matter of the death of the hostess of the Ship. His mind was engrossed in his own troubles.

As soon as old Clutch had his shoe fitted on, and the other shoes looked to, Bideabout pursued his way.

His progress was not fast. Clutch was personally unaffected by the failure of the bank, and could not be induced to accelerate his speed. Beating only made him more stubborn, and when Bideabout stretched his legs out to the furthest possible extent apart that was possible, and then brought them together with a sudden contraction so as to dig his heels into the horse's ribs, that brought Clutch to an absolute standstill.

On reaching Godalming, the worst anticipations of Jonas were confirmed. The bank was closed; his savings were lost. Nothing had been withdrawn in time to secure them by giving him a hold on the squatter settlements of his neighbors. And he himself had incurred liabilities that might bring him into the same pit that he had digged for his fellows.

He turned homewards in great discouragement and acridity of heart. His fellows in the Punch-Bowl had never regarded him with cordiality; now they would be his combined enemies. The thoughts of his heart were gloomy. In no direction could he see light. He now did not urge Clutch along beyond the pace at which the old horse had made up his mind to go; it was immaterial to Jonas whether he were on the road or at home. Nowhere would he be free from his trouble.

He would, perhaps, have turned into the Ship for a glass of spirits but, remembering that he had been told the hostess was dead, he did not feel inclined to enter a house where he would be still further depressed. He had not, however, gone far out of the village, before he heard his name called from behind, and on turning his head saw Joe Filmer in pursuit.

The ostler came up to him, panting and said—

"Ter'rible news, ain't it? The old lady gone. But that ain't why I've stopped you. 'Tis she bade me give your missus a message—as she hadn't forgot the bequest of money. But we're that muddled and busy at the Ship, I can't go to the Punch-Bowl, so I just runned after you. You'll take the message for me, won't you?"

"Money!" exclaimed Bideabout, reining in old Clutch, who now objected to be stayed on his way to the familiar stable. "Money!" repeated Bideatout, and then lugged at old Clutch's rein till he had turned the brute about.

The horse had sufficient obstinacy in him to persist in his intentions of not being stopped on the high-road, and though turned round he continued to scramble along in the reverse direction to his home.

"Hang you, you old toad!" exclaimed Jonas. "If you will, I don't care. Be it so. We will go to the Ship. I say, Joe! What was that about money?"

"It was that the missus made me promise to inform your missus, that she'd not forgotten her undertakin', but had made provision that she should have the money as she wished."

"The money—how much?"'

"I do not know. She did not say."

"And she has left money to Matabel?"

"I suppose so. She was always amazin' fond of her. She was a savin' woman, and had put away something of her own."

"I'll go to the Ship. I will, certainly. I ought not to have passed without a word with Simon on his loss. I suppose he's sure to know how much it is?"

"I suppose so. Missus would consult him. She made a show o' that always, but nevertheless followed her own head."

"And Simon is terrible cut up?"

"Bears it like a man."

"Here, take old Clutch; give him some oats, and kick him, he deserves it, he's been so unruly. But, stay—no. Hold his head, and I'll kick him, afore he's had his oats. He's a darned malicious old Radical. Put in some pepper to his nose when he's done his oats."

Bideabout went into the house, through the porch, and entered the bar.

Simon was seated there smoking a long clay, with his feet on the fender, before a glowing fire, and with a stiff glass of hot punch on the table at his side.

"Sorry for you," was Jonas's brief address of salutation and condolence.

Mr. Verstage shook his head. "That's what my old woman said."

Seeing an expression of surprise and query in the Broom-Squire's face, he explained: "Not after, afore, in course. She said, 'Very sorry for you, Simon, very. It's wus for you than for me, I shall die—you'll make yourself ridic'lous.'"

"What did she mean?"

"Can't think," answered Simon, with great solemnity. "Will you have a drop of something? In this vale of tears we want consolation." Then, in a loud voice, "Polly—another glass."

After looking steadily and sadly into the embers, Mr. Verstage said: "I don't believe that woman ever made a mistake in her life—but once."

"When was that?"

"When she gave Matabel to you. We wanted her in this house. Her proper place was here. It all comes wi' meddlin' wi' what ort to be let alone—and that is Providence. There's never no sayin' but Iver—"

Dimly the old host saw that he was floundering upon delicate ground. "My doctrine is," said he, "let things alone and they'll come right in the end."

Bideabout moved uneasily. He winced at the reference to Iver. But what he now really was anxious to arrive at was the matter of money left by Mrs. Verstage to Mehetabel.

"Now," said Simon, looking after the serving-maid, as she left the bar, when she had deposited the tumbler beside Bideabout. "Now, my old woman was amazin' set against that girl. Why—I can't think. She's a good girl when let alone. But Sanna never would let her alone. She were ever naggin' at her; so that she upset the poor thing's nerve. She broke the taypot and chucked the beer to the pigs, but that was because she were flummeried wi' my old woman going on at her so. She said to me she really couldn't bear to think how I'd go on after she were gone. I sed, to comfort her, that I knowed Polly would do her best. 'She'll do the best she can for herself,' answered Sanna, as sharp as she said 'Yes, I will,' when we was married. I don't know what her meanin' was. You won't believe it, but it's true what I'm going to tell you. She said to me, did Susanna, 'Simon there was Mary Toft, couldn't die, because there were wild-fowl feathers in her bed. They had to take her off the four-poster and get another feather-bed, before she could die right off. Now,' said Sanna, 'it's somethin' like that with me. I ain't got wild-bird feathers under me, but there's a wild fowl in the house, and that's Polly. So long as she's here die I can't, and die I won't.' 'Well, old woman,' sed I, if that's all, to accommodate you, I'll send Polly to her mother,' and so I did—and she died right on end, peaceable."

"But Polly is here."

"Oh, yes—when Sanna were gone—we couldn't do wi'out her. She knowed that well enough and came back—runnin' like a long dog, and very good and thoughtful it was of her. Most young wimen ain't considerate like that."

This was all wide of the subject that engrossed the interest of Bideabout, and had induced him to revisit the Ship. As the host made no allusion to the topic, the Broom-Squire plunged into the matter, headforemost.

"Joe Filmer," said he, "called me back. I didn't wish to come in and trouble you now. But Joe said as how you wanted to speak to me about some money as your wife had left with you for my Matabel; and I thought it might be botherin' your mind when you wanted to turn it to religious thought, and so I came back to say I'd relieve you of it and take it at once."

"Money! Oh!" Mr. Verstage was a little difficult to turn from one line of thought to another. "Polly never stood out for higher wages. Not like some who, when they've been with you just long enough to learn the ways of the house, and to make themselves useful, and not to break everything they handle, and spoil everything they touch, ask, 'Please will you advance my wages?' Polly never did that."

"I am not speakin' of Polly," said Jonas, peevishly, "but of some money that Joe Filmer told me you wanted to tell me about. Something that your poor wife desired you to give to Matabel."

"Oh, you mean that hundred pounds. I wasn't against it. On the contrary, I said I'd add fifty to it. I always said Sanna did wrong in giving Matabel to—I mean flying in the face of Providence."

"I shall be very glad to take it, and thus relieve your mind of all care."

"Oh, it's no care at all."

"It must be, and besides—it must interfere with your turning your mind to serious thoughts."

"Oh, not at all. I can't give you the money. It is not for you."

"No; but it is for Matabel, and we are one."

"Oh, no; it's not for Matabel."

"The hundred and fifty pounds is not for Matabel? And yet you said it was intended to make up to her for something you did not exactly explain."

"No, it is not for Matabel. Matabel might have had it, I daresay, but my old woman said she was set against that."

"Then we are to be deprived of it by her folly?" The Broom-Squire flushed purple.

"Oh, no. It is all right. It is for the child."

"For the child! That is all the same. I am the father, and will take care of the money."

"But I can't give it you."

"Have you not got it?"

"The money is all right. Sanna's hundred pounds—I know where that is, and my fifty shall go along with it. I was always fond of Matabel. But the child was only baptized to-day, and won't be old enough to enjoy it for many years."

"In the meantime it can be laid out to its advantage," urged Bideabout.

"I daresay," said Simon, "but I've nothin' to do with that, and you've nothin' to do with that."

"Then who has?"

"Iver, of course."

"Iver!" The Broom-Squire turned livid as a corpse.

"You see," pursued the host, "Sanna said as how she wouldn't make me trustee, I was too old, and I might be dead, or done something terrible foolish, before the child came of age to take it on itself, to use her very words. So she wouldn't make me trustee, but she put it all into Iver's hands to hold for the little chap. She were a won'erful shrewd woman were Sanna, and I've no doubt she was right."

"Iver trustee—for my child!"

"Yes—why not?"

The Broom-Squire stood up, and without tasting the glass of punch mixed for him, without a farewell to the landlord, went forth.

CHAPTER XXXIII. — MARKHAM

The funeral of Mrs. Verstage was conducted with all the pomp and circumstance that delight the rustic mind. Bideabout attended, and his hat was adorned with a black silk weeper that was speedily converted by Mehetabel, at his desire, into a Sunday waistcoat.

In this silk waistcoat he started on old Clutch one day for Guildford, without informing his wife or sister whither he was bound.

The child was delicate and fretful, engaging most of its mother's time and engrossing all her thought.

She had found an old cradle of oak, with a hood to it, the whole quaintly and rudely carved, the rockers ending in snakes' heads, in which several generations of Kinks had lain; in which, indeed, Jonas had spent his early infancy, and had pleaded for his mother's love and clamored for her attention. Whether with the thought of amusing the child, or merely out of the overflow of motherly love that seeks to adorn and glorify the babe, Mehetabel had picked the few late flowers that lingered on in spite of frost, some pinched chrysanthemums, a red robin that had withstood the cold, some twigs of butcher's broom with blood-red berries that had defied it, and these she had stuck about the cradle in little gimlet holes that had been drilled round the edge, probably to contain pegs that might hold down a cover, to screen out glaring sun or cutting draught.

Now, as Mehetabel rocked the cradle and knitted, singing to the sobbing child, the flowers wavered about the infant, forming a wreath of color, and freshening the air with their pure fragrance. Each flower in itself was without much perceptible savor, yet the whole combined exhaled a healthy, clean, and invigorating waft as of summer air over a meadow.

The wreath that surrounded the child was not circular but oblong, almost as though engirding a tiny grave, but this Mehetabel did not see.

Playing the cradle with her foot, with the sun shining in at the window and streaking the foot, she sang—

"My heart is like a fountain true

That flows and flows with love to you;
As chirps the lark unto the tree,
So chirps my pretty babe to me.
And it's O! sweet, sweet! and a lullaby."

But the answer was a peevish moan from the bed. The young mother stooped over the cradle.

"Oh, little lark! little lark! this is no chirp,
Would you were as glad and as gay as the lark!"

Then, resuming her rocking, she sang,

"There's not a rose where'er I seek
As comely as my baby's cheek.
There's not a comb of honey bee,
So full of sweets as babe to me.
And it's O! sweet, sweet! and a lullaby."

Again she bowed over the crib, and all the rocking flowers quivered and stood still.

"Baby, darling! Why are there such poor roses in your little cheek? I would value them above all the China roses ever grown! Look at the Red Robin, my sweet, my sweet, and become as pink as is that."

"There's not a star that shines on high
Is brighter than my baby's eye.
There's not a boat upon the sea
Can dance as baby does to me.
And it's O! sweet, sweet, and a lullaby."

"No silk was ever spun so fine
As is the hair of baby mine.
My baby smells more sweet to me
Than smells in spring the elder tree.
And it's O! sweet, sweet, and a lullaby!"

The child would not sleep.

Again the mother stayed the rocking of the cradle, and the swaying of the flowers.

She lifted the little creature from its bed carefully lest the sharp-leafed butcher's broom should scratch it. How surrounded was that crib with spikes, and they poisonous! And the red berries oozed out of the ribs of the cruel needle-armed leaves, like drops of heart's blood.

Mehetabel took her child to her bosom, and rocked her own chair, and as she rocked, the sunbeam flashed across her face, and then she was in shadow, then another flash, and again shadow, and from her face, when sunlit, a reflection of light flooded the little white dress of the babe, and illumined the tiny arm, and restless fingers laid against her bosom.

"A little fish swims in the well,
So in my heart does baby dwell.
A little flower blows on the tree,
My baby is the flower to me.
And It's O! sweet, sweet! and a lullaby!"

A wondrous expression of peace and contentment was on Mehetabel's face. None of the care and pain that had lined it, none of the gloom of hopelessness that had lain on it, had left now thereon a trace. In her child all her hope was centred, all her love culminated.

"The King has sceptre, crown and ball.
You are my sceptre, crown and all,
For all his robes of royal silk.
More fair your skin, as white as milk.
And it's O! sweet, sweet, and a lullaby!

"Ten thousand parks where deer may run,
Ten thousand roses in the sun.
Ten thousand pearls beneath the sea.
My babe, more precious is to me.
And it's O! sweet, sweet, and a lullaby!"

Presently gentle sleep descended on the head of the child, the pink eyelids closed, the restless hand ceased to grope and clutch, and the breath came evenly. Mehetabel laid her little one again in its cradle, and recommenced the rocking with the accompanying swaying of the flowers.

Now that the child was asleep Mehetabel sat lightly swinging the cradle, afraid to leave it at rest lest that of her infant should again be broken.

She thought of the death of her almost mother Susanna Verstage, the only woman that had shown her kindness, except the dame of the school she had attended as a child.

Mehetabel's heart overflowed with tender love towards the deceased, she fully, frankly forgave her the cruel blow whereby she had wounded her, and had driven her out of her house and into that of Jonas. And yet it was a deadly wrong: a wrong that could never be redressed. The wound dealt her would canker her heart away; it was of such a nature that nothing could heal it. Mehetabel was well aware of this. She could see brightness before her in one direction only. From her child alone could she derive hope and joy in the future. And yet she forgave Mrs. Verstage with a generous forgiveness which was part of her nature. She would forgive Jonas anything, everything, if he would but acknowledge his wrong, and turn to her in love.

And now she found that she could think of Iver without a quickening of her pulses.

In her love for her babe all other loves had been swallowed up, refined, reduced in force. She loved Iver still, but only as a friend, a brother. Her breast had room for one prevailing love only—that of her child.

As she sat, slightly rocking the cradle, and with a smile dimpling her cheek, a knock sounded at the door, and at her call there entered a young man whom she had seen during the winter with Jonas. He was a gentleman, and she had been told that he had lodged at the Huts, and she knew that he had engaged the Broom-Squire to attend him, when duck-shooting, at the Fransham ponds.

Mehetabel apologized for not rising as he entered, and pointed to the cradle.

"My name is Markham," said the young man, "I have come to see Mr. Kink. This is his house, I believe?"

"Yes, sir; but he is not at home."

"Will he be long absent?"

"I do not know. Will you please to take a chair?"

"Thank you." The young gentleman seated himself, wiped his brow, and threw his cap on the floor.

"I want some fishing. I made Mr. Kink's acquaintance, shooting, during the winter. Excuse me, are you his sister or his wife?"

"His wife, sir."

"You are very young."

To this Mehetabel made no reply.

"And uncommonly pretty," pursued Mr. Markham, looking at her with admiration. "Where the deuce did the Broom-Squire pick you up?"

The young mother was annoyed—a little color formed in her cheek. "Can I give a message to Jonas?" she asked.

"A message? Tell him he's a lucky dog. By heaven! I had no idea that a pearl lay at the bottom of the Punch-Bowl. And that is your baby?"

"Yes, sir."

Mehetabel lightly raised the sheet that covered the child's head.

The stranger stooped and looked at the sleeping child, that seemed to be made uneasy by his glance, and turned moaning away.

"It looks as if it were for another world—not this," said the gentleman.

The flush spread over Mehetabel's brow. "Sir," she said in a fluttering voice, "You are not a doctor, are you?"

"Oh, dear, no!—a barrister."

"Then," said she, in a tone of relief, "you do not know. The child is very well, but young."

"That may be."

The young man returned to his seat.

"I have left a fishing-rod outside," he said. "I wanted Kink to accompany me on one of the ponds where there is a punt. There must be plenty of fish in these sheets of water?"

"I believe there are, sir. As Jonas is away, perhaps Samuel Rocliffe can help you. He is my husband's nephew, and lives in the cottage, a little further down."

"Thank you, I'll look him up. But, hang me, if I like to leave—with such attractions here I do not care to leave."

After standing, considering a moment, hardly taking his eyes off Mehetabel, he said—"My pretty little hostess, if ever I begrudged a man in my life, I begrudge Jonas Kink—his wife. Come and tell me when you find him intolerable, and see if I cannot professionally help you to be rid of such a curmudgeon. Who knows?—the time may come! My name is Markham."

Then he departed.

CHAPTER XXXIV. — THE PICTURE

Meanwhile Bideabout was on his way to the town of Guildford. He made slow progress, for old Clutch had no mind for speed. The horse was mistrustful as to whither he was going, and how he would be treated on reaching his destination. No amount of beating availed. He had laid on his winter growth of hair, which served as a mat, breaking the force of the strokes administered. He was proof against kicks, for whenever Jonas extended his legs for the purpose of bringing his heels sharply against the sides of Clutch, the old horse drew a deep inspiration and blew himself out; thus blunting the force of the heels driven into him.

At length, however, Jonas and old Clutch did reach Guildford. To old Clutch's great astonishment he found himself in a town new to him, more populous than Godalming; and being strongly convinced that he had done enough, and that every house was an inn open to receive him, and being eager to make himself comfortable, he endeavored to carry his master into a china-shop, then into a linen-draper's shop, and next into a green-grocer's.

Jonas was constrained to stable his obstinate steed in the first tavern he came to, and to make the rest of his way on foot.

Guildford is, to this day, a picturesque old town, dominated by the ruins of a fine royal castle, and with a quaint Grammar School and hospital. At the present time it is going through immense transformation. It has become a favorite retiring place for old officers of the army, supplanting in this respect Cheltenham. But at the period of this tale it was a sleepy, ancient, county town that woke to life on market days, and rested through the remainder of the week. It did not work six days and keep one Sabbath, but held the Sabbath for six days and woke to activity on one only.

Now nobody quite knows who are all the new people that flow into the villas, and flood the suburbs. At the period whereof we tell there were no invaders of the place. Everybody knew every one else in his own clique, and knew of and looked down on every one else in the clique below him, and thanked God that he only knew of him, and did not know him; and looked up at and slandered every one else in the clique above him.

At the time of which we tell there was no greater joy to those in each of the many cliques than to be able to stare at those who belonged to a clique esteemed lower, and to ask who those people were, and profess never to have heard their names, and to wonder out of what dungheap they had sprung.

At that time the quintessence of society in the town consisted of such as were called upon and returned the calls of the county families. Now, alas, almost every country gentleman's house in the neighborhood is no longer occupied by its ancient proprietors, and is sold or let to successful tradespeople, so that the quintessence of society in the town plumes itself on not knowing the occupants of these stately mansions.

At that time the family that inhabited a house which had been built fifty years before regarded with contempt those who occupied one built only thirty years before. At that time those who had a remote connection by cousinship twice removed with an Honorable, deemed themselves justified in considering every one else, not so privileged, as dishonorable.

Now all this is past, or is in process of passing away, and in Guildford and its suburbs, as elsewhere, the old order changeth, and the poll of a Parish Council teaches men their levels in the general estimation.

Without much difficulty, Jonas Kink was able to discover where the artist, Iver Verstage, had his house and his studio. The house was small, in a side street, and the name was on the door.

Jonas was ushered into the workshop by an elderly maid, and then saw Iver in a blouse with his arms tied about with string; a mahl-stick in one hand and a brush in the other.

Iver was surprised to see the Broom-Squire, and indisposed to welcome him. He purposely retained stick and brush in his hands, so as not to be able to strike palms with the man who had deprived him of the woman he admired and loved best in the world; and whom he suspected of misusing her.

Jonas looked about the studio, and his eye was caught by a picture of Mehetabel at the well head. The young artist had devoted his best efforts to finishing his study, and working it up into an effective and altogether charming painting.

The Broom-Squire held in the right hand the stick wherewith he had thrashed old Clutch, and this he now transferred to the left, whilst extending his right hand and forcing a smile on his leathery face. The artist made a pretence of seeking out some place where he could put down the articles encumbering his hands, but finding none, he was unable to return the salutation.

"Let bygones be bygones," said Jonas, and he dropped his hand. "Fine pictur' that, very like my wife. What, now, have you sold that for?"

"It is not sold at all. I do not think I shall part with the painting."

"Why not?" asked Jonas, with a malevolent twinkle in his eyes and a flush on his cheek-bones.

"Because it is a good sample of my ability which I can show to such as come as customers, and also because it reminds me of an old friend."

"Then you may take my portrait," said Jonas, "and sell this. Mine will do as well, and you knowed me afore you did Matabel."

"That is true," laughed Iver, "but I am not sure that you would make so striking subject, so inspiring to the artist. Did you come all the way from the Punch-Bowl to see the painting?"

"No, I didn't," answered Jonas.

"Then had you business in the town?"

"None particular."

"Was it to give me the pleasure of seeing you and asking after old friends at Thursley?"

"Old friends," sneered Bideabout; "much the like o' you cares for them as is old. It's the young and the bloomin' as is to your fancy. And I reckon it ain't friends as you would ask about, but a friend, and that's Matabel. Well, I don't mind tellin' of yer that she's got a baby, but I s'pose you've heard that, and the child ain't over strong and healthy, such as ort to be in the Punch-Bowl, where we're all hard as nails."

"Aye, not in physique only?"

"I don't know nothin about physic. I didn't take it when I were poorly, and nobody ever did in the Punch-Bowl as I've heard tell on. I sent once to Gorlmyn (Godalming) for a sleepin' draught, when I were bad wi' that shot in my shoulder as you knows of. But I never took it, not I."

"So you've come to see me?"

"Oh, yes, I've come, civil and neighbor-like, to see you."

"What about? Will you sit down?"

"Thanky, I just about like to stand. Yes, I've come to see you—on business."

"On business!"

"Yes, on business. You're trustee, I hear, for the child."

"To be sure I am. Mother put away a hundred pounds, and father has added fifty to it—and it is for your little one, some day."

"Well," said Jonas, "what I've come about is I wants it now."

"What, the hundred and fifty pounds?"

"Aye, I reckon the hundred and fifty pounds."

"But the money is not left to you."

"I know it b'aint; I want it for the child."

"You are not going to have it."

"Look here. Master Iver Verstage, you never ort to ha' been made trustee for my child. It's so much as puttin' a slight and an insult on me. If that child be mine then I'm the one as should have the trust. Don't I know best what the child wants? Don't I know best how to lay it out for its advantage? The money ort to ha' been put in my hands and in none other. That's my opinion."

"Bideabout!" answered Iver, "it is not a question as to what my father and mother should have done. I did not seek to be made trustee. It was a freak on the part of my dear mother. As she has done it, there it is; neither you nor I can alter that."

"Yes. You can renounce trusteeship."

"That will not help. Then I suppose the money would go into Chancery, and would be consumed there without any of it reaching the child."

Jonas considered, and then shook his head.

"You can hand it over to me."

"Then I should be held responsible and have to refund when the little fellow comes of age."

"He may never come of age."

"That neither you nor I can tell."

"Now look here," said the Broom-Squire, assuming an air of confidence, "between you and me, as old acquaintances, and me as gave you the feathers out o' a snipe's wing to make your first brush—and, so to speak, launched you in your career of greatness—between you and me I'm in an awkward perdic'ment. Through the failure of the Wealden Bank, of which you've heard tell, I've lost pretty much everything as I had managed to save through years of toil and frugality. And now I'm menaced in my little property. I don't know as I shall be able to hold it, unless some friend comes to the help. Well, now, who'll that little property go to but my son—that there precious darlin' baby as we're talkin' about. He'll grow out o' his squawlin', and he'll want his property unincumbered and clear, as it came to me. That I can't give him unless helped. I don't ask that there hundred and fifty pounds for myself. I know very well that I can't have it for myself. But I demand it for the child; it is now or never can the little estate in the Punch-Bowl be saved from fallin' into the hands of them darned lawyers. A stitch in time saves nine, and a little help now may be all that is wanted to keep the property clean and clear and unembarrassed wi' debt. If once we get our heads under water we'll all get drowned, me and Matabel and the kid—sure as crabs ain't garden apples."

"That may be very true, Bideabout," answered Iver, "but for all that I cannot let the money out of my control."

"Ain't you bound to spend it on the child?"

"I am bound to reserve it whole and intact for the child."

"But can you not see," persisted Jonas, "that you are doing that for the child, it would wish above all, when come to years of discretion."

"That is possible, but my hands are tied."

"In truth you will not."

"I cannot."

"I don't believe you. It is because you want to spite me that you will not help."

"Not at all, Bideabout. I wish well to the child and its mother, and, of course, to you. But I cannot break a trust."

"You will not?"

"If no other word will suit you—be it so—I will not."

Jonas Kink fumed blood red.

"You think to have me there. I shouldn't be surprised but it's you who are at the bottom of all—and will buy me up and buy me out, that you and Matabel may have the place to yourselves. It shall never be. I know what was meant when Sanna Verstage made you trustee. I am to be reckoned with. I can assure you of that. I shall find means to keep my property from you and my wife also."

He raised his stick and fell to beating the picture of Mehetabel with it; till it was rent to rags.

"Not even her picture shall you have—and I would it were her I were slashin' and breakin' to pieces as I've done to this picture. It may come to that in the end—but out of my power and into your hands she shall never go."

CHAPTER XXXV. — THE ONLY CHANGE

Jonas Kink, after much objurgation and persuasion, had induced old Clutch to leave his stable at Guildford, and return home by way of Godalming.

But the horse was unfamiliar with the road. He had been ridden along it in reverse direction in the morning, but, as every one knows, a way wears quite a different aspect under such circumstances. Old

Clutch was mistrustful. Having been taken such an unprecedentedly long journey, he was without confidence that his master might not prolong the expedition to a still further distance. Accordingly he was exceedingly troublesome and unmanageable on the road from Guildford, and his behavior served to work the temper of Jonas to the extremity of irritability.

The horse, on approaching Godalming, began to limp. Bideabout descended, and examined each hoof. He could see no stone there, nothing to account for the lameness of old Clutch, which, however, became so pronounced as he entered the street of the little town that he was obliged to stable the beast, and rest it.

Then he went direct to the offices of a small attorney of the name of Barelegs, who had been engaged on his business.

As he entered the office, Mr. Barelegs looked up from a deed he was reading, turned his head, and contemplated his client.

There was something in his manner that angered Jonas, already excited and inclined to be annoyed at trifles, and he said irritably,—

"You look at me. Mister Barelegs, just as does old Clutch when I come into the stable, expectin' a feed of corn, he does."

"And no doubt he deserves it."

"He thinks he does, but he don't."

"And no doubt he gets his feed."

"There is doubt about it. He gets it when I choose to give it, not when he glowers at me—that way, he's wonderful artificial is old Clutch."

"I dare be sworn, Mr. Kink, if he has served you well, he expects to be paid for it."

"He's an owdacious old Radical," observed Jonas. "Just now he's shamming lame, becos I rode him into Guildford, and he likes the inn here. There's an old broken-winded, galled gray mare, I reckon he's set his fancy on in the same yard, and I'm pretty sure this lameness means nothin' more nor less than that he wants to be a-courtin'. To see them two hosses, when they meet, rubbin' heads, is enough to make a fellow sick. And Clutch, at his age too—when he ort to be thinkin' of his latter end!"

"We've all our little weaknesses, Mr. Kink, man and beast alike. You courted—not so long ago."

"I never courted in the ridic'lous fashion of other folks. I'd none of your yardin', and aiblen' to aiblen', and waistin'."

"What do you mean, Mr. Kink?"

"Don't you know the three stages o' courtin here? Fust o' all, the young pair walks each other about a yard apart—that's yardin'. Then they gits more familiar, and takes each other's arms. That's wot we calls in these parts aiblen' to aiblen', and last, when they curls their arms round each other, won'erful familiar, that's called waistin'. No, I never went through none o' them courses in my courtship. I weren't such a fool. But I was tellin' you about old Clutch."

"I want to hear about that party. What if he does not receive his feed. Doesn't he kick?"

Jonas laughed ironically.

"He tried that on once. But I got a halter, and fastened it to his tail by the roots, and made a loop t'other end, and when he put up his heels I slipped one into the loop, and he nigh pulled his tail off at the stump."

"Then, perhaps he bites."

"He did try that on," Jonas admitted, "but he won't try that on again."

"How did you cure him of biting?" asked the solicitor.

"I saw what he was up to, when I was a-grooming of him. He tried to get hold of my arm. I was prepared for him. I'd slipped my arm out o' my sleeve and stuffed the sleeve with knee-holm (butcher's broom), and when he bit he got the prickles into his mouth so as he couldn't shut it again, but stood yawnin' as if sleepy till I pulled 'em out. Clutch and I has our little games together—the teasy old brute—but I'm generally too much for him." After a little consideration Bideabout added, "It's only on the road I find him a little too cunnin' for me. Now he's pretendin to be lame, all 'long of his little love-affair with that gray hoss. Sometimes he lies down in the middle of the road. If I had my fowlin' piece I'd shoot off blank cartridge under his belly, and wouldn't old Clutch go up all fours into the air; but he knows well enough the gun is at home. Let old Clutch alone for wickedness."

"Well, Mr. Kink, you haven't come here to get my assistance against old Clutch, have you?"

"No," said Bideabout. "That's gospel. I ain't come here to tell about old Clutch; and it ain't against him as I want your assistance. It is against Iver Verstage, the painter chap at Guildford."

"What has he been doing?"

"Nuthin'! that's just it. He's made treasurer, trustee, or whatever you're pleased to call it, for my baby; and I want the money out."

"Out of his pocket and into yours?"

"Exactly. I don't see why I'm to have all the nussin' and feedin' and clothin' of the young twoad, and me in difficulties for money, and he all the while coaxing up a hundred and fifty pounds, and laying of it out, and pocketin' the interest, and I who have all the yowls by night, and the washin' and dressin' and feedin' and all that, not a ha'penny the better."

"How does this person you name come to be trustee for the child?"

"Becos his mother made him so; and that old idjot of a Simon Verstage, his father, goes and makes the sum bigger by addin' fifty pounds to her hundred, so now there's this tidy little sum lies doin no good to nobody."

"I cannot help you. You cannot touch the principal till the child is of age, and then it will go to the child, and not you."

"Why! that's twenty-one years hence. That's what I call reg'lar foreright (awkward); and worse than foreright, it's unreasonable. The child is that owdacious in the cradle, I shouldn't be surprised when he's of age he would deny me the money."

"The interest will be paid to you."

"What is that—perhaps sixpence in the year. Better than nuthin', but I want the lot of it. Look you here, Master Barelegs, I know very well that I owe you money. I know very well that unless I can raise two hundred pounds, and that pretty smart, I shall have to mortgage my little bit of land to you. I don't forget that. But I daresay you'd rather have the money down than my poor little bit of lean and ribby take out o' the common. You shall have the money if you'll help me to get it. If I can't get that money into my fingers—I'm a done man. But it's not only that as troubles me. It is that the Rocliffes, and the Snellings, and the Boxalls, and Jamaica Cheel will make my life miserable. They'll mock at me, and I shall be to them just as ridic'lous an object as was Thomas Rocliffe after he'd lost his Countess. That's twenty-three years agone, and he can't get over it. Up comes the Countess Charlotte on every occasion, whenever any one gets across with him. It will be the same with me. I told 'em all to their faces that I had got them into my power, and just as the net was about to snap—then the breaking of the bank upset all my reckonings, and spoiled the little game—and what is worse, has made me their sport. But I won't stand no nonsense from old Clutch, nor will I from them."

"I confess I do not quite understand about this money. Was it left by will?"

"Left by will right enough," answered Bideabout. "You see the old woman, Sanna Verstage, had a bit of property of her own when she married, and then, when it came to her dyin', she set to write a will, and wanted to leave a hundred pounds to the little twoad. But she called up and consulted Simon, and he sed, 'Put on another fifty, Sanna, and I'll make that up. I always had a likin' for Matabel.' So that is how it came about as I've heard, and a hundred pound came out of her estate, and Simon made up the other fifty. And for why—but to spite me, I dun know, but they appointed Iver to be trustee. Now, I'm in difficulties about the land. I reckon when I'm dead it will go to the little chap, and go wi' all the goodness drained out of it—acause I have had to mortgage it. Whereas, if I could touch that money now, there'd be nothing of the kind happen."

"I am very sorry for you," remarked the lawyer. "But that bequest is beyond your reach so long as the child lives."

"What's that you say?"

"I say that unless the poor little creature should die, you cannot finger the money."

"And if it did die, would it be mine?"

"Of course it would. By no other way can you get it, but, please Heaven, the child may grow to be a strong man and outlive you."

"It's wonderful weakly," said Jonas, meditatively.

"Weakly in the cradle is sturdy at the table," answered the solicitor, slightly altering a popular maxim.

"It's that peevish and perverse—"

"Then it takes after its father," laughed Mr. Barelegs. "You can't complain of that, Kink."

The Broom-Squire took his hat and stick and rose to leave.

Mr. Barelegs stayed him with a wave of the hand, and, "A word with you further, Mr. Kink. You gracefully likened me, just now, to your horse Clutch expecting his feed of oats after having served you well. Now I admit that, like Clutch, I have spent time and thought and energy in your service, and, like Clutch, I expect my feed of oats. I think we must have all clear and straight between us, and that at once. I have made out my little account with you, and here it is. You will remember that, acting on your instructions, I have advanced money in certain transactions that have broken down through the unfortunate turn in your affairs caused by the failure of the Wealden Bank. There is a matter of two hundred, and something you owe me for payments made and for services. I daresay you are a little put about now, but it will be useful to you to know all your liabilities so as to make provision for meeting them. I will not be hard on you as a client, but, of course, you do not expect me to make you a present of my money, and my professional service."

Jonas took the account reluctantly, and his jaw fell.

"I dare say," pursued the solicitor, "that among your neighbors you may be able to borrow sufficient. The Rocliffes, your own kinsmen, are, I fear, not very flush with money."

"Ain't got any to bless themselves with," said Jonas.

"But the Boxalls are numerous, and fairly flourishing. They have probably put away something, and as neighbors and friends—"

"I've quarrelled with them. I can't borrow of them," growled Bideabout.

"Then there are the Snellings—"

"I've offended them as well."

"But you have other friends."

"I haven't one."

"There is Simon Verstage, a warm man; he could help you in an emergency."

"He's never been the same with me since I married Matabel, his adopted daughter. He had other ideas for her, I fancy, and he is short and nasty wi' me now. I can't ask him."

"Have you then, really, no friends?"

"Not one."

"Then there must be some fault in you, Kink. A man who goes through life without making friends, and quarrels even with the horse that carries him, is not one who will leave a gap when he passes out of the world. I shall expect my money. If you see no other way of satisfying me, I must have a mortgage on your holding. I'll not press you at once—but, like Clutch, I shall want my feed of oats."

"Then," said Jonas, surlily, as he turned his hat about, and looked down into it, "I don't see no other chance of gettin the money than—"

"Than what?"

"That's my concern," retorted the Broom-Squire. "Now I'm goin' to see whether old Clutch is ready—or whether he be shammin' still."

CHAPTER XXXVI. — THE SLEEPING DRAUGHT

Jonas found that old Clutch was not lavishing endearments on the gray mare over the intervening partition of stalls, but was lying down on the straw. Nothing said or done would induce the horse to rise, and the hostler told Bideabout that he believed the beast was really lame. It had been overworked at its advanced age, and must be afforded rest.

"He's a Radical," said the Broom-Squire. "You move that gray into another stable and Clutch will forget about his lameness, I dare swear. He's twenty-five and has a liquorish eye, still—it's shameful."

Bideabout was constrained to walk from Godalming to the Punch-Bowl, and this did not serve to mend his humor. He reached home late at night, when the basin was full of darkness, and the only light that showed came from the chamber where Mehetabel sat with her baby.

When Jonas entered, he saw by the rushlight that she was not undressed, and heard by her voice that she was anxious.

"The baby is very unwell, Jonas," she said, and extending her hand, lit a tallow candle at the meagre flame of the rushlight.

As the wick flared, so did something flare up in the face of the Broom-Squire.

"Why do you look like that?" asked Mehetabel, for the look did not escape her.

"Main't I look as I choose?" he inquired surlily.

"It almost seemed as if you were glad to hear that my poor darling is ill," complained she.

"Ain't I glad to be home after bein' abroad all day a-wackin', and abusin' of old Clutch, and then had to walk from Gorlmyn (Godalming), and the aggravation of knowin' how as the hoss be shakin' his sides laughin' at me for doin of it. Wot's up with the kid?"

"I really cannot tell, Jonas; he's been restless and moaning all day. I have not been able to get him to sleep, and I am sure he has had one or two fits. He became white and stiff. I thought he'd a-died, and then my heartstrings were like breaking."

"Oh, drat your heartstrings, I don't care to hear of them. So, you thort he was dyin'. Perhaps he may. More wun'erful things happen than that. It's the way of half the babies as is born."

"It will kill me if mine is taken from me!" cried Mehetabel, and cast herself on her knees and embraced the cradle, regardless of the sprigs of spiked leaves she had stuck round it, and burst into an agony of tears.

"Now look here," said Jonas; "I've been tried enough wi' old Clutch to-day, and I don't want to be worreted at night wi' you. Let the baby sleep if it is sleepin', and get me my vittles. There's others to attend to in the world than squawlin' brats. It's spoilin' the child you are. That's what is the meanin' of its goings-on. Leave it alone, and take no notice, and it'll find out quick enough that squeals don't pay. I want my supper. Go after the vittles."

Mehetabel lay in her clothes that night. The child continued to be restless and fretted. Jonas was angry. If he was out all day he expected to rest well at night; and she carried the cradle in her arms into the spare room, where the peevishness of the child, and the rocking and her lullaby could not disturb her husband. As she bore the cradle, the sprigs of butcher's broom and withered chrysanthemums fell and strewed her path, leaving behind her a trail of dying flowers, and of piercing thorns, and berries like blood-drops. No word of sympathy had the Broom-Squire uttered; no token had he shown that he regarded her woes and was solicitous for the welfare of his child. Mehetabel asked for neither. She had learned to expect nothing from him, and she had ceased to demand of him what he was incapable of giving, or unwilling to show.

Next morning Mehetabel was prompt to prepare breakfast for her husband. The day was fine, but the light streaming in through the window served to show how jaded she was with long watching, with constant attention, and with harrowing care.

Always punctilious to be neat, she had smoothed her hair, tidied her dress, and washed the tears from her face, but she could not give brightness to the dulled eye or bloom to the worn cheek.

For a while the child was quiet, stupefied with weariness and long crying. By the early light Mehetabel had studied the little face, hungering after tokens of recovering powers, glad that the drawn features were relaxed temporarily.

"Where are you going to-day, Bideabout?" she asked, timidly, expecting a rebuff.

"Why do you ask?' was his churlish answer.

"Because—oh! if I might have a doctor for baby!"

"A doctor!" he retorted. "Are we princes and princesses, that we can afford that? There's no doctor nigher than Hazelmere, and I ain't goin' there. I suppose cos you wos given the name of a Duchess of Edom, you've got these expensive ideas in your head. Wot's the good of doctors to babies? Babies can't say what ails them."

"If—if—" began Mehetabel, kindly, "if I might have a doctor, and pay for it out of that fifteen pound that father let me have."

"That fifteen pound ain't no longer yours. And this be fine game, throwin' money away on doctors when we're on the brink of ruin. Don't you know as how the bank has failed, and all my money gone? The fifteen pound is gone with the rest."

"If you had but allowed me to keep it, it would not have been lost now," said Mehetabel.

"I ain't goin' to have no doctors here," said Bideabout, positively, "but I'll tell you what I'll do, and that's about as much as can be expected in reason. I'm goin' to Gorlmyn to fetch old Clutch; and I'll see a surgeon there and tell him whatever you like—and get a mixture for the child. But I won't pay more than half-a-crown, and that's wasted. I don't believe in doctors and their paint and water, as they gives us."

Jonas departed, and then the tired and anxious mother again turned to her child. The face was white spotted with crimson, the closed lids blue.

There was no certainty when Bideabout would return, but assuredly not before evening, as he walked to Godalming, and if he rode home on the lame horse, the pace would be slower than a walk.

Surely she could obtain advice and help from some of the mothers in the Punch-Bowl. Sally Rocliffe she would not consult. The gleam of kindness that had shone out of her when Mehetabel was in her trouble had long ago been quenched.

When the babe woke she muffled it in her shawl and carried the mite to the cottage of the Boxalls. The woman of that family, dark-skinned and gypsy-like, with keen black eyes, was within, and received the young mother graciously. Mehetabel unfolded her treasure and laid it on her knees—the child was now quiet, through exhaustion.

"I'll tell y' what I think," said Karon Boxall, "that child has been overlooked—ill-wished."

Mehetabel opened her eyes wide with terror.

"That's just about the long and short of it," continued Mrs. Boxall. "Do you see that little vein there, the color of 'urts. That's a sure sign. Some one bears the poor creature no love, and has cast an evil eye on it."

The unhappy mother's blood ran chill. This, which to us seems ridiculous and empty, was a grave and terrible reality to her mind.

"Who has done it?" she asked below her breath.

"That's not for me to say," answered the woman. "It is some one who doesn't love the babe, that's sure."

"A man or a woman?"

Mrs. Boxall stooped over the infant.

"A woman," she said, with assurance. "The dark vein be on the left han' side."

Mehetabel's thoughts ran to Sally Rocliffe. There was no other woman who could have felt ill-feeling against the hapless infant, now on her lap.

"What can I do?" she asked.

"There's nothin'. Misfortune and wastin' away will be to the child—though they do say, if you was to take it to Thor's Stone, and carry it thrice round, way of the sun, you might cast off the ill-wish. But I can't say. I never tried it."

"I cannot take it there," cried Mehetabel, despairingly, "the weather is too cold, baby too ill."

Then clasping the child to her bosom, and swaying herself, she sobbed forth—

"A little fish swims in the well.
So in my heart does baby dwell,
The king has sceptre, crown and ball,
You are my sceptre, crown and all."

She went home sobbing, and hugging her child, holding it away from the house of Sarah Rocliffe, lest that woman might be looking forth at her window, and deepen by her glance the spell that held and broke down her child.

Towards evening fall Jonas returned.

Directly he crossed the threshold, with palpitating eagerness Mehetabel asked—

"Have you seen the doctor?"

"Yes," he answered curtly.

"What did he say?"

"He'd got a pass'l o' learned names of maladies—I can't recollect them all. Tain't like as I should."

"But—did he give you any medicine?"

"Yes, I had to pay for it too."

"Oh, Jonas, do give it me, and tell me, are you quite sure you explained to him exactly what ailed baby?"

"I reckon I did."

"And the bottle, Jonas?"

"Don't be in such a won'erful hurry. I've other things to do than get that put yet. How is the child?"

"Rather better."

"Better!" he echoed, and Mehetabel, who looked intently in his face, saw no sign of satisfaction, rather of disappointment.

"Oh, Jonas!" she cried, "is it naught to you that baby is so ill? You surely don't want him to die?"

He turned fiercely on her, his face hard and gray, and his teeth shining—

"What makes you say that—you?"

"Oh, nothin', Jonas, only you don't seem to care a bit about baby, and rather to have a delight in his bein' so ill."

"He's better, you say?"

"Yes—I really do think it."

There was an unpleasant expression in his face that frightened her. Was it the eye of Jonas that had blighted the child? But no—Karon Boxall had said that it was ill-wished by a woman. Jonas left the room, ascended the stairs, and strode about in the chamber overhead.

Swaying in her chair, holding the infant to her heart, the sole heart that loved it, but loved it with a love ineffable, she heard her husband open the window, and then hastily shut it again. Then there was a pause in his movement overhead, and he came shortly after down the stairs. He held a phial in his hand—and without looking at Mehetabel, thrust it towards her, with the curt injunction, "Take."

"Perhaps," said the young mother, "as my darling is better, I need not give him the medicine."

"That's just like your ways," exclaimed the Broom-Squire, savagely. "Fust I get no rest till I promise to go to the doctor, and then when I've put myself about to go, and bring the bottle as has cost me half-a-crown, you won't have it."

"Indeed—it is only—"

"Oh, yes—only—to annoy me. The child is ill. I told the doctor all, and he said, that this would set it to rights and give it sleep, and rest to all of us." He was in a bad temper. Mehetabel did not venture to say more. She took the phial and placed it on the table. It was not wrapped up in paper.

Then Jonas hastily went forth. He had old Clutch to attend to.

Mehetabel remained alone, and looked at the medicine bottle; then she laid the infant on her knees and studied the little face, so blanched with dark rings round the eyes. The tiny hands were drawn up on the breast and clasped; she unfolded and kissed them.

Then she looked again at the phial.

There was something strange about it. The contents did not appear to have been well mixed, the upper portion of the fluid was dark, the lower portion white. How came this about? Jonas had ridden old Clutch home, and the movements of the horse were not smooth. The bottle in the pocket of Bideabout must have undergone such shaking as would have made the fluid contents homogeneous and of one hue. She held the bottle between herself and the light. There was no doubt about it, either the liquid separated rapidly, or had never been mixed.

She withdrew the cork and applied the mouth of the phial to her nose.

The scent of the medicine was familiar. It was peculiar. When had she smelt that odor before. Then she started. She remembered the little bottle containing laudanum, with the death's head on it, in the closet upstairs.

Hastily, her heart beating with apprehension, she laid her babe in the cradle, and taking the light, mounted to the upper chamber. She possessed the key of the cabinet in the wall. She had retained it because afraid to give it up, and Jonas had manufactured for himself a fresh key.

Now she unlocked the closet, and at once discovered the laudanum bottle.

It was half empty.

Some of it had been used.

How had it been used? Of that she had little doubt. The dangerous, sleep-bringing laudanum had been put into the medicine for the child. It was to make room for that that Jonas had opened the window and poured forth some of the contents.

A drop still hung on the top of the phial.

She shut and relocked the cupboard, descended, with dismay, despair in her heart, and taking the bottle from the table, dashed it into the fire upon the hearth. Then she caught her babe to her, and through floods of tears, sobbed: "There is none love thee but I—but I—but only I! O, my babe, my babe! My sceptre, crown, and all!"

In the blinding rain of tears, in the tumult of passion that obscured her eyes, that confused her brain, Mehetabel saw, heard nothing. She had but one sense—that of feeling, that thrilled through one fibre only attached to the helpless, suffering morsel in her arms—the infant she held to her breast, and which she would have liked to bury in her heart away from all danger, concealed from the malevolent eye, and the murderous hand.

All the mother's nature in her was roused and flared into madness. She alone loved this little creature, she alone stood between it and destruction. She would fight for it, defend it to her last breath, with every weapon wherewith she was endowed by nature.

After the first paroxysm of passion was passed, and a lull of exhaustion ensued, she looked up, and saw Bideabout enter, and as he entered he cast a furtive glance at the table, then at the child.

In a moment she resolved on the course she should adopt.

"Have you given the babe the draught?" he asked, with averted face.

"Not all."

"Of course, not all."

"Will it make baby sleep?" asked Mehetabel.

"O, sleep—sleep! yes—we shall have rest for one night—for many, I trust. O, do not doubt. It will make it sleep!"

CHAPTER XXXVII. — A MENACED LIFE

As soon as the Broom-Squire had gone out again to the "hog- pen," as a pigstye is called in Surrey, to give the pig its "randams and crammins," because Mehetabel was unable to do this because unable to leave the child, then she knelt by the hearth, put aside the turves, and, regardless of the fire, groped for the fragments of the broken phial, that nothing might betray to Bideabout her having rejected the medicine with which he had tampered.

She cut and burnt her fingers, but in the excitement of her feelings, was insensible to pain.

She had removed and secreted the glass before he returned. The babe was sleeping heavily, and snoring.

When Jonas came in and heard the sound from the cradle, a look of expectation came over his face.

"The child's burrin' like a puckeridge (night-jar)," he said. "Shouldn't wonder if the medicine ain't done him a lot o' good. It don't need a doctor to come and see to prescribe for a baby. All that little ones want is good sleep, and natur' does the rest."

Owing to the annoyance caused to Bideabout by the child's fretfulness during the night, Mehetabel occupied a separate chamber, the spare bedroom, along with her babe, and spent her broken nights under the great blue and white striped tent that covered the bed.

She had enjoyed but little sleep for several nights, and her days had been occupied by the necessary attention to the suffering child and the cares of the household. Because the babe was ill, that was no reason why his father's meals should be neglected, and because the mother was overwrought, he was not disposed to relieve her of the duties to the pigs and cows save on this one occasion.

That the poor little infant was really more at ease was obvious to the mother's watchful eye and anxious heart, but whether this were due to its malady, whatever that was, having taken a felicitous turn, or to mere exhaustion of powers, she was unable to decide, and her fears almost overbalanced her hopes.

She retired to sleep that night without much expectation of being able to obtain sleep. Her nerves were overstrung, and at times thought in her mind came to a standstill; it was as though a sudden hush came on all within her, so that neither did heart beat nor breath come. But for these pauses, her mind might have given way, a string have snapped, and her faculties have fallen into disorder.

It is said of Talleyrand that he needed no sleep, as his pulse ceased to beat after a certain number of strokes, for a brief space, and then resumed pulsation. During that pause, his physical and mental powers had time for recuperation. Be that as it may, it is certain that to some persons whose minds and feelings are put to extraordinary tension, greatly prolonged, there do come these halts in which all is blank, the brain ceases to think, and the heart to feel, and such gaps in the sequence of thought and emotion have a salutary effect.

Mehetabel did not undress. She had not put off her clothing for several nights. The night was cold, and she would probably have to be incessantly on the move, to meet the little sufferer's necessities, as they arose, and to watch it, whenever her fears prevailed over her hopes, and made her think that a protracted quiet was ominous.

The only light in the room emanated from a smouldering rush, sustained in a tall iron holder, the lower end of which was planted in a block of oak, and stood on the floor. Such holders, now become very scarce, were furnished with snuffers, so contrived that the rushlight had to be taken out of its socket and snuffed by them, instead of their being brought to the rush.

Of rushlights there were two kinds, one, the simplest, consisted of a dry rush dipped in a little grease. The light emitted from such a candle was feeble in the extreme. The second, a superior rushlight, had the rush pealed of its bark with the exception of one small strip which held the pith from breaking. This pith was dipped in boiling fat, and when the tallow had condensed it was dipped again, and the candle given as many coats as was desired. Such a rushlight was a far more useful candle, and if it did not emit as large a flame and give forth so much light as a dip which had a cotton wick it was sufficient to serve most purposes for which in a farmhouse artificial illumination was required.

The first and inferior sort of rushlight was that which Matabel allowed herself for the sick-room.

When she laid her head on the pillow and threw the patched-work quilt over her shoulders the cool of the pillow struck through her head and relieved the fire that had raged therein.

She could not sleep.

She thought over what had happened. She considered Bideabout's action as calmly as possible. Was it conceivable that he should seek the life of his own child? He had shown it no love, but it was a far cry from lack of parental affection to deliberate attempt at murder.

What gain would there be to him in the death of his child? She was too innocent and simple to think of Mrs. Verstage's bequest as supplying the motive. As far as she could find there was nothing to account for Jonas' desire to hasten the child's death save weariness at its cries which distressed him at night, and this was no adequate reason. There was another, but that she put from her in disgust. Bad as Bideabout might be she could not credit him with that.

What was that bottle which Jonas had been given by the doctor when his arm was bound up? Of laudanum she knew nothing, but remembered that it had been recommended as a means for giving him the rest he so required. It was a medicine intended to produce sleep. He had refused it because afraid lest he should administer to himself, or have administered to him, an overdose which would cause him to sleep too soundly, and slide away into the slumber of death.

It was possible that the surgeon at Godalming knew that Jonas possessed this phial, and had given him the medicine for the child along with instructions as to how many drops of the laudanum he was to add to the mixture, to make it serve its proper purpose.

If that were so, then the Broom-Squire had acted as directed by a competent person and for the good of his child, and she, his wife, had cruelly, wickedly, misjudged him. Gentle, generous, incapable of harboring an evil thought, Matabel at once and with avidity seized on this solution, and applied it to her heart to ease its pain and relieve the pressure that weighed on it.

Under the lightening of her anxiety caused by this Mehetabel fell asleep, for how long she was unable to guess. When she awoke it was not that she heard the cry of her child, but that she was aware of a tread on the floor that made the bed vibrate.

Instead of starting up, she unclosed her eyes, and saw in the room a figure that she at once knew was that of Jonas. He was barefooted, and but partially dressed. He had softly unhasped the door and stolen in on tip-toe. Mehetabel was surprised. It was not his wont to leave his bed at night, certainly not for any concern he felt relative to the child; yet now he was by the cradle, and was stooping over it with his head turned, so that his ear was applied in a manner that showed he was listening to the child's breathing. As his face was turned the feeble light of the smouldering rushlight was on it.

Mehetabel did not stir. It was a pleasing revelation to her that the father's heart had warmed to his child, and that he was sufficiently solicitous for the feeble life to be disturbed thereby at night.

Jonas remained listening for a minute, then he rose erect and retreated from the chamber on tiptoe and closed the door noiselessly behind him.

A smile of pleasure came on Mehetabel's lips, the first that had creamed them for many a week, and she slipped away again into sleep, to be aroused after a brief period by the restlessness and exclamations of the child that woke with hunger.

Then promptly she rose up, went to the cradle, and lifted the child out, coaxed it and sang to the infant as she seated herself on the bedside nursing it.

As she swayed herself, holding the child, the door that was ajar opened slightly, and by the feeble light of the rush she could discern something without, and the flame was reflected in human eyes.

"Is that you, Jonas?" she called.

There was no reply, but she could hear soft steps withdrawing in the direction of his room.

"He is ashamed of letting me see how anxious he is, how really fond of the poor pet he is in heart." As the child's hands relaxed, and it sobbed off to sleep, Mehetabel laid it again in the cradle. It was abundantly evident that the infant was getting better. In a couple of days, doubtless, it would be well.

Glad of this, relieved of the care that had gnawed at her heart, she now slipped between the sheets of the bed. The babe would probably sleep on till dawn, and she could herself enjoy much-needed rest.

Then she dreamt that she and her little one were in a fair garden full of flowers; the child had grown somewhat and could enjoy play. She thought that she was plucking violets and making a crown for her baby's head, and then a little staff covered with the same purple, fragrant flowers, to serve as sceptre, and that she approached her little one on her knees, and bent to it, and sang:—

"The king has sceptre, crown and ball,
You are my sceptre, crown, and all!"

But then there fell a shadow on them, and this shadow cut off all light from her and from her child. She looked and saw Jonas. He said nothing, but stood where the sun shone and he could obscure it.

She lifted her babe and moved it away from the blighting shadow into warmth and brightness once more. Yet was this but for a moment, as again the shadow of Jonas fell over them. Once more she moved the child, but with like result. Then with a great effort she rose from her knees, carrying the child to go away with it, far, far from Jonas—and in her effort to do so woke.

She woke to see by the expiring rush-candle and the raw light of early dawn, that the Broom-Squire was in the room, and was stooping over the cradle. Still drunk with sleep, she did not stir, did not rally her senses at once.

Then she beheld how he lifted the pillow from under the infants head, went down on his knees, and thrust the pillow in upon the child's face, holding it down resolutely with a hand on each side.

With a shriek of horror, Mehetabel sprang out of bed and rushed at him, stayed his arms, and unable to thrust them back, caught the cradle and plucked it to her, and released the babe, that gasped—seized it in her arms, glued it to her bosom, and dashing past Jonas before he had risen to his feet, ran down the stairs, and left the house—never to enter it again.

CHAPTER XXXVIII. — SHUT OUT

A raw gray morning.

Mehetabel had run forth into it with nothing over her head, no shawl about her shoulders, with hair tangled, and eyes dazed, holding her child to her heart, with full resolve never again to set foot across the threshold of the farmhouse of Jonas Kink.

No doubt whatever remained now in her mind that the Broom-Squire had endeavored to compass the death of his child, first by means of poison, and then by suffocation.

Nothing would ever induce her again to risk the precious life of her child at his hands. She had no thought whither she should go, how she should live—her sole thought was to escape from Jonas, and by putting a distance between herself and him, place the infant beyond danger.

As she ran up the lane from the house she encountered Sally Rocliffe at the well head.

"Where be you goyne to, like that; and with the child, too?" asked the woman.

Mehetabel drew the little face of the babe to her, lest the eye of its aunt should light on it. She could not speak, palpitating with fear, as she was.

"What be you runnin' out for this time o' the mornin'?" asked Mrs. Rocliffe again.

"I cannot tell you," gasped the mother.

"But I will know."

"I shall never, never go back again," cried Mehetabel.

"Oh! he's kicked you out, has he? That's like Jonas."

"I'm runnin' away.

"And where be yo goyne to?"

"I don't know."

"But I do," said Mrs. Rocliffe with a chuckle.

Mehetabel gave no thought to her words. She thrust past her, and ran on.

Fear, love, gave strength to her limbs. She had no consideration for herself, that she was dishevelled and incompletely clad, that she had eaten nothing; she sped up the side of the Common, to escape from the Punch-Bowl, the place where she had weltered in misery. There was no hope for her and her child till she had escaped from that.

In the cold air, charged with moisture, the larks were singing. A ploughboy was driving his horses to the field that was to be turned up by the share.

As she passed him he stared at her with surprise. She reached the village. The blacksmith was up and about; he was preparing to put a tire on a cart-wheel. For this purpose he had just kindled a fire of turf "bats," that were heaped round the fire on the ground outside the forge. He looked up with astonishment as Mehetabel sped past, and cast to her the question, "Wot's up?" which, however, she did not stay to answer.

She made no tarry till she reached the Ship Inn. There she entered the porch, and would have gone through the door into the house, had she not been confronted by Polly, the maid, who at that moment was coming up the passage from the bar.

Polly made no attempt to give room for Mehetabel to pass; she saluted her with a stare and a look at her from head to feet, full of insolence.

"Wot do you want?" asked the girl.

"I wish to see and speak to father," answered Mehetabel.

"I always heard as your father lies in Thursley Churchyard," answered the servant.

"I mean I should like to speak with Mr. Verstage."

"Oh! the landlord?"

"Yes; the landlord. Where is he?"

"Don' know. Somewhere about, I reckon."

"It is cold, and my child is ill. I would go into the kitchen, by the fire."

"Why don't you then go home?"

"I have no home."

"Oh! it's come to that, is it?"

"Yes. Let me in."

"No, indeed. This ain't the place for you. If you think you're goyne to be mistress and order about here you're mistaken. You go along; I'm goyne to shut the door."

Mehetabel had not the spirit to resent this insolence.

She turned in the porch and left the inn, that had once been her home, and the only home in which she had found happiness.

She made her way to the fields that belonged to Simon Verstage, and after wandering through a ploughed glebe she found him.

"Ah, Matabel!" said he, "glad to see you. What brings you here so early in the day?"

"Dear father, I cannot tell you all, but I have left Bideabout. I can stay with him no longer, something has happened. Do not press me to tell—at least not now. I can never return to the Punch-Bowl. Will you take me in?"

The old man mused.

"I'll consult Polly. I don't know what she'll say to it. I'm rather dependent on her now. You see, I know nothing of the house, I always put that into Susanna's charge, and now poor Sanna is gone, Polly has taken the management. Of course, she makes mistakes, but wun'erfully few. In fact, it is wun'erful how she fits into Sanna's place, and manages the house and all—just as if she had been brought up to it. I'll go and ask her. I couldn't say yes without, much as I might wish."

Mehetabel shook her head.

The old man was become feeble and dependent. He had no longer a will of his own:

"I will not trouble you, dear father, to ask Polly. I am quite sure what her answer will be. I must go further. Who is Guardian?"

"That's Timothy Puttenham, the wheelwright."

Then Mehetabel turned back in the direction of the village and came in front of the shop. Puttenham and his apprentice were engaged on the fire, and Mehetabel stood, with the babe folded in her arms, watching them at work. They might not be disturbed at the critical period when the tire was red hot and had to be fitted to the wheel.

A circle of flame and glowing ashes and red-hot iron was on the ground. At a little distance lay a flat iron disc, called the "platform"; with a pole in the centre through which ran a spindle. On this metal plate lay a new cast wheel, and the wright with a bar screwed a nut so as to hold the cart-wheel down firmly on the "platform."

"Now, boy, the pincers!"

Then he, grasping a long pair of forceps, his apprentice with another, laid hold of the glowing tire, and raising it from the fire carried it scintillating to the wheel, lifted it over the spindle, and dropped it about the woodwork. Then, at once, they seized huge hammers and began to belabor the tire, to drive it on to the wheel, which smoked and flamed.

"Water, boy, water!"

The apprentice threw water from a pitcher over the tire throughout its circumference, dulling its fire, and producing clouds of steam.

Mehetabel, well aware that at this juncture the wright must not be interfered with, drew close to the fire, and kneeling by it warmed herself and the sleeping child, whilst she watched the sturdy men whirling their hammers and beating the tire down into place around the wheel.

At length the wright desisted. He leaned on his great hammer; and then Mehetabel timidly addressed him.

"Please, Mr. Puttenham, are you not Guardian of the Poor?"

"Certainly, Mrs. Kink."

"May I be put in the Poors' House?"

"You!"

The wheelwright opened his eyes very wide.

"Yes, Mr. Puttenham, I have no home."

"Why, Matabel! What is the sense of this? Your home is in the Punch-Bowl."

"I have left it."

"Then you must return to it again."

"I cannot. Take me into the Poors' House."

"My good girl, this is rank nonsense. The Poor House is not for you, or such as you."

"I need its shelter more than most. I have no home."

"Are you gone off your head?"

"No, sir. My mind is sound, but to the Punch-Bowl I cannot, and will not, return. No, never!"

"Matabel," said the wheelwright, "I suppose you and Jonas have had a quarrel. Bless you! Such things happen in married life, over and over again, and you'll come together and love each other all the better for these tiffs. I know it by experience."

"I cannot go back! I will not go back!"

"It is not cannot or will not—it is a case of must. That is your home. But this I will do for you. Go in and ask my old woman to let you have some breakfast, and I'll send Jack"—he signed to his apprentice— "and bid him tell Bideabout where you are, and let him fetch you. We mustn't have a scandal."

"If Jonas comes, I shall run away."

"Whither?"

That Mehetabel could not say.

"Where can you go? Nowhere, save to your husband's house. For God's sake!" he suddenly exclaimed, knocking his hammer on the tire, "don't say you are going to Guildford—to Iver Verstage."

Mehetabel raised her heavy eyes, and looked the wheelwright frankly in the face. "I would rather throw myself and baby into one of the Hammer Ponds than do that."

"Right! You're a good gal. But there was no knowing. Folks talk. Come in! You shall have something—and rest a while."

The kind, well-intentioned man laid his large hand on her shoulder and almost forced her, but gently, towards the house. She would not enter the door till he had promised not to send for Jonas.

Selena Puttenham, the wright's wife, was a loquacious and inquisitive woman, and she allowed Mehetabel no rest. She gave her bread and milk with readiness, and probed her with questions which Mehetabel could not answer without relating the whole horrible truth, and this she was resolved not to do.

The wright was busy, and could not remain in his cottage. The wife, with the kindest intentions, was unable to restrain herself from putting her guest on the rack. The condition of Mehetabel was one to rouse curiosity. Why was she there, with her baby, in the early morning? Without having even covered her head; fasted and jaded? Had there been a quarrel. If so—about what? Had Bideabout beaten her? Had he thrust her out and locked the door? If so, in what had she offended him? Had she been guilty of some grievous misdemeanor?

At length, unable further to endure the torture to which she was subjected, Mehetabel sprang up, and insisted on leaving the cottage.

Without answering Mrs. Puttenham's question as to whither she was going, what were her intentions, the unhappy girl hastened out of the village clasping in her arms the child, which had begun to sob.

And now she made her way towards Witley, of which Thursley was a daughter parish. She would find the Vicar, who had always treated her with consideration, and even affection. The distance was considerable, in her weary condition, but she plodded on in hopes. He was a man of position and authority, and she could trust him to protect her and the child. To him she would tell all, in confidence that he would not betray her secret.

At length, so fagged that she could hardly walk, her arms cramped and aching, her nerves thrilling, because the child was crying, and would not be comforted, she reached the Vicarage, and rang at the back door bell. Some time elapsed before the door was opened; and then the babe was screaming so vociferously, and struggling in her arms with such energy, that she was not able to make herself heard when she asked for the Parson.

The woman who had answered the summons was a stranger, consequently did not know Mehetabel. She made signs to her to go away.

The cries of the child became more violent, and the mother's efforts were directed towards pacifying it. "Let me come in, I pray! I pray!" she asked with a brow, in spite of the cold, bathed in perspiration.

"I cannot! I must not!" answered the woman. She caught her by the arm, drew her aside, and said—"Do you not know? Look! the blinds are all down. He died in the night!"

"Dead!" cried Mehetabel, reeling back. "My God! whither shall I go?"

CHAPTER XXXIX. — AT THE SILK MILL

Mehetabel sank on the grass by the drive.

"I am worn out. I can go no further," she said, and bowed her head over the child.

"You cannot remain here. It is not seemly—a house of mourning," said the woman.

"He would not mind, were he alive," sobbed Mehetabel. "He would have cared for me and my babe; he was always kind."

"But he is not alive; that makes the difference," said the servant. "You really must still the child or go away."

"I cannot go another step," answered Mehetabel, raising her head and sinking it again, after she had spoken.

"I don't know what to do. This is unreasonable; I'll go call the gardener. If you won't go when asked you must be removed by force."

The woman retired, and presently the gardener came up. He knew Mehetabel—that is to say, knew who she was.

"Come," said he, "my cottage is just yonder. You must not remain here on the green, and in the cold. No wonder the child screams. There is a fire in my house, and you can have what you like for a while, till you are rested. Give me your hand."

Mehetabel allowed him to raise her, and she followed him mechanically from the drive into the cottage, that was warm and pleasant.

"There now, missus," said the man; "make yourself comfortable for an hour or two."

The rest, the warmth, were grateful to Mehetabel. She was almost too weary to thank the man with words, but she looked at him with gratitude, and he felt that her heart was over full for her to speak. He returned to his work, and left her to herself. There was no one else in the cottage, as he was a widower, and had no family.

After a considerable time, when Mehetabel had had time to recruit her strength, he reappeared. The short winter day was already closing in. The cold black vapors rose over the sky, obscuring the little light, as though grudging the earth its brief period of illumination.

"I thought I'd best come, you know," said the man, "just to tell you that I'm sorry, but I can't receive you here for the night. I'm a widower, and folk might talk. Why are you from home?"

"I ran away. I cannot return to the Punch-Bowl."

"Well, now. That's curious!" said the gardener. "Time out of mind I've had it in my head to run away when my old woman was rampageous. I've knowed a man who actually did run to Americay becos his wife laid on him so. But I never, in my experience, heard of a woman runnin' away from her husband, that is to say—alone. You ain't got no one with you, now?"

"Yes, my baby."

"I don't mean that. Well, it is coorious, a woman runnin' away with her baby. I'm terrible sorry, but I can't take you in above another half-hour. Where are you thinking of goyne to?"

"I know of no where and no one."

"Why not try Missus Chivers at Thursley. You was at her school, I suppose?"

"Yes, I was there."

"Try her, and all will come right in the end."

Mehetabel rose; her child was now asleep.

"Look here," said the gardener. "Here's a nice plaid shawl, as belonged to my missus, and a wun'erful old bonnet of hers—as the cat has had kittens in since she went to her rest—and left me to mine. You are heartily welcome. I can't let you turn out in the cold with nothing on your head nor over your shoulders."

Mehetabel gladly accepted the articles of clothing offered her. She had already eaten of what the man had placed on the table for her, when he left the house. She could not burden him longer with her presence, as he was obviously nervous about his character, lest it should suffer should he harbor her. Thanking him, she departed, and walked back to Thursley through the gathering gloom.

Betty Chivers kept a dame's school, in which she had instructed the children of Thursley in the alphabet, simple summing, and in the knowledge and fear of God. With the march of the times we have abolished dames schools, and cut away thereby a means of livelihood from many a worthy woman; but what is worse, have driven the little ones into board schools, that are godless, where they are taught to despise manual labor, and to grow up without moral principle. Our schools are like dockyards, whence expensively-equipped vessels are launched provided with everything except ballast, which will prevent their capsizing in the first squall. The Vicar of Witley had been one of those men, in advance of his time, who had initiated this system.

Whatever of knowledge of good, and of discipline of conscience Mehetabel possessed, was obtained from Mrs. Susanna Verstage, or from old Betty Chivers.

We are told that if we cast our bread on the waters, we shall find it after many days. But simple souls are too humble to recognize it.

So was it with Goodie Chivers.

That Mehetabel, through all her trials, acted as a woman of principle, clung to what she knew to be right, was due very largely to the old dame's instructions, but Betty was too lowly-minded for one instant to allow this, even to suspect it.

Our Board School masters and mistresses have quite as little suspicion that they have sowed the seed which sprung up in the youths who are dismissed from offices for defalcation, and the girls who leave menial service to walk the streets.

Mrs. Chivers was glad to see Mehetabel when she entered. She had heard talk about her—that she had run away from her husband, and was wandering through the country with her babe; and having a tender heart, and a care for all her old pupils, she had felt anxious concerning her.

Mehetabel pleaded to be taken in for the night, and to this Mrs. Chivers readily consented. She would share her bed with the mother and the child, as well as her crust of bread and cup of thin tea. Of milk, in her poverty, the old woman allowed herself but a few drops, and of butter with her bread none at all.

Yet what she had, that she cheerfully divided with Mehetabel.

On the morrow, after a restful sleep, the young wife started for a silk mill on one of those Hammer ponds that occupied a depression in the Common. These ponds were formed at the time when iron was worked in the district, and the ponds, as their name implies, were for the storage of water to beat out the iron by means of large hammers, set in motion by a wheel. When these ponds were constructed is not known. The trees growing on the embankments that hold back the water are of great size and advanced age.

One of these ponds, at the time of our tale, was utilized for a silk mill.

On reaching the silk mill, she timidly asked for the manufacturer. She knew him slightly, as he had been occasionally to the "Ship," where he had lodged a guest at one time when his house was full, and at another to call on a fisherman who was an acquaintance, and who was staying there. He was a blunt man, with a very round head and a very flat face. His name was Lilliwhite. He had exchanged words with Mehetabel when she was at the inn, and had always been kindly in his address.

When she was shown into his office, as ill-luck would have it at once the child became fretful and cried.

"I beg your pardon," said Mehetabel. "I am sorry to trouble you, but I wish you would be so good, sir, as to let me do some work for you in the mill."

"You, Mehetabel! Why, what do you mean?"

"Please, sir, I have left the Punch-Bowl. I cannot stay there any longer. Do not ask me the reasons. They are good ones, but I had rather not tell them. I must now earn my own livelihood, and—" She was unable to proceed owing to the wailing of the infant.

"Look here, my dear," said the silk weaver, "I cannot hear you on account of the noise, and as I have something to attend to, I will leave you here alone for a few minutes, whilst I look to my business. I will return shortly, when the young dragon has ceased rampaging. I dare say it is hungry."

Then the good-natured man departed, and Mehetabel used her best endeavors to reduce her child to quiet. It was not hungry, it was not cold. It was in pain. She could feed it, she could warm it, but she knew not how to give it that repose which it so much needed.

After some minutes had elapsed, Mr. Lilliwhite looked in again, but as the child was still far from pacified, he retired once more.

Twenty minutes to half-an-hour had passed before the feeble wails of the infant had decreased in force, and had died away wholly, and then the manufacturer returned, smiling, to his office.

"'Pon my soul," said he, "I believe this is the first time my shop has been turned into a nursery. Come now, before the Dragon of Wantley is awake and roaring, tell me what you want."

Mehetabel repeated her request.

"There is no one I would more willingly oblige," said he. "You have ever conducted yourself well, and have been industrious. But there are difficulties in the way. First and foremost, the Dragon of Wantley."

"I beg your pardon, sir."

"I mean the child. What will you do with it? If you come here, engaged by me, you must be at the mill at seven o'clock in the morning. There is an hour for dinner at noon, and the mill hands are released at five o'clock in the afternoon in winter and six in summer. What will the Dragon do all the time its mother is spinning silk? You cannot have the creature here—and away, who will care for it? Who feed it?"

"I had thought of leaving my baby at Mrs. Chivers'."

"That is nonsense," said the silk weaver. "The Dragon won't be spoon-fed. Its life depends on its getting its proper, natural nourishment. So that won't do. As for having it here—that's an impossibility. Much you would attend to the spindles when the Dragon was bellowing. Besides, it would distract the other girls. So you see, this won't do. And there are other reasons. I couldn't receive you without your husband's consent. But the Dragon remains as the insuperable difficulty. Fiddle-de-dee, Matabel! Don't think of it. For your own sake, for the Dragon's sake, I say it won't do."

CHAPTER XL. — BY THE HAMMER POND

Discouraged at her lack of success, Mehetabel now turned her steps towards Thursley. She was sick at heart. It seemed to her as if every door of escape from her wretched condition was shut against her.

She ascended the dip in the Common through which the stream ran that fed the Hammer ponds, and after leaving the sheet of water that supplied the silk mill, reached a brake of willow and bramble, through which the stream made its way from the upper pond.

The soil was resolved into mud, and oozed with springs; at the sides broke out veins of red chalybeate water, of the color of brick.

She started teal, that went away with a rush and frightened her child, which cried out, and fell into sobs.

Then before her rose a huge embankment; with a sluice at the top over which the pond decanted and the overflow was carried a little way through a culvert, beneath a mound on which once had stood the smelting furnace, and which now dribbled forth rust-stained springs.

The bank had to be surmounted, and in Mehetabel's condition it taxed her powers, and when she reached the top she sank out of breath on a fallen bole of a tree. Here she rested, with the child in her lap, and her head in her hand. Whither should she go? To whom betake herself? She had not a friend in the world save Iver, and it was not possible for her to appeal to him.

Now, in her desolation, she understood what it was to be without a relative. Every one else had some one tied by blood to whom to apply, who would counsel, assist, afford a refuge. A nameless girl, brought up by the parish, with—as far as she was aware—but one relative in the world, her mother's sister, whose name she knew not, and whose existence she could not be sure of—she was indeed alone as no other could be.

The lake lay before her steely and cold.

The chill wind hissed and sobbed among the bulrushes, and in the coarse marsh grass that fringed the water on all sides except that of the dam.

The stunted willows shed their broad-shaped leaves that sailed and drifted, formed fleets, and clustered together against the bank.

The tree bole on which she was seated was rotting away; a huge fleshy fungus had formed on it, and the decaying timber emitted a charnel-house smell.

Now the babe in Mehetabel's arms was quiet. It was asleep. She herself was weary, and quivering in all her limbs, hot and yet cold, with an aguish feeling. Her strength of purpose was failing her. She was verging on despair.

She could not remain with Betty Chivers without paying for her lodging and for her food. The woman did but just maintain herself out of the little school and the post-office. She was generous and kind, but she had not the means to support Mehetabel, nor could Mehetabel ask it of her.

What should she do? What the silk manufacturer had said was quite true. The babe stood in her way of getting employment, and the babe she must not leave. That little life depended on her, and her time, care, thought must be devoted to it.

Oh, if now she could but have had that fifteen pounds which Simon Verstage in his providence had given her on her wedding day! With that she would have been easy, independent.

When Jonas robbed her of the sum he cut away from her the chance of subsistence elsewhere save in his house—at all events at such a time as this.

She looked dreamily at the water, that like an eye exercised a fascination on her.

Would it not be well to cast herself into this pool, with her babe, and then both would be together at rest, and away from the cruel world that wanted them not, that rejected them, that had no love, no pity for them?

But she put the thought resolutely from her.

Presently she noticed the flat-bottomed boat usually kept on the pond for the convenience of fishers; it was being propelled over the stream in her direction. A minute later, a man seated in the boat ran it against the bank and stepped out, fastened the point to a willow stump, and came towards her.

"What—is this the Squiress?"

She looked up and recognized him.

The man who came to her and addressed her was Mr. Markham, the young barrister, who had been to the Punch-Bowl to obtain the assistance of Jonas in wild-duck shooting.

She recalled his offensively familiar manner, and was troubled to see him again. And yet she remembered his last remark on leaving, when he had offered his services to help her to free herself from her bondage to Jonas. The words might have been spoken in jest, yet now, she caught at them.

He stood looking at her, and he saw both how pale she was, with a hectic flame in her cheek, and a feverish glitter in her eye, and also how beautiful she thus was.

"Why," said he, "what brings you here?"

"I have been to the silk mill in quest of work."

"Work! Broom-Squiress, one such as you should not work. You missed your vocation altogether when you left the Ship. Jonas told me you had been there."

"I was happy then."

"But are you not so in the Punch-Bowl?"

"No. I am very miserable. But I will not return there again."

"What! fallen out with the Squire?"

"He has made it impossible for me to go back."

"Then whither are you bound?"

"I do not know."

He looked at her intently.

"Now, see here," said he. "Sit down on that log again from which you have risen and tell me all. I am a lawyer and can help you, I daresay."

"I have not much to tell," she answered, and sank on the tree bole. He seated himself beside her.

"There are things that have happened which have made me resolve to go anywhere, do anything, rather than return to Jonas. I promised what I could not keep when I said I would love, honor, and obey him."

Then she began to sob. It touched her that this young man should express sympathy, offer his help.

"Now listen to me," said Mr. Markham; "I am a barrister. I know the law, I have it at my ringers' ends, and I place myself, my knowledge and my abilities at your disposal. I shall feel proud, flattered to do so. Your beauty and your distress appeal to me irresistibly. Has the Squire been beating you?"

"Oh, no, not that."

"Then what has he done?"

"There are things worse to bear than a stick."

"What! Oh, the gay Lothario! He has been casting his eye about and has lost his leathery heart to some less well-favored wench than yourself."

Mehetabel moved further from him on the tree-bole.

He began picking at the great lichen that grew out of the decaying tree, and laughed.

"Have I hit it? Jealous, eh? Jealousy is at the bottom of it all. By Jove, the Broom-Squire isn't worth expending a jealous thought on. He's a poor sordid creature. Not worthy of you. So jealous, my little woman, eh?"

Mehetabel turned and looked steadily at him.

"You do not understand me," she said. "No Jonas has not sunk so low as that."

"He would have been a fool to have cast aside a jewel for the sake of quartz crystal," laughed Markham. "But, come. A lawyer is a confessor. Tell me everything. Make no reservations. Open your heart to me, and see if the law, or myself—between us we cannot assist you."

Mehetabel hesitated. The manner in which the man offered his services was offensive, and yet in her innocent mind she thought that perhaps the fault lay in herself in not understanding and receiving his address in the way in which it was intended. Besides, in what other manner could she obtain relief? Every other means was taken from her.

Slowly, reluctantly, she told him much that she had not told to any one else—only not that Jonas had endeavored to kill the child. That she would not relate.

When she had finished her tale, he said, "What you have told me is a very sad story, and makes my heart ache for you. You can rely on me, I will be your friend and protector. We have had a case on lately, of a woman who was equally unhappy in her married life; her name was Jane Summers. You may have seen it in the papers."

"I'll never see the papers. How did Jane Summers manage?"

"She had a crabbed, ill-conditioned husband, and she was a fine, handsome, lusty woman. He fell ill, and she did not afford him all that care and attention which was requisite in his condition. She went out amusing herself, and left him at home with no one to see to his necessities. The consequence was that he died, and she was tried for it, but the case against her broke down. It could not be proved that had she been devoted to him in his sickness he would have recovered. The law takes cognizance of commission of a crime, and not of neglect of duty."

Mehetabel opened her eyes. "If Jonas were ill I would attend him day and night," she said. "But he is not ill—never was, till the shot entered his arm, and then I was with him all day and all night."

"How did he receive your ministry?"

"He was very irritable. I suppose the pain made him so."

"You got no thanks for your trouble?"

"None at all. I thought he would have been kinder when he recovered."

"Then," said the young man, laughing; "the man is not to be cured. You must leave him."

"I have done so."

"And you are seeking a home and a protector?"

"I want to earn my living somewhere."

"A pretty young thing like you," said the stranger, "cannot fail to make her way. Come! I have offered you my aid," he put his arm round her and attempted to snatch a kiss.

"So!" exclaimed Mehetabel, starting to her feet. "This is the friend and protector you would be! I trusted you with my troubles, and you have taken advantage of my trust. Let me alone! Wherever I turn there hell hath opened her mouth! A moment ago I thought of ending all my troubles in this pond—that a thousand times before trusting you further."

With beating heart—beating with anger—proudly raising her weary head, she walked away.

CHAPTER XLI. — WANDERERS

It occurred to Mehetabel that the rector of Milford had been over at Thursley several times to do duty when the vicar of Witley was ill, and she thought that perhaps she might obtain advice from him.

Accordingly she turned in the direction of that village as soon as she had reached the road. She walked wearily along till she arrived in this, the adjoining parish, separated from Thursley by a tract of healthy common. At her request, she was shown into the library, and she told the parson of her trouble.

He shrugged his shoulders, and read her a lecture on the duties of wife to husband; and, taking his Bible, provided her with texts to corroborate what he said.

"Please, sir," she said, "I was married when I did not wish it, and when I did not know what I could do, and what was impossible. As the Church married me, can it not undo the marriage, and set me free again?"

"Certainly not. What has been joined together cannot be put asunder. It is not impossible to obtain a separation, legally, but you will have to go before lawyers for that."

Mehetabel flushed. "I will have nothing to do with lawyers," she said hastily.

"You would be required to show good cause why you desire a separation, and then it would be expensive. Have you money?"

"Not a penny."

"The law in England—everywhere—is only for the rich."

"Then is there nothing you can advise?"

"Only that you should go home again, and bear what you have to bear as a cross laid on you."

"I will never go back."

"It is your duty to do so."

"I cannot, and will not."

"Then, Mrs. Kink, I am afraid the blame of this domestic broil lies on your shoulders quite as much as on those of your husband. Woman is the weaker vessel. Her duty is to endure."

"And a separation—"

"That is legal only, and unless you can show very good cause why it should be granted, it may be refused. Has your husband beaten you?"

"No, but he has spoken to me—"

"Words break no bones. I don't think words would be considered. I can't say; I'm no lawyer. But remember—even if separated by law, in the sight of God you would still be one."

Mehetabel left, little cheered.

As she walked slowly back along the high-road, she was caught up by Betsy Cheel.

"Halloo!" said this woman; "where have you been?"

Mehetabel told her.

"Want to be separated from Jonas, do you? I'm not surprised. I always thought him a bad fellow, but I doubt if he's worse than my man, Jamaica."

After a while she said: "We'll walk together. Then we can chat. It's dull going over the Common alone. I've been selling eggs in Milford. They're won'erful dear now; nine a shillin'; but the hens feel the cold, and don't lay this time of the year much. How's the child? You didn't ort to be carryin' it about in this weather and at this time o' the year."

"I have nowhere that I can leave it, and its only home is against my heart, in my arms."

"You've run away?"

"Yes; I shall not go back to Jonas."

"I don't call that sense," said Bessy. "If you run away, run away with some one who'll take care of you. That's what I did. My first husband—well, I don't know as he was a proper husband. He called me names, and took the stick to me when drunk; so I went off with Jamaica. That I call reasonable. Ain't you got no one to run away with?"

Mehetabel did not answer. She hastened her pace—she did not relish association with the woman. "I'd have run away from Jamaica scores o' times," continued Mrs. Cheel, "only I ain't so young as I once as, and so the opportunities don't come. There's the pity. I didn't start and leave him when I was good-looking and fresh. I might have done better then. If you think a bad, cross-crabbed man will mend as he grows older, you make a mistake. They grow wusser. So you're right to leave Jonas. Only you've gone about in the wrong way. There's Iver Verstage. I've heard talk about him and you. He don't live such a terrible distance off. I hear he's doin' purty well for himself at Guildford. Why don't you go to him? He's more suitable in age, and he's a nice-lookin' young fellow."

"Mrs. Cheel," said Mehetabel, standing still, "will you go forward a little faster? I cannot walk with you. I do not ask you for any advice. I do not want to hear what you have to say. I have been to the parson. It seems to me that I can get no help from heaven, but that hell is holding out hands on all sides, offering assistance. Go on your way. I shall sit here for half an hour. I am too weary to walk at your pace."

"As you will," said Bessy Cheel. "I spoke out of good will, and told what would be the best for you. If you won't take my opinion—that's no odds to me, and it may turn out wuss for you."

Mehetabel drew aside, to a nodule of ironstone rock that capped the first elevation of the Common, the first stage of the terraces that rise to Hind Head.

Here she remained till all chance of association with Mrs. Cheel was over. Then she went on to Thursley village, to find the Widow Chivers in great excitement. Jonas Kink had been in the village inquiring for his wife and child; and had learned that both had been given shelter by the dame.

He had come to the school, and had demanded his wife and his little son. Betty had taken charge of the infant and laid it to sleep in her own bed and happily at this time it was asleep. When she told Bideabout that Mehetabel had left the house in quest of work, he had happily concluded that she had carried the child with her, and had asked no further questions; but he had been violent and menacing. He had threatened to fetch the constable and recover his child, even if he let the mother go where she liked.

Mehetabel was greatly alarmed.

"I cannot stay here," she said, "in no case will I give up the babe. When Iver Verstage baptized me it was lest I should become a wanderer. I suppose the christening was a poor one—for my wandering is begun, and it is not I only who am condemned to wander, but my little child also."

With a heavy heart she left the dame's school. Had she been alone she would have run to Godalming or Hazelmere, and sought a situation as a domestic servant, but that was not possible to her now, cumbered with the child.

Watching her opportunity, that none of the villagers might observe her leaving the school and note the direction she took, she ran out upon the heath, and turned away from the high-road.

On all sides, as already intimated at the opening of this tale, the sandy commons near Thursley are furrowed as though a giant plough had been drawn along them, but at so remote a period that since the soil was turned the heather had been able to cast its deep brown mantle of velvet pile over every irregularity, and to veil the scars made in the surface.

These gullies or furrows vary in depth from ten to forty feet, and run to various lengths. They were the subaerial excavations and open adits made by miners in quest of iron ore. They are probably of all dates from prehistoric antiquity to the reign of the Tudors, after which the iron smelting of the weald came to an end. The magnificent oaks of the forest of Anderida that stretched from Winchelsea, in Kent, a hundred and twenty miles west, with a breadth of thirty miles between the northern and southern chalk downs—these oaks had been hewn down and used as fuel, in the fabrication of military armor and weapons, and just as the wood was exhausted, coal was discovered in the north, and the entire industry of iron in the weald came to an end.

Mehetabel had often run up these gullies when a child, playing on the commons with Iver, or with other scholars of Dame Chivers school.

She remembered now that in one of these she and Iver had discovered a cave, scooped out in the sandrock, possibly the beginning of an adit, probably a place for storing smuggled goods. On a very small scale it resembled the extraordinary labyrinth of subterranean passages at Puttenham, that may be explored at the present day. During the preceding century and the beginning of that in which we live, an extensive business in smuggled spirits, tea, and tobacco was carried on from the coast to the Thames; and there were certain store places, well-known to the smugglers in the line of trade. In Thursley parish is a farm that is built over vast vaults, carefully constructed, with the entrance of them artfully disguised.

The Puttenham labyrinth has its openings in a dense coppice; and it had this advantage, that with a few strokes of the pick a passage could be blocked with sand from the roof.

The cave that Mehetabel had discovered, and in which she had spent many a summer hour, opened out of the side of one of the most profound of the trenches cut in the surface after ore. The entrance was beneath a projecting slab of ironstone, and was concealed by bushes of furze and bramble. It did not penetrate beyond thirty feet into the sand rock, or if it had done so formerly, it was choked when known to Mehetabel, with the falling in of the roof. These sandstone caves are very dry, and the temperature within agreeable.

Here Mehetabel resolved to bide for a while, till she had found some place of greater security for herself and the child.

She did not leave Mrs. Chivers without having arranged with her for the conveyance of food to a place agreed on between them.

With the shawl so kindly given her by the gardener, Mehetabel could exclude all wintry air from her habitation, and abundance of fuel was at hand in the gully, so that she could make and maintain a fire that would be unnoticed, because invisible except to such as happened to enter the ravine.

Mehetabel left the village and emerged on the path bearing that precious but woeful burden, her little babe, in her arms folded about it. Then, all at once, before her she saw that same young lawyer who had insulted her at the Hammer Pond. He recognized her at once, as she did him. She drew back and her heart beat furiously.

"What, Queen of the heath?" said he, "still about with your baby?"

She would not answer him. She stepped back.

"Do not be afraid; I wish you well—you and your little one. Come, for the sake of that mite, accept my offer. What will you say to yourself—how excuse yourself if it die through exposure, and because of your silly scruples?"

She would not listen to him. She darted past, and fled over the down.

She roamed about, lost, distracted. In her confusion she missed the way to the cave, and the darkness was gathering. The moaning little morsel of her flesh could not be comforted. She rocked it violently, then gently. In neither way could she give it relief. She knew not which direction she had taken, on what part of the heath she was straying.

And now rain began to fall, and Mehetabel had to protect her child from being drenched. For herself she had no thought. The rain came down first in a slight sprinkle, and then in large drops, and a cold wind swashed the drops into her face, blinding her.

All at once, in the uncertain light, she saw some dark gap open before her as a grave. She would have fallen headlong into it had she not arrested her foot in time. Then, with a gasp of relief she recognized where she was.

She stood at the edge of the old mining ravine. This trench, cut in the sandy down, had looked like a little bit of Paradise to the child-eyes of the pupils of Betty Chivers in summer, when the air was honey-sweet with the fragrance of the flowering furze, and musical with the humming of bees; and the earth was clotted with spilt raspberry cream—the many-tinged blossom of the heather—alas! it was now sad, colorless, dripping, cold, and repellent.

CHAPTER XLII. — THE CAVE

Mehetabel made her way down the steep side of the gully, and to the cave, burdened with the babe she carried in her arms. She bore a sack over her back that contained some dry turves, shavings, and a few potatoes, given her by the school-dame. The place of refuge had obviously been frequented by children long after the time when Mehetabel and Iver had retired to it on hot summer days. The sides of the entrance had been built up with stones, with moss driven into their interstices. Within, the floor was littered with dry fern, and in one place was a rude hearth, where fires had been kindled; this was immediately under a vertical opening that served as chimney, and prevented the smoke of a fire from filling the cave.

The young mother laid her child on the shawl she spread over the bracken, and proceeded to kindle a fire with a tinder-box lent her by Mrs. Chivers. It amused the babe to watch the sparks as they flew about, and when the pile of turves and sticks and heather was in combustion, to listen to the crackle, and watch the play and leap of the flames.

As the fire burnt up, and the blue smoke stole through the natural chimney, the whole cave glowed orange.

The air was not cold within, and in the radiation from the fire, the place promised to be warm and comfortable.

The child crowed and stretched its feet out to the blaze.

She looked attentively at the babe.

What did that wicked young lawyer mean by saying that it would die through exposure? It had cried and moaned. All children cry and moan. They have no other means of making their wants known. Wet the little creature was not; she had taken every precaution against that, but her own garments steamed in the heat of the fire she had kindled, and leaving the babe to watch the dancing flames, she dried her wet gown and stockings in the glow.

Then by the reflection Mehetabel could see on the nether surface of the sandstone slab at the entrance the initials of herself and Iver that had been cut by the latter many years ago, with a true-lover's knot uniting them. And there on that knot, lost in dream, was a peacock butterfly that had retired to hibernate. The light from the fire glowed in its purple and gold eyes, and the warm ascending air fluttered the wings, but did not restore animation to the drowsy insect. In corners were snails at the limit of their glazed tracks, also in retreat before winter. They had sealed themselves up in their houses against cold.

Mehetabel was constrained to pass in and out of her habitation repeatedly so as to accumulate fuel that might serve through the night. Happily, on her way she had noticed a little shelter hut, probably constructed by a village sportsman, under which he might conceal himself with his gun and await the game. This was made of dry heather, and branches of fir and chestnut. She had no scruple in pulling this to pieces, and conveying as much as she could carry at a time to her cave.

The child, amused by the fire, did not object to her temporary desertion, and it was too feeble and young to crawl near to the flames.

After several journeys to and fro Mehetabel had contrived to form a goodly pile of dry fuel at the back of her habitation, and now that a sufficiency of ash had been formed proceeded to embed in it the potatoes that Betty Chivers had given her.

How often had she and Iver, as children, talked of being savages and living in wigwams and caves, and now she was driven to a life of savagery in the midst of civilization. It would not, however, be for long. She would search the neighborhood round for work, and when she had got it move away from this den in the Common.

A stoat ran in, raised its head, looked at the fire, then at her, with glistening eyes devoid of fear, but at a movement of the child darted away and disappeared.

A Sabbath sense of repose came over Mehetabel. The babe was content and crooning itself to sleep. Her nerves in tension all day were now relaxed; her wearied body rested. She had no inquisitive companion to worry her with questions, none overkind to try her with injudicious attentions. She could sit on the fragrant fern leaves, extend her feet, lean her head against the sandstone, and watch the firelight play over the face of her child.

A slight sound attracted her attention. It was caused by a bramble leaf caught in a cobweb, drawn in by the draught produced by the fire, and it tapped at and scratched the covering stone. Mehetabel, roused from her languor, saw what occasioned the sound, and lost all concern about it. There were particles in the sand that sparkled. It afforded her a childish pleasure to see the twinkles on every side in the rise and fall of the flames. It was no exertion to cast on another branch of heather, or even a bough of pine. It was real pleasure to listen to the crackle and to see the sparks shoot like rockets from the burning wood. The cave was a fairy palace. The warmth was grateful. The potatoes were hissing in the embers. Then Mehetabel dreamily noticed a black shadow stealing along the lower surface of the roof stone. At first she saw it without interest, without inquiry in her mind, but little by little her interest came, and her attention centred itself on the dark object.

It was a spider, a hairy insect with a monstrous egglike belly, and it was creeping slowly and with caution towards the hibernating butterfly. Perhaps its limbs were stiff with inaction, its blood congealed; perhaps it dreaded lest by precipitation it might alarm its prey and lose it.

Mehetabel put out her hand, picked up a piece of furze, and cast it at the spider, which fell.

Then she was uneasy lest it would crawl along the ground and come to her baby, and sting it. She inherited the common superstition that spiders are poisonous insects.

She must look for it.

Only now, as she tried to raise herself, did she discover how stiff her joints had become. She rose to her knees, and raked out some of the potatoes from the ashes, and swept the floor where the spider had dropped with a brush of Scottish pine twigs.

Then, all at once, she remained motionless. She heard steps and voices outside, the latter in low converse. Next a face looked in, and an exclamation followed, "Jamaica! There, sure enough, she be!"

The voice, the face—there was no mistaking either. They belonged to Sally Rocliffe.

The power to cry out failed in Mehetabel. She hastily thrust her child behind her, into the depths of the cave, and interposed herself between it and the glittering eyes of the woman.

"Come on, Jamaica, we'll see how she has made herself comfortable," said Mrs. Rocliffe, and she entered, followed by Giles Cheel. Both had to stoop at the opening, but when they were a few feet within, could stand upright.

"Well, now, I call this coorious," said Sarah; "don't you, Jamaica? Here's all the Punch-Bowl turned out. Some runnin' one way, some another, all about Matabel. Some sez she's off her head; some thinks she has drownded herself and the child. And there's Jonas stormin', and in a purty takein'. There is my Thomas—gone with him—and Jamaica and I come this way over the Common. But I had a fancy you might be at the bottom o' one of them Hammer Ponds. I was told you'd been to the silk mill."

"What be you run away for? What be you a hidin' for—just like a wild beast?" asked Giles Cheel.

Mehetabel could not answer. How could she declare her reason? That the life of the child was menaced by its own father.

"Now come back with us," said Jamaica, in a persuasive tone.

"I will not. I never will return," exclaimed Mehetabel with energy. She was kneeling, with her hands extended to screen her child from the eye of Sally Rocliffe.

"I told you so, did I not?" asked the woman.

"She sed as much to me yesterday mornin when I saw her run away."

"I will not go back. I will never go back," repeated Mehetabel

"Where is the child?" asked Sally.

"It is behind me."

"How is it?"

"It is well now, now we are out of the Punch-Bowl, where all hate it and wish it dead."

"Now, look here, Matabel," said Cheel, "you be reasonable, and come peaceably."

"I will not go back; I never will!" she answered with increased vehemence.

"That's all very fine sayin'," pursued Giles Cheel. "But go back you must when Jonas fetches you."

"I will not go back! Never! never!"

"He'll make you."

"Not if I will not go."

"Aye, but he can. If you won't go when he axes, he can get the constable to force you to go home. The law of the land can help him thereto."

"I will not go back! Never!"

"Where he is just now, I can't say," pursued Cheel. "But I have a notion he's prowlin' about the moor, thinkin' you may have gone to Thor's Stone. Come he will, and he'll take you and the baby, and you may squeal and scratch, go back with him you must and will. So I say go peaceable."

"I will not go back!" cried Mehetabel. She picked up a lump of ironstone and said, passionately, "I will defend myself. I am as strong as he. I am stronger, for I will fight for my child. I will kill him rather than let him take my baby from me."

"Hear her!" exclaimed Sally Rocliffe. "She threatens she'll do for Jonas. Every one knows she tried that on once afore, wi' his gun."

"Yes," said Mehetabel, fiercely, "I will even do that. Rather than go back and have my baby in that hated place again, I will fight and kill him. Let him come here and try."

She set her teeth, her eyes glared, her breath came snorting through her nostrils.

"I say, Gilly, I'll go back. It ain't safe here. She's possessed with seven devils."

"I am not possessed, save with mother's love. I will never, never go back and take my babe to the Punch-Bowl. Never, never, allow you, Sally, to look at its innocent face again, nor Jonas to touch it. There is no one cares for it, no one loves it, no one who does not wish its death, but me, and I will fight, and never—"

Her strength gave way, her hands sank in the sand, and her hair fell over her face, as she broke into a storm of sobs and tears.

"I say, Jamaica, come out," whispered Mrs. Rocliffe. "We'll talk over wot's to be done."

Giles Cheel and Sally Rocliffe crept out of the cave backwards. They did so, facing Mehetabel, with mistrust. Each believed that she was mad.

When the two were outside, then Jonas's sister said to her companion "I'll tell you what, Jamaica, I won't have nuthin' more to do with this. There's somethin' queer; and whether Jonas has been doin' what he ort not, or whether Matabel be gone rampagin' mad, that's not for me to say. Let Jonas manage his own affairs, and don't let us meddle no more."

"I am sure it's 'as nuthin' to me," said Cheel. "But this is a fine thing. At the christenin' of that there baby he had words to say about me and my Betsy, as if we was a disgrace to the Punch-Bowl, becos we didn't always agree. But my Betsy and me never came to such a pass as this. I'm willin'. Let's go back and have our suppers, and let her be where she is."

"You need not tell Jonas that we have found her."

"No; not if you wishes."

"Let the matter alone altogether; I reckon she's in a dangerous mood, and so is Jonas. Something may come of it, and I'd as lief be out of it altogether."

"That's my doctrine, too," said Giles.

Then he put his head in at the cave door, and said "Good-night, missus!"

CHAPTER XLIII. — AT COLPUS'S

On the morrow Mehetabel, carrying her babe, revisited the schoolmistress, at an early hour, before the children assembled.

Betty Chivers received her with joy.

"Matabel," she said, "I've been thinking about you. There's James Colpus and his daughter are in want of a woman. That girl, Julia Caesar, as has been with them, got at the barrels of ale, and has been givin' drink all round to the men, just when they liked. She'd got a key to the cellar unbeknown to Master Colpus; so she has had to walk off. Polly Colpus, she knows you well enough, and what a managing girl you are. They couldn't do better than take you—that is, if they can arrange with Bideabout, and don't object to the baby."

Accordingly, somewhat later, Mehetabel departed for the farm of James Colpus, that adjoined the land occupied by old Simon Verstage.

James Colpus was preparing to go out fox-hunting when Mehetabel arrived. He wore a tight, dark-colored suit, that made his red face look the redder, and his foxy hair the foxier. His daughter had a face like a full moon, flat and eminently livid;' fair, almost white eyebrows, and an unmistakable moustache. She was extraordinarily plain, but good-natured. She was pouring out currant brandy for her father when Mehetabel arrived.

"Well!" exclaimed Colpus. "Here is the runaway wife. Tally-ho! Tally-ho! We've got her. All the parish has been out after you, and you run to earth here, do you?"

"If you please," said Mehetabel, "I have come to offer my services in the place of Julia Caesar, who has been sent away. You know I can work. You know I won't let nobody have the tap o' the beer—and as for wages, I'll take what you are willing to give."

"That's all very fine, Miss Runaway, but what will Bideabout say to that?"

"I am not going back to Bideabout," answered Mehetabel. "If you cannot take me, I shall go to every farm and offer myself, and if none in Thursley or Witley will have me, I'll beg my bread from door to door, till I do find a house where I may honestly earn it. Go back to the Punch-Bowl I will not."

"I'd like to take you," said Colpus. "Glad to have you. Never a better girl anywhere, of that I am quite certain—only, how about the Broom-Squire? I'm constable, and it must not be said that the constable is keeping a man's wife away from him."

"You will not keep me from him. Nothing in the world will make me go back to him."

"Then—what about the baby? Can you let Bideabout have that?"

Mehetabel flushed almost as red as Colpus and his daughter.

"Never!" she said, firmly.

"But, look here," said the farmer, "if I did agree to take you, why, after a day or two, you'd be homesick, and wantin' to be back in the arms of Jonas. It's always so with women."

"I shall never go back," persisted Mehetabel.

"So you say. But before the week is out you'll be piping another song."

"You may bind me to stay—three months—six—a year,"

"That is all very well to say. Bind me, but how? What bind will hold—when the marriage tie does not?"

"The marriage tie would have held me till death," answered Mehetabel gravely, "if Jonas had not done that which makes it impossible for me to remain. It is not for my sake that I am away. Had I been alone I would have borne all till I died. But I have other duties now. I am a mother. Here is my darling, a charge from God. I owe it to God to do what I am here for—to find another home, a place away from the Punch-Bowl."

"What do you mean?"

"I cannot explain."

"Is the Punch-Bowl unhealthy for the child?"

"Yes, it would die there."

"Who told you so?"

"I know it. My heart says so."

"Now look here," said Colpus, getting red as a poppy, "there's a lot of talk in the place about you. Some say that Bideabout is in the wrong, some say that the wrong lies with you. It is reported that he beat you, and there are folks that tell as how you gave him occasion. You must let me know the right of it all, or I can't take you."

"Then I must go," said Mehetabel, "I cannot tell you all. You may think ill of me if you choose, I cannot help that."

Colpus rubbed his foxy whiskers and head.

"You're a won'erful active woman, and do more work than three ordinary gals. I'd like to have you in the house. But then—what am I to say if Kink comes to claim you?"

"Say you will not give me up."

"But I ain't so sure but what he can force me to surrender you."

"You are the strongest man in Thursley."

"'Tain't that," said Colpus, gratified by the compliment. "'Tis he might bring the law against me. I don't know nuthin' about law, though I'm constable, but I reckon, if I was to keep a cow of his as had strayed and refused to give her up, he could compel me. And what's true of a cow is true of a wife. If I could be punished for stealin' his goose I might be summonsed all on account of you. Then there's the babe—that might be brought in as kidnappin'! I daren't risk it."

"But, father," put in Polly. "How would it do for a time, just to try."

"There's something in that, Polly.

"And Julia Caesar have left things in a terrible mess. We must have all cleared up before another comes in. What if we take Matabel by the day to clear up?"

"Look here, Polly," said Colpus, who visibly oscillated in mind between his wishes to engage Mehetabel and his fears as to what the consequences might be. "It's this," he touched his forehead, and made a sign towards the applicant. "Folk do say it."

"Matabel," said the good-natured farmer's daughter, "you go along to Thursley, and father and I will talk it over. If we think we can take you—where shall we send to find you?"

"To Betty Chivers' house."

"Well, in half an hour I trust we shall have decided. Now go."

As Mehetabel withdrew, Polly said, "It's all gammon, father, about her not being right in her head. Her eye is as steady as the evenin' star. And it's all lies about there bein' any fault in her. Matabel is as honest and true as sunlight."

Then old Colpus shouted after Mehetabel, who was departing by the lane. "Don't go that way, over the field is the path—by the stile. There's a lot o' water in the lane."

The young mother turned, thanked him with an inclination of the head, and pressing her cheek to the child she bore, she took the path that crossed a meadow, and which led to a tuft of holly, near which was the stile, into the lane. She walked on, with her cheek resting on the child's head, and her eyes on the trodden, cropped wintry grass, with a flutter of hope in her bosom; for she was almost certain that with the influence of Polly engaged on her side, old Colpus would agree to receive her.

She did not walk swiftly. She had no occasion for haste. She hoped that the objections of the farmer would give way before she had reached the hedge, and that he would recall her.

She had almost arrived t the turf of holly, singing in a low tone to the child in her arms, when, a voice made her start and cry out.

She looked up. Jonas was before her.

Unobserved by her he had entered the field. From the lane he had seen her, and he had crossed the stile and come upon her.

She stood frozen to the spot. Each muscle became rigid; the blood in her arteries tingled as though bees were making their way through every vein. Her brows met in a black band across her face. She trembled for a moment, and then was firm. A supreme moment, the supreme moment in her life was come.

"So I have found you at last," sneered Jonas. Hatred, fury, were in him and sent a quiver through the tones of his voice.

"Yes, you have found me," she answered with composure.

"You—do you know what you have done? Made me a derision and a talk to all Thursley, a jest in every pot-house."

"I have not done this. It is your doing."

"Is it not enough that I have lost my money, but must I have this scandal and outrage in my home?"

She did not answer him. She looked steadily at him, and he dared not meet her eyes.

"You must come with me at once," he said.

"I will not go with you."

"I will make you."

"That you cannot."

"You are mad. You must be put under restraint."

"I will go to the madhouse, but not to the Punch-Bowl."

"You shall be forced to return."

"How?"

"I will have you tied. I will swear you are crazed. I will have you locked up, and I will beat you till you learn to obey and behave as I would have you."

"Jonas," said Mehetabel, "this is idle talk. Never, never will I go back to you."

"Never!"

He approached, his eyes glaring, his white fangs showing, like those of a dog about to bite.

Instinctively she put her hand into her pocket and drew forth a lump of ironstone, that she had brandished the previous evening before Sally Rocliffe and Giles Cheel; and which she carried with her as her only weapon of defence.

"Jonas," said Mehetabel. "You may threaten, but your threats do not move me. I can defend myself."

"Oh, with a stone? he scoffed.

"Yes, if need be with a stone. But I have better protection than that."

"Indeed—let me hear it."

"If you venture to touch me—venture to threaten any more—then I shall appeal for protection."

"To whom—to Iver?"

"Not to Iver," her heart boiled up, and was still again.

"To whom—to Farmer Colpus?"

"To the law."

"The law!" jeered Jonas. "It is the law that will send you back to me."

"It is the law which will protect me from you," answered Mehetabel.

"I am fain to learn how."

"How! I have but to go before a magistrate and tell how you tried to poison your own child—how, when that failed, you tried to smother it. And, Jonas," she added—as she saw his face grow ashen, and a foam bubble form on his lips—"and, Jonas," she stepped forward, and he backed—his glassy eyes on her face, "and, Jonas," she said, "look here, I have this stone. With the like of this you sought to kill me in the moor." She raised it above her head, "you would-be murderer of your wife and your child—I am free from you." She took another step forward—he reeled back and vanished—disappeared instantly from her sight with a scream—instantly and absolutely, as when the earth opened its mouth at the word of Moses and swallowed up Korah.

CHAPTER XLIV. — AGAIN: IRONSTONE

Mehetabel heard shouts, exclamations, and saw Thomas Rocliffe and his son, Samuel, come up over the stile from the lane, and James Colpus running towards her.

What had happened? Whither had Jonas vanished? She drew back and passed her hand, still holding the ironstone, over her face.

Then she saw Thomas and Samuel stoop, kneel, and Thomas swing himself down and also disappear; thereupon up came the farmer.

"What is it? Has he fallen in—into the kiln?"

That the reader may understand what had occurred, it is necessary that a few words of explanation should be given.

At the time when the country was densely wooded with oaks, then the farmers were wont annually to draw chalk from the quarries in the flank of the Hog's Back, that singular ridge, steep as a Gothic roof, running east and west from Guildford, and to cart this to their farms. On each of these was a small brick kiln, constructed in a sand-bank beside a lane, so that the chalk and fuel might be thrown in from above, where the top of the kiln was level with the field, and the burnt quicklime drawn out below and shovelled into a cart that would convey it by the road to whatever field was thought to require such a dressing.

But fuel became scarce, and when the trees had vanished, then sea coal was introduced. Thereupon the farmers found it more convenient to purchase quicklime at the kiln mouth near the chalk quarry, than to cart the chalk and burn it themselves.

The private kilns were accordingly abandoned and allowed to fall to ruin. Some were prudently filled in with earth and sand, but this was exceptional. The majority were allowed to crumble in slowly; and at the present day such abandoned kilns may be found on all sides, in various stages of decay.

Into such a kiln, that had not been filled in, Jonas had fallen, when he stepped backwards, unconscious of its existence.

Polly Colpus had followed her father, but kept in the rear, alarmed, and dreading a ghastly sight. The farmer bent with hands on his knees over the hole. Samuel knelt.

"Have you got him?" asked Colpus.

"Lend a hand," called Thomas from below, and with the assistance of those above the body of Jonas Kink was lifted on to the bank.

"He's dead," said the farmer.

Then Mehetabel laughed.

The three men and Polly Colpus turned and looked at her with estrangement.

They did not understand that there was neither mockery nor frivolity in the laugh, that it proceeded involuntarily from the sudden relaxation of overstrained nerves. At the moment Mehetabel was aware of one thing only, that she had nothing more to fear, that her baby was safe from pursuit. It was this thought that dominated her and caused the laugh of relief. She had not in the smallest degree realized how it was that this relief was obtained.

"Fetch a hurdle," said Colpus, "and, Polly, run in and send a couple of men. We must carry him to the Punch-Bowl. I reckon he's pretty well done for. I don't see a sign of life in him."

The Broom-Squire was laid on the gass.

Strange is the effect of death on a man's clothes. The moment the vital spark has left the body, the garments hang about him as though never made to fit him. They take none of the usual folds; they lose their gloss—it is as though life had departed out of them as well.

Mehetabel seated herself on a bit of swelling ground and looked on, without understanding what she saw; seeing, hearing, as in a dream; and after the first spasm of relief, as if what was being done in no way concerned her, belonged to another world to her own. It was as though she were in the moon and saw what men were doing on the earth.

When the Broom-Squire had been lifted upon a hurdle, then Polly Colpus thought right to touch Mehetabel, and say in a low tone: "You will follow him and go to the Punch-Bowl?"

"I will never, never go there again. I have said so," answered Mehetabel.

Then to avoid being pressed further, she stood up and went away, bearing her child in her arms.

The men looked after her and shook their heads.

"Bideabout has had a blow on the forehead," said Colpus.

Mehetabel returned to the school, entered without a word, and seated herself by the fire.

"Have you succeeded?" asked the widow.

"How?"

"Will Farmer Colpus take you?"

"I don't know."

"What have you in your hand?"

Mehetabel opened her fingers and allowed Betty Chivers to remove from her hand a lump of ironstone.

"What are you carrying this for, Matabel?"

"I defend baby with it," she answered.

"Well, you do not need it in my house," said the dame, and placed the liver-colored lump on the table.

"How hot your hand is," she continued. "Here, let me feel again. It is burning. And your forehead is the same. Are you unwell, Matabel?"

"I am cold," she answered dreamily.

"You have been over-worried and worked," said the kind old woman. "I will get you a cup of tea."

"He won't follow me any more and try to take my baby away," said Mehetabel.

"I am glad of that."

"And I also."

Then she moved her seat, winding and bending on one side.

"What is it, my dear?" asked Betty.

"His shadow. It will follow me and fall over baby."

"What do you mean?"

Mehetabel made no reply, and the widow buried herself in preparation for the midday meal, a very humble one of bread and weak tea.

"There's drippin' in the bowl," she said, "you can put some o' that on the bread. And now, give me the little chap. You are not afraid of trusting him to me?"

"Oh, no!"

The mother at once surrendered the child, and Mrs. Chivers sat by the fire with the infant in her lap.

"He's very like you," she said.

"I couldn't love him if he were like him," said Mehetabel.

"You must not say that."

"He is a bad man."

"Leave God to judge him."

"He has judged him," answered the girl, looking vacantly into the fire, and then passed her hand over her eyes and pressed her brow.

"Have you a headache, dear?"

"Yes—bad. It is his shadow has got in there—rolled up, and I can't shake it out."

"Matabel—you must go to bed. You are not well."

"No—I am not well. But my baby?"

"He is safe with me."

"I am glad of that, you will teach him A B C, and the Creed, and to pray to and fear God. But you needn't teach him to find Abelmeholah on the map, nor how many gallons of water the Jordan carries into the Dead Sea every minute, nor how many generations there are in Matthew. That is all no good at all. Nor does it matter where is the country of the Gergesenes. I have tried it. The Vicar was a good man, was he not, Betty?"

"Yes, very good."

"He would give the coat off his back, and the bread out of his mouth to the poor. He gave beef and plum pudding all around at Christmas, and lent out blankets in winter. But he never gave anything to the soul, did he, Betty? Never made the heart warm. I found it so. What I got of good for that was from you."

"My dear," said the old woman, starting up. "I insist on your going to bed at once. I see by your eye, by the fire in your cheek, that you are ill."

"I will go to bed; I do not want anything to eat, only to lay my head down, and then the shadow will run out at my ear—only I fear it may stain the pillow. When I'm rich I will buy you another. Baby is rich; he has got a hundred and fifty pounds. What is his is mine, and what is mine is his. He will not grudge you a new pillow-case."

Mehetabel, usually reserved and silent, had become loquacious and rambling in her talk. It was but too obvious, that she was in a fever, and wandering. Mrs. Chivers insisted on her taking some tea, and then she helped her upstairs to the little bedroom, and did not leave her till she was asleep. The school children, who came in after their dinner hour, were dismissed, so that Mrs. Chivers had the afternoon to devote to the care of the child and of the sick mother, who was in high fever.

She was in the bedroom when she heard a knock at the door, and then a heavy foot below. She descended the rickety stairs as gently as possible, and found Farmer Colpus in the schoolroom.

"How do you do, Mrs. Chivers? Can you tell me, is Matabel Kink here?"

"Yes—if you do not mind, Mr. Colpus, to speak a little lower. She is in bed and asleep."

"Asleep?"

"She came in at noon, rather excited and queer, and her hand burnin' like a hot chestnut, so I gave her a dish o' tea and sent her upstairs. I thought it might be fever—and her eyes were that strange and unsteady—"

"It is rather odd," said the constable, "but my daughter observed how calm and clear her eye was—only an hour before."

"Maybe," said Mrs. Chivers, "and yet she was that won'erful wanderin' in her speech—"

"You don't think she was shamming?"

"Shammin'! Lord, sir—that Matabel never did, and I've knowed her since she was two-year old. At three and a half she comed to my school."

"By the way, what is that stone on your table?" asked Colpus.

"That, sir? Matabel had it in her hand when she comed in. I took it away, and then I felt how burnin' she was, like a fire."

"Oh! she was still holding that stone. Did she say anything about it?"

"Yes, sir, she said that she used it to defend herself and baby."

"From whom?"

"She didn't say—but you know, sir, there has been a bit of tiff between her and the Broom-Squire, and she won't hear of goin back to the Punch-Bowl, and she has a fancy he wants to take the baby away from her. That's ridic'lous, of course. But there is no getting the idea out of her head."

"I must see her."

"You can't speak to her, sir. She is asleep still." Colpus considered.

"I'll ask you to allow me to take this stone away, Betty. And I must immediately send for the doctor. He has been sent for to the Punch-Bowl, and I'll stop him on the way back to Godalming. I must be assured that Matabel is in a fit state to be removed."

"Removed, whither?"

"To the lock-up."

"The lock-up, sir?"

"To the lock-up. Do you know, Mrs. Chivers, that Jonas Kink is dead, and that very strong suspicions attach to Matabel, that she killed him?"

"Matabel killed him!"

"Yes, with that very stone."

CHAPTER XLV. — IN HOPE

When the surgeon, on his return from the Punch-Bowl was called in to see Mehetabel, he at once certified that she was not in a condition to be removed, and that she would require every possible attention for several days.

Accordingly, James Colpus allowed her to remain at the Dame's School, but cautioned Betty Chivers that he should hold her responsible for the appearance of Mehetabel when required.

Jonas Kink was not dead, as Colpus thought when lifted out of the kiln into which he had been precipitated backwards, but he had received several blows on the head which had broken in the skull and stunned him. Had there been a surgeon at hand to relieve the pressure on the brain, he might perhaps have recovered, but there was none nearer than Godalming; the surgeon was out when the messenger arrived, and did not return till late, then he was obliged to get a meal, and hire a horse, as his own was tired, and by the time he arrived at the Punch-Bowl Jonas had ceased to breathe, and all he could do was to certify his death and the cause thereof.

Mehetabel's nature was vigorous and elastic with youth. She recovered rapidly, more so, indeed than Mrs. Chivers would allow to James Colpus, as she was alarmed at the prospect of having to break to her that a warrant was issued against her on the charge of murder.

When she did inform her, Mehetabel could not believe what she was told.

"That is purely," she said. "I kill Jonas! If he had touched me and tried to take baby away I might have done it. I would have fought him like a tiger, as I did before."

"When did you fight him?"

"In the Moor, by Thor's Stone, over the gun—there when the shot went off into his arm."

"I never knew much of that, though there was at the time some talk."

"Yes. I need say nothing of that now. But as to hurting Jonas, I never hurt nobody in my life save myself, and that was when I married him. I don't believe I could kill a fly—and then only if it were teasin' baby."

"There is Joe Filmer downstairs, has somethin' to say. Can he come up?"

"Yes," answered Mehetabel. "He was always kind to me."

The ostler of the Ship stumbled up the stairs and saluted the sick girl with cordiality and respect.

"Very sorry about this little affair. 'Tis a pity, I sez, that such a fuss be made over trifles. There's been the crownin' of the body, and now there's to be the hearin' of you afore the magistrates, and then they say you'll have to go to the 'sizez, and there'll come the hangin'. 'Tis terrible lot o' fuss all about Jonas as wasn't worth it. No one'll miss him and if you did kill him, well, there was cause, and I don't think the wuss o' you for it."

"Thank you, Joe, but I did not kill him."

"Well—you know—it's right for you to say so, 'cos you'll have to plead not guilty. Polly, at our place never allows she's broke nothin', but the chinay and the pipkins have got a terrible way of committin' felo de se since she came to the Ship. She always sez she didn't do it—and right enough. No one in this free country is obliged to incriminate hisself. That's one of our glorious institootions."

"I really am guiltless," urged Mehetabel.

"Quite right you should say so. Pleased to hear it. But I don't know what the magistrates will say. Most folks here sez you did, and all the Punch-Bowl will swear it. They sez you tried to kill him wi' his own gun, but didn't succeed as you wished, so now you knocked him on the head effectual like, and tippled his dead body down into the kiln. He was an aggravatin' chap, was Bideabout, and deserved it. But that is not what I come here to say."

"And that was—"

"Well, now, I mustn't say it too loud. I just slipped in when nobody was about, as I don't want it to be known as I am here. The master and I settled it between us."

"Settled what, Joe?"

"You see he always had a wonderful liking for you, and so had I. He was agin you marryin' the Broom-Squire, but the missus would have it so. Now he's goyne to send me with the trap to Portsmouth. He's had orders for it from a gent as be comin' wild fowl shootin' in the Moor. So my notion is I'll drive by here in the dark, and you'll be ready, and come along wi' me, takin' the baby with you, and I'll whip you off to Portsmouth, and nobody a penny the wiser. I've got a married sister there—got a bit o' a shop, and I'll take you to her, and if you don't mind a bit o' nonsense, I'll say you're my wife and that's my baby. Then you can stay there till all is quiet. I've a notion as Master Colpus be comin' to arrest you to-morrow, and that would be comical games. If you will come along wi' me, and let me pass you off as I sed, then you can lie hid till the wind has changed. It's a beautiful plan. I talked it over with the master, and he's agreeable; and as to money—well, he put ten pound into my hand for you, and there's ten pound of my wages I've saved and hid in the thatchin' of the cow-stall, and have no use for; that's twenty pound, and will keep you and the baby goin' for a while, and when that's done I daresay there'll be more to be had."

"I thank you, Joe," began Mehetabel, the tears rising in her eyes.

He cut her short. "The master don't want Polly to know nothin' of it. Polly's been able to get the mastery in the house. She's got the keys, and she's a'most got the old chap under lock. But it's my experience as fellows when they get old get won'erful artful, and master may be under her thumb in most things, but not all. And he don't fancy the notion of your bein' hanged. So he gave me that ten pound, and when I sed I'd drive you away afore the constable had you—why, he just about jumped out o' his breeches wi' joy. Only the first thing he said then was—'Not a word to Polly.'"

"Indeed, Joe, you are good, but I cannot go."

"You must go either to Portsmouth or to Gorlmyn. You may be a free woman, but in hidin', or go to prison. There's the choice before you. And if you b'ain't a fool, I know what you will take."

"I do not think it right to run away."

"Of course if you killed him deliberate, then you may go cheerful like and be hanged for it. But wot I sez and most sez, but they in the Punch-Bowl, is that it worn't deliberate. It were done under aggravatin' sarcumstances. The squatters in the Bowl, they have another tale. They say you tried to shoot him, and then to poison him, and he lived in fear of his life of you, and then you knocked him head over heels into the kiln, and served him right is my doctrine, and I respect you for it. But then—wot our people in Thursley sez is that it'll give the place a bad name if you're hung on Hind Head. They've had three hangin' there already, along of wot they did to your father. And to have another might damage the character of the place. I don't fancy myself that farmer Colpus is mighty keen on havin' you hanged."

"I shall not be hanged when I am guiltless," said Mehetabel.

"My dear," answered the hostler, "it all depends not on what you are but on what the judge and jury think, and that depends on the lawyers what they say in their harangues. There's chances in all these things, and the chance may be as you does get found guilty and be sentenced to the gallows. It might cause an unpleasantness here, and that you would wish to avoid I don't say as even Sally Rocliffe and Thomas would like it, for you're related to them somehow, and I'm quite sure as Thursley villagers won't like it, cos we've all respected you and have held Jonas cheap. And why we should have you hanged becos he's dead—that's unanswerable I say. So I'll be round after dark and drive you to Portsmouth."

"No, indeed, I cannot go."

"You can think it over. What about the little chap, the baby? If they hang you, that'll be wuss for him than it was for you. For you it were bad enough, because you had three men hanged all along of your father, but for he it'll be far more serious when he goes about the world as the chap as had his mother hanged."

"Joe, you insist on imagining the worst. It cannot, it will not, be that I shall be condemned when guiltless."

"If I was you I'd make sure I wasn't ketched," urged the hostler. "You may be quite certain that the master will do what he can for you; but I must say this, he is that under Polly that you can't depend on him. There was old Clutch on the day when Bideabout was killed. The doctor came from Gorlmyn on a hired hoss, and it was the gray mare from the inn there. Well, old Clutch seems to have found it out, and with his nose he lifted the latch of the stable-door and got out, and trotted away after the doctor or the old mare all the road to Gorlmyn; and he's there now in a field with the mare, as affable as can be with her. It's the way of old horses—and what, then, can you expect of old men? Polly can lead the master where she pleases."

"Joe," said Mehetabel, "I cannot accept your kind offer. Do not think me ungrateful. I am touched to the heart. But I will not attempt to run away; that would at once be taken as a token that I was guilty and was afraid of the consequences. I will not do anything to give occasion for such a thought. I am not guilty, and will act as an innocent person would."

"You may please yourself," answered Filmer; "but if you don't go, I shall think you what I never thought you before—a fool."

"I cannot help it; I must do what is right," said Mehetabel. "But I shall never forget your kindness, Joe, at a time when there are very few who are friends to me."

The period of Mehetabel's illness had been a trying one for the infant, and its health, never strong, had suffered. Happily, the little children who came to the Dame's school were ready and suitable nurses for it. A child can amuse and distract a babe from its woes in an exceptional manner, and all the little pupils were eager to escape A B C by acting as nurses.

When the mother was better, the babe also recovered; but it was, at best, a puny, frail creature.

Mehetabel was aware how feeble a life was that which depended on her, but would not admit it to herself. She could not endure to have the delicacy of the child animadverted upon. She found excuses for its tears, explanations of its diminutive size, a reason for every doubtful sign—only not the right one. She knew she was deceiving herself, but clung to the one hope that filled her—that she might live for her child, and her child might live for her.

The human heart must have hope. That is as necessary to its thriving as sun is to the flowers. If it were not for the spring before it, the flower-root would rot in the ground, the tree canker at the core; the bird would speed south never to return; the insect would not retreat under shelter in the rain; the dormouse would not hibernate, the ant collect its stores, the bee its honey. There could be no life without expectation; and a life without hope in man or woman is that of a machine—not even that of an animal. Hope is the mainspring of every activity; it is the spur to all undertakings; it is the buttress to every building; it runs in all youthful blood; it gives buoyancy to every young heart and vivacity to every brain. Mehetabel had hope in her now. She had no thought for herself save how it concerned her child. In that child her hope was incorporate.

CHAPTER XLVI. — A TROUBLED HOPE

On the following morning Mehetabel was conveyed to Godalming, and was brought before the magistrates, assembled in Petty Sessions.

She was in no great anxiety. She knew that she was innocent, and had a childlike, childish confidence that innocence must come out clear of stain, and then only guilt suffered punishment.

Before the magistrates this confidence of hers was rudely shaken. The evidence that would be produced against her at the Assizes was gone through in rough, as is always done in these cases, and the charge assumed a gravity of complexion that astonished and abashed her. That she and her husband had not lived in harmony was shown; also that he had asserted that she had attempted his life with his gun; that he was afraid she would poison him if trusted with the opiate prescribed for him when suffering from a wound. It was further shown by Giles Cheel and Sarah Rocliffe that she had threatened to kill her husband with a stone, if not that actually used by her, and then on the table, by one so like it as to be hardly distinguishable from it. This threat had been made on the night previous to the death of Jonas Kink. On the morning she had encountered her husband in a field belonging to Mr. James Colpus, and this meeting had been witnessed by the owner of the field, his daughter, and by Thomas Rocliffe and his son Samuel.

Colpus and his daughter had been at some distance in the rear, but Thomas and Samuel Rocliffe had been close by, in a sunken lane; they had witnessed the meeting from a distance of under thirty feet, and were so concealed by the hedge of holly and the bank as to render it improbable that they were visible to the accused.

James Colpus had seen that an altercation took place between Mehetabel and the deceased, but was at too great a distance to hear what was said. He had seen Mehetabel raise her hand, holding something— what he could not say—and threaten Jonas with it; but he did not actually see her strike him, because at that moment he turned to say something to his daughter.

The evidence of Mary Colpus was to much the same effect. The accused had come to her to ask for a situation vacant in the house, through the dismissal of Julia Caesar, her former servant, and some difficulty had been raised as to her reception, on account of the doubt whether Jonas would allow his wife to go out into service, and leave her home. She and her father had promised to consider the matter, and with this understanding Mehetabel had left, carrying her babe.

Just as she reached the further extremity of the field, she met her husband, Jonas Kink, who came up over the stile, out of the lane, apparently unobserved by Mehetabel; for, when he addressed her, she started, drew back, and thrust her hand into her pocket and pulled out a stone. With this she threatened to strike him; but whether she carried her threat into execution, or what occasioned his fall, she could not say, owing to her father having spoken to her at that moment, and she had diverted her eyes from the two in the field to him. When next she looked Jonas had disappeared, and she heard the shouts, and saw the faces of Thomas and Samuel Rocliffe, as they came through the hedge.

Then her father said, "Something has happened!" and started running. She had followed at a distance, and seen the Rocliffes pull the body of Jonas Kink out of the kiln and lay it on the grass.

Thomas Rocliffe was a stupid man, and the magistrates had difficulty with him. They managed, however, to extract from him the following statement on oath:

He and Samuel had been out the previous day along with Jonas Kink, his brother-in-law, looking for Mehetabel. Jonas thought she had gone to the Moor and had drowned herself, and he had said he did not care "such a won'erful sight whether she had."

On the morning of the event of his death Jonas had come to them, and asked them to attend him again, and from what he, Thomas, had heard from Sally, he said that they had been on the wrong scent the night before, and that they must look for Matabel nigher, in or about the village.

They had gone together, he and Jonas and his son Samuel, along the lane that led out of the Punch-Bowl towards Thursley by the Colpus's farm, and as they went along, in the deep lane, Jonas shouted out that he saw his wife coming along. Then he, Thomas and Samuel looked, and they also saw her. She was walking very slow, and "was cuddlin' the baby," and did not seem to know where she was going, for she went wide of the stile. Then Jonas got up over the stile, and told Thomas and Samuel to bide where they were till he called them. They did so, and saw him address Mehetabel, who was surprised when he spoke to her, and then something was said between them, and she pulled a big stone out of her pocket and raised it over her head, stepped forward, "sharp-like," and knocked him with it, on the head, so that he fell like one struck with a thunderbolt, backward into the kiln. Thereupon he and Samuel came up over the hedge, and he jumped into the kiln, and found his brother-in-law there, huddled up in a heap at the bottom. He managed with difficulty to heave him out, and with the assistance of Samuel and Farmer Colpus, to lay him on the grass, when all three supposed he was dead.

When they said that he was dead, then Mehetabel laughed.

This statement produced a commotion in court. Then they got a hurdle or gate, he couldn't say which, and lifted the deceased on to it and carried him home to the Punch-Bowl. It was only when they laid him on the bed that they saw he still breathed. They heard him groan, and he moved one hand—the right. He was rather stiff and awkward with his left since his accident.

This evidence was corroborated at every point by the testimony of Samuel, who was quite positive that Mehetabel had struck Jonas on the head. Like all stupid people, the two Rocliffes were ready to swear to and maintain with tenacity those points which were false or inaccurate, and to hesitate about asserting with confidence such as were true, and could not be other than true. It is not always in the power of a wise and observant man to discriminate between facts and imagination, and a dull and undeveloped intelligence is absolutely incapable of distinguishing between them.

The evidence of the surgeon was to the effect that Jonas Kink had died from the consequences of fracture of the skull, but whether caused by a blow from a stone or from a fall he was unable to state. There were contusions on his person. He probably struck his head against the bricks of the kiln as he fell or was thrown into it. Abrasions of the skin were certainly so caused. When he, the witness, arrived at the Punch-Bowl, Kink was already dead. He might have been dead an hour, the body was not absolutely cold. When asked whether the piece of ironstone on the table might have dealt the blow which had broken in the skull of Jonas, he replied, that it might have done so certainly, and the fracture of the skull was quite compatible with the charge advanced that it had been so caused.

The next witness summoned was Betty Chivers, who gave her evidence with great reluctance, and with many tears. It was true that the stone produced in court had been taken by her from the hand of the accused, and that immediately on her return from the farm of Mr. Colpus. Mehetabel had not told her that she had met her husband, had not said that he was dead, but had admitted that she had armed herself with the stone for the purpose of self-defence against Jonas, her husband, who, she believed, desired to take the child from her.

Mehetabel was asked if she had anything to say, and when she declined to say anything, was committed for trial at the ensuing assizes at Kingston.

Throughout the hearing she had been uneasy. The cell where she had been confined was close to the court, and she had been obliged to leave her child with a woman who had attended to her; and with this person the infant would not be at rest. Faintly, and whenever there was a lull in the court, she could hear the wail of her child, the little voice rising and falling, and she was impatient to be back with it, to still its cries and console the little heart, that was frightened at the presence of strangers and separation from its mother.

Through all the time that she was in court, Mehetabel was listening for the voice of the little one, and paying far more attention to that, than to the evidence produced against her.

It was not till Mehetabel was removed to Kingston on Thames and put in the prison to await her trial, that the full danger that menaced was realized by her, and then it was mainly as it affected her child, that it alarmed her. Life had not been so precious, that she valued it, save for the sake of this feeble child so dependent on her for everything.

Her confidence in justice was no longer great. Ever since her marriage—indeed, ever since Mrs. Verstage had turned against her, she had been buffeted by Fortune, devoid of friends. Why should a Court of Justice treat her otherwise than had the little world with which she had been brought in contact.

In Kingston prison the wife of the jailer was kind, and took a fancy to the unhappy young mother. She sat with and talked to her.

"If they hang me," said Mehetabel, "what will become of my baby?"

"It will go to a relation."

"It has no relations but Sally Rocliffe, and she has ill-wished it. She will be unkind to it, she wants it to die; and if it lives, she will speak to my child unkindly of me."

She wiped her eyes. "I cannot bear to think of that. I might make up my mind to die, if I knew my baby would be kindly cared for and loved—though none could love it and care for it as I do. But I could not die thinking it was taught that I was a bad woman, and heard untrue things said of me every day. I know Sally, she would do that. I had rather my child went on the parish, as I did, than that Sally Rocliffe should have it. I was a charity girl, and I was well cared for by Susanna Verstage, but that was a chance, or rather a Providence, and I know very well there are not many Susanna Verstages in the world. There is not another in Thursley, no, nor in Witley either."

"Your child could not go on the parish. Your husband, as I have been told, had a freehold of his own and some money."

"He lost all his money."

"But the farm was his, and that must be worth a few hundred pounds, so that it would not be possible for the child to go on the parish."

"Then it must go to Sally Rocliffe. There is no other relation."

This was now the great trouble of Mehetabel. She had accepted the inevitable, that wrong judgment would be pronounced, and that she would be hung. Then the thought that her little darling would be placed under the charge of the woman who had embittered her married life, the woman who believed her to be guilty of murder,—this was more than she could endure.

She had passed completely from confidence that her innocence would be acknowledged and that she would at once be released, a condition in which she had rested previous to her appearance before the magistrates at Godalming, into the reverse state, she accepted, now that she was in prison, awaiting her trial, as a certainty that she would be condemned and sentenced to the gallows.

This frame of mind in which she was affected the jailer's wife, and made her suppose that Mehetabel was guilty of the crime wherewith she was charged.

All Mehetabel's thoughts and schemings were directed towards the disposal of her child and its welfare after she was taken from it. All the struggle within her torn heart was to reconcile herself to the parting, and to have faith in Providence that her child would be cared for when she was removed.

How that could be she saw not; and she came at length to hope that when she was taken away the poor little orphan babe would follow her. In that thought she found more comfort than in the anticipation of its living, ill-treated by its aunt, and brought up to be ashamed of its mother.

"You say," said Mehetabel to the jaileress, "that they don't hang women in chains now. I am glad of that. But where will I be buried? Do you think it could be contrived that if my baby were to die at some time after me it might be laid at my side? That is the only thing I now desire—and that—oh! I think I could be happy if I were promised that."

CHAPTER XLVII. — BEFORE THE JUDGE

Previous to the Assizes, Joe Filmer arrived in Kingston in a trap drawn by old Clutch. He was admitted into the prison on his expressing his desire to see Mehetabel.

After the first salutations were passed, Joe proceeded to business. "You see, Matabel," said he, "the master don't want you to think he won't help you out o' this little mess you've got into. But he don't want Polly to know it. The master, he's won'erful under that young woman's—I can't say thumb, but say her big toe. So if he does wot he does about you, it's through me, and he'll sit innercent like by the fire twiddlin' of his thumbs, and talkin' of the weather. Master would be crafty as an old fox if he weren't stupid as an owl. I can't think how he can have allowed himself to get so much into Polly's power. It is so; and when he wants to do a thing without her knowin', he has to do it underhand ways. Well, he thort if he let our 'oss and trap go, as Polly'd be suspectin' something, and Polly's terrible set against you. So he told me to take a holiday and visit a dyin' aunt, and borrow old Clutch and a trap from the Angel at Gorlmyn. Clutch have been there all along, ever since your affair. There's no keepin' him away. So I came here; and won'erful slow Clutch was. When I came to Kingston I put up at the Sun, and sez I to the ostler: Be there a good lawyer hereabouts, think you? 'Well,' sez he, 'I'm a stranger to Kingston. I were born and bred at Cheam, but I was ostler first in Chertsey, and then for six months at Twickenham. But there's a young woman I'm courtin', I think she does the washin' for a soort of a lawyer chap, and I'll ax she at my dinner time.' So he did, and he came back and told me as the gal sed her master was a lawyer. She didn't think much of the missus, she was mean about perquisates, but the master was decent enough, and never came pokin into the kitchen except when he wanted to have his socks dried. So I reckon he'll do the job for you. Well, I gave that there ostler threepence, and axed him to do me the favor of tellin' that there lawyer that I'd be glad to stand him a glass o' ale if he'd step over to the bar of the Angel. I'd got a bit of business I wanted to consult him about. Well, he came, affable enough, and I told him all—as how I wanted him to defend you, and get you out of this tidy hobble you was in, and wot it 'ud cost. Then he thought a bit, and said that he could get up the case, but must engage counsel. He was only a turnkey, or some name like that; I sed, sed I, he was to manage all, and he might take it or lump it on these terms: Five and twenty pounds if he got you off clear, and if he didn't, and you was hanged, then nuthin'."

Joe smiled and rubbed his hands in self-satisfaction. Then he continued: "You know the master stands behind me. He'll find the money, so long as Polly don't know; but he thort, and so does I, as it could be done cheapest if I took it on me. So I sed to the lawyer chap, who was makin' faces as if he'd got a herrin' bone in his teeth, sez I, 'I'm nort but an ostler in a little country inn, and it's not to be supposed I've much savin's. Nor is Matabel any relation, only she wos maid in the inn whilst I wos ostlin', so I feels a sort o' a likin' for the girl, and I don't mind standin' five and twenty pound to get her off. More I can't give.' That, Matabel, was gammon. The master wouldn't stick at five and twenty, but he told me to try on this little game. He's deep is the master, for, all the innercence he puts on. I said to the ostler I'd give him half-a-crown for the gal as washes, as she introduced me to the lawyer. That there turnkey, as he calls himself, he sez he must get the counsel, and I sez, that, of course, and it comes out of the five and twenty. Then he made more faces, but I stuck to it, and I believe he'll do it. He axed me about particulars, and I sed he wos to consult you. The master sed that durin' the trial I wos to be nigh the lawyer, and if he seemed to flag at all I wos to say, 'Another five pound, old ginger, if you gets her off.' So I think we shall manage it, and Polly be never the wiser."

The Assizes began. Mehetabel, in her prison, could hear the church bells ring merry peals to welcome the judge. She was in sore anxiety about the child, that had failed greatly of late. The trouble in which its mother had been involved had told on its never strong constitution. Even had she been occupied with her own defence and ultimate fate, the condition of the babe imperiously demanded that the main solicitude of its mother should be devoted to it, to still its cries, to relieve its pains, to lull it to necessary sleep.

When Mahetabel knew that she was in a few minutes to be summoned to answer in court for her life, she hung over the little sufferer, clasped it and its crib in her arms, and laid her cheek beside its fevered face on the pillow. She could rest in no other position. If she left the child, it was to pace the cell—if she turned her thoughts to her defence, she was called back by a peevish cry to consider the infant.

When finally summoned to the court she committed the babe to the friendly and worthy jaileress, who undertook to care for it to the best of her abilities. The appearance of Mehetabel in the court produced at once a favorable impression. Her beauty, her youth, the sweetness and pathos of expression in her intelligent face, and the modesty with which she bore the stare of the crowd, sent a wave of sympathy through all present, and stirred pity in every heart. When Mehetabel had recovered the confusion and alarm into which she was thrown by finding herself in the dock with heads all about her, eyes fixed upon her, and mouths whispering comments, she timidly looked up and around.

She saw the judge in his robes under the Royal arms, the barristers, in gowns and wigs, she looked in the direction of the jury, and with a start recognized one amongst them. By a strange chance Iver Verstage had been chosen as one of the petty jury, and the prosecution not suspecting that he was in any way mixed up in the matter before the court, not knowing that he was acquainted with the prisoner, that he came from the neighborhood of the scene of the murder, suffered him to pass unchallenged. Iver did not turn his face her way, and avoided meeting her eye.

Then she saw Joe Filmer's honest countenance; he sought what Iver avoided, and greeted her with a smile and a nod.

There was one more present whom Mehetabel recognized, and that in spite of his wig. She saw in the barrister who was to act as counsel in the prosecution that same young man who had insulted her on the dam of the Hammer Pond.

There was little fresh evidence produced beyond that elicited before the magistrates. Almost the only new matter was what was drawn from the two Rocliffes relative to the conversation that had passed between the prisoner and the deceased previous to his death. But neither father nor son could give a clear account, and they contradicted each other and themselves. But both were confident as to Mehetabel having struck Jonas on the head.

The counsel for the defence was able to make a point here. According to their account they were in a lane, the level of which was considerably lower than that of the field in which the altercation took place. There was a hedge of holly intervening. Now holly does not lose its leaves in winter. Holly does not grow in straggling fashion, but densely. How were these two men able to see through so close a screen? Moreover, if they could see the prisoner then it was obvious she could see them, and was it likely that she would strike her husband before their eyes. Neither Samuel nor Thomas Rocliffe was able to explain how he saw through a hedge of holly, but he had no hesitation in saying that see he did. They were both looking and had chosen a spot where a view was possible, and that Mehetabel did not know they were present was almost certain, as she was looking at Jonas all the while and not in their direction. The counsel was disappointed, he had hoped to make much of this point.

Mehetabel was uneasy when she noticed now that the bewigged young man who had spoken with her at the Hammer Pond labored to bring out from the witnesses' admissions that would tell against her. He was not content with the particulars of the death of Jonas, he went back to the marriage of Mehetabel, and to her early history. He forced from the Rocliffes, father and son, and also from Colpus and his daughter the statement that when Mehetabel had been told her husband was dead she had laughed.

Up to this the feeling of all in court had been unmistakably in her favor, but now, as in the petty sessions, the knowledge that she had laughed turned the current of sympathy from her.

When all the evidence had been produced, then the counsel for the prosecution stood up and addressed the court. The case, said he, was a peculiarly painful one, for it exhibited the blackest ingratitude in one who owed, he might say, everything to the deceased. As the court had heard—the accused had been brought up in a small wayside tavern, the resort of sailors on their way between London and Portsmouth, where she had served in the capacity of barmaid, giving drink to the low fellows who frequented the public-house, and he need hardly say that such a bringing up must kill all the modesty, morality, sense of self-respect and common decency out of a young girl's mind. She was good-looking, and had been the object of familiarities from the drunken vagabonds who passed and repassed along the road, and stayed to slake their thirst, and bandy jokes with the pretty barmaid. From this situation she had been rescued by Jonas Kink, a substantial farmer. Having been a foundling she had no name. She had been brought up at the parish expense, and had no relatives either to curb her propensities for evil, or to withdraw her from a situation in which no young woman, he ventured to say, could spend her early years without moral degradation. It might almost be asserted that Jonas Kink, the deceased, had lifted this unfortunate creature from the gutter. He had given her his name, he had given her a home. He had treated her with uniform kindness—no evidence had been produced that he had ever maltreated her. On the contrary, as the widow Chivers had admitted—the prisoner said herself that the deceased had never struck her with a stick. That there had been quarrels he freely admitted, that the deceased had spoken sharply was not to be denied. But he asked: What husband would endure that the young wife who was indebted to him for everything, should resume her light and reprehensible conduct, or should show inclination to do so, after he had made her his own? No doubt whatever that the prisoner at the bar felt the monotony of a farmhouse irksome after the lively existence in a public house. No doubt she missed the society of topers, and their tipsy familiarities. But was that reason why she should kill her husband?

He believed that he had been able to show that this murder had been planned; that the prisoner had provided herself with the implement wherewith it was her purpose to rid herself of the husband who was distasteful to her. With deliberate intention to free herself, she had waited to catch him alone, and where she believed she was unobserved. The jury must consider how utterly degraded a woman must be to compass the death of the man to whom she had sworn eternal fidelity and love. A woman who could do this was not one who should be suffered to live; she was a scandal to her sex; she dishonored humanity.

The counsel proceeded to say: "Gentlemen of the jury, I have anxiously looked about for some excuses, something that might extenuate the atrocity of this crime. I have found none. The man who steals bread to support his starving children must suffer under the law for what he has done. Can you allow to go free a woman, because young, who has wilfully, wantonly, and deliberately compassed the murder of her husband, merely, as far as we can judge, because he stood in her way pointing the direction to morality and happiness. Whatever may be said in defence of this unfortunate prisoner now on her trial, gentlemen of the jury, do not mistake your office. You are not here to excuse crime and to forgive criminals, but to judge them with justice. Do not be swayed by any false feeling of commiseration because of the sex and youth of the accused. Remember that a wife guilty of the murder of her husband, who is allowed to run free, encourages all others, possibly even your own, to rid themselves of their husbands, whenever they resent a look or a word of reproach. I will lose no more words, but demand a sentence of guilty against Mehetabel Kink."

The young mother had hardly been able to endure the sense of shame that overwhelmed her during the progress of the speech of the counsel. Flushes of crimson swept through her face, at his insinuations and statements affecting her character, and then the color faded leaving her deadly white. This was an agony of death worse than the gallows. She could have cried out, "Take my life—but spare me this dishonor."

Joe Filmer looked troubled and alarmed; he worked his way to the back of the bench, where sat the counsel for the defence, and said: "Old Crock, five guineas—ten, if you'll get her off. Five from the master, and five from me. And I'll kick that rascal who has just spoken, as he comes out; I will, be Jiggers!"

When the counsel for the defense stood up, Mehetabel raised her shame-stricken face. This man, she knew, would speak a good word for her—had he not done so already? Had not all his efforts been directed towards getting out of the witnesses something favorable to her, and to showing contradictions in their statements which told against her?

But she looked timidly towards him, and dared not meet the glances of the crowd in the court. What must they think of her—that she was an abandoned woman without self-restraint; a disgrace to her sex, as that young barrister had said.

Again, it must be said, she was accustomed to injustice. She had been unfairly treated by Susanna Verstage. She had met with cruel wrong from her husband. By the whole of the Punch-Bowl she had been received without generosity, without that openness of mind which should have been manifested towards a stranger claiming its hospitality. She had not received the kindness that was her due from her sister-in-law. Even the well-disposed Joe Filmer believed her to be guilty of murder. But perhaps she could have borne all this better than the wounding insults offered her by the counsel for the prosecution, blasting her character before the world.

The barrister engaged to defend her did his utmost, and did it with ability. He charged the jury not to be deceived into believing that this was a case of premeditated murder, even if they were satisfied that Jonas had been killed by the stone carried by the defendant.

As he had brought out by the evidence of the widow Betty Chivers, and by that of the surgeon, the prisoner had been off her head, and was not responsible for what she said or did. What more likely then that she raved in delirium when she asserted that she would kill her husband, and what more evident token of having her brain overbalanced than that she should be running about the country hiding in caves, carrying her child with her, under the impression that her husband desired to take it from her, and perhaps do it an injury. That was not the conduct of a sane woman. Why should a father seek to rob her of her child? Could he suckle it? Did he want to be encumbered with an unweaned infant? Then as to the alleged murder. Was the testimony of the two men, Thomas and Samuel Rocliffe, worth a rush? Was not this Thomas a fool, who had been enveigled into a marriage with a tramp who called herself a countess? Did he not show when under cross-examination that he was a man of limited intelligence? And was his son Samuel much better? There was a dense holly hedge betwixt them and the prisoner. He put it to any candid person, who can see so clearly through a holly bush as to be able to distinguish the action of parties on the further side? These two witnesses had fallen into contradiction as to what they had heard said, through the holly hedge, and it was much easier to hear than to see athwart such an obstruction.

There was enough to account for the death of Jonas Kink without having recourse to the theory of murder. He had received a blow on his head, but he had received more blows than one; when a man falls backwards and falls down into a kiln that yawns behind him he would strike his head against the side more than once, and with sufficient force to break in his skull and kill him. How could they be sure that he was not killed by a blow against the bricks of the kiln edge? The accused had charged the deceased with having tried to murder her baby. That was what both the witnesses had agreed in, though one would have it she had asserted he tried to poison it, and the other that he had endeavored to strangle it. Such a charge was enough to surprise a father, and no wonder that he started back, and in starting back fell into the kiln, the existence of which he had forgotten if he ever knew of it. He the counsel, entreated the jury not to be led away by appearances, but to weigh the evidence and to pronounce as their verdict not guilty.

No sooner had he seated himself than he was nudged in the back, and Joe Filmer said, in a loud whisper, "Famous! Shake hands, and have a drop o' Hollands." Then the ostler thrust forward a bottle that had been in his pocket. "It's first-rate stuff," he said. "The master gave it me."

The Judge summed up and charged the jury. As Joe Filmer described his address afterwards, "He said that there were six things again' her, and about a half-a-dozen for her; there was evidence as went one road and evidence as went t'other way. That she was either guilty or not guilty, and the gem'men of the jury was to please themselves and say wot they liked."

Thereupon the jury withdrew.

Now when the twelve men were in the room to which they had retired, then the foreman said:—"Well, gents, what do you think now? You give us your opinion, Mr. Quittenden."

"Then, sir," answered the gentleman addressed, an upholsterer. "I should say 'ang 'er. It won't do, in my opinion, to let wives think they can play old Harry with their 'usbands. What the gentleman said as acted in the prosecution was true as gospel. It won't do for us to be soft heads and let our wives think they can massacre us with impunity. Women ain't reasonin' creatures, they're hanimals of impulse, and if one of us comes 'ome with a drop too much, or grumbles at the children bein' spoiled, then, I say, if our wives think they can do it and get let off they'll up wi' the flat iron and brain us. I say guilty. Ang 'er."

"Well, sir," said the foreman, "that's your judgment. Now let us hear what Josias Kingerle has to say."

"Sir," said the gentleman addressed, who was in the tannery business, "if she weren't so good-lookin' I'd say let her off."

As an expression of surprise found utterance Mr. Kingerle proceeded to explain.

"You see, gentlemen of the jury, and you, Mr. Foreman, I have a wife, and that good lady was in court, an' kept her eye on me all the time like a rattlesnake. I couldn't steal a peep at the prisoner but she was shakin' of her parasol handle at me, and though she didn't say it with words yet I read it in her eye, 'Now then, Josiah, none o' your games and gushes of pity over pretty gals.' It's as much as my domestic felicity is worth, gentlemen, to say not guilty. My wife would say, and your wives would all say, 'O yes! very fine. Because she was 'andsome you have acquitted her. Had we—' I'm speakin' as if it was our wives addressin' of us, gentlemen—'Had we been in the dock, or had there been an ugly woman, you would have said guilty at once.' So for peace and quietness I say guilty. 'Ang 'er."

"Well, Mr. Kingerle," said the foreman, "that is your opinion; you agree with Mr. Quittenden. Now then, what say you, Mr. Wrist?"

The juryman addressed was a stout and heavy man. He stretched his short legs, seated himself in his chair, and after a long pause said, "I don't know as I care particular, as far as I'm concerned. But it's better in my opinion to hang her, even if innocent, than let her off. It's setting an example, a fine one, to the wimen. I agree with Mr. Quittenden, and say—guilty. 'Ang 'er.'

"Now then, Mr. Sanson."

"I," answered a timid little apothecary, "I wouldn't wish to differ from any one. I had rather you passed me over now, and just asked the rest. Then I'll fall in with the general division."

"Very well, then—and you, Mr. Sniggins."

"I am rayther hard of hearing," answered that gentleman, "and I didn't catch all that was said in evidence, and then I had a bad night. I'd taken some lobster last evening, and it didn't agree with me, and I couldn't sleep, and it was rayther hot in the court, and I just closed my eyes now and again, and what with being hard of hearing and closing my eyes, I'm not very well up in the case, but I say—guilty. 'Ang 'er."

"And you, Mr.—I beg your pardon, I did not catch your name."

"Verstage."

"Not a Kingston gent?"

"Oh, no, from Guildford,"

"What say you, sir?"

"I—emphatically, not guilty." Iver threw himself back in his chair, extended his legs, and thrust his hands into his trouser pockets. "The whole thing is rank nonsense. How could a woman with a baby in her arms knock a man down? You try, gents, any one of you—take your last born, and whilst nursing it, attempt to pull your wife's nose. You can't do it. The thing is obvious." He looked round with assurance. "The man was a curmudgeon. He misused her. He was in bad circumstances through the failure of the Wealden Bank. He wanted money, and the child had just had a fortune left it—something a little under two hundred pounds."

"How do you know that?" asked the foreman. "That didn't come out in evidence."

"P'raps you shut your ears, as Mr. Sniggins shut his peepers. P'raps it came out, p'raps it didn't. But it's true all the same. And the fellow wanted the money. Matabel—I mean the prisoner at the bar thought— rightly or wrongly matters not—that he wished for the death of his child, and she ran away. She was not crazy; she was resolved to protect her child. She swore that she would defend it. That Giles Cheel and Mrs. Rocliffe said. What mother would not do the same? As for those two men, Thomas and Samuel Rocliffe, they never saw her knock down Jonas Kink, for the good reason that she was holding the baby, and couldn't do it. But when she told him, he was seeking his child's life—all for the money left it—then he stumbled back, and fell into the kiln—not guilty. If I sit here till I starve you all—not guilty."

"But, sir, what you state did not come out in the evidence."

"Did it not? So much the worse for the case. It wasn't properly got up. I'll tell you what, gents, if you and me can't agree, then after a time the jury will be dismissed, and the whole case will have to be tried again. Then the evidence will come up that you think you haven't heard now, and she'll be acquitted, and every one will say of this jury—that we were a parcel of noodles."

"Well, sir, not guilty," said the foreman. "What do you say, Mr. Lilliwhite?"

"Sir," answered the gentleman addressed, "I'd like to know what the cost to the county will be of an execution. I say it can't be done under a hundred pounds, if you calculate the carpentering and the timber, and the fees, and the payment of the constables to keep order, and of the hangman. I say it ain't worth it. There'll be another farthing stuck on the rates, all along of this young woman. I'm again' it. Not guilty. Let 'er go."

"And I," said the next juryman, "am averse to capital punishment. I wrote a little tract on the subject. I do not know if any of you gentlemen have seen it. I have copies in my pocket. I shall be happy to present each of you with a copy. I couldn't possibly say guilty and deliver her over to a violent death, without controverting my published opinions, and, so to speak, stultifying myself. So, really, sir, I must positively say not guilty, and would say as much on behalf of the most ferocious murderer, of Blue Beard himself, rather than admit anything which might lead to a sentence of capital punishment. Not guilty."

Nearly an hour and a half elapsed before the jury returned to the court. It was clear that there had been differences of opinion, and some difficulty in overcoming these, and bringing all the twelve, if not to one mind, at all events to one voice.

A silence fell on the whole court.

Mehetabel who had been allowed a seat, rose, and stood pale as death, with her eyes fixed on the jurymen, as they filed in.

The foreman stepped forward, and said: "We find the prisoner not guilty."

Then, in the stillness with which the verdict was received, Mehetabel's voice was heard, tremulous and pleading. She had dropped a curtsey, and said, "Thank you, gentlemen." Then turning to the judge, and again dropping a curtsey, she raised her eyes timidly, modestly, to the judge, and said, "Please, sir, may I go to my baby?"

CHAPTER XLIX. — WELCOME

Mehetabel was not able to leave Kingston for several days. Her child was too ill to bear the journey to Thursley; and the good-natured jailer's wife kindly urged her to remain as her guest till she thought that the little being might be removed with safety. Joe Filmer would drive her back, and Joe consented to tarry. He had business to discharge, the settlement of the account with the solicitor, or turnkey as he called him, to haggle over the sum, and try to get him to abate a sovereign because paid in ready money. He had also to satisfy the girl who had recommended the attorney, and the ostler who had consulted the girl, and old Clutch, who having found his quarters agreeable at the stable of the Sun, was disinclined to depart, and pretended that he had the strangles, and coughed himself into convulsions. At length, towards the end of the week, Mehetabel thought the child was easier, and Joe having satisfied all parties to whom he was indebted, and Clutch having been denied his food unless he came forth and allowed himself to be harnessed, Mehetabel departed from Kingston, on her return journey.

The pace at which old Clutch moved was slow, the slightest elevation in the ground gave him an excuse for a walk, and he turned his head inquiringly from side to side as he went along, to observe the scenery. If he passed a hedge, or a field in which was a horse, he persisted in standing still and neighing. Whereupon the beast addressed, perhaps at the plough, perhaps a hunter turned out to graze, responded, and till the conversation in reciprocal neighs had concluded to the satisfaction of the mind of Clutch, that venerable steed refused to proceed.

"I suppose you've heard about Betty Chivers?" said Joe.

"About Betty! What?"

"She got a bad chill at the trial, or maybe coming to it; and she is not returned to Thursley. I heard she was gone to her sister, who married a joiner at Chertsey, for a bit o' a change, and to be nussed. Poor thing, she took on won'erful about your little affair. So you'll not see her at Thursley."

"I am sorry for that," said Mehetabel, "and most sorry that I have caused her inconvenience, and that she is ill through me."

"I heard her say it was damp sheets, and not you at all. Old wimen are won'erful tender, more so than gals. And, of course, you've heard about Iver."

"Iver! What of Iver?" asked Mehetabel, with a flush in her cheek.

"Well, Mister Colpus, he had a talk wi' Iver about matters at the Ship. He told him that the girl Polly were gettin' the upper hand in everythin', and that if he didn't look smart and interfere she'd be marryin' the old chap right off on end, and gettin' him to leave everythin' to her, farm and public house and all his savings. Though she's an innercent lookin' wench, and wi' a head like a suet puddin' she knows how to get to the blind side of the master, and though she's terrible at breakages, she is that smooth-tongued that she can get him to believe that the fault lies everywhere else but at her door. So Iver, he said he'd go off to Thursley at once, and send Polly to the right-abouts. And a very good thing too. I'll be glad to see the back of her. 'Twas a queer thing now, Iver gettin' on to jury, weren't it?"

"Yes, Joe, I was surprised."

"I reckon the Rocliffes didn't half like it, but they made no complaint to the lawyer, and so he didn't think there was aught amiss. You see, the Rocliffes be won'erful ignorant folk. If that blackguard lawyer chap as sed what he sed about you had known who Iver was, he'd have turned him out. That insolent rascal. I sed I'd punish him. I will. They told me he comes fishin' to the Frensham Ponds and Pudmoor. He stays at the Hut Inn. I'll be in waitin' for him next time, and give him a duckin' in them ponds, see if I don't."

The journey home was not to be made in a day when old Clutch was concerned, and it had to be broken at Guildford. Moreover, at Godalming it was interrupted by the obstinacy of the horse, which—whether through revival of latent sentiment toward the gray mare, or through conviction that he had done enough, refused to proceed, and lay down in the shafts in the middle of the road. Happily he did this with such deliberation, and after having announced his intention so unequivocally, that Mehetabel was able to escape out of the taxcart with her baby unhurt.

"It can't be helped," said Joe Filmer, "we'll never move him out but by levers; what will you do, Matabel? Walk on or wait?"

Mehetabel elected to proceed on foot. The distance was five miles. She would have to carry her child, but the babe was not a heavy weight. Gladly would she have carried it twice the distance if only it were more solid and a greater burden. The hands were almost transparent, the face as wax, and the nose unduly sharp for an infant of such a tender age.

"I daresay," said Joe aside, "that if I can blind old Clutch and turn him round so that he don't know his bearin's, that I may get him up and to run along, thinkin' he's on his way back to Gorlmyn. But he's deep—terrible deep."

Accordingly Mehetabel walked on, and walked for nearly two hours without being overtaken. She reached that point of the main road whence a way diverges on the right to the village of Thursley, whereas the Ship Inn lies a little further forward on the highway. She purposed going to the dame's schoolhouse, to ascertain whether Mrs. Chivers had returned. If she had not, then Mehetabel did not know what she should do, whither she should go. Return to the Punch-Bowl she would not. Anything was preferable to that. The house of Jonas Kink was associated with thoughts of wretchedness, and she could not endure to enter it again.

She reached the cottage and found it locked. She applied at the house of the nearest neighbor, to learn whether Betty Chivers was expected home shortly, and also whether she had left the key. She was told that news had reached Thursley that the schoolmistress was still unwell, and the neighbor added, that on leaving, Betty had carried the key of the cottage with her.

"May I sit down?" asked Mehetabel; her brow was bathed in perspiration, and her knees were shaking under her, whilst her arms ached and seemed to have lost the power to hold the precious burden any longer. "I have walked from Gorlmyn," she explained; "and can you tell me where I can be taken in for a night or two. I have a little money, and will pay for my lodgings."

The woman drew her lips together and signed to a chair. Presently she said in a restrained voice: "That there baby is feverish, and my man has had a hard day's work and wants his rest at night, and though 'tis true we have a spare room, yet I don't see as we can accommodate you. So they let you off—up at Kingston?"

"Yes, I was let off," answered Mehetabel, faintly.

"Hardly reckoned on it, I s'pose. Most folks sed as you'd swing for it. You mustn't try on them games again, or you won't be so lucky next time. The carpenter, Puttenham, has a bed at liberty, but whether he'll take you in I don't know."

Mehetabel rose, and went to the cottage of the wheelwright. The man himself was in his shop. She applied to his wife.

"I don't know," said Mrs. Puttenham. "They say you was off your head when you did it. How can I tell you're right in your intellecks now? You see, 'twould be mighty unpleasant to have anything happen to either Puttenham or me, if we crossed you in any way. I don't feel inclined to risk it. I mind when owd Sammy Drewitt was daft. They did up a sort of a black hole, and stuck he in, and fed him through a kind of a winder in the side, and they had the place cleaned out once a month, and fresh straw littered for him to lie on. Folk sed he ort to ha' been chained to the wall, but they didn't do that. He never managed to break through the door. They found him dead there one winter mornin' when the Hammer Ponds was froze almost a solid block. I reckon there's been nobody in that place since. The constable might send a man, and scrape it out, and accommodate you there. It's terrible dangerous havin' a maniac at large. Sammy Drewitt made a won'erful great noise, howlin' when the moon was nigh full, and folk as lived near couldn't sleep then. But he never knocked nobody on the head, as I've heard tell. I don't mind givin' you a cup o' tea, and some bread and butter, if you'll be quiet, and not break out and be uproarious. If you don't fancy the lock-up, there is a pound for strayed cattle. I reckon of that Mister Colpus keeps the key—that is if it be locked, but mostly it be open. But then there's no roof to that."

Mehetabel declined the refreshment offered her so ungraciously, and went to the cottage of Mrs. Caesar, the mother of Julia who had been dismissed from the service of Mr. Colpus.

Of her she made the same request as of the two last.

"I call that pretty much like cheek, I do," replied Mrs. Caesar. "Didn't you go and try to get into Colpus's, and oust my daughter?"

"Indeed, indeed, I did not."

"Indeed, you did. I heard all about it, as how you wanted to be took in at Colpus's when Julia was out."

"But Mrs. Caesar, that isn't ousting her. Julia was already dismissed!"

"Dismissed! Hoity-toity! My daughter gave notice because she was too put upon by them Colpuses. They didn't consider their servants, and give 'em enough to eat, and holidays when they wanted to go out with their sweethearts. And you had the face to ax to be taken there. No, I've no room for you;" and she shut the door of the house in Mehetabel's face.

The unhappy girl staggered away with her burden, and sank into a hedge. The evening was drawing on, and she must find a house to shelter her, or else seek out the cave where she had lodged before.

Then she recalled what Joe Filmer had said—that Iver had returned to the Ship. A light flashed through her soul at the thought.

Iver would care for her. He who had been her earliest and dearest friend; he, who through all his years of absence, had cherished the thought of her; he who had told her that the Ship was no home to him without her in it; that he valued Thursley only because she lived there; he who had clasped her with his arm, called her his own and only one; to him—to him—at last, without guilt, without scruples; she could fly to him and say, "Iver, I am driven from door to door; no one will receive me. Every one is suspicious of me, thinks evil of me. But you—yourself, who have known me from infancy—you who baptized me to save me from becoming a wanderer—see, a wanderer, homeless, with my poor babe, I come to you—do you provide that I may be housed and sheltered. I ask not for myself so much as for my little one! To Iver—to Iver—as my one refuge, my only hope!"

Then it was as though her heart were light, and her heels winged. She sprang up from where she had cast herself, and forgetful of her weariness, ran, and stayed not till she had reached the familiar porch of the dear old Ship.

And already through the bar window a light shone. The night had not set in, yet a light was shining forth, a ray of gold, to welcome the wanderer, to draw her in, with promise of comfort and of rest.

And there—there in the porch door stood Iver.

"What! Mehetabel! come here—here—after all! Come in at once. Welcome! A word together we must have! My little Mehetabel! Welcome! Welcome!"

CHAPTER L. — MOVE ON

"Come in, little friend! dear Matabel! come into the kitchen, by the fire, and let us have a talk." His voice was cheery, his greeting hearty, his manner frank.

He drew her along the passage, and brought her into the little kitchen in which that declaration had taken place, the very last time she had been within the doors of the inn, and he seated her in the settle, the very place she had occupied when he poured out his heart to her.

Mehetabel could not speak. Her bosom was too full. Tears sparkled in her eyes, and ran down her cheeks. The glow of the peat and wood fire was on her face, and gave to it a color it did not in reality possess. She tried to say something, but her voice gave way. Half laughing in the midst of tears she stammered, "You are good to me, Iver."

He took the stool and drew it before the fire that he might look up into her agitated face.

"How have you come?" asked he.

"I walked."

"Where from—not Kingston?"

"Oh, no! only from Gorlmyn."

"But that is a long way. And did you carry the child?"

"Yes, Iver! But, oh! he is no weight. You have not seen him. Look at him. He is quiet now, but he has been very troublesome; not that he could help it, but he has been unwell." With the pride and love of a mother she unfolded the wraps that concealed her sleeping child, and laid it on her knees. The dancing light fell over it.

Iver drew his stool near, and looked at the infant.

"I am no judge of babies," he said, "but—it is very small."

"It is small, that is why I can carry him. The best goods are wrapped in the smallest parcels."

"The child looks very delicate—ill, I should say."

"Oh, no! it has been ill, but is much, much better now. How could even a strong child stand all that my precious one has had to go through without suffering? But that is over now. Now at length we shall have rest and happiness, baby and me, in each other." Then catching the child to her heart, she rocked herself, and with tears of love flowing, sang—

"Thou art my sceptre, crown and all."

She laid the child again on her lap and sat looking at it admiringly in the rosy light of the fire that suffused it. As the flames had given to her cheek a fictitious color, so did they now give to the infant a glow as of health that it did not actually possess.

"You must be tired," said Iver.

"I am tired; see how my limbs shake. That is why my baby trembles; but as for my arms, they are past tiredness, they are just one dead ache from the shoulder to the wrist."

"Are you hungry, Matabel?"

"Oh, no! All I want is rest, rest. I am weary."

Presently she asked, "Where is father?"

"He is away. Gone to the Dye House to see a cow that is bad. They sent for him, to have his opinion. Father is thought a great authority on cows."

"And Polly?"

"Oh! Polly," laughed Iver, "she's bundled off. Father has borne it like a philosopher. I believe in his heart he is rather pleased that I should have turned her neck and crop off the premises. It was high time. She had mastered the old man, and could make him do what she pleased."

"Whom have you got in her place?"

"Julia Caesar. She was sent away from the Colpuses for drawing the beer too freely. Well, here she can draw it whenever there are men who ask for drink, so she will be in her proper element. But she is only a stop gap. I engaged her because there really was for the moment no one else available, but she goes as soon as we can find a better."

"Will you take me?" asked Mehetabel, with a smile, and with some confidence that she would be gladly accepted.

"We shall see—there is another place for you, Matabel," said Iver. "Now let us talk of something else. Was it not a piece of rare good luck that I was stuck on the jury? Do you know, I believe all would have gone wrong but for me. I put my foot down and said, 'Not guilty,' and would not budge. The rest were almost all inclined to give against you, Matabel, but there was a fellow with a wist in his stupid noddle against capital punishment. He was just as resolute as I was, and between us, we worked the rest round to our way of thinking. But I should like to know the truth about it all, for it is marvellous to me."

"There is nothing for me to say, Iver," answered Matabel, "but that some words I uttered made Jonas spring back, and neither he nor I knew that there was a kiln behind, it was so overgrown with brambles, and he fell down that."

"And you laughed."

"Oh, Iver! I don't know what I did. I was so frightened, and my head was so much in a whirl that I remember nothing more. You do not really think that I laughed."

"They all said you did."

"Iver, you know me too well to believe that I was other than frightened out of my wits. There are times when a laugh comes because the tears will not break out—it is a gasp of pain, of horror, nothing more. I remember, at my confirmation, when the Bishop laid his hands on us, that the girl beside me laughed; but it was only that she was feeling more than she could give token of any other way."

"That's like enough," said Iver, and taking the poker he put the turf together to make it blaze; "I say, Matabel, they tell me that Jonas was a bad loser by the smash of the Wealden Bank, and that he was about to mortgage his little place. Of course, that is yours now—or belongs to the young shaver. There are a hundred pounds my mother left, and fifty given by my father, that I hold, and I don't mind doing anything in reason with it to prevent having the property get into the lawyer's hands. I wouldn't do it for Jonas; but I will for you or the shaver. Shall you manage the farm yourself? If I were you I would get Joe Filmer to do that. He's a good chap, honest as daylight, and worships you."

"I don't know or think anything about that," said Mehetabel.

"But you must do so. The Rocliffes have invaded the place, so my father says. They took possession directly Jonas was dead, and they are treating the farm as if it were their own. You are going to the Punch-Bowl at once, and I will assert your rights."

"I am not going to the Punch-Bowl again," said Mehetabel, decisively.

"You must. You have no other home."

"That can be no home to me."

"But—where are you going to live?"

"I ask—" she looked at Iver with something of entreaty in her eyes—"May I not come and be servant here? I will do my duty, you need not doubt that."

"I have no doubt about that," he answered. "But—but—" he hesitated, and probed the fire again, "you see, Matabel, it wouldn't do."

"Why not?"

"Oh, there are three or four reasons."

She looked steadily at him, awaiting more.

"In the first place," he said, with a little confusion, "there has been much chatter about me being on the jury, and some folk say that but for me you'd have been found guilty, and—" He did not complete the sentence. He had knocked a burning turf down on the hearth. He took the tongs, picked it up and replaced it. "I won't say there is not some truth in that. But that is not all, Matabel. I'm going to give up Guildford and live here."

"You are!" Her eyes brightened.

"Yes, at the Ship. For one thing, I am sick of giving lessons to noodles. More than half of those who take lessons are as incapable of making any progress as a common duck is of soaring to the clouds. It's drudgery giving lessons to such persons. The only pictures they turn out that are fit to be looked at are such as the master has drawn and corrected and finished off for them. I'll have no more of that."

"I am glad, Iver. Then you will be with the dear old father."

"Yes. He wants some one here to keep an eye on him. But, just because I shall be here, it is not possible for you to be in the house. There has been too much talk, you know, about us. And this matter of my being on the jury has made the talk more loud and unpleasant for me. I shall have to be on my P's and Q's, Mattie; and I doubt if I am acting judiciously for myself in bringing you into the house now. However, it is only for an hour, and the maid Julia is out, and father is at the Dye House, and no one was in the road; so I thought I might risk it. But, of course, you can't remain. You must go."

"I must go! What, now?"

"I won't hurry you for another ten minutes, but under the circumstances I cannot allow you to remain. There is more behind, Matabel. I have got engaged to Polly Colpus!"

"Engaged—to Polly Colpus?"

"Yes. You see she is the only child of James Colpus, and will have his land, which adjoins ours, and several thousand pounds as well. Her mother left her something, and her father has been a saving man; so I could not do better for myself. I have got tired of teaching imbeciles to draw and daub. You see, I knew nothing about a farm, but father will manage that, and when he is too infirm and old, then Mr. Colpus will work it along with his own, and save me the trouble. Polly is clever and manages very well, and I can trust her to govern the Ship and make money out of that. So my idea is to be here when I like, and when tired of being in the country, to go to London and sell my pictures, or amuse myself. With the farm and the inn I shall be free to do that without the worry of giving lessons. So you understand that not only must I avoid any scandal among the neighbors by harboring you here, but I must not make Polly

Colpus jealous; and she might become that, and break off the engagement were you taken into the house. She is a good girl, and amiable, but might become suspicious. There are so many busybodies in a little place, and the smaller the place is the more meddlesome people are. It would not do for my engagement to be broken through any such an injudicious act on my part, and I should never forgive myself for having given occasion for the rupture. Consequently, as is plain as a pike-staff, we cannot possibly take you into the Ship. Not even for to-night. As for receiving you as a servant here, that is out of the question. There is really no place for you but the Punch-Bowl."

"I will not go back to the Punch-Bowl," said Mehetabel, her heart sinking.

"That is unreasonable. It is your natural home."

"I will not go back. I said so when I ran away. Nothing will induce me to return."

"Then I wash my hands of all concerning you," said Iver, irritably. "There really seems to be ill-luck attending you, and affecting all with whom you are brought in touch. Your husband—he is dead, and now you try to jeopardize my fortunes. 'Pon my word, Matabel," he stood up. "It cannot be. We are willing enough to take in most people here, but under the circumstances cannot receive you."

"The door," said the girl, also rising, "the door was open at one time to all but to you. Now it is open to all but to me."

"You must be reasonable, Matabel. I wish you every good in the world. You can't do better than take Joe Filmer and make yourself happy. Every one in this world must look first to himself; then to the things of others It is a law of Nature and we can't alter it."

Leisurely with sunk head on her bosom, Metabel moved to the door.

"If I can assist you with money," suggested Iven

She shook her head she could not speak.

"Or if you want any food—"

She shook her head again.

But at the door she stood, leaned against the jamb turned, and looked steadily at Iver.

"You are going to the Punch-Bowl?" he asked.

"No, I will not go there!"

"Then, where do you go?"

"I do not know, Iver—you baptized me lest I should become a wanderer, and now you cast me out, me and my baby to become wanderers indeed."

"I cannot help myself, dear Matabel. It is a law of Nature, like that of the Medes and Persians, unalterable."

CHAPTER LI. — THOR'S STONE AGAIN

Stunned with the sense that her last hope was taken from her, the cable of her one anchor cut, Mehetabel left the Ship Inn, and turned from the village. It would be in vain for her to seek hospitality there. Nothing was open to her save the village pound and the cell in which the crazy man, Sammy Drewitt, had perished of cold. There was the cave in which she had found refuge the night before the death of Jonas. She took her way to that again, over the heath.

There was light in the sky, and a star was shining in the west, above where the sun had set.

How still her baby was in her arms! Mehetabel unfolded the shawl, and looked at the pinched white face in the silvery light from the sky. The infant seemed hardly to breathe. She leaned her cheek against the tiny mouth, and the warm breath played over it. Then the child uttered a sob, drew a long inspiration, and continued its sleep. The fresh air on the face had induced that deep, convulsive inhalation.

Mehetabel again covered the child's face, and walked on to the gully made by the ancient iron-workers, and descended into it.

But great was her disappointment to find that the place of refuge was destroyed. Attention had been drawn to it by the evidence of Giles Cheel and Sally Rocliffe. The village youths had visited it, and had amused themselves with dislodging the great capstone, and breaking down the sandstone walls. No shelter was now obtainable there for the homeless: it would no more become a playing place for the little children of the Dame's school.

She stood looking dreamily at the ruin. Even that last place of refuge was denied her, had been taken from her in wantonness.

Leisurely she retraced her steps; she saw again the light in the window of the Ship, and the open door. She, however, turned away—the welcome was not for her—and entered the village. Few were about, and such as saw her allowed her to pass without a salutation.

She staggered up some broken steps into the churchyard, and crossed it, towards the church. No friendly light twinkled through the window, giving evidence of life, occupation, within. The door was shut and locked. She seated herself wearily in the porch. The great building was like an empty husk, from which the spirit was passed, and it was kept fast barred lest its emptiness should be revealed to all. The stones under her feet struck a chill through her, the wall against which she leaned her back froze her marrow, the bench on which she sat was cold as well. Why had she come to the porch? She hardly knew. The period at which Mehetabel lived was not one in which the Church was loved as a mother, nestled into for rest and consolation. She performed her duties in a cold, perfunctory manner, and the late Vicar had, though an earnest man, taught nothing save what concerned the geography of Palestine, and the weights and measures of Scripture—enough to interest the mind, nothing to engage the heart, to fill and stablish the soul.

And now, as Mehetabel sat in the cold porch by the barred door, looking out into the evening sky, she extended, opened, and closed her right hand, as though trying to grasp, to cling to something, in her desolation and friendlessness, and could find nothing. Again a horror came over her, because her child lay so still. Again she looked at it, and assured herself that it lived—but the life seemed to be one of sleep, a prelude to the long last sleep.

She wiped her brow. Cold drops stood on it, as she struggled with this thought. Why was the child so quiet now, after having been so restless? Was it that it was really better? Was this sleep the rest of exhausted nature, recovering itself, or was it—was it—she dared not formulate the thought, complete the question.

Again, in the anguish of her mind, in her craving for help in this hour of despondency, she put forth her hand in the air gropingly, and clutched nothing. She fully opened her palm, extended it level before her, and then, wearily let it fall.

From where she sat she could not see even the star that had glimmered on her as she crossed the common.

She heard the crackling of the gravel of the path under a foot, and a figure passed the porch door, then came back, and stood looking at her.

She recognized the sexton.

"Who are you there?" he asked.

She answered him.

"Do you want to see where Jonas is laid? Come along with me, and I'll show you."

She shrank back.

"He's where the Kinks all are. You must look and see that it is all right. I haven't been paid my fee. Them Rocliffes buttoned up their pockets. They sed it was for you to pay. But I hear they have put their hands on the property. They thought you would be hanged, but as you ain't they'll have to turn out, and you'll have to pay me for buryin' of Jonas, I reckon."

The old fellow was much bowed, and hard of hearing. He came into the porch, laid hold of Mehetabel, and said, "I'm goin to lock the gate. You must turn out; I can't let you bide in the churchyard till you come to bide there forever. Be that your baby in your arms?"

"Yes, Mr. Linegar, it is."

"It don't make much noise. Ain't a very lively young Radical."

"Would you like to see my baby?" asked Mehetabel, timidly, and she uncovered the sleeping child.

The sexton bowed over the little face, and straightening himself as much as he could, said, "It seems not unlike as that the child be comin' to me."

"What do you mean?" Her heart stood still.

"If you hadn't showed it me as alive, I'd ha' sed it were dead, or dyin'. Well, come and tell me where it's to be laid. Shall it go beside Jonas?"

"Mister Linegar!" Mehetabel stood still trembling. "Why do you say that? My babe is well. He is sleeping very sound."

"He looks won'erful white."

"That's because of the twilight. You fancy he is white. He has the most beautiful little color in his lips and cheeks, just like the crimson on a daisy."

"Well, come along, and choose a place. It'll save comin' again. I'll let you see where Jonas lies. And if you want to put up a monument, that's half-a-guinea to the passon and half-a-crown to me. There, do you see that new grave? I've bound it down wi' withies, and laid the turf nice over it. It's fine in the sun, and a healthy situation," continued the sexton, pointing to a new grave. "This bit of ground is pretty nigh taken up wi' the folks of the Punch-Bowl, the Boxalls, and the Nashes, and the Snellings, and the Kinks, and the Rocliffes. We let 'em lie to theirselves when dead, as they kep' to theirselves when livin'. Where would you like to lie, you and the baby—you may just as well choose now—it may save trouble. I'm gettin' old, and I don't go about more than I can help.

"If anything were to happen, Mr. Linegar, then let us be laid—me and my darling—on the other side of the church, where my father's grave is."

"That's the north side—never gets no sun. I don't reckon it over healthy."

"I would rather lie there. If it gets no sun on that side, my poor babe and I have been in shade all our lives, and so it fits us best to be on the north side."

"Well, there's no accountin for tastes," said the sexton. "But I've hear you be a little troubled in the intellecks."

"Is it strange," answered Mehetabel, "that one should wish to be laid beside a father—my poor father, who is alone?"

"Come, come," said the old man, "it is time for me to lock up the churchyard gate. I only left it open because I had been doing up Jonas Kink's grave with withies."

He made Mehetabel precede him down the path, saw her through the gate, and then fastened that with a padlock.

"Even the dead have a home—a place of rest," she said. "I have none. I am driven from theirs."

It was not true that she had no home, for she had one, and could claim it by indefeasible right, the farmhouse of the Kinks in the Punch-Bowl. But her heart revolted against a return to the scene of the greatest sorrows. Moreover, if, as it was told her, the Rocliffes had taken possession, then she could not enter it without a contest, and she would have perhaps to forcibly expel them. But even if force were not required, she was quite aware that Sally Rocliffe would make her position intolerable. She had the means, she could enlist the other members of the squatter community on her side, and how could she—Mehetabel—maintain herself against such a combination? To return to the Punch-Bowl would be to enter on ignoble broils, and to run the gauntlet of a whole clique united to sting, wound, bruise her to death. How could she carry on the necessary business of the farm when obstructed in every way? How manage her domestic affairs, without some little assistance from outside, which would be refused her?

She entertained no resentment against Iver Verstage for having excluded her from the inn, but a sense of humiliation at having ventured to seek his help unsolicited. Surely she had an excuse. He had always been to her the one to whom her thoughts turned in confidence and in hope. It was in him and through him that all happiness was to be found. He had professed the sincerest attachment to her. He had sought her out at the Punch-Bowl, when she shrank from him; and had she not been sacrificed—her whole life blighted for his sake? Surely, if he thought anything of her, if he had any spark of affection lingering in his heart for her, any care for her future, he would never leave her thus desolate, friendless, houseless!

She wandered from the churchyard gate, aimless, and before she was aware whither she was going, found herself in the confines of Pudmoor. How life turns in circles! Before, when she had run from the Ship, self-excluded, she had hasted to Pudmoor. Now, again, excluded, but by Iver, she turned instinctively to Pudmoor. Once before she had run to Thor's Stone, and now, when she found help nowhere else, she again took the same direction. She had asked assistance once before at the anvil, she would ask it there again. Before she had asked to be freed from Iver. She had no need to ask that now, he had freed himself from her. She would seek of the spirits, what was denied her by her fellow-men, a home where she might rest along with her baby.

The first time she had sought Thor's Stone she had been alone, with herself only to care for, though indeed for herself she had cared nothing. Now, on this second occasion, she was burdened with the child infinitely precious to her heart, and for the sake of which even a stumble must be avoided. The first time she had been fresh, in the full vigor of her strength. Now she was worn out with a long tramp, and all the elasticity gone out of her, all the strength of soul and body broken.

Slowly, painfully she crept along, making sure of every step. The full moon did not now turn the waters into gold, but the illumined twilight sky was mirrored below—as steel.

She feared lest her knees should fail, and she should fall. She dared not seat herself on a ridge of sand lest she should lack power to rise again. When she came to a crabbed fir she leaned against it and stooped to kiss her babe.

"Oh, my golden darling! My honeycomb! How cold you are! Cling closer to your mother's breast. She would gladly pour all the warmth out of her heart into your little veins."

Then on again, amidst the trilling of the natterjacks and the croaking of the frogs. Because of their noise she could not hear the faint breath of her infant. Although she walked slowly, she panted, and through panting could not distinguish the pulsation of the little one she bore from the bounding of her own veins. At last she saw, gleaming before her—Thor's Stone, and she hasted her steps to reach it.

Then she remembered that she was without a hammer. That mattered not. She would strike on the anvil with her fingers. The spirits—whatever they were—the good people—the country folk called them, would hear that. She reached the stone, and sank exhausted below it She was too weary to do more than lie, with her child in her lap, and hold up her face bathed in sweat, for the cool evening wind to wipe it, and at the same time feed with fresh breath her exhausted lungs.

Then looking up, she saw the little star again, the only one in the light-suffused heavens, but it twinkled faintly, with a feeble glitter, feeble as the frail life of the child on her lap.

And now a strange thing occurred.

As she looked aloft suddenly the vault was pervaded with a rosy illumination, like the flushing of a coming dawn, and through this haze of rosy light, infinitely remote, still flickered the tiny spark of the star.

What was this? Merely some highly uplifted vapor that caught the sun after it had long ceased to shine on the landscape.

There were even threads of amber traced in this remote and attenuated glory—and, lo—in that wondrous halo, the little star was eclipsed.

Suddenly—with an unaccountable thrill of fear, Mehetabel bent over her babe—and uttered a cry that rang over the Mere.

The hand she had laid on Thor's Stone to tap struck it not. She had nothing to ask; no wish to express. The one object for which she lived was gone from her.

The babe was dead in her lap.

Her hand fell from the stone.

CHAPTER LII. — THE ROSE-CLOUD

Joe Filmer, driving old Clutch, drew up at the door of the Ship Inn. Iver Verstage came out and welcomed him.

"I've had a trouble with Clutch," said the ostler. "He lay down as we got out of Gorlmyn, and neither whip nor kicks 'ud make him stir. I tried ticklin', but t'wern't no good neither. How long this 'ud have gone on I dun know; I took him out o' th' shafts, and got him back to Gorlmyn, because some men helped me wi' him, and pulled at his tail, and twisted his carcass about till his nose pointed to the stable of the Angel. Then he condescended to get up and go to the inn. I shouldn't ha' got him away at all but that a notion came into my head as helped. I got the ostler to saddle and bride the gray mare, and mount her afore old Clutch's naked eyes. And I told the ostler to ride ahead a little way. Then, my word! what airs and jinks there were in Clutch; he gambolled and trotted like a colt. It was all a show-off afore the gray mare. The ostler—I knew him very well, he's called Tom Tansom, and it's a coorious thing now, he only cut his wise teeth about three months afore, and suffered won'erful in cutting 'em. But that's neither here nor there. Tom Tansom, he rode ahead, and old Clutch went after as if he were runnin' with the hounds. But I must tell you, whilst I was in Gorlmyn, that Widow Chivers came with the carrier, and as she was wantin' a lift, I just took her up and brought her on. She's been ter'ible bad, she tells me, with a cold, but she's better now—got some new kind o' lozenges, very greatly recommended. There's a paper given along wi' 'em with printed letters from all sorts o' people as has benefited by these lozenges. They're a shillin' and a ha'penny a box. Betty sez they've done her a power of good."

"Go on with your account of old Clutch. You're almost as bad as he with your stoppages."

"I'm tellin' right along. Well, the ostler he trotted on till he came to a turn in the road, and then he went down a lane out o' sight. But old Clutch have been racin' on all the way, thinkin' the mare had got a distance ahead. I'd a mighty difficulty to make him stop at the corner to set down Betty Chivers, and again here. Though he's roarin' like the roarin' of the sea, he wants to be on again and ketch up the gray mare. It's a pleasure that I've dun the old vagabond. Has Matabel been here?"

"Yes, she has; and has gone."

"Where to?"

"Of course, home, to the Bowl."

"Not she. She's got that screwed into her head tight as a nut, that she'll never go there again. There was the sexton at the corner, and he helped Betty with her bag, he said he turned Matabel out of the church porch."

"Then she may be in the churchyard."

"Oh, no, he turned her out of the churchyard, and the last he seed of her was goin' down to the Pudmoor. If she's queer in her head, or driven distracted wi' trouble—she oughtn't to be allowed to go there."

"Gone to Pudmoor!" exclaimed Iver. "I shouldn't wonder if she has sought Thor's Stone. She did that once before."

"I'll clap old Clutch in the stable, then go and look for her. Will you come, Mr. Iver?"

"Well—yes—but she cannot be received in here."

"No, there is no need. Betty Chivers will take her in as before. Betty expects her. I told her as we comed along that Matabel were before us, and we almost expected every minute to take her up. Though how we should ha' managed three in the trap I don't know, and Clutch would have been in an outrageous temper. Do you hear him snortin' there? That's because he's angry—the Radical!"

Beside Thor's Stone Iver and Joe Filmer found Mehetabel rocking her child, she had bared her bosom and held the little corpse against her palpitating heart, in the desperate hope of communicating to it some of her own heat; and if love could have given life the baby would have revived.

Again, as when her husband died, her brain was for a while unhinged, but she had the same kind and suitable nurse, the widow, Betty Chivers.

And now this story is all but done. Little more remains to be told.

Never again did Mehetabel return to the Punch-Bowl—never revisit it. The little property was sold, and after the debts of Jonas were paid, what remained went for her sustenance, as well as the money bequeathed by Susanna Verstage and that laid aside by Simon.

Years passed. Betty Chivers was gathered to the dust and in her place Mehetabel kept the Dame's school. It was thought that Joe Filmer had his eye on her, and on more than one occasion he dressed himself in his Sunday best and walked towards the school, but his courage ebbed away before he reached it, and he never said that which he had resolved to say.

On the north side of the church, near the monument of the murdered sailor, was a tiny mound, ever adorned with flowers, or when flowers were unattainable, with sprigs of holly and butcher's broom set with scarlet berries. At the beginning of the present century the decoration of a grave was rarely if ever practised. It was looked on as so strange in Mehetabel, and it served to foster the notion that she was not quite right in her head.

But in nothing else did the village schoolmistress show strangeness: in school and out of school she was beloved by her children, and their love was returned by her.

We live in a new age—one removed from that of Dame schools. A few years has transformed the system of education in the land.

In one of the voyages of Lemuel Gulliver, he reached the island of Lagado, where the system of construction adopted by the natives in the erection of an edifice was to begin at the top, the apex of a spire or roof, and to build downwards, laying the foundations last of all, or leaving them out altogether.

This is precisely the system of primary education adopted in our land, and if rent and ruin result, it is possibly due to the method being an injudicious one.

The face of Mehetabel acquired a sweetness and repose that were new to it, and were superadded to her natural beauty. And she was happy, happy in the children she taught, happy in the method she pursued, and happy in the results.

Often did she recall that visit to Thor's Stone on the night when her child died, and she remembered her look up into the evening sky. "I thought all light was gone from me, when my star, my little feeble star, was eclipsed, but instead there spread over the sky a great shining, glorious canopy of rosy light, and it is so,"—she looked after her dispersing school—"my light and life and joy are there."

The Vicar came up.

There had been a great change in the ecclesiastical arrangements of Thursley. It was no longer served occasionally and fitfully from the mother church. It had a parson of its own. Moreover a change had been effected in the church. It was no longer as a house left desolate.

"I have been thinking, Mrs. Kink," said the Vicar, "that I should much like to know your system of education. I hear from all quarters such good accounts of your children."

"System, sir!" she answered blushing, "oh, I have none."

"None, Mrs. Kink?"

"I mean," she answered, "I teach just what every child ought to know, as a matter of course."

"And that is?"

"To love and fear God."

"And next?"

With a timid smile:

"That C A T spells cat, and D O G spells dog."

"And next?"

"That two and two makes four, and three times four makes twelve."

"And next?"

She raised her modest dark eyes to the Vicar, and answered, smiling, "Mine is only a school for beginners. I lay the foundations. I do not profess to finish."

"You teach no more than these?"

"I lay the foundations on which all the rest can be raised," she answered.

"And you are happy?"

She smiled; it was as though the sun shone out of her face.

"Happy! Oh, so happy! I could not be happier." Then, after a pause, "Except when I and my own little one are together again, and that would be too much happiness for my heart now. But it will be able to bear the joy—then."

Sabine Baring-Gould – A Concise Bibliography

Sabine Baring-Gould's full bibliography consists of over 1200 works. Many of these are songs and hymns with the best known being 'Onward Christian Soldiers'.

A Book of the Pyrenees (1907)

Court Royal (1891)
A Book of Dartmoor (1900)
A Book of North Wales (1903)
A Book of Ghosts (1904)
A Book of South Wales (1905)
A Book of the Rhine from Cleve to Mainz (1906)
A Book of The West: Being An Introduction To Devon and Cornwall (2 Volumes, 1899)
A First Series of Village Preaching for a Year
A Garland of Country Songs (with Henry Fleetwood Sheppard) (1895)
A Second Series of Village Preaching for a Year
An Old English Home and its Dependencies, London, 1898
Arminell
Bladys of the Stewponey (1919)
Cliff Castles and Cave Dwellings of Europe
Cornish Characters (1909)
Curiosities of Olden Times (1896)
Curious Myths of the Middle Ages (1866)
Dartmoor Idylls (1896)
Devon (1907) (Methuen's Little Guide on Devonshire)
Devon Characters and Strange Events (1908)
Domitia (1898)
English Fold Songs for Schools (1907)
Eve
Family Names and their story (1910)
Grettir the Outlaw: a story of Iceland (1890)
Iceland, Its Scenes and Its Sagas
In the Roar of the Sea (1891)
In Troubadour Land: A Ramble in Provence and Languedoc (1890)
John Herring
Lives of the Saints, in sixteen volumes (1897)
Legends of the Patriarchs and Prophets (from the fall of the angels to the death of Solomon).
Mehalah, A Story of the Salt Marshes (1880)
Noemi
Old Country Life (1889)
Pabo, The Priest (1899)
Red Spider (1887)
Sermons on the Seven Last words
Sermons to Children
Songs & Ballads of the West (in 4 Volumes 1881-1891)
Songs of the West: Folksongs of Devon & Cornwall (1905)
The Book of Were-Wolves, being an account of a terrible superstition (1865)
The Broom-Squire (1896)
The Gaverocks
The Life of Napoleon Bonaparte (1908)
The Lives of the Saints – a sixteen-volume collection (1872 and 1877)
The Mystery of Suffering
The Pennycomequicks
The Preacher's Pocket

The Tragedy of the Caesars (1892)
The Village Pulpit (1886)
The Vicar of Morwenstow, being a life of Robert Stephen Hawker (1876)
Urith
Village Preaching for Saints' Days